THE PROBLEM WITH PLAYERS

BRITTAINY CHERRY

THE PROBLEM WITH PLAYERS

Brittainy Cherry

The Problem with Players

By: Brittainy Cherry
The Problem with Players
Copyright © 2024 by Brittainy Cherry
All rights reserved.

Published: Brittainy Cherry 2024

Developmental Editing: Ana Teresa Ribeiro Siqueira

Editing: Editing4Indies, Virginia Tesi Carey, My Brother's Editor

Cover Design: Staci Hart

❀ Created with Vellum

AUTHOR'S NOTE

This story is a tale about two individuals who fall in love. While this is a contemporary romance with a lot of elements of humor, it also deals with deep conversations and reflections of personal growth and personal struggles.

For those reasons, I'd like to note that parts of this story may be sensitive to a few readers due to the subject matter, which includes depression and conversations of self harm.

For the eldest child:
May you find your sunbeams.

1

AVERY

"Don't miss that catch, don't miss that catch! *OH, COME ON!*" I hollered, hopping up from the side of the tub as I held my cell phone in my hands. Never in my life did I witness such a heartbreaking play. The football game was only in the first quarter, and for the life of me, I couldn't understand why the quarterback decided to throw the ball to Mr. Butterfingers.

They were lucky the throw wasn't intercepted like the one a few plays back. My team was making way too many mistakes too early into the game.

A knock on the door startled me.

"Avery? Are you coming out?" my fiancé, Wesley, asked from the other side of the door.

I glanced around the bathroom, slightly panicked, before shoving my phone into my bra.

It was a no-technology event that evening at Wesley's and my house, which made no sense to me, seeing how it was freaking Super Bowl Sunday. Who had no-tech nights during the Super Bowl?

That seemed like a good enough reason to call off an

engagement. Especially when the score was so close. It was anyone's game, and I was going to miss it. After the foreseeable breakup, Wesley and I would tell people we had "irreconcilable differences" and go on our way.

The following year, I'd throw a Super Bowl party.

Okay, maybe breaking up over a game was a little far-fetched, but it wasn't every year that your favorite team played at the game of all games. It would probably be another thirty years before we made it back to the Super Bowl.

My dad was probably celebrating at his place with my sisters, Yara and Willow, my brother-in-law, Alex, and our aunt-by-choice, Tatiana, who helped raise me and my two sisters. Tatiana was our mother's best friend, and after Mama passed away, she stepped up to make sure we had a woman figure in our lives.

Tatiana always made the best dang buffalo chicken dip for Daddy's Super Bowl parties.

A heavy sense of jealousy raced through me knowing Yara would eat all that dip without me while Willow ate her vegan dip.

"You good?" Wesley asked.

"Yeah, yeah, sorry," I called out. I smoothed my hands over my black dress and combed my straight black hair behind my ears. I looked in the mirror and saw Mama's brown eyes staring back at me. I had so many of her features, which felt equally like a blessing and a curse. From her round nose and high cheekbones to her dark-brown skin and jet-black hair.

I took a deep breath and released it slowly, mentally preparing to socialize with a group I didn't know. I wasn't the best at striking up a conversation with strangers. Then again, I wasn't really into striking up conversations with people I knew either. The best types of human beings were the ones who shut up. Or at least the ones who didn't try to talk to me.

At the ripe age of thirty-six, I was hoping I'd met all the new people I'd ever have to meet in my life, outside of my students. Unfortunately for me, my rocket scientist fiancé was a social butterfly. Even worse, the people he socialized with were very intelligent. Like *super* smart. The kind of brilliance that made me feel like a box of rocks. I was talking about IQs of 150 and up.

What was I supposed to talk to those people about? Clearly not the Super Bowl. That was for certain.

When it was just Wesley and me, I could handle his intelligence. We had a normal relationship, except when he was excited about statistics. I didn't know a man could love stats and probabilities so much until I met him. When he finally convinced me to date him, he showed up with a whole pie chart, breaking down why someone as cold and closed-off as me was a perfect match for his vibrant and social personality.

I couldn't disagree with the numbers.

We were a match made in a science lab.

Still, the idea of spending the rest of the evening with his close college friends was enough to make me want to break out into hives. I'd been to a few of his work functions and dealt with colleagues of his before, and I always left feeling less than those around me. I didn't think they did it on purpose, either. They just spoke in a language I didn't understand. I was pretty sure they'd feel the same way if I had gone full-blown sports talk with them.

Needless to say, I was scared of having nothing in common with the people who meant the most to Wesley.

I swung the bathroom door open and smiled at Wesley. "Sorry, sorry. Got a little backed up."

He smirked and raised an eyebrow. "Is that so?"

"Yup. That's so."

He reached forward , dug into my bra, and pulled out my cell phone. "So you weren't just cussing at your cell phone watching the World Series?"

"The *Super Bowl*," I corrected, snatching my phone back from him. "And no. I wasn't watching that. Of course not. Not when we decided on a technology-free evening."

"Good. I'm guessing that means you won't mind if I keep this," he said, taking the phone back from me. He slid it into his back pocket and kissed my cheek. "Now, come on. It's about time you meet my friends. They just texted that they are about two minutes away."

Wesley and I had been dating for over three years, yet I'd never met a handful of his closest friends. He moved from Charlotte, North Carolina, to Illinois for a job position over five years ago, leaving most of his close friends in North Carolina. This was the first time his three friends had come to visit him in small-town Honey Creek.

It would be nice to meet his groomsmen finally. I'd heard many stories about Patrick, Lance, and Drew, though Drew wasn't in the wedding. I only had my sisters standing up for me, so it would've been an odd number. It did feel odd that Wesley said Drew was his best friend, yet he didn't ask him to be his best man. Wesley offered that role to Lance instead. When I asked about it, Wesley shrugged it off. I guess guy friendships were different.

The four of them went to undergrad together and kept close contact even after going their separate ways for graduate school. As far as I knew, they were all super brains, too, like Wesley.

When the doorbell rang, I followed Wesley to the foyer, ready to be as social as possible. I put on a big smile as Wesley opened his front door, and the three individuals stood there with huge grins. They all shouted big hoorays, holding up bottles of champagne as they rushed over to Wesley and pulled him into a big hug.

They laughed and celebrated a warm reunion as I stood

back, taking in the situation. Once they released their grip on Wesley, they walked into the foyer and smiled my way.

Wesley walked over and wrapped an arm around my waist. "You guys, this is my beautiful, talented, breathtaking fiancée, Avery. Avery, this is Patrick, Lance, and Drew," he stated, gesturing toward each individual.

I shook hands with each of them, a little thrown off when it came to the last hand I shook, Drew's. It appeared to me that there had been some kind of miscommunication along the line when it came to Wesley's best friend.

Drew Jacobson was a woman.

A very beautiful woman with long blond hair and the bluest of blue eyes.

I tried my best to play it cool as I was introduced to them all, but I couldn't get over the fact that I had no clue his best friend was a very beautiful *woman* with long blond hair and the bluest of blue eyes.

Lovely.

I wasn't an insecure woman, but seeing Drew sent a wave of discomfort through me. Especially based on how she looked at Wesley with heart-shaped eyes. Maybe it was my imagination, but Drew seemed to hug Wesley a little *too* long for my liking. There was always a slight bit of discomfort when another woman hugged a taken guy a little too long. Last year, I almost got into a fistfight with our town's gossip, Milly West, when she put her grimy hands around Alex on his and Yara's wedding day. Willow informed me it would've been unladylike to beat up a woman in her sixties on our sister's wedding day, but I considered it. That was until Alex grimaced and peeled Milly's hands away from him. He instantly wrapped himself around Yara and rolled his eyes at Milly.

One thing Alex Ramírez would always do was roll his eyes and sit in annoyance with anyone and everyone who wasn't his wife. He loathed human interaction as much as I did. One of the things he and I had in common. The other thing? Our love for my younger sister.

Alex was a good, loyal man like my father. Wesley was on the list, too.

I'd only dated one man before Wesley, when I was a very young eighteen-year-old. That only lasted for a summer, too. Since then, I've spent most of my life single, and I didn't have a problem with that. It wasn't until Wesley came around that I saw the real possibility of being with someone again, of loving someone else. Before him, I was content with the idea of being an old maid and living my life to the fullest. I knew I didn't need a man to have a happy life. Overall, the male species kind of annoyed me.

My youngest sister, Willow, the free spirit that she was, made sure to always remind Yara and me that the greatest love stories were with the ones staring back at us in our reflections, and men were just fun play toys that we could pick up and put down whenever we wanted.

I thought that was her way of excusing her promiscuous ways when it came to her picking up and putting down quite the array of play toys herself. Still, I believed her. I never let my life revolve around men. To be honest, I thought most of them were arrogant, smelly, and low in value. So when I found myself falling for Wesley, I knew he was different. He made me question all my sour beliefs about the male species.

At least, I thought so until I sat in our living room playing a game of charades with his friends.

With *Drew*.

Drew, the woman.

A few facts I'd learned about Drew over the past thirty minutes: she had a hyena laugh; when she lied, her mouth twitched; and she avoided refined sugar with every fiber of her spirit. Though, based on the twitch of her mouth, that was a lie.

Also, the more champagne the woman drank, the more obnoxious she became.

Drew stood in front of everyone, pulling her long hair into a ponytail and clapping her hands together. She made the hand gesture as if she were operating an old-fashioned camera.

"It's a movie!" Wesley called out. A little too elated if you asked me. He hadn't stopped smiling since that woman—and his other friends—entered our house. I swear, I'd never seen all his teeth before that night. My gosh, did he still have his wisdom teeth? Wesley was normally much more reserved with his smiles and somber with his expressions.

Drew nodded in agreement. She then put up one finger.

"One word!" Wesley shouted.

She nodded again, then started acting out a scene—poorly. She looked like a wild child, holding her hands out into the air, and Wesley stared at her as if she were Meryl Streep in an Oscar-winning movie. That was when my Spidey senses began to tingle. Something was amiss with how my fiancé was staring at another woman. Some might've called me paranoid, but my father taught me at a young age to never go against a hunch. And my hunch told me something was odd about Drew and Wesley's connection.

Patrick and Lance laughed at Drew's actions, having no clue what she was doing. I was just as lost as I studied the woman trying her best. I guessed her best wasn't good enough. She might've been a rocket scientist, but the woman was not a charades queen.

"Come on!" Drew said, clapping her hands toward Wesley. "We did this for our first date, on the boat!" she urged.

And there it is.

My hunch had been hunched.

First date?

We weren't just going to skip past that comment.

Or perhaps we were because Wesley shot up from his seat

and clapped his hands together. "*Titanic!*" he shouted, doing wild karate chops in the air as he exploded with excitement.

This. Dickhead.

I stayed planted on the couch in an indescribable state of shock.

"Yes!" Drew replied, rushing over to *my* fiancé and wrapping him in a big embrace. He hugged her back tightly as if that was the right thing to do. My blood began to boil like no other as I sat there like an idiot, taking in the romantic scene unfolding before me.

What.

The.

Actual.

Fuck?

I stared at the two as if they had grown three heads. I was stuck in a state of complete disbelief. They might as well take off their clothes and start going at it on the living room rug, for all I cared. The amount of disrespect happening right in front of me was mind-blowing.

When they finally let one another go, I said, "It doesn't count."

Everyone looked at me, confused.

Drew narrowed her eyes. "What doesn't count?"

"Your point for the game. It doesn't count. You're not allowed to use words during charades."

Wesley laughed and sat down beside me. He raked his hand through his reddish-brown hair and shrugged. "I think we can make up the rules as we go."

Did he just somehow become less attractive to me?

I swear, earlier that day, I found him much more handsome.

Now, the sound of his voice sounded like nails on a chalkboard.

Oh my gosh, I was engaged to an ugly man!

"Why would we make up the rules as we go? There are

already rules to the game," I remarked. "The whole point of charades is not to speak. That's the literal definition of charades."

"Charades can also mean an absurd pretense intended to create a pleasant appearance," Drew urged with laughter. I was glad she was still having a bang-up time.

"Yeah, well, that's not what this game is. So you don't get a point." I crossed my arms as the whole energy of the room shifted. Instantly, I felt like a jerk because I was the one who caused it. Me and some newly unlocked insecurities that I didn't know how to deal with. I didn't even know I could get insecure! Over a *man*?! How deeply disappointed I was in myself. What was happening to me?

"It's not that serious, darling," Wesley said, leaning over to me. The way he said darling came off as condescending to me. Or maybe I was simply overthinking every syllable that fell from his ugly tongue. He kissed my cheek lightly. "I think we just need some more champagne."

I glanced over at the kitchen counter, where Patrick stood, holding the empty bottles. "Sadly, we are all out of champagne," he mentioned.

I hopped up from the couch. "I'll run down to the corner store and get some more. I'll be back."

"Oh, you don't have to—" Lance started.

I shook my head. "No, it's fine. You all continue the game of talking charades. I'll be back before you know it." I didn't look back toward Wesley because I was almost certain his eyes would be packed with confusion by my oddities. But also, screw him.

Because why was his best friend someone that he used to date? Not only did they date, but they reenacted scenes from *Titanic*. That was love!

I grabbed my purse and jacket before heading out the door. As the chilled February breeze smacked my cheeks, my overheated body relaxed slightly. Maybe that was all I needed—some fresh air to calm down. I couldn't imagine what my blood pressure numbers would've been from a simple game of charades.

Walking down the semi-snow-covered sidewalk to Jackie's Beer & Spirits store, I muttered how stupid I was for getting so upset over a game. Did I overreact? Maybe, but Wesley was wrong for never mentioning that his best friend was a woman. A woman he once-upon-a-time dated, nonetheless. I felt as if I had every right to be upset. Yet what bothered me the most was how dramatic I looked in front of his friends. It was a terrible first impression, and now they probably thought I was some kind of psychopath.

As I walked into Jackie's, I felt a breath of relief as I heard one of my favorite sounds—a sports anchor speaking on the television screen. I grabbed a few bottles of champagne and headed to the front of the store, where Jackie sat behind her counter watching the Super Bowl game.

"Hey, Avery. Kind of surprised you pulled yourself away from this game. Did you see the halftime show? Miley Cyrus came out as a surprise guest!" Jackie said, taking the bottles of champagne from me and ringing them up.

I grumbled to myself and shook my head. "I missed it."

"You? Miss Sports Lady herself missed it?"

"Yeah, not watching the game tonight," I muttered, staring at the television. My team was up by three points in the fourth quarter, and I wanted to shit a few bricks trying to figure out how they got to that point. I paid for the champagne, took the three bottles by their necks, and kept my eyes on the screen. The crowd went wild as the opposing team threw the ball, which Jameson intercepted.

"*Oh shit!*" I shouted, tossing my hands up in victory. I couldn't believe I made it down to the liquor store to witness one of the greatest interceptions ever. Jameson not only caught the ball but ran down the field as if he were running from a masked murderer, sprinting as if his life depended on it. "*Go, go, go!*" Jackie and I shouted together. My heart pounded wildly as Jameson crossed into the end zone, scoring another touchdown.

"Oh my gosh!" I said, jumping up and down in glee.

"That was wild!" Jackie said, shaking her head in disbelief.

"You're right. That was intense," a deep, velvety voice said from behind me, spooking me back into my body. I turned around and bumped straight into a big, firm body, causing me to lose grip on the bottles in my hands. They began to fall, but the man was quick with his response time to catch all three bottles within his arms.

Massive. F**king. Arms.

"Whoa, nice save there, Nathan," Jackie mentioned before returning to the game.

My eyes rose as my heart began to pound against my rib cage when I met his stare. This time, the pounding of said heart wasn't from excitement. It was from disgust.

Nathan. F**king. Pierce.

As if my evening could get any worse.

Nathan stood there with my champagne bottles in his arms. He had enough nerve to smile at me with his toothy, all-American grin. I hated that smile more than anything, and I went out of my way to avoid said smile since he had moved back to Honey Creek, Illinois.

Nathan Pierce wasn't simply the boy who got away—he was the one who freaking sprinted. I wasn't certain I hated anyone with a deeper passion than that man standing in front of me. With an annoyingly impressive physique sculpted through countless hours on the baseball field, his powerful six-five frame made me feel tiny beside him. I wasn't even short at my five-nine height, but Nathan made me feel like a pathetic ant when he stood near me.

Not only was he massive in size but he was massive in heart, too. His features were so warm and welcoming, which drove me up a wall. Everyone in town loved the man. Probably because he was once-upon-a-time famous. People in Honey Creek loved anything that had a touch of success attached to it. Even though Nathan's career did crash and burn.

Since his return to town, I had watched him from a distance. His deep-set brown eyes were intense and expressive. He could express a million words solely with his eyes, and once upon a time, I could decipher every syllable. He had rich, smooth ebony skin that seemed to glow with health, even in the wintertime. His smile drew people in with its warmth, and the rugged handsomeness about him made women toss themselves at him as if they were at a 1980s New Kids on the Block concert. The light stubble that framed his jawline and the way he wore his baseball hat with a very prominent bend to the bill brought him an amount of effortless charm and attractiveness.

For anyone other than me, that was.

To me, he looked stupid.

Stupid and ugly.

Ugly and stupid.

His smile stretched wider. It made my skin crawl like a million spiders were unleashed over my whole body. I'd never had a smile that made me want to upchuck until I received one from Nathan Pierce.

"Hey, Avery," he said.

My gosh.

I wished he had forgotten my name because the last thing I needed to hear was it rolling off his tongue. Wesley was my current love, and Nathan was my first. He was the man who made me hate men. My man-hating villain story, one might say. The one who left scars on my heartbeats many years before he ran off to win the World Series for California.

Twice.

Wesley was the redemption arc for my hatred of men. Well, until pretty Miss Drew showed up.

Now I was back to hating all men again.

Especially the one holding my champagne.

I snatched the bottles from his hold as I stared at him with piercing hostility. "Don't talk to me," I ordered with sharp disdain. I didn't say another word as I walked out of the liquor store and stomped my feet all the way back home.

Leave it to Nathan to ruin a perfectly happy touchdown moment with his mere existence.

———

"Okay, I get it," Wesley said as he twirled some dice between his fingers after his friends left for the evening. "You're upset."

"Am I?" I huffed as I took the emptied bottles of champagne to the recycling bin. I hated when he did that—when he told me what I'd been. If I was upset, I wanted to come to that realization on my own. I didn't need Wesley to tell me I was upset. That only annoyed me more.

After returning from the liquor store, I had to put on a brave smile and function as if I wasn't bothered so Wesley's friends wouldn't think I was some raging drama queen. Even though I was, indeed a raging drama queen. I started noting every little comment Drew made toward Wesley, and I counted every time she found a way to touch my fiancé.

Forty-seven times.

She touched him forty-seven freaking times!

"You are, and that's completely understandable," Wesley said as he followed me to the kitchen with the almost-empty charcuterie board. "I should've told you about Drew."

"You mean you should've mentioned that your best friend was a woman and that you two used to date each other? You should've mentioned that your ex-girlfriend was coming to our place instead of having me find that information out during a game of charades? Yes. Yes, you should've. You've never even mentioned dating anyone before me."

"That's because no one mattered before you."

"Nice try, smooth talker. How long did you two date?"

"Not long." He tossed his hands in the air in surrender. "It was really short."

"How short is short?"

"Like three, four years."

"*Four years*?!" I gasped, stunned by the news I was discovering.

He's so ugly!

"I know that sounds bad, but honestly, Avery, it was so long ago. We were in a college relationship. It is ancient history."

"It didn't seem really ancient to her," I muttered. "She's in love with you."

He laughed and shook his head. "She's not in love with me."

"She spent the whole game night talking about how wonderful you are and how you taught her everything she knows about thrust-to-weight ratio, which sounds highly inappropriate to me."

"Oh no. That's not some weird sex thing if that's what you're thinking. Thrust-to-weight ratio is what compares the thrust produced by an engine to the weight of the vehicle and—"

I placed a hand on his forearm. "Wesley."

"Yes?"

"I might not know rocket science, but I know women. She was talking about you thrusting your weight into her vehicle."

He shook his head. "You're overreacting."

"Don't say that. Otherwise, I will truly overreact, and you'll end up sleeping on the couch. All I'm saying is it would've been nice to have a heads-up that you were bringing an ex to our house for game night. When the only game we should've been watching was the Super Bowl."

He narrowed his eyes. "Is that what this is all about? The fact that you missed your football game?"

"No, it's not about missing the game even though rumor has it that it turned out to be one of the most exciting games in the history of football. It's about the lack of communication. I was put into an uncomfortable situation, and I didn't like that, Wesley. I don't like being blindsided."

"You're right." He moved over to me, placed his hands against my shoulders, and kissed me. "I'm wrong." He kissed me again. "I'm sorry." *Kiss.* "Forgive me."

I grumbled but kissed him back. "Fine. But only if you watch the replays from the game tonight."

"Deal. But tell me... What did you think of my friends?"

I liked Lance and Patrick. They were funny and down-to-earth in a way that I appreciated. But Drew? Yeah, screw her. I didn't want to tell him the truth, though, because that seemed mean, and I was almost certain he'd just chalk it up to me being insecure. Nothing drove me crazier than the idea of a man thinking I was insecure due to him.

Still, I didn't want to lie because that seemed wrong, too. So I told him the only thing I could think to say. "They're smart," I complimented them. "Very, very smart."

He smiled as a burst of pride shot through his system. "I know, right?"

2

AVERY

A fter the Super Bowl, I went straight into my favorite season: baseball. I was head of the physical education department at our town's high school, and for the past five years, I'd been the assistant coach for our baseball team. That was until this year, when Head Coach Erikson stepped down, giving me a real shot at running the team. Over the past few years, my sisters considered me the head coach even though it wasn't an official title. Coach Erikson made sure to keep me beneath him, making it hard for me to help the team.

He had a lot of old-school coaching thoughts. He was in his late sixties, and he and I butted heads often. I was looking forward to proving that the Honey Creek Hornets weren't a bad team—they simply had bad leadership behind them.

The first weeks of February were our preseason, and I was thrilled to get started again. I took pride in the sport more than anything even though our team wasn't the best. Still, we had some pretty impressive players I thought could make it to the big leagues. I believed in those boys and knew they could do amazing things on the field if given the right direction.

Cameron Fisher was one of those players. At least he had been until he went through a big personal loss last semester. I could see it in his game that losing his mother did quite a number on him. I was still trying to figure out how best to help the kid, seeing how he was a junior now and scouts were highly interested in his game. That was until recently.

Don't cry, don't cry, don't cry...

Oh balls. The kid was going to cry.

Cameron stood at the plate, biting his bottom lip to push down the tears cooking in the back of his eyes. He was already two strikes down, and based on his lip-biting and elbow-trembling, he was about to get his third out.

Lately, Cameron has had stage fright. He was easily the best player on the team. That boy could hit a home run with his eyes closed during baseball practice, yet when it came to playing against another team, he froze up like a TV dinner left in the back of a freezer for over a year.

I sat in the dugout with my hands clenched together, silently chanting the same thing I chanted every time Cameron was up to bat.

Don't cry, don't cry, don't cry...

He stepped into his batting stance and held his bat in the perfect position. His fellow teammates cheered him on, clapping from the dugout. They knew exactly what I knew was about to happen, but they still cheered him on because that meant being a good teammate.

I glanced at the scouts in the stands. What an awful game to come see Cameron play. He was better than this, but all they were seeing was the opposite of that fact. It wasn't fair, but the kid was living too much in his head and not enough in his heart as of late. I didn't blame him. After I lost my mother, I moved through life as if in quicksand, getting nowhere at all. Still, I hated that it was happening to Cameron at such a defining moment of his baseball career.

The scouts were early anyway. We were still in preseason, and these games didn't count for much.

Cameron took a deep breath as I held mine.

The pitch was released, Cameron swung, and he missed.

A swing and a miss.

Damn.

The crowd from the opposite team erupted with cheers while our small handful of fans booed. The loudest boos came from Cameron's own father, Adam Fisher, who stood in the stands, probably drunk.

"What was that, Cam? Dammit!" Adam shouted, gesturing as if the greatest tragedy had just taken place. "Come on!"

The look on the scouts' faces told me everything I needed to know as they packed up their stuff and left the stands. They'd seen enough, which upset me because they didn't see anywhere near enough of that kid. He was so much more talented than his current grief-stricken state.

I found my father in the stands, too. Daddy had attended every home game since I started five years ago. He gave me a small smile and shrugged. I could hear his comments without him even speaking: *You win some, you lose some, but no matter what, you keep playing the game.*

Matthew Kingsley was the father of the century. He got me into the sport, and his quiet support kept me going throughout the season. I only wish Adam Fisher had taken a note out of my father's handbook of supportive parenting.

Cameron grumbled and stomped off to the dugout. A few teammates tried to pat him on the back and tell him it was okay, but Cameron shrugged them away as he moved to the back corner of the dugout. He took off his helmet and threw it to the ground.

Don't cry. Don't cry. Don't cry...

"Fuck!" he blurted out, covering his face with his hands. He broke down into tears.

Crap.

Every time he did that, I felt my own heart shatter.

I walked over to him and sat on the bench beside him. I clasped my hands together and remained silent for a moment. I wasn't good with seeing others cry. I didn't show emotions at the level of the average human. The last time I cried, I was eighteen years old—almost two decades ago—so seeing other people cry made me feel highly uncomfortable. It was probably something I should've seen a therapist about, but to see a therapist, one had to open up, and well, no, thank you.

I grimaced as I raised my hand and patted Cameron on the shoulder. "There, there," I muttered. "You'll get them next time, Cam. This is just preseason anyway. This game doesn't count."

"You said every game counts, Coach K," he replied.

"Did I? Well, yeah. But this one didn't. Every game but this one. You'll get it next time."

I stood and removed myself from the situation because it felt odd to remain sitting there. If I were falling apart, I wouldn't want people to be around, watching me and giving me pitiful shoulder pats. I gave him space and privacy to pull himself together.

I coached the rest of the game, only for us to lose by a handful of runs. Cameron would probably beat himself up for striking out, but it wasn't a huge deal. Our team sucked every single year. I was kind of surprised that the school district didn't cancel our baseball team to save a few bucks, but they did invest a lot of money into the state-of-the-art sports facility after Nathan's success in the Major Leagues. The district was convinced they could become the breeding ground for Major League players. It hadn't happened much, especially with the baseball team that yours truly had overseen.

Maybe this year will be different with Coach Erickson gone. One could only hope.

THE FIRST WEEK OF MARCH, I was called into the principal's office only to realize that the district had been discussing our team's bad performance. Instead of canceling the team altogether, Principal Raymond, or Ray as I called him, had gathered an even worse idea. One that made my blood boil from irritation as I sat across from him at his desk.

"You're bringing on another coach?" I asked, stunned. "Without giving me a chance to vet them?"

Ray combed his hand through his thinning blond hair. "I really hope you understand, Avery. We truly believe in your coaching abilities and your team's talent."

"So why the heck would you bring in another coach without asking my thoughts? Frankly, I don't know if I need another coach. I have the team under control. The season is just beginning. We're just getting our sea legs back on the field."

"Yes, I understand that. But, well, you haven't won a game in three years, Avery."

Had it really been three years since we'd won a game? No way.

There was that one time back in—oh crap.

We hadn't won a game in over three years. That wasn't the best look.

"That was because of Coach Erikson. I'm not him."

"Still...three years."

"But another coach?" I grumbled. "Why don't you just cancel the program?" I sarcastically said.

"Because it's a great program and a good way for the students to build up their skills. Yet we think having another coach could benefit us in ways we couldn't even imagine. I know you wouldn't want to lose the program, either. You've invested a lot in this. This is a good thing, Avery. This is a *great* thing."

He was right. I'd hate to lose the program. A lot of the kids relied on baseball to keep their heads above water with whatever home issues they were dealing with. It was their outlet, their haven, and I didn't want to remove that for them. As a teacher and coach, I always swore to put the students' needs before mine. The only problem was that I was a lone wolf. I didn't work well with others. I spent the past five years fighting Coach Erikson tooth and nail on every topic. The idea of another coach coming in was enough to make my skin crawl.

"Do I get to be involved in the hiring process?" I asked, almost knowing the answer already by how Ray was acting.

"We went ahead and handled that for you. They should be here any second now," Ray said as he glanced at his watch.

I arched an eyebrow. "You already hired someone?"

Before he could respond, a person came darting into the office in a flurry.

"Sorry I'm late. Got held up a little bit at my brother's shop."

I turned around to meet Nathan's eyes.

Nathan. F**king. Pierce.

No way.

My jaw all but dropped to the floor as a wave of disgust landed in the pit of my stomach. No way did Ray hire Nathan Pierce to be my assistant coach. No freaking way!

"Cancel the program," I blurted out as I turned back to face Ray. "Cancel the whole thing," I hissed with unyielding resentment. I was now adding Ray to my list of men who pissed me off. His name was right under the jerk who cut me off in line at the coffee shop this morning.

"Now, Avery," Ray started, but I was already pushing myself up from my desk chair to shoot out of that office space. No way was I going to stay in that room and breathe the same air as that...that...*man.*

I hurried past Nathan and headed straight for the hallway.

Seconds later, I heard him calling my name. He was chasing me, but I wasn't going to turn around.

"Avery! Wait up!" he called as I darted between students.

"Oh my gosh! Dude! You're Nathan Pierce!" a few students remarked as they noticed him. I glanced over my shoulder and rolled my eyes as I saw Nathan push out one of his all-star smiles toward the easily impressed students.

Give me a break.

He wasn't *that* amazing.

You won one or two World Series, and people acted like your poop didn't stink. News flash: celebrities went number two in toilets just like us regular folks. They probably just used overpriced, oil-infused tissue to wipe their bums.

I kept on my way to my office in the gym. Once I reached it, I slammed the door and took a breath. Seconds later, my door opened, and lo and behold, it was Nathan.

Lovely.

Freaking stalker.

It was no secret that Nathan was back in our little town of Honey Creek, Illinois, after his career took a nosedive. He'd been around for the past year or so, and I prided myself on being able to avoid crossing paths with him for a long time. I hated that he broke that record on Super Bowl Sunday, but I was quick to start it up again. I was a month strong before this awful encounter took place.

Something about crossing paths with one's ex-boyfriend was so uncomfortable. And crossing paths with your famous ex-boyfriend was extra uncomfortable. Especially when no one else but your two sisters knew you had a relationship with said man.

We dated the summer after our senior year. Three months. I knew it seemed ridiculous to feel so deeply about someone who I'd only dated for three short months, but that was the thing about love—it didn't follow timelines. It showed up when people least expected it. When I fell for Nathan, I fell hard. I was more certain than ever that I was his, he was mine, and we'd be us forever.

When he abruptly ended things with me, my heart never fully recovered. I never knew something like love could lead to so many trust issues.

"Hey." Nathan stood there with an annoyingly attractive smirk.

I wanted to smack the smile off his smug face. One of the worst things about running into an ex was seeing how attractive they'd become over the years. Nathan was always handsome, but now he looked like a diamond dipped in gold. His arms were muscular and massive as he crossed them over his chest. His brown skin looked ridiculously hydrated. His dark-brown hair was cut in a fade, and his ears were pierced with diamond studs. His brown eyes still reminded me of heaven, and his wicked smile reminded me of hell.

He wore a dark gray pullover that was probably one size too small based on how his biceps were showcased, black jogger pants, and some overpriced sneakers.

I hated how beautiful and *big* he was. Not many men in town could make me feel small, but standing near Nathan did exactly that.

Which was why I puffed out my chest and narrowed my eyes. "What do you want, Nathaniel?" I hissed, annoyed by his proximity and the fact that he was trying to ruin my life again after all these years.

"Nathaniel." He chuckled. "Using the full name to show how much you missed me, huh?"

"I only use your full name as a sign of hatred."

"You used to say it for very different reasons."

I felt my skin heat from his words. "Yes, well, I was a dumb kid. Now it's used for hatred."

He stepped toward me. "So you hate me, Ave?"

"With a passion," I said. "A deep, skull-crushing passion."

He scratched his beard, which had grown quite a bit since last month. "And to think, I was hoping we'd let bygones be bygones."

"Yeah, that would have happened if you would've stayed *gone*. It was an unwritten agreement. You break my heart, and you stay gone." For a split second, a look of guilt flashed across his face. Before he could feel bad for breaking my heart, I rolled my eyes dramatically just to make sure he noticed. "Don't get a big ego about it. I'm over you breaking my heart. I'm engaged now," I remarked, holding up my ring finger. "To a rocket scientist," I exclaimed. Why was I word-vomiting to him? Why was I telling him anything about my life?

Shut up, Avery.

"I heard," he replied. "Congratulations."

"I don't want your congratulations. I want you to be gone."

He slid his hands into the pockets of his joggers. "That's going to be an issue, seeing how I'm now coaching the baseball team with you."

"No," I urged. "You're not. This is my thing."

"Yeah, but Raymond said—"

"I don't care what he said, Nathan. I'd rather this program burn to the ground before I coach with you. What, do you think you're some kind of genius because you played in the Major Leagues? I was ten times a better baseball player than you could've ever been."

"I know," he said quickly. "I never said I was better than you."

"So you understand why I don't need you? Good."

"No." He shook his head. "You do need me. I've been to a few of your preseason games. Your team is a bit..." He waved his hand in a disapproving fashion. "Lacking."

"*Lacking?*"

"Yeah. That's no offense to you. I'm sure you're doing the

best you can, but I think I can bring a lot to the table with what I've learned in the industry and my personal strengths. And with you being my assistant coach—"

"I'm sorry, come again? Assistant coach?" There was absolutely no way he said assistant. As if he was now the head coach of a team I'd been managing for years. The nerve of this guy!

"I figured Raymond told you—"

Before he could finish, I marched toward Principal Raymond's office. I barged back into the office space without an invitation and began to holler. "Ray, what does this man mean he's head coach now?"

Raymond looked up from his paperwork with fear in his eyes. Rightfully so. I was seconds away from ripping his eyeballs out of their sockets as rage built within me.

"Now, listen, Avery," he started. His calmness felt belittling in a way. Or perhaps I was being overly emotional, but who could blame me? The one thing I had that was mine—my team—was being ripped from beneath me without any warning.

How could the school district think that demoting me was the right choice? Without even talking to me about it first? This was beyond humiliating. It was insulting to my character and position of authority.

What was with people not telling me things before I had to find out in such hurtful ways? It had been a month, and I still wasn't over the reveal of Drew, and now this was happening.

"What you've done for the team has been amazing," Raymond stated. "But with an actual Major League Baseball player as head coach, we're certain we can get these players where they need to be. Maybe even make it to the playoffs. And who knows? These boys could end up getting college offers with the right team leadership beneath them."

With the right team leadership.

Which meant I was the wrong team leadership.

They didn't even give me a chance.

That cut deep, but I stood firm.

I couldn't let him know that he hurt my feelings.

I couldn't let anyone ever know they hurt my feelings.

The school bell rang for second period to begin, and I felt sick, knowing I had a class to get to.

"This is crap, and you know it, Ray," I huffed, crossing my arms over my chest. "There should've been a conversation."

"Well, let's consider this the conversation and move forward from here on out. Or you do have the option to step down from the team. There's no pressure to stay, Avery. You are more than able to let it all go. Then maybe you can focus your energy on something else. Something that makes you happy. I mean, truthfully, do you even like coaching these boys? Because I can't tell."

That felt like the biggest slap to my soul.

I loved coaching those kids.

They were the highlight of my year. The highlight of my life. I loved the game more than most people. More than Nathan Pierce. Sure, he got to the big leagues, but that didn't mean the game belonged to him. A million people would never get the chance Nathan had presented to him. That didn't mean they were any less deserving or passionate.

"I love my job," I said, my voice cracking as my emotions began to build within me. I felt like I was on the chopping block, and being told that I didn't care about something I deeply cared for didn't make me feel good at all. It felt hurtful at the least, infuriating at the most.

"Then show it. Show that even with a slight demotion, you will still show up for the students the way they need you to. For now, perhaps you should get to your other students waiting for you to teach them today."

He broke his stare from me and looked back down at his paperwork, a clear sign that the conversation was sealed closed, and nothing I would say could change his mind.

I was officially demoted from my head coach position, only to have my ex-boyfriend take on the role.

I wanted to throw up.

I headed out of the office, and the moment I stepped into the empty hallways, my eyes landed on Nathan, who stood by a locker. When he looked up, he gave me a pathetic frown, which only made me want to slam my fist into his face.

He stepped toward me. "Avery, I didn't know—"

"Do you get off on this?" I whisper-shouted, moving in toward him. "Do you get off on coming back and taking the one thing away that meant everything to me?"

"Avery—"

"Whatever it is you're about to say, I don't care to hear it. I'm already struggling enough," I snapped. I hated that those words slipped out, because the last thing I wanted was for Nathan to know he was getting under my skin. But he had been. Every piece of me felt enraged from him stepping into my realm and taking control of the things I'd loved most.

I'd struggled with my mental health throughout the whole year. That was no secret to me. Depression was an unwanted visitor who knocked at my door throughout the seasons, and at times, it would swallow me whole. Yet baseball season was the one thing I had to look forward to. It was my safe place in a world that sometimes felt so heavy. It was my return to self after months of living in shadows. He was taking that from me. He was taking away the small breaths of relief I found throughout the year.

He rubbed his hand over his head. "If you let me explain—"

"Go to hell, Nathaniel," I spat. "Or at least do me the smallest favor and stay out of my way."

As I stormed off to get to class, he said, "We'll talk after the weekend!"

"I HATE HIM!" I exclaimed as I marched into The Pup Around the Corner, Yara's dog spa. She was at the register checking a customer out, when I barged in and interrupted the interaction. "I *hate, hate, hate* him!"

Yara raised an eyebrow toward me and then looked at the customer. "Thanks again, Sally. We'll see you in a few weeks for Eddie's trim."

Sally glanced at me and shook her head in disapproval. "That loud shouting isn't very ladylike, Avery Kingsley."

"Yeah, well, I never claimed to be ladylike. Bye, Sally."

She scowled before walking out of the store with her dog. I was almost certain she'd tell her friends how short and snappy I'd been. Then word would spread through the small town about how I was the mean Kingsley sister, the one people avoided like the plague.

Whatever. I didn't care what people thought of me. At least, that was the lie I liked to tell.

Yara turned toward me with her kind smile. My sister was the master of kind smiles. She was probably the favorite sister in town. Willow would've been tied with her if she ever stayed in Honey Creek long enough to interact with others. Instead, she was always hurrying off on some wild adventure.

Yara walked around the counter to join me on the other side, and I smirked a little at her growing stomach, almost forgetting how annoyed I'd been. Yara and Alex were expecting a baby in a few months. My favorite little family. Alex and Yara defined opposites attract, and they worked out. His grumpy mixed so well with her sunshine.

Yara stood in her overalls with her natural hair in two big puffs on top of her head, looking as cute as ever, but I couldn't let her cuteness distract me from my bad mood. "I *hate* him," I continued.

"You hate all men, so I'll need you to be more specific about which man you currently hate," she quipped.

That was no secret to anyone, really. I did hate all men. Sure, Wesley was one of the good ones, but at the end of the day, he was still a walking dick. And walking dicks always had a small chance of dicking a woman around. Even the good ones.

Exhibit A: Drew.

"Nathan," I said.

"Nathan who?"

"What do you mean, Nathan who? My Nathan. Well, not my Nathan, but *that* Nathan. Nathan Pierce."

Her eyes widened as her jaw dropped. "You interacted with Nathan Pierce?"

"Yes." My pits sweated just thinking about it.

"After working so hard to avoid him?"

"Yup. It's even worse than that. Ray hired Nathan to be a coach for the baseball team with me."

"No!" she exclaimed, shocked like no other. I was thankful she was as flabbergasted as I'd been. If it wasn't for her animated reactions, I might've thought I overreacted.

"Yes!" I said, tossing my hands up in the air. "And! Not just to be a coach. The *head* coach!"

"*Nooo!*" she shouted. She then began wiggling her hips as she crossed her legs. "Oh my gosh, I just peed a little."

"Yeah, I pretty much shit myself when I heard the news, too."

"No, I mean, I actually just peed a little. It's been happening on and off all day."

An alarm shot through me. "Uh, do you have to go to the bathroom or something?"

She waved it off. "No. I'm wearing a pad. It's fine. Keep going."

Pregnant Yara was wild. Yet I didn't want to stop my freak-out over the fact that Nathan somehow weaseled his way into my job and took my position. Like the little snake he'd been.

"I'm so mad." I sighed. "Ray told me either I step down to

assistant coach and let Nathan run the team for this season or he'd have to let me go from the team altogether."

"Can he do that?"

"Yup. That isn't in my teaching contract. He could cut me from the team without a second thought. He also told me I was being childish, so I told him to suck a cock."

"Avery, you didn't!"

"No," I groaned. "But I wanted to. I can't believe this is happening. These kids and this game mean everything to me, and to have Mr. Major League sweep in and take it without a moment of hesitation just seems so wrong."

"Well, look at it this way. His knowledge will benefit everyone. It is about the kids, right?"

I narrowed my eyes at her with a disgusted look. "Whose side are you on?"

"Yours, obviously. Always yours. Screw Nathan Pierce. Sorry. Pregnancy brain has me saying bizarre things sometimes," she joked.

"Right. Okay. Good. Because if I'm going to be delusional with my anger, I need you to be on the same page."

"Yeah, of course, but..."

"*But*?!"

"But," she continued, "last week, you did say that you wished something would give with the team. So you could make them the best they could ever be. This could be your gift from the universe."

"Nathan Pierce? A gift? *Psh.*" I waved in dismissal. "You're sounding a little too hippie-like. Have you been hanging out with Willow?"

"She did bring me a special tea blend this morning," she mentioned, speaking of our free-spirited little sister. Willow Kingsley was the opposite of me. Where I walked on solid ground, Willow floated high in the clouds. The perks of being the youngest child. They seemed to have a lot more freedom with life than the eldest.

"But I do stand by what I said about the gift from the universe," Yara said.

"What's the return policy on universe gifting?" I muttered as I crossed my arms.

"I know it's awkward for you, Avery, but this could be good for the team. I know it's probably uncomfortable with Nathan, but you're both adults now and can work past any old drama you had. I know you can because you're a badass who can work through anything. Even ex-boyfriends."

3

NATHAN

I had a strong distaste for people who lied to get their way. Nothing rubbed me the wrong way more than a liar.

"You said you told Avery about me being the head coach and that she was on board with the idea," I remarked as I stood in Raymond's office, floored that he didn't tell Avery. I felt like a major dick for blindsiding her like that. If Raymond had told me Avery did, in fact, not know about the arrangement, I would've told him to tell her as soon as possible. I wouldn't have agreed to the position without her approval.

Nothing good came from surprising Avery Kingsley.

I'd learned that the hard way.

"I might have told a little lie. The truth is, I know you would've turned down the head coaching position if you knew Avery didn't approve. I think you'll be the greatest gift to the team, Nathan. I couldn't risk losing you."

"You wouldn't have lost me, but I wouldn't have accepted the head coach position."

"Listen, I know you don't know Avery as well as I do, but she can be a handful. She's hotheaded and would've had this explosive reaction regardless of how gently we revealed the news. I figured yanking the Band-Aid off was the best bet."

"This should've been discussed. Now I have an irritated coach who doesn't trust me. That only makes things more challenging."

"Not exactly. I told Avery if she didn't find your addition to the team a good fit, she could remove herself completely from the coaching staff. And if she gives you a hard time, I'll remove her myself."

Was he joking?

That was messed up.

He had enough nerve to flip Avery's world upside down and then threaten to remove her.

What a dick.

"It will be fine," I told him. My mind was still trying to wrap around everything that was happening. I only considered coaching the baseball team when I was approached with the opportunity because my mother was worried about me focusing too much on the family farm. She said I needed hobbies. Real hobbies outside of balancing the books. Plus, I'd missed the game.

Did a part of me want to be near Avery Kingsley, too? Sure. Maybe.

But the connection we had all those years ago was old and buried. I didn't want to dig it up. If anything, it was a simple curiosity of wanting to know the type of woman Avery grew up to become.

Okay. That ws a lie. Maybe I did want to dig up our connection a tad bit. I couldn't help it. She was a part of the happiest time in my life when I was younger. It was almost impossible to not think about her and what we once were.

I'd heard whispers in town about Avery. Gossiping townsfolk calling her rude and harsh. Most people in Honey Creek looked at Avery and said she grew up to be bitter and cold, but when I looked into her eyes, I saw the same thing I'd seen all those years before—someone I wanted to know more about.

Her brown eyes were still beautiful, yet colder than I'd remembered.

I wondered what made them so cold.

I wondered what made her heart harden so much over the years.

And due to my curiosity, I needed her to stay around for a while. I couldn't have her quit the team or be let go. I also didn't want her to have some awful thoughts about who I'd grown up to be. After my career-ending injury, I went through a bit of a spiral with my mental health. It wasn't only due to the injury, but around the same time, I'd lost one of my best friends to a tragedy. I wasn't in a good place, and the media ran with their stories about how I was a drug addict and a has-been. I knew what it was like to be judged from the outside. I didn't like that Raymond or the people of Honey Creek judged Avery in that same fashion.

And even if she was cold, the world probably made her that way. People's hearts didn't harden by choice. They hardened due to traumatic inflictions of pain caused by others.

Maybe this was my opportunity to reintroduce myself to her. To start anew. To leave our past behind us and work together to make the team the best it could be. Because if there was one thing Avery knew, it was baseball. She lived and breathed the sport. I didn't join the team to have her talents overlooked. I joined in order to help highlight them.

Now, I had to make sure she realized that. I needed her to see that I wasn't out to steal her job but to make things better for her. Raymond, of course, didn't make that easier for me.

AFTER LEAVING THE SCHOOL, I headed to my brother's butcher shop in downtown Honey Creek. I came from a big family. I had the most amazing mother and four brothers who meant the world to me. Said brothers are also a pain in my ass. I was certain I was a pain in theirs, too. As the eldest brother, I felt a big responsibility to make sure they always had everything they needed. Especially after our father passed away years ago.

If it weren't for the near financial ruin my father left us in when he passed, I would've probably stayed in Honey Creek instead of signing a baseball contract. Yet our family needed the money—*bad*—so it seemed like the best option at the time. I didn't regret my choice. It ended up saving the family farm.

My family ran Honey Farms, one of the best farms in all the Midwest. We had everything you could think of, from goats, chickens, pigs, and cows to almost every vegetable known to humankind. We partnered with some stellar businesses across Illinois. Not long ago, I scored a contract to get all our produce into the restaurant owned by Avery's brother-in-law, Alex. Alex and I were currently discussing getting some meat on his menu from our butcher shop.

My twin brothers, Evan and Easton, ran the butcher shop. They were two years younger than me and the complete opposite of one another. Not only based on their looks, as they were fraternal, but also on how they lived their lives. In a different realm, I wouldn't have been shocked if Easton was a leading man in romantic comedy movies, while Evan would've been some grumpy surgeon who took everything far too seriously. Instead, the two of them ended up in a butcher shop. A shop that was our father's dream.

As I walked through the door, Easton was at the register, chatting with a few customers about the oxtails they had in the store's freezer section.

"You'll be amazed at how tender these bad boys will get," Easton told them. "Toss in some of our mom's pork belly mac and cheese and greens from the fridge section, and boom! You have a whole meal."

"That's kind of a high price tag for so little meat on the bones," the customer remarked with a look of disappointment.

Easton shook his head. "You're paying for quality with Pierce's Meat. Hear me out. Let me ring you up for your first order of these, maybe four packs, and if you aren't satisfied, come on back and I'll refund you. But you also have to remember my cooking instructions, all right? I promise you, your family will be kissing your feet over these."

I smirked as I stood back, watching my brother influence those folks into buying over one hundred bucks of oxtails.

Easton's superpower was selling a product. Lucky for us, he wasn't lying about the superior quality of the meat. If the Pierce family did one thing well, it was crafting great products. Easton was just a mastermind at making people spend money on said products. That big-ass smirk he always gave to people probably didn't hurt. Being a friendly face came in handy. People trusted him and for good reason. After Easton sold the products, we'd always get happy returning customers.

As he rang up their items, he thanked them, walked around the counter, shook their hand, and handed them a flyer with the daily specials for the following week.

"I tossed my business card into your bag, too, with my private number on it. Give me a call if you need extra help with those oxtails," Easton offered with a friendly wink.

After they left, he turned toward me with his big, goofy grin still plastered on his face. "Hey, big brother." He playfully batted his fist against my chest. "You need to get back in the gym. You're looking a bit small there, buddy."

"Still strong enough to kick your ass," I said, pulling him into a headlock. "Where's Evan?"

"In the back, chopping up some ribs. You need him?" Easton asked, wiggling his way out of the headlock.

"Nah. It's all good. I'm here to pick up the sample box to take over to Isla Iberia. We need Alex to add our pork to his menu."

"Get him the pork belly, too!" Evan hollered from the back room. He came out with a slab of ribs, plopped them down onto brown parchment paper, and wrapped them up. "Give him this and the pork belly. I know he only asked for chops and bacon, but he needs to sample these too. The rest is in the storage locker."

Evan rocked the same grimace he always did, but every now and then, the corner of his mouth would turn up in an almost smirk. When it came to the twins, Easton must've swallowed up all the smiling genetics. Evan lived his days frowning.

"You coming out for the birthday celebrations tomorrow?" Evan asked as he removed his gloves and tossed them into a trash bin. "River and Grant got us a table at O'Reilly's." He said he *got us a table* as if O'Reilly's was a VIP situation instead of a simple hole-in-the-wall bar in downtown Honey Creek.

"Wouldn't miss it," I mentioned, speaking about our other younger brothers, River and Grant, turning twenty-six. Yup, that's right. I had two sets of twin brothers. I felt like the odd man out growing up. Whenever we had family drama when we were younger, it felt like everyone except for me had someone in their corner to turn to. I was bitter about it for a while, but over time, I realized that I did fine on my own. Plus, my brothers were good guys. They worked hard to make me not feel left out, even when it was next to impossible.

River and Grant helped Mom a lot on the actual farm. River ran the business side of things, and Grant tended to the animals and managed the staff.

For how hardworking they both were, they loved to celebrate their birthdays even harder. I knew a night at O'Reilly's would end up being a drunken night where we wouldn't end up home until well after five in the morning.

Correction—*they* wouldn't end up home until after five in the morning. I took pride in my escaping skills. I was a professional at exiting stage left from any celebration that went past ten at night. I was too old to keep up with my younger brothers and their drinking, but I was more than willing to show up for a beer or two. The ten-year age gap between the youngest twins and I sure showed up when I tried to keep up with their drinking.

"Don't pussy out and ditch us before midnight, Cinderella," Easton teased, shoving my shoulder.

"You know I'll turn into a pumpkin if I stay out past that time," I joked as I opened the storage fridge and grabbed the container to take to Alex's restaurant.

Easton smirked. "If you stay up late, there's a better chance you could get laid, Grandpa. How long has it been since you've seen the beautiful workings between a woman's legs?"

"Not everyone's getting laid as often as you, brother," I said. "Some of us have restraints *and* standards."

"I have standards!" Easton dramatically exclaimed, slapping his hands over his chest as if I'd just told him he was the biggest scumbag on earth.

Evan huffed out laughter at the idea of Easton having standards. He moved over to the sink and washed his hands. "You having standards is the most absurd thing I've heard in a while. You'll screw any woman."

Easton shrugged. "That's me having standards. I can't help it that all women have this tempting mystical land resting right between their legs. It's like an amusement park down there, and I'm just a man who wants to show them my raging bull while they allow me to tilt-their-whirl. Sure, each theme park is different. Some have more waterslides than others, but the price of admission is always worth it."

I chuckled. "You're ridiculous."

"No, I'm a lover boy. Drake taught me well. Nine tomorrow night at O'Reilly's, brother."

"*Nine?*" I groaned. What kind of events started at nine at night? What was this? A college frat party? "I thought we agreed on six."

"That was before Mom said she wanted to do cake and ice cream at her place. You can make it a late night for yourself, old balls," Evan said, tossing the wrapped-up slab of ribs and pork belly into the carton in my hands. "If I have to be out, then you do, too. Now, go sell our goods."

I took on one of Evan's grimaces before heading out to Isla Iberia to pitch the products to Alex. I was already dreading the fact that I'd be staying up past ten on Saturday night. I liked to live a boring life where I worked all day and slept all night. My bedtime routine was my favorite part of every day, and one day off made my whole week feel unstable.

"I figured you forgot about the drop-off," Alex mentioned as I walked into the kitchen of Isla Iberia through the back alleyway entrance.

"Not a chance. Got all the best pork for you to sample." I set the container down on his countertop. He quickly washed and dried his hands with a rag before inspecting the goods.

He arched an eyebrow and tossed the rag over his shoulder. "I only asked for chops and bacon."

"We figured you deserved more than chops and bacon, Chef."

He narrowed his eyes as he began to examine the meat. He lifted the extras Evan tossed in. "Pork belly?"

"Pork belly."

He grumbled, patting the meat with his hand. "I actually wanted some pork belly to test out a few recipes."

I grinned. "It's almost like we should go into business with one another."

"Don't get smart about it, all right? I said I would try your meat. I didn't say I'd add it to my menu. I already get some quality stuff from a team in Chicago."

"You'll get better quality here and won't have to pay to have it brought over, Chef. I'm telling you, once you taste Pierce meat, you won't regret it."

"I'm already on board with your produce, which has proved to be a good thing. But if I'm honest, you're putting me in a bit of an uncomfortable situation here, Nate."

"How so?"

"When we made our deal for produce, I wasn't with Yara. Now that she's my wife, it adds a bit of a challenge to the whole situation of us working together."

"What do you mean by that?"

He cocked an eyebrow and shook his head. "I think you know what I mean by that."

"I honestly have no idea."

He crossed his arms and leaned back against his counter. "I got a visit from Yara earlier today. She was extra emotional about something that went down with Avery and you today at the high school."

Oh.

That.

I flicked my thumb against the bridge of my nose before crossing my arms, too, standing tall. "Oh?" I said, trying to play it cool.

"Yes, oh." He shook his head. "You got a pregnant woman coming over to me in distress because she's convinced her older sister is going to have a mental breakdown from losing the one position that means the world to her. Now, you see how it could add unnecessary beef to my life if I have to tell her that I'm adding your family's *beef* to my restaurant?"

"To be fair, it's more than just beef. You have pork now, and we also have chicken—"

"Nathan. You already know I like you, and I hate most

people. You and your family have been easy as hell to work with over the past two years. But the idea of pissing off my pregnant, hormonal wife and Avery—a woman who scares me to this day—is a big risk to my...well...life expectancy."

I sighed. "I know it's a bad look."

"It's an *awful* look."

"What if I told you I wasn't taking the head coaching position? What if I left that for Avery? Would you then consider a partnership?"

He narrowed his eyes. "Perhaps..."

I held a hand out toward him. "Deal."

"There's no way it's that easy."

"It's that easy. There was a miscommunication with the whole head coach thing anyway. I don't want the position if it means taking it from Avery. Between you and me, I just missed the game. I'd be more than happy being an assistant coach beside her."

Alex brushed his hand against the back of his neck but then shook my hand. "All right. Give Avery her position back, and I'll continue to consider a partnership. Thanks."

"Not a problem. And congratulations again on the baby."

Alex wasn't one to smile much, but his lips turned up slightly. "Thanks. We're excited." You could tell how happy Yara made him. He could hardly avoid smiling when it came to talking about his family. Seeing a grump like him smile as much as he had about his partner and soon-to-be newborn was good. Maybe our grumpy Evan would find himself a Yara someday. It might ease his harsh temperament.

"Don't screw me over, though," Alex warned. "The moment I hear back from my wife that Avery is the head coach again, then we can chat."

"Deal. Thanks again for the shot, Chef."

He shook his head. "I'm still not going to get used to the MVP Nathan Pierce calling me Chef."

"Tell Avery I'm sorry if you see her before I do," I mentioned.

"There's no way I'm telling her anything. I'm not getting in the middle of whatever the two of you have going on. I learned a long time ago to stay out of other people's affairs."

"Isn't you telling me that you'll only do a deal with me if I give Avery the head coaching position being involved in our affairs?"

Alex parted his mouth and hesitated for a minute. I'd stumped him. He rubbed his hand against his brows and grumbled under his breath, "*sal de mi maldita cocina.*"

"What does that mean?"

"It means get the fuck out of my kitchen."

I smirked. "Yes, Chef."

→ love triangle
→ she's not good at her job
→ make him love her job ∵ she's unable to put
   & kids first

4

NATHAN

The second Saturday night rolled around, it was time to celebrate River and Grant. I loved my brothers, but I was already dreading each moment as we drove together from Mom's to O'Reilly's. I even tried to weasel my way out of a night of drinking by offering to help Mom clean up after the big meal she'd cooked for us boys.

She, of course, turned down the request and told me to go have fun with the guys.

"You don't get enough brotherly time, and you definitely don't get enough social time. Enjoy it," Mom said, swatting me out of her kitchen. That was the second time I'd been kicked out of kitchens that week.

"Twenty-six is going to be my year," River announced, rubbing his hands together in the passenger seat of the car as I drove to O'Reilly's. Grant was sandwiched in the back seat between Evan and Easton, looking squashed between the two guys. No way were the three of them comfortable based on their size alone. If there was one thing about the Pierce brothers, it was the fact that we didn't skip arm day. Or leg day, for that matter.

I told them we should've taken different cars, but they forced me to drive, claiming I couldn't sneak out if I was the driver for the evening.

The three sat scrunched up back there like idiots, smiling from ear-to-ear as if they were in for the best night of their lives.

"It's going to be my year, too, asshat," Grant replied to his twin.

Unlike Evan and Easton, Grant and River were identical twins. If a person were to look at the two of them side by side, they'd just believe they were seeing double images of the same person. From their wide, toothy grins to their bushy brows and dreadlocks, those two were remarkably the same. It didn't help that they dressed alike, too. They were both sneakerheads with an addiction to expensive designer clothing.

They even had damn near the same voice. If I closed my eyes and one of them said something, I wouldn't know which brother spoke. They used to get in a lot of trouble for doing *The Parent Trap* and switching spots with one another when they were kids.

Mom had her hands full with those troublemakers growing up. I missed a lot of that period because I was off playing baseball, but it was nice to see they grew up to be decent, good men.

When it came to the youngest twins' dating lives, River and Grant were a mixture of their three older brothers. They didn't need companionship. They were fine on their own, like Evan and me, but every now and again, they had a soft lover boy side to them, too, like Easton.

River was one to fall fast for a woman. That didn't always bode well for his sensitive heart. Yet after every breakup, he always hit his personal records with deadlifting in the gym, so that could be seen as a silver lining. It was only about a week ago that he found out his ex-girlfriend Sarah had been cheating on him with his so-called best friend. I figured that was why the guys were so hell-bent on having me stay out with them. Our little River needed to get his mind off a girl who wasn't good enough for him.

That kind of made me want to stop being a jerk about going out. There wasn't much that I wouldn't do to make sure my family was safe and good. If my going out would've helped make River happier, then I'd do it. He had his fair share of heartbreak, even at a younger age. I've only gone through one heartbreak myself, though I have been known to break others' hearts without trying.

Which was why I'd kept my heart—and my dick—to myself as of late. I didn't see any reason to send any woman mixed signals.

As we pulled up to O'Reilly's, I parked the car, and the guys hopped out, clapping their hands with excitement. They walked into the bar as if they were walking into some Vegas strip club instead of a small-town, hole-in-the-wall bar that served their drinks in plastic cups.

The amount of swag dripping off the sets of twins was ridiculous.

I hated how good they looked, too. They knew they were handsome, looking like our father. Evan was damn near a heartthrob with his thick-ass beard. If he didn't love his solitude so much and put off that stay-the-hell-away-from-me energy everywhere he went, women would throw themselves at him.

I followed them, still dreading the whole evening. That was until I looked over at the bar and saw a doe-eyed bartender standing there serving drinks. Probably the most beautiful woman I've ever seen.

Avery Kingsley bartended at O'Reilly's?

Well, that shifted my mood a good amount.

"Does she still think you're a dick?" Evan murmured toward me as we sat at a back table, watching the other guys taking yet another shot at the bar.

"Who?"

He gave me a you-know-who look. "Avery. The woman you've been hung up on since you were nineteen."

"Eighteen," I corrected. "And watch your mouth." I shoved him in the arm. "I'm not hung up on her. Never have been," I lied. "Don't go around spreading that rumor."

"Can't spread rumors if I keep to myself. But you've been staring at her nonstop since we walked in here. I know I'm the only one who knows you had a short thing with Avery, but if you keep staring at her like you are, everyone in town will know."

Evan was the only brother who knew about Avery and me. It wasn't that I was trying to keep her a secret. If anything, at one point, I wanted to shout from the rooftop about Avery and how much I loved her. But it was so short-lived that I didn't even get a chance to do so. Evan only knew about the whole situation because he walked in on Avery and me once when I was helping her around the farm. He found us making out next to the horse stables.

I averted my eyes away from Avery and grumbled as I took a swig of my beer. "I'm coaching baseball at the high school."

Evan arched an eyebrow. "No shit. To be closer to Avery?"

"No," I urged. "To get back into the game I love. I miss it. When the school district came to me with the idea, I ran with it."

"It didn't hurt that she's a coach there, too, huh?"

No, it didn't.

He didn't need to know that, though.

"I missed the game," I explained. "That's it, that's all. But I'm pretty sure Avery hates my guts now. The school put me as the head coach. I was under the impression Avery knew about that until she snapped at me."

"Is that why she's giving you a solid fuck-off stare whenever she looks your way?"

"That could be the reason, yeah. She still doesn't know I'm not taking the position. I'm going to be her assistant coach. Alex said he wouldn't consider partnering with us if I didn't step down."

"That's pretty messed up."

"It's loyalty to his sister-in-law. I can't be mad at a man with family values. I would've done the same thing if the roles were reversed," I said, looking back in Avery's direction. When I did, she locked eyes with me, and a deep scorn fell on her face before she looked away. She turned to my brothers and smiled brightly, pouring them another shot.

It's not family values, it's manipulation. She's not good at her job

Why did they get her happy smiles?

That didn't seem fair at all.

"Just a heads-up, she's engaged," Evan mentioned as he took a sip of his beer.

I arched an eyebrow. "Why would I care that she's engaged?"

Evan almost smiled, but before he could reply, we were being called to the bar to take a shot with the other guys. We headed to join them and found a line of shots set out. Easton turned and handed one to me and another to Evan.

"Sweet Miss Avery made some birthday shots for the boys," Easton said as Avery pulled out a lighter.

"Happy Birthday, River and Grant. This is your year, boys," Avery stated. Seeing her treat my brothers so kindly while she handled me as if I was scum annoyed me. The tinge of jealousy hit me hard.

River patted his twin's chest. "See? Told you it's my year!"

"And mine!" Grant urged.

Avery looked like she was in a damn good mood. She

placed the birthday boys' shots in front of her, sprinkled something on top, and lit them on fire. "Happy Birthday, boys. Make a wish."

River and Grant shut their eyes for a moment, then blew out the shots.

"Give a toast, Nathan!" Grant requested as he picked up his shot. "You always give the best toasts."

I smiled and held up my shot glass. "River and Grant, life was a lot less hectic before you came along, but it wasn't anywhere near as fun. Here's to the birthday boys, who've been copying and pasting each other since day one. May your nights be as long as your arguments and your hangovers be as short as your differences. Cheers, brothers!"

"Cheers!" they all shouted, tapping their glasses on the bar countertop before downing the shots. The moment I put my shot glass on the countertop, I caught Avery's stare.

It wasn't packed with the same hatred as before. Her look seemed more curious this time. Soft. Unalert. With haste, she shook off the stare and gathered the shot glasses to clean up.

The guys headed off to play a round of darts, leaving me sitting at the bar as Avery cleaned. She was the only one working behind the counter, but that seemed fine, seeing as how the place wasn't packed. It had a handful of regulars, my brothers, and me that night. Most people in town went over to Stan's Bar and Grill on Saturday nights. That was why the boys preferred O'Reilly's—they had more opportunities to get wasted and take over the jukebox.

"Since when are you a bartender?" I asked when I had built up enough courage to speak to Avery. I didn't know why, but that woman made me nervous. I wasn't used to getting nervous around people, but she sure knew how to shake me.

She glanced over her shoulder toward me before returning to drying the shot glasses. "Since I get paid a teacher's salary."

"I always thought it was awful how little teachers got paid.

Other professions shouldn't be making anywhere near what they do, compared to teachers."

"Says the fancy MLB player offered multimillion-dollar contracts," she huffed. She tossed her towel over her shoulder and placed a hand against her hip. Her hip that she'd popped out. Her hip that my eyes fell straight toward. The way that body curved...

"You need another drink?" she asked.

"No, I still have my beer over at the table."

"Then stop taking up my bar space."

I scanned the empty bar. "No one's here."

"I like to keep my counter space open if people do wander in. So if you could please leave," she said as she began to tie up a trash bag. She pulled it from the container and started heading for the back door. I sat in my seat for a moment, still feeling the urge to talk to her about what happened yesterday at the high school. So I stood and I followed her outside to the gated area with the giant trash bins. As I stepped outside, I closed the still-opened door, swinging it shut behind me.

"Hey, Avery. I was hoping we could talk about—"

She turned quickly at the sound of the slamming door and shouted, "No!" She hurried over to the door right after it clicked shut. Her hand wrapped around the doorknob, and she pulled it repeatedly, but it didn't budge.

Oh shit.

We were locked out.

"Dammit!" she yipped as she pounded her hands against the door, trying to make as much noise as possible. Unfortunately, the music inside was too loud from the jukebox, which my brothers added more coins to with every passing minute.

She turned to me with a murderous look in her eyes. I could feel her rage from the intensity of her stare. If possible, I wouldn't have been shocked if smoke started shooting out of her ears.

"What are you doing?!" she shouted, flailing her arms in the air. "That door locks from the inside when it shuts!"

"Why would they make a door that locks from the inside?"

"Why would you follow me out here?" she countered.

Good rebuttal.

I rubbed my hand on the back of my neck. "I was hoping we could talk."

"Talk?" she grumbled. "By the trash bins?"

"To be fair, you didn't want me at your bar counter," I replied.

She didn't find humor in anything I said. She stared blankly at me for a few moments before returning to the door and pounding against it. "Hey, open up the door!" she shouted. "Let me in!"

No one came, and I felt pretty shitty about it.

I glanced around the area to see if there was an easy way out, but it was enclosed by a fence that went higher than my wannabe Spider-Man self could climb.

Avery gestured toward me. "Do you have your phone? Call your brother."

"Yeah, of course." I reached into my back pocket and patted it, only to find no phone. I'd placed it on the table beside my beer before taking the shot with my brothers. "Actually..."

"Oh my goodness," she groaned as she slapped her hand to her face. "I'm the only one working tonight, Nathan, and the bar is unattended. Do you know how much trouble I could get into for this?"

"I'm sorry. I didn't mean to—"

"To what?" She cut in. "Disrupt my life? Because it seems you're on a nice campaign to do exactly that."

I grimaced as she said those words. Sure, I hadn't made the best impressions over the past forty-eight hours, but the last thing I wanted to do was cause Avery any trouble. If anything, I wanted to make things right between us. Yet somehow, I'd managed to keep screwing that up.

"Yeah," I said. "That."

She rolled her eyes. "I shouldn't be surprised. You're the same as you've always been."

"I'm not the same boy you knew back then, Avery. I'm better than that."

"No, you aren't. People don't change. At least not for the better." →*sha 36and she think people dont change*

"So you're telling me that you're the same person you were when you were eighteen?"

"No," she disagreed. "I'm a lot harder and a lot more distrusting. That's what life does to people. It makes them cynics."

"Not everyone," I argued.

"Most." She tugged on the door again, as if the more she pulled, the more likely it would open. She then pounded against it with her open hand, mumbling something under her breath. Probably a few cuss words. With a weighted sigh, she groaned and surrendered from pounding.

"I'm sorry," I said as I watched her defeated body fall against the cobbled wall.

She shut her eyes and tilted her head up toward the sky. "For what? Getting me locked out here or taking my job? Either way, I don't forgive you."

"For both," I offered. I stood beside her, resting my back against the building. "I didn't mean to make things harder for you, Avery. That was never my plan. And to be clear, the school district informed me that you were on board with me taking the head coach position. They even made it sound like it was your idea."

"Does that sound anything like me?"

"Well, looking back on it, no. I just thought…" I didn't know what I thought. I suppose I didn't think it through at all. All I saw was a chance to get back into at game that I loved and amend things with the woman I once loved. Sure, I knew it wouldn't be easy to get in her good graces, but such a big part of me wanted to prove to her that I wasn't the selfish, hurtful kid I had been. One of my biggest regrets was how I ended things with Avery all those years before.

Yet now I felt as if I had only dug a deeper hole with her on my path to forgiveness.

She glanced over long enough for me to catch her rolling her eyes. "Just forget about it, Nathan. I don't care, okay? I'm probably going to lose this job, too, thanks to you. My boss is going to kill me when he realizes I got myself locked out by the trash bins."

Add that to my pile of screwups.

The list kept growing.

"I'll talk to your boss. I'll make sure he knows it was my mistake," I told her. "I know I shouldn't have followed you out here. I just wanted an opportunity to talk to you and apologize."

"Cool. You did that. Now, if you could just leave me alone, that would be marvelous."

"Av—"

"Gah!" she shouted as she pushed herself away from the wall. "What is it with you, huh? Are you on some kind of redemption arc? Are you trying to come back to town to right all your wrongs? What do you want from me, Nathaniel? You want me to forgive you?" She tossed her hands in the air out of frustration. "Fine. I forgive you. You want my coaching position? Okay. It's yours. I just don't see why you keep trying with me. We're never going to be friendly with one another, okay? Just make peace with that."

That felt like a knife to my gut. A knife that stabbed repeatedly.

Before I could even conjure up a response, the locked door

swung open, and Easton popped his head out. "Oh shit! There you are," he said to me.

"Keep the door open!" Avery shouted as she darted over to the door. She hurried inside, not looking back once. I stood there a moment, still trying to recover from the word bullets Avery shot me with. I didn't blame her for her coldness. If anything, I deserved every single word that fell from her mouth. Still, it didn't make it easy.

"Did you two get locked out here?" Easton asked with narrowed eyes. "Are you good, brother?"

"Yeah." I walked toward him and patted his back. "I'm good. Let's get another drink."

5

AVERY

Whatever Laurelin and Reed Pierce mixed when they birthed their five sons, it must've been laced with gold. The Pierce boys were the definition of fantastic genetics. All five of them—including Nathan, unfortunately—were beyond good-looking. I'd known the boys since they were kids, as I worked at Honey Farms as a teenager. That was how I'd met Nathan. Though, at that point, everyone knew who he was. He was the all-star athlete who attended college on a full-ride baseball scholarship. He was a celebrity to us in Honey Creek. During that time at the farm, I was able to get to know Nathan. It only took one summer of young love for me to fall for him on Honey Farms, and then it only took one day for him to shatter said love into a million pieces.

Seeing all the guys in the bar that evening was odd because it was clear that both pairs of twins were no longer the little boys who used to help me around the farm. They were fully grown men who each looked as if they should've been featured on the cover of *GQ*.

Evan emanated a grown-man-who-didn't-care-about-anyone energy whenever he walked into any room. He was the hermit of the group—the grumpy one, most would say. It seemed the only things he cared about were his work and his teenage daughter, Priya. I always thought he had to grow up a little faster than the others, seeing how he had a kid at eighteen, but he stepped up to the plate. His twin, Easton, was the poet of the group. The most romantic man I'd ever witnessed and a massive flirt with any and everyone. And I meant everyone. Whether a man or woman, Easton would give said person a stare that made them feel flustered.

The younger twins, River and Grant, were a ball of fun. They never took anything too seriously, other than making sure their haircuts were always fresh and neat. Women in town were in love with those two guys, but they didn't seem too interested in the attention. River, I heard, just ended things with his girlfriend, and Grant... Well, he had a few situationships of his own.

Outside of the guys looking like Greek gods, they were some of the nicest individuals I'd ever crossed paths with— even Evan and his grumpiness. He wasn't rude—just...reserved. I understood that. I liked to keep to myself and my family, too.

And if I didn't have my own feelings toward Nathan, I would've thought he was one of the most charming people in the world, too, like his brothers. Maybe that was the issue, though. I knew Nathan on a personal level, which tainted my viewpoint of him.

I wished I could look at him the same way I viewed his brothers—as if he was simply a handsome, remarkable man who could make any person blush with a simple "hello." I was almost certain half of Easton and Evan's business at their butcher shop came from women coming in just to hear Easton compliment them on their looks.

The Pierce charm was a real infectious illness that a lot of people fell for. Luckily for me, I had my vaccine.

After I closed O'Reilly's that night, I was left on high alert.

The interactions with Nathan were more than I was ready to deal with, and I could not for the life of me understand why he got under my skin so much.

When I got home, I showered, washed my face, and climbed into my bed, where Wesley was already sleeping. As I lay down, he snuggled closer to me, wrapping his arms around me, as he did every night I crawled into bed with him.

He gently kissed my shoulder blade and whispered, "Good night."

I didn't fall asleep right away.

Instead, I lay in my fiancé's arms, thinking about another man.

6

AVERY

Get up, Avery.

Every now and then, I would wake up in bed and be unable to move.

I had never told anyone about the struggles of not being able to physically pull myself out of bed, but lately, it had been happening a lot more than I felt comfortable with. On those mornings, I felt breathless. It was as if the weight of the world sat heavily on my chest, and I couldn't remove it, no matter how hard I tried.

That morning was one of those mornings.

Wesley had already left for his morning workout. He always woke before me, before the sun, too, and he'd be gone by the time my eyes opened.

I lay in bed as the weight of my own breath felt like a boulder on my chest. The sunlight crept through the curtains, a slimmer of light in the darkness of my room, mocking the darkness that currently clung to me like a second skin. I hated these moments. The moments when I slipped into a type of sadness I couldn't make sense of.

I'm not depressed.

I'm not depressed.

I'm fine.

I'm fine.

Those words kept playing repeatedly through my mind. They were trying to push out the other thoughts that seemed to grow louder and louder with every passing second.

Stay down.

What's the point of getting up?

I hated days like today. Days when the battle inside me raged fiercer than I'd had the strength to fight. Depression was an uninvited guest to my soul, and it had thrown a shroud over my will, leaving me paralyzed in the sanctuary of my bed.

The digital clock on my nightstand kept changing, a relentless reminder of the world moving forward without me. I wanted to get up and shake off the despondency sticking to me, but my body refused to obey my wants.

I was tired.

So desperately exhausted.

It was as if my limbs were tethered to the mattress, each attempt to move quashed by an invisible force.

"Get up, get up, get up, Avery," I whispered to the hollowness, a feeble attempt to summon any shred of willpower. My voice sounded foreign to my own ears, as though it belonged to another person. I felt as if my own soul had abandoned my body, and I was left with nothing more than emptiness.

I had many reasons to be happy.

Sure, a few things had gone wrong lately, but there was more good than bad. I was getting married in three weeks. In three short weeks, I'd be saying "I do" to someone who loved me. Someone who chose me even though I never felt good enough.

I wasn't good enough.

"No," I murmured, knowing those thoughts were not my

own. It was the depression seeping in, feeding me with its devilish lies—lies I was trying my hardest to fight.

As I lay there, my phone suddenly rang, breaking me out of the small trance I found myself in. Yara's name flashed across the screen. I stared at it but didn't answer.

She called back again.

And again.

It was clear she needed me when the fourth call came in. That was enough to slice through the room's silence—people needed me. Her persistent calls were a telltale sign of that fact. I didn't have time to freeze because people outside counted on me to defrost myself to help them with their own issues.

I reached for the phone with shaky hands.

"Hello?" I asked as my voice croaked.

"Avery," Yara cried with a frantic tone, a tone that mirrored the turmoil within my own soul, yet it was external, real, and urgent. Not like my issues. My issues were not as important.

Her tearful tone made me prop myself up to a sitting position.

"Yara. What is it? Are you okay? Is the baby all right? What do you need?" I said, pushing down my own issues to focus on hers. That was the quickest way to knock me out of my darkness. I'd focus on other people's issues and put mine on the back burner.

"The baby's fine. It's just...can you come over? I need you."

I need you—three words that got me out of bed. I didn't have time to be sad. I was needed by others. At that moment, the fog of depression that clouded my thoughts began to lift slightly. Not enough to dispel it, but enough to give me a sliver of energy to go to my sister's to make sure she was all right. That was my job as an older sister, after all. To be altogether for others so they felt safe enough to fall apart.

With a resolve that seemed to come from outside myself, I swung my legs off the bed. My body protested, but I forced myself to stand. The room swayed around me, a sign of the effort it took for me to simply exist at that moment.

I steadied myself.

I had to.

For her.

I'd always steady myself for my sisters.

"I'm on my way. Be there soon," I told her before hanging up the phone.

After I hung up, I stood still for a moment. I shut my eyes and took in a few deep inhales. Each one was a reminder that I was still here, I was still breathing, and I could still go on.

Then I shook off the shadows hanging on tightly and headed over to Yara's to make sure she was all right.

"I'M SO SORRY," Yara cried, covering her mouth with her hand. She was in a state of full panic as she stood before me wearing her bridesmaid dress, which was clearly too small. The black silk gown set tightly around her stomach as she had a full-blown meltdown. "I tried everything, and I mean everything, to get it on," she swore. "I even laid down on my stomach to try to have Alex zip it that way, but it wouldn't get past my hips." She sobbed.

I sat in front of her on her couch with a slight snicker slipping through me.

"Avery! It's not funny!" she ordered. "Your wedding is in three weeks, and my dress doesn't fit! How can I be your matron of honor if my gown doesn't fit?"

My wedding was in three weeks.

That sent a panic through my system that I wasn't prepared for.

"It doesn't matter," I swore. "You could wear a trash bag, and it would look good, Yara. Who cares?"

"A trash bag is all I'll be able to fit in soon enough," she said, still crying, still convinced she would ruin my big day. Truthfully, though, I didn't care. If I had it my way, my bridesmaids could've worn any dress that they felt comfortable in. Wesley had a very different idea of what our wedding would be, though. I never really saw myself as a woman who'd have a wedding, let alone be married, but I knew it was important to Wesley. Therefore, I let him take the lead.

He wanted a formal black-tie event, with the ceremony in our small town, then the reception at a fancy mansion on the outskirts of Chicago, which cost more than I was willing to admit.

Daddy covered many of the wedding costs even though I told him not to. It was just last year when he paid so much for Yara and Alex's nuptials, yet he said it was not a big deal at all. "I'd been saving up for these days," he told me. I asked what he would have done with the money if we didn't get married. He replied, "Given you a big check to use of your free will."

That was a tempting option to me instead of having a whole wedding. I did not like the spotlight on me, and the idea of wearing a wedding gown all day instead of jeans and a T-shirt was enough to make me groan from discomfort. A nice courtroom wedding would've been fine with me. I didn't need the glints and glimmer. Unfortunately, my fiancé did.

"How about this?" I took Yara's shaky hands into mine and led her to the couch. As she sat, I heard the seams of the dress rip more, which brought on more tears. I tried my best not to laugh, but it was slightly funny. "We will go into Chicago a few days before the wedding and pick out a black dress that fits you perfectly. We'll try all department stores until you feel at your utmost comfortable."

"I won't match Willow's dress," she warned.

"Willow will come with us, and she'll get the same dress as you. It's not a big deal. And even if your dresses don't match,

they are both black, which is wonderfully close enough to me."
I wiped at her tears. "This is not a reason to fall apart, okay?"

She sniffled and nodded. "Okay." She wiped her tears away
and shook her head. "I just feel so bad. I want this day to be
perfect for you. I don't want to be the reason things look bad in
pictures."

"You could never look bad in pictures, Yara. Get those
thoughts out of your head. And all I care about is saying 'I do.'
Nothing else really matters. I'm just ready to have a husband."

I think.

Maybe.

How did people know when they were ready for marriage?

"They are pretty nice when you get the right ones," she
agreed.

"Speaking of good husbands, where is Alex?"

"Oh, he didn't know how to manage my breakdown, so he
went to buy me donuts."

"Smart man."

"The smartest man." She shook her head and gently chuckled. "Gosh, I'm so sorry for being a hot mess. My emotions are
all over the place lately. The past few weeks have been so wild.
Pregnancy is intense."

"But beautiful," I told her. I couldn't wait to hold my niece
or nephew one day. Alex and Yara weren't finding out the baby's
gender until birth. My anxiety could never wait that long but to
each their own. What mattered most was their having a healthy
baby to bring home.

A part of me felt selfish for the thoughts that raced through
my head when I learned my sister was pregnant. There was a
touch of jealousy, of longing, that I felt from the news. Don't get
me wrong, I was truly happy for Alex and Yara. They would
both be amazing parents. I just thought that by age thirty-six, I
would already have the things my younger sister was expe-
riencing.

Of course, I never spoke about my fear of falling behind. I didn't want to make anyone else feel bad or have pity for me. Still, my heart longed for children someday. At least Wesley and I were on the same page about that. We planned to start our family shortly after our wedding. Only three weeks until the rest of my life took off, like my sister's.

"Enough about me and my tears," Yara said, wiping away the final emotions falling from her eyes. "How are you?"

For a moment, my mind traveled back to my morning struggles. My heart beat faster as I thought about the panic I'd felt as I lay in the darkness, not wanting to get up at all. Almost unable to move from the shadows of the hovering depression that floated over every inch of my being.

I couldn't tell Yara that.

It would've broken her heart, and her sweet heart was already fragile.

Besides, I'd be fine.

I'd always be fine.

Being fine was my default setting.

The sprouts of depression were only something that came every now and again. It wasn't anything worth making others feel bad about.

Instead of telling her the truth, I pushed out a smile and said, "I'm good."

7

NATHAN

I slept awfully all weekend. The boys kept me out way too late on Saturday, and I worked around the farm from sunrise to sunset on Sunday. No one talked about how much work it took to run a farm as large as my family's. We had a solid crew of employees, but I still felt as if it was never enough.

Mom told me I was a workaholic, but I liked being busy. The more I kept my mind occupied with other things, the less time I had to overthink things. Or to overthink people. People like Avery.

Still, even while I worked all Sunday, thoughts of her would slice through my brain. I couldn't stop thinking about the way I'd made such an ass of myself in front of her on Saturday night. Not only did I jeopardize her job by following her outside and getting us locked out but I also looked damn near like a stalker.

Not exactly the vibe I was going for.

I just wanted her to know I wasn't trying to ruin her life. In my attempt, though, I almost proceeded to ruin her life.

When Monday afternoon came and it was time to meet the

team at practice, I felt a heaviness sitting against my chest. As I approached Avery's office, I knocked against her open door.

"Knock, knock," I said.

She sat at her desk, looking down at her paperwork. "You don't have to say knock, knock if you're going to actually knock, Nathaniel."

Nathaniel.

A telltale sign that she still, indeed, hated me.

I crossed my arms over my chest and stepped into her office. My eyes danced around the space, taking it in for the first time. When I chased her into her office last Friday, I didn't get a chance to see her space. I was too focused on trying to get her not to hate me.

The space wasn't huge, but it was a decent size. Much bigger than the office I was given down the hall. Framed photographs of past teams and motivational quotes covered the walls. One was a sign with the word "heart" written over the word "head." A reminder to lead with one's heart on the field, more than one's head. She was the one who taught me that lesson when we were young. I was nervous about my baseball career, and she told me that if I led with my heart, I'd end up at home plate every single time. Heart over head was the saying that changed my confidence, which in turn changed my game.

It was clear she still believed in that technique, which was odd to me, seeing how she seemed to live a lot more in her head than her heart from what I'd noticed.

Her large and well-worn desk sat in the middle of the space. It was covered with lineup sheets, player stats, and a few too many coffee mugs that needed a good washing. In a fancy case was an autographed baseball. I couldn't help but wonder who signed that thing, but I knew I couldn't approach it or ask her about it. I was probably already crossing her boundaries by even breathing the same air as her.

A whiteboard filled with practice schedules and game

strategies was on the right wall. The number of scribbles over her work showed how much she changed her mind once she found a better game plan. The markings looked like a beautiful disaster, something that probably only made sense to Avery's brain. I wished I could learn how her thoughts worked in that day and age. How she figured things out and pieced together her strategies.

In the left corner of her office was a bookshelf with a collection of baseball books. Everything from manuals and inspirational memoirs to...was that a baseball romance novel?

That's slightly shocking, Coach.

I arched an eyebrow, wanting to know more about said book, but Avery cut my curiosity in half as she snapped my way. "What do you want?" she barked. "Or let me guess, you're here to tell me you're taking my office space, too."

Her harsh personality wouldn't go away anytime soon, so I had to learn to deal with it. I wasn't afraid of a hard Avery Kingsley. She was hard when I first met her all those years ago on the farm. It took her a little while to warm up to me, let alone fall in love.

I figured it would take some time for her to warm up to my grown-up version, too. Though, I didn't need her to fall in love with me this time. I just needed her to dip her toe into "like" territory. Because if we were going to make this team the best it could be, there had to be at least some kind of mutual respect between us coaches.

"I was going to head out to meet the guys. I figured it might be good to have you out there with me."

She glanced down at her watch and muttered something under her breath. She pushed herself away from her desk and grabbed her clipboard. As she walked over to me, she said, "Fine. Let's get this over with."

"Sounds good."

"Can you do me a favor, though?"

"Sure. What's that?"

A flash of sadness raced through her brown eyes as they fell on mine. "Don't make me seem too much like a loser when you tell them that you're the new head coach."

I swallowed hard as I slid my hands into my pockets. "I'll do my best, Coach."

She nodded and walked away. "And don't call me Coach. I hate that."

We headed out to the indoor gym facility, which was pretty impressive. When I went to school at Honey Creek High, we did not have the next-level equipment that the school now had. It would make our late-winter, early-spring workouts much more enjoyable. The space was equipped with batting cages, pitching machines, and a huge area for fielding practices.

It was no wonder the school didn't want to ditch the whole baseball program. They'd clearly invested a lot of money in it.

Not only did they have all this inside but they also had a beautiful outdoor field and a batting cage along with a gigantic gym for strength and conditioning. I knew we would have amazing weightlifting, plyometrics, and other fitness routines in that space.

"This place still blows my mind," I remarked as we entered the indoor space.

"Get a student who goes off to win two World Series, and the school makes it their whole personality," Avery mumbled. "They call it the Nathan Pierce effect."

"They did this because of me?"

She rolled her eyes. "Don't be so shocked. It's like when Taylor Swift wins a Grammy and acts like it's such a surprise."

She was so snappy, and I didn't know if she knew it, but it made me oddly more intrigued to break through that wall she had built up. The ruder she grew, the kinder I'd become. Though I was almost certain that made her angry, too.

As we approached the guys, who were all talking to each

other, laughing and joking around, Avery clapped her hands together as she held her clipboard under her arm. "All right, boys, listen up. We have some changes coming on. I want to introduce you to Coach Pierce. He's going to be helping us out a bit." Avery gestured toward me, giving me the sign to take it from there.

I cleared my throat and slid my hands into the pockets of my black joggers. "Hey there. I'm Nathan Pierce, and I'm excited to join the team as the assistant coach to Coach K. You can call me Coach P. I'm excited to be back at Honey Creek to help take this already strong team to a stronger level under Coach Kingsley's leadership. If I'm honest, I learned my best baseball traits from her back when we were young, and it's an honor to be able to work beside her again."

I saw the somberness on Avery's face as I spoke, but I tried not to take it in too much. The surprise on her face from the announcement that I was taking the assistant coach as opposed to the head coach seemed to lift a weight off her shoulders.

"So before we get started, I want you all to know this first week, I'm just here to observe. I want to see how you all move, how you all work, and I want to get to know you each on a personal level. Don't be afraid to reach out and ask me any questions. A coach is only as strong as the safe place that they make for their team, and I want you all to feel comfortable coming to me with anything and everything. Does anyone have any questions off the bat? Nothing's off-limits."

"You're going to regret saying that," Avery muttered.

I arched an eyebrow at her, but before I could ask why, a bunch of hands shot up.

I gestured to one of the guys. "Yeah? What's your name and question?"

"Yeah, hi, Coach P. I'm Ryan. I'm a right fielder. I was wondering, is it true you were found on the Vegas Strip wasted out of your mind and on drugs?"

Well.

They sure didn't pull any punches.

I looked back over at Avery, searching for a bit of help.

She didn't look as if she felt bad for me at all as she shrugged. "You should never say to teenage boys that nothing is off-limits."

Fair enough.

I cleared my throat and crossed my arms. "Being in the spotlight as a famous figure brought me a lot of highs. It also brought some low moments. Yet I like to think we aren't our best or worst moments. We are the moments in-between."

Another player raised his hand. I called on him.

"Hey, Coach. I'm Caleb. Third baseman."

"Nice to meet you, Caleb," I said. "And your question?"

"So yeah, uh, is that a yes to Ryan's question?" he asked.

I cleared my throat and looked around. "Any more questions?"

More hands shot back up.

Avery stepped forward and slid her hands into the pockets of her joggers. "Any questions that aren't about Coach P being famous, about his past partying behavior, about who he may or may not have dated, about how much money is in his account, or about his injury?"

All the hands slowly went down.

Avery smirked a little. It was clear she knew the guys inside and out. It would take me a little time to catch up to her level of knowledge, but I was ready to take it all in and play catch-up.

"All right, then. Let's get to work. We're going to split up into teams." She used her hand to split the guys down the middle. "Caleb, you're leading your team on hitting drills. I want to see pepper work, soft toss, and tee work. Cameron, you're team leader for pitching drills. Start with bullpen sessions, then toss in some towel drills. Let's go! Move, move, move."

The guys responded to Avery's orders with haste.

One thing was clear—the team respected her. That was a good thing. A coach with no respect from their team was no coach at all.

———————

"WHAT WAS THAT?" Avery whisper-shouted after practice as she followed me into my office. "Why did you tell them you were the assistant coach after Ray said you were the head coach?"

"I turned down the position. He told me you knew and agreed to the first arrangement, and when it became achingly clear that that wasn't the truth, I told him I'd only be the assistant coach or I'd walk. So"—I slightly bowed—"I'm here to assist, Coach."

She rolled her eyes. Leave it to Avery Kingsley to somehow make eye-rolling attractive. "You're so annoying."

I arched an eyebrow. "I'm annoying for letting you keep your head coach position?"

"You didn't *let* me keep it."

"Technically, yeah, I did."

"Technically, piss off," she replied.

I smirked.

She rolled her eyes again. "Stop smirking, Nathaniel. Your smugness is annoying."

"I get the feeling you think everything about me is annoying."

"That's because it is. You, as a whole human being, are annoying."

"I missed you, too, Coach."

The rage that shot through her system erupted into a burst of shouting and hand gestures. "*You* are a *pain* in my *ass*, Nathaniel, and I cannot *stand* you." She sighed and pinched the bridge of her nose. "But if we are forced to work together, we have to have some ground rules."

"I'm more of a rule breaker."

"Trust me, I know. I saw your baseball stats."

I smiled slyly. "So you've followed my stats?"

"Deflate your big head, Mr. Ego. I study all the top baseball players' stats."

I smiled wider. "So you think I'm one of the best?"

She crossed her arms over her chest and narrowed her eyes. "Rule number one," she scolded. "You'll respect my decisions around the boys. If you disagree, you discuss it with me in private."

"Does that go both ways?"

"Of course. I don't need the boys thinking there's an issue between us coaches. Coach Erikson didn't adhere to that rule. It made the past few years of my life hell. We don't need to show-case a disconnect."

"Even though there is a clear disconnect, based on the room's energy right now."

"We are as disconnected as two people could ever be."

"I'd like to take an opportunity to plug us back together."

"That sounds highly inappropriate, which brings me to the next rule. No inappropriate comments toward me."

I arched an eyebrow and dramatically slammed my hand over my heart. "When have I ever been inappropriate?"

She cocked an "are you shitting me right now" eyebrow.

I chuckled. "Okay, no inappropriate commentary."

"Rule number three—"

"How many rules are there?"

"A lot. There are a lot of rules." She smoothed her hands over her hoodie and rolled her shoulders back. "No talk about us."

"I can't talk about us?"

"No. Not the old us, at least. Not like...what we once were."

"You mean how we were in love?" I questioned.

Avery's cheeks flushed as she moved over to my door and

shut it. She continued to whisper-shout as she looked my way. "Exactly that! No talk about any of that. No one even knows about that whole situation."

"I'm sure Yara and Willow do. Didn't you tell your sisters?"

She pointed a stern finger my way. "I would answer that, but that's breaking rule number three, and we will not break these rules."

"Whatever you say, Coach."

She rolled her eyes—*again*. It was as if whenever I spoke, she displayed a heavy level of disgust. I'd never had someone react so intensely to my mere existence. It was as if whenever I spoke, Avery got a damn hairball stuck in her throat that she wanted to hack up.

Most women had the complete opposite reaction to me. Not to sound cocky, but Avery made me feel like a slimy alien that she loved to belittle. ⟶ cringe

Oddly enough, that only made me want to be closer to her.

Call it a shame kink, if you will.

I took a seat in my office chair and spun around. "Any more rules?"

She narrowed her eyes and shrugged. "Don't baby these boys. They need a tough love training."

"They need a bit of soft love, too. How about you play bad cop, and I'll be good cop?"

"Why would I be the bad cop?"

"Because you said tough love. That's not very good cop of you."

Another eye roll!

I should've gotten a cookie every time I got her to roll those beautiful brown eyes.

"Just don't take it easy on them, Nathan. We're here to coach them, not to change their diapers."

I didn't argue with her because I got lost in those eyes of hers. Avery Kingsley was the kind of beauty that people wrote songs about. She'd only gotten better with age, too. I'd been back in Honey Creek for a while and watched her from afar. Mainly because she did everything in her power to avoid me.

It was clear as day that she was determined not to interact with me. When we were on the same sidewalk, she'd always cross the street. She'd dip into stores, too, if she saw me coming. Once, we were in the grocery store at the same time, and she'd abandoned her cart just to avoid meeting me by the grated cheese.

Clearly, some closure was needed between us, yet I wasn't allowed to even bring that up due to rule number three.

But since I returned to Honey Creek, I noticed her. I noticed her so much that I'd find myself dreaming about her some nights simply based on the small times I'd crossed her during the daylight. Avery had the kind of smile that made others want to smile, too, though most of the time, her smile was reserved for a select few. When one unlocked her smiles, it felt like finally making it to Narnia. A gift that kept giving. Yet when she wasn't smiling, she was grimacing. Still, her grimaces were oddly attractive to me. She made resting bitch face seem sexy.

Her deep brown skin was smooth and always moisturized. She wasn't one to wear makeup, and if you looked closely enough, you could see the two small birthmarks resting against her left cheek. I, myself, always looked closely enough.

Her black natural hair sat slightly below her shoulders when she let it down, but she usually had it tossed up in a messy bun on top of her head. She was also a professional at wearing oversized clothes that didn't show off her body, but a few months ago, I saw her at her sister's wedding. She wore a tight black gown that reminded me of how remarkable each curve on her body had been.

"Nathaniel?! Hello?! Earth to Nathaniel," Avery said, waving her hands in front of me.

I snapped out of the trance I had found myself in as I fell into her eyes. "Uh, sorry, repeat that?"

"I said rule number five is to learn about who these kids are. They're good kids, and I don't want them to feel overlooked. Having you here will help them get the attention they deserve in a way I couldn't do alone."

"Did you just say you're happy I'm here, Coach?"

"Oh, shut it, Nathaniel. See you tomorrow afternoon. We'll go over the details before practice. I'll meet you in my office at three."

"Looking forward to it, Coach."

"Don't," she said before marching out of my office.

8

AVERY

"Rumor has it, there's a new coach on your team," Tatiana mentioned when stopping by my house after I returned home. She always stopped by a few times a week with food. It was her love language. Plus, she worked at Alex's restaurant, Isla Iberia, which meant she usually brought some of the tastiest treats.

"That rumor is true." I sighed as I stepped to the side of my door to let her in.

She headed straight for the kitchen and started to put her containers into the fridge. "That's a fun twist."

"If by fun, you mean annoying as fu—"

"*Language.*" She pointed a stern finger my way. "My virgin ears can't hear the word 'fuck' out loud," she joked.

I smiled and took a seat on the barstool in front of the countertop. If I knew anything about Tatiana Silva, it was that she had a filthy mouth and a vibrant wardrobe. Her closet dripped with neon colors, and her mouth dripped with f-bombs.

I opened one of the containers. "What's this?"

"Slow-roasted pork belly bites over jalapeño slaw. It's heavenly," she cooed. "But be warned, it's from the Pierce Meat Butcher Shop."

"That's fine. I just hate Nathan, not his brothers," I said as I picked up the piece of pork belly and took a bite. My eyes rolled backward from pure bliss. Thank goodness I didn't hate his brothers. That meat was tender and delicious. However I was certain it had more to do with Alex and less with the Pierce brothers.

"Dang, that's tasty," I said.

"I work at the best spot," she agreed. She leaned against the countertop and smiled my way. "So you and Nathan Pierce. How do you think it will be working with him?"

Hell.

A pain in my ass.

I shrugged. "It will be fine."

"He's handsome, isn't he?" she asked, popping a piece of pork belly into her mouth.

I had to remind myself that Tatiana didn't know about Nathan's and my short-lived past. If she had known, she wouldn't have been so freely speaking of his praises. Or maybe she would've. Tatiana often gave people second and third chances.

I wasn't.

"I didn't notice," I lied.

I did notice how handsome Nathan had been. I noticed so much that it made me want to vomit. I just wish I could *un-*notice.

"How could you not notice? I know you're an engaged girl, but woman to woman, I think we can both agree that he hit the lottery with his looks. Did you witness that man walk away, too? He has the perfect, plump baseball butt."

"Tatiana, too much info."

She shrugged and opened another container. "I'm just saying. I like his butt. I envy his butt. It made me almost want to do squats to tighten my own. But then again, the thought of working out makes my eye twitch, so I started watching *The Office* again for the eighteen-millionth time."

"Seems like the right choice to me."

"Same here. So." She handed me a fork to taste the rice dish in front of her. "Tell me how everything's going with wedding planning. We're right around the corner, huh?"

"Yup, and I am not ready."

She smiled. "We never really are."

We talked the rest of the evening about anything and everything—except for Nathan. I was happy his name didn't circle back around. The last thing I needed to do was speak more about his bubble butt.

And yeah, okay. I've seen the behind of Nathaniel Pierce once or twice as he walked away.

Those two cheeks of his might've made me want to do a few squats, too.

———

AFTER WORKING SO hard to avoid Nathan, I'd now have to spend time with him at least five days a week. I felt a strong amount of annoyance every time I saw his face. Each time I saw him, I was reminded of how he walked out on me and chose baseball over our love.

I hated him.

I knew it was silly, and I should've gotten over it after all these years, but there was something so cocky about him reappearing in my life, getting a job on my team, and acting like we were just supposed to be good friends after all that transpired between us.

I knew Yara was into her enemies-to-lovers romance novels, but this felt more like a lovers-to-enemies plotline without a cheesy happily ever after.

Everything about him made my skin crawl.

I hated how the guys on the team idolized him. How their eyes lit up with interest whenever Nathan spoke to them. I hated how he smiled his cocky smile whenever he'd teach the guys something, and they'd excel at it. I hated how he told me I was doing a great job.

Screw you, Nathaniel! Of course, I know I'm doing a great job!

I didn't need his praise. If anything, I needed him to shut up.

I loathed that man. I hated how he smiled, how he spoke, how he smelled like oak trees soaked in lemon drops. I hated how he chewed gum. How he clapped his hands. How he wore a backward baseball hat. I hated his breathing pattern, and his eyes, and his stupid dimples.

How he cleared his throat.

How he snickered.

How he patted me on the back whenever I made a good call.

Don't touch me, Nathaniel!

I hated everything about that man. I honestly didn't know hate could be so strong, which made it quite confusing to me when my stomach would sometimes flutter whenever he was near me. Then again, there were those small glimpses of him that I didn't completely despise. Those quiet moments when he interacted with the guys on the field.

After Nathan's first few practices, I stood back and studied how Nathan coached Jackson Perk on Friday night. The practice was over for the rest of the team, but Nathan volunteered to stay back to help Jackson out.

Jackson was a solid player but he never enjoyed the attention. Nathan took notice of him, though. Nathan focused on the guys who hung out in the shadows more than the others who shone in the spotlight.

Jackson was quiet. I hardly ever heard him make a peep all

practice, and he'd been on my team for the past three years. Yet as I watched Nathan teach Jackson how to reposition his batting stance, I noticed Jackson's eyes sparkle with interest more than ever before.

"It's all about the follow-through," Nathan explained to Jackson as he held a bat in his hand, flexing every muscle in his arm as he demonstrated the swing in slow motion. "And don't hold the bat too tightly. I know that's a normal habit, but loosen up, and you'll see it soar. Here, you try," he told Jackson, handing him the bat.

Nathan placed a ball on the batting tee in front of the two, and Jackson got into place. With a slight sigh, Jackson rolled his shoulders back, gripped the bat, and swung as Nathan had instructed.

He struck the ball, and it went flying across the field.

Well, I'll be damned.

I smirked, seeing the pride that shot through Jackson's system. It was as if a wave of confidence filled every inch of his being.

"Hell yeah," Nathan said as pure bliss fell against his face. He playfully shoved Jackson. "How did that feel?"

"Good," Jackson quietly said with a nod. "Great."

"Good, good." Nathan placed another ball on the tee. "Now do it again and step into it more. Don't be afraid to follow the swing."

Jackson nodded in understanding and hit the ball with even more power. The smile on his face grew bigger. "Holy crap," he breathed out, shaking his head in disbelief.

Nathan stood there proudly. He seemed to believe in the players more than they believed in themselves. "Told you. You got this, buddy. So it's time you stop playing it small, all right?" He patted Jackson on his shoulder. "You are a star. Time to start shining brighter."

Jackson laughed, shaking his head. "Thanks, Coach P."

The joy shooting through Jackson made my heart feel as if it would explode with an overflow of happiness. I'd never seen that kid look so thrilled in my life.

Maybe I did hate Nathan, but it was clear he was good at what he did.

"All right, get home and get all your homework done. Remember, if you need help with your algebra test coming up, I'm more than willing to lend a hand," Nathan said to Jackson.

And that hatred I felt for him?

It stupidly started to lessen.

"Thanks again, Coach P. I'll see you tomorrow!" Jackson said, hurrying over to grab his duffel bag before he jogged toward the parking lot.

When Nathan turned to face me, I still wore my goofy grin. The second we locked eyes, I shook it off. He walked over toward me with his hands in his sweatpants pockets.

"You see that?" he asked me, speaking of Jackson. "He's a powerhouse."

"He is," I agreed. I crossed my arms, trying to shake off the confusion in my head. How could I hate the man but still be so damn impressed with his skill level? "Good job with him. He needed that boost."

Nathan arched an eyebrow. "Was that a compliment?"

"It was a observation from one coach to another. Nothing more, nothing less."

His smile stretched. "Just admit it...I'm growing on you."

"Like an annoying wart I want surgically removed. I'm almost shocked at how easy it is for me to dislike you. You might be a great coach, but you're still a bad person."

"You have no idea who I am," he stated. "You haven't even given me a chance to show you who I am."

I was going to responde with a sarcastic reply, but a somberness hit his stare. For some reason, I felt a bit guilty for my coldness toward him. It looked as if my words struck a chord, and his truths slipped through his stare. I stood there for a moment, wanting to decipher what that stare meant. I knew I'd been giving Nathan a lot of crap over the past few weeks, but that was the first time it seemed that my words affected him.

Before, it felt as if he was playing along. As if we had a playful game of "I hate you, Nathan Pierce" going on. Normally, he'd shoot back a witty comment at me, but at that moment, his lack of comebacks, paired with his pained expression, left me feeling...bad.

He cleared his throat and nodded once toward me. "Night, Coach," he said, walking off toward the building.

"Nathan," I called out.

He looked over his shoulder and arched a brow. "Yeah?"

"You did great," I told him. "With Jackson. With all the guys. You're a great coach."

His serious stare remained. "Do you really think I'm a bad person?"

Yes.

No.

Maybe.

I don't know.

Ever since Nathan reappeared in my life, I felt more confused than ever before.

My lips parted, and he shook his head. "Don't answer that," he told me. "I forgot about your rules. We don't get personal." He turned away from me and continued his way to his car, leaving me with a guilty conscience.

Maybe one day you should stop being such a jerk, Avery.

Did I hold some resentment toward him from our past? Yes. But were we still those thoughtless, young, stupid kids who fell in love? Not in the slightest.

When I got home after practice, Wesley was nowhere to be found. That was odd because he was normally home well before me unless he worked late. Whenever he worked late, he'd text me, though, and let me know. A sudden panic hit my stomach as I tried to call him. Unfortunately, his phone went straight to voicemail, showing me it was not on.

I had dinner on the table waiting for him, and by the time it got cold, I tossed it into the fridge. As panic rose with every passing moment, I thought about calling the local hospital and the hospitals in Chicago to make sure he wasn't involved in an accident.

My mind began to think the worst. Ever since I was a little girl, I had an unnatural fear of something happening to the people I cared about the most. After Mama passed away, I'd become so paranoid about the safety of my sisters and father. I remembered that whenever Daddy would be gone during storms, I'd sit at the window and stare outside until I saw the headlights of his car pull up. Whenever Willow would go on one of her travel adventures, I'd obsessively check in to make sure she was all right. When Yara had a health scare at the start of her pregnancy, I didn't sleep for days, thinking each night I'd wake up with a text message saying something went wrong with her or the baby.

Paranoia was strong within me when it came to my loved ones and their well-being. I couldn't count the number of sleepless nights I'd lived as I set up with a worrisome mind. And now Wesley being missing in action was only feeding into that fear of mine.

When I heard a car pull into our driveway, I darted over to my front door to make sure he was okay. To my surprise, I saw him climbing out of the passenger seat of a BMW. Out of the driver's seat came Drew.

What was she doing here?

She tossed her head back, laughing at something Wesley said as he held leftover food containers in his hands. He laughed just as hard as her, going as far as to snort out a chuckle.

Within seconds, my worry turned into rage. A simmering rage that I had to push down as they both approached the front porch.

The moment Wesley's eyes found mine, his smile stretched. "Hey, sweetheart." He walked up the steps and kissed my cheek. "What's going on?"

"What's going on?" I whisper-shouted, stunned by his nonchalant approach. "Where have you been? What is she doing here?"

I could've said it more nicely, but I didn't see a reason to be nice at that moment. I'd spent the past few hours thinking my fiancé was dead in a ditch, only to find him rolling out of a car with his best woman—who was still his ex-girlfriend, by the way—laughing and giggling together.

He narrowed his confused eyes. "I thought I told you she and her work colleagues were coming into Chicago to present my boss with a presentation over the next two weeks."

"You definitely didn't tell me that," I said.

"I'm sure I did. You were probably just wrapped up in your baseball stats and schoolwork," he replied.

"No. I would've recalled your ex-girlfriend of four years coming to work with you for two weeks," I sharply countered.

Wesley looked at me, stunned by my words. His voice dropped. "Don't start, Ave…"

Don't start?

"It's actually a really exciting project. I think it could cause this guy to reach new levels in his career," Drew stated as she walked up the steps, grinning ear to ear as she entered a conversation she wasn't invited to join. She then rubbed her hand up and down Wesley's arm. "He's a brilliant mind. We might as well use the best of that brain of his."

I tilted my head and stared at her hand on Wesley's arm. I then looked at him, and the look was enough for him to shake Drew's touch from his arm.

I never wanted to stab two people in the eyes more than at that very moment. Yet I still managed to push out a smile. "Lovely."

"Don't worry, I'm not crashing at your place. I was just hoping to use your bathroom before I headed back to my hotel in Chicago," Drew mentioned as she scooted past me and walked into my house without an official invite.

Wesley must've noticed my bewilderment. There was so much to unpack from the interaction, including why Drew was driving him home that afternoon.

"My car died, and I needed a ride home," he quickly explained. "Drew was already in the office, and it made sense for her to give me a ride home. Shortly after, my phone died. We ended up staying at my office for a while, talking to other people. You know, nerd stuff. Then she said she was hungry, so we stopped for a quick bite." He held up the food containers. "I brought you leftovers."

"I already ate," I snipped. "The dinner I made for us."

He frowned. "Sorry. I should've found a way to reach out to you."

"You should've also gotten me a whole meal of my own. Not your doggy bag," I grumbled.

"You're right. I messed up." He kissed my cheek. "I'm sorry. I love you. I'll make sure things are clearer moving forward."

"Swear?"

"Swear."

Drew came back out on our front porch, wiping her hands against her thighs to dry them. "Thanks for the toilet, Avery. And thanks for buying me dinner, Wes. It was delicious."

He *bought* her dinner? She called him *Wes*? He hated being called Wes. At least that was what he told me. I wasn't a jealous girl, but based on the level of anger building within me, I was seconds away from punching Wesley in his privates.

I never knew I could hate someone more than I hated

Nathan, yet Drew and Wesley were shooting for first place on my shit list. Anyway, currently, my hatred meter for Nathan seemed a bit...off. But alas. Life came at you quickly.

Drew hugged Wesley—or *Wes*, as she called him—a little too long if you ask me. I stood there stunned as her hands rubbed his back as if her fingertips were trying to find their way through his jacket and clothing so she could touch his bare skin. Listen, I wasn't one to hate women. I was a girls' girl through and through, but *screw that woman*. I needed someone to send her back to hell, where she came from.

As she let him go, she had enough wisdom in her not to try a hug with me.

"See you at the wedding, Avery!" she sang before hurrying to her car and driving away.

I stood on the porch quietly with Wesley, unable to find the exact words to express my anger.

"How far in the doghouse am I?" he asked. I narrowed my eyes at him and gave no response before I headed inside, only to hear him say, "That far in, huh?"

WESLEY SLEPT in our guest room, which was for the best. I didn't sleep much at all, but somewhere between the few hours of rest I did receive, Wesley placed a note beside my bed that said, "I'm sorry for yesterday. Took an Uber to pick up my car. Let me make it up to you tonight by cooking you dinner. Love you."

I read the note a few times before I sighed and fell back against my pillow.

The pressure was back, resting heavily against my chest as I lay in my bed. I wondered if anyone else in the world ever struggled the way I did with getting out of bed some mornings. It was as if every inch of them was kidnapped by an invisible source, which made it impossible to move as the judgmental voices in their heads grew louder and louder with every passing second.

That Saturday marked two weeks until my wedding.

Two weeks until forever.

And I couldn't move.

Get up, Avery.

My alarm went off over an hour ago. I needed to get up because I had to get to work, but I couldn't move.

The thought of making it through another day felt extra heavy that morning. I didn't know why. I never knew why my brain would allow itself to spiral to dark places the way it did. Sure, I had issues, but they weren't big issues. Not in the way that others suffered. Some people had illnesses. Others had trauma. I simply couldn't muster up the mental energy to pull myself away from my sheets.

It was as if a gravitational pull was tethering me to the bed with invisible strings.

Get up, Avery.

I shut my eyes as a few tears rolled down my face. The voices in my head condemning me were much louder than those in my head that fought for my strength.

I bet Drew gets up each morning easily.

She's so light and fluffy and easy to get along with.

I bet she never has bad days.

Why can't you be like her? Wesley laughs more with her than he has ever laughed with you.

My mind played tricks on me, and I couldn't believe I let those thoughts overtake me. I wasn't a jealous woman. Still, my heart hurt knowing that my wedding was in two weeks, and for the first time ever, I felt unstable in my relationship.

Get up, Avery.

Wesley had been consistent for years. That was why we worked. We weren't overly emotional and lovey-dovey, but we had a mutual respect for one another, which seemed good enough for me. That was until he threw that mutual respect for me out the window when it came to Drew.

He took her to dinner.

When was the last time he took you to dinner, Avery? Did you see how he laughed when he climbed out of her car? He would never laugh with you like that. You're not funny like her.

Also, you made Nathan feel like crap. He wasn't even being rude. What's the matter with you? Why are you always so angry? This is why people don't like you, outside of your family.

You'd be alone forever if Wesley didn't pity you.

The sunbeams spread through the windows as I stayed in bed. I did not have time for this. I didn't have time to fall apart. It was Saturday, and the team was having a late afternoon practice. I still had so much work to do over at my office. People were counting on me. The guys would show up to the field and expect me to be their head coach. Still, the thought of facing another day, of going through the motions in a world that felt so vibrantly alive while I felt so irrationally tired inside, felt overwhelming.

I wish I could be better.

I wish I was nicer.

Still, something kept me from breaking down this hardened exterior that seemed to keep people at a distance. Including my own fiancé. I didn't even know Wesley could look as vibrant as he had with Drew, which broke my heart slightly. I didn't know he could reach such a level of...joy.

9

NATHAN

EASTON

Hey. I'm not feeling great today. Can you cover for me at the butcher shop?

I stared at the message from my brother on Saturday morning as I stood in the horse stables, brushing Lightning, my favorite animal on the farm. I'd heard a little flu was going around the farm, and I was doing my best to avoid getting it. The last thing I needed was to be down for a few days when there was so much work to do.

NATHAN

I got you covered.

EASTON

Thanks. I'll remember this as I lay on my deathbed.

If Easton would be one thing, it would be dramatic. Each of us guys dealt with being sick very differently. The younger twins were pretty much the type to disappear into their rooms until they emerged well. I kept to myself, too, and tried every home remedy to get rid of the virus as soon as possible. I didn't normally have time to be sick. Too much life needed to be tended to, especially now that I was coaching baseball. Evan became an even bigger grump than he'd already been, but he hardly ever got sick. I couldn't recall the last time I'd seen him under the weather. He had the immune system of a god. And our Easton became the biggest crybaby in the entire world.

One sniffle and he was convinced he had the deadliest of diseases.

NATHAN

Don't be so dramatic.

EASTON

Are you sure you want those to be your last words to me?

NATHAN

No. You're right. I meant to say don't be so dramatic, you little shit.

EASTON

Love you, too, big brother. Bring me home some bone broth from the shop. Mom said she'd make me homemade soup.

Spoiled brat.

Then again, if Mom was making him soup, I'd get some, too. Hopefully with her homemade sourdough bread. The perks of living a few doors down from my mother. She always had something delicious cooking.

I liked taking over the front of the house at the butcher shop. I was better at dealing with the customers than with the pressure of cutting the meat in the back of the house. That was all Evan's territory, though, and that guy never took a day off. He not only had a perfect high school attendance record but the same was also true at Pierce Butcher Shop. He would only consider taking off if my niece, Priya, needed him for something. He put being a father above everything else in his life.

Now that Priya was sixteen, though, she was in the shop as much as her father, helping as a cashier up front.

"Hey, Uncle Nate," she said as I walked into the butcher shop. She had a big smile on her face as she finished counting the money in the drawer. We had about fifteen minutes before we opened, and she was already at work with that big ole smile.

Not to be biased, but I had the most beautiful niece in the goddamn world. Priya was the definition of stunning. She looked equal parts like my brother and like her mother, a beautiful Indian woman who she was named after, Priya Patel. My niece's mother was not in her life at all and signed over full parental rights to Priya when she was born. She said having a child at that age was too much, and she didn't want anything to do with her.

Evan was able to choose the name for his daughter, and he chose to name her after her own mother because he wanted her to have a piece of the woman he loved, even if it was only by them sharing the same first name.

I felt bad for Priya's biological mother because she not only missed out on a beautiful daughter but she also let go of Evan, who I was more than certain would've loved her forever if given the chance. Then again, they were young, both only eighteen when Priya was born. I tried my best not to judge both parents' choices. I couldn't imagine how hard it was to leave and also how hard it was to stay.

Both sides of the coin came with struggles.

Evan just so happened to end up with the greatest gift, too.

"Hey, Squirt," I said as I walked over to her and wrapped her in a hug. I kissed her forehead. "How goes it?"

"Good. I'm a bit annoyed with you, though," she warned as she pulled away from me and sassily placed her hands against her hips.

"What did I do this time?" I asked as I checked the display window with all the items we were selling that day.

"Well, you've been hanging around the high school a lot more since you started coaching the baseball team."

"And that's an issue?"

"Yes," she said, tossing her hands up in irritation. "A huge issue. I was at lunch the other day when you came in through the cafeteria from the parking lot."

"And...?"

"And my friends saw you!" she remarked.

My brows knitted together. "I'm sorry, I didn't know I was supposed to be invisible when I entered the school."

"Well, you should figure out how to be invisible because they called you *hot!*" She shivered as if the idea of me being good-looking was the most disturbing thing she'd ever heard of in her life. "They kept going on about how they'd love for you to coach them in different...ways. I even overheard teachers talking about how handsome you are."

I laughed. "It's not that serious."

"It is. It's so gross. So if you can just not look so much like you, that would be great."

I smirked and flexed my arms. "I can't help it that I'm so ridiculously handsome, Squirt. It's a gift, it's a curse."

She rolled her eyes. "If only they knew how corny you are."

I flexed my arms behind me. "Too bad they'll never know because they are so wrapped up in my hotness."

"It's like you want to make me physically ill like Uncle Easton," she complained.

I laughed. "Is he texting you that he's on his deathbed, too?"

"Yes. He's asking me to make my famous chocolate chip cookies as a farewell gift."

"Don't you dare make him those cookies." I brushed my hand over my chin. "Unless you make me a dozen, too."

"Uncle River said the same thing. You guys really need to

look into your cookie addiction. I'm surprised you don't all weigh a million pounds."

I flexed one more time. "What can I say? It's genetics."

She made more gagging sounds before we got to work. After a while, I flipped the "open" sign on the door. A few customers already waited outside for us to open, which wasn't surprising. The shop always buzzed with business. Evan and Easton truly created a remarkable place. I wondered what our father would've thought of their success. He always wanted to open that shop before he passed away, but he never saw it come to fruition. That wasn't due to anyone's doing but his own, seeing how he gambled away the funds to make it come to life.

Still, sometimes I wondered if he would've been proud of them.

Then again, it wasn't very characteristic for that man to have pride in anything other than himself.

A woman walked into the shop, laughing like a freaking hyena. Falling closely, *very* closely behind her was Wesley, Avery's fiancé. He had an ice cream cone in his hands, and the woman turned to face him and slapped her hand against his chest. Wesley caught her hand in his grip. Oh shit. They were holding hands. At least for a split second. The woman leaned forward and licked the ice cream from the cone in Wesley's hand.

She *licked* his ice cream.

"You're so ridiculous, Wes!" she sang, shaking her head in laughter as she wiped dripping ice cream from her chin. "There's no way you thought that."

"I one hundred percent thought that," he said with a smug look on his face as he licked the ice cream.

They both licked from the same ice cream cone. They could've been having sex in public, as far as I was concerned. Not to be dramatic, but if I found out my fiancée was licking another man's cone in public, that would be enough to call off a wedding.

Perhaps a part of me wanted to find any reason for Avery to call off her wedding.

Still... It felt inappropriate.

I stood behind the cash register with my arms crossed, annoyed by their mere existence. I'd never interacted with the guy in town, though I'd seen him around enough because he was with Avery and her family most of the time. Other than knowing he was about to marry Avery in a few weeks, I knew nothing about the man. Yet seeing how he was with a woman who wasn't Avery made a newfound rage bubble up within me.

It only took me two seconds to notice something extremely inappropriate going on between the two individuals. I may not have known them personally, but I knew body language. And theirs was loud and clear.

Wesley looked up toward me and smiled as if he didn't realize I hated his guts by him allowing that woman to put her hands on him in such a flirtatious way.

Avery deserved better.

He then turned toward the woman and said, "Drew, help me out here."

Drew.

What a stupid, ugly name.

Stupid and ugly.

Drew walked over to the display window and slammed her hands against it, leaving her grimy fingerprints on it. Now, I'd have to clean off her prints after they left.

"Hey! Aren't you like...that famous baseball guy?" she asked, gesturing toward me. "I came into town and heard people talking about you."

"That's me," I mumbled.

"Nathan, right?" she asked. "Nathan Pierce?"

I nodded.

Wesley looked at me, and his smile somewhat faded. "Avery's assistant coach?"

"Yup," I dryly replied.

He held a hand out for a shake. "Oh, hey, man. I've heard a lot about you."

I shook his hand even though I didn't want to. "I would say hopefully good things, but if they came from Avery, probably not."

He laughed and retracted his hand. "So you know my lady's personality well."

I ignored his comment. "What can I get you?"

He glanced at the display as Drew kept hanging all over it. He raked his hand through his messy red hair and pointed. "We'll take some of the pork belly."

"Just what this guy needs," Drew said, poking Wesley in his gut. My eyes fell to the gesture, and when I moved back to Wesley's eyes, he must've noticed the daggers I was shooting his way because he took a step away from Drew.

He crossed his arms over his chest. "About five pounds of it. I'm making a special dinner for Avery. A little treat-before-marriage type of meal. She's been a bit overwhelmed, and I want to make sure she feels loved," he told me.

"I'm sure what you're doing will make her feel that way," I taunted.

"Yeah, and I'm just working as his sous chef," Drew chimed in. "I'll have to make sure he doesn't cut off a finger, seeing how he hardly knows how to cook," she said, playfully swatting his chest.

I took notes of the hits again.

Wesley took note of me noting said hits.

"Chill out, Drew," he said with a forced laugh.

She leaned in and licked his ice cream again. It appeared she had no chill-out mode.

"Do you need anything else?" I asked curtly, still annoyed.

"Just two ribeyes, and we'll be ready to go," Wesley said, sensing the uncomfortable energy in the space.

Priya began collecting the order. When she finished, I rang them up and checked Wesley out. He thanked me for the order. I didn't say anything back. They left, but before I knew it, Wesley walked back inside.

"Hey, man. I know you and Avery have practice later today. Do you think you can keep the whole dinner and our interaction here to yourself? I want it to be a surprise."

"You want me to keep Drew licking your fucking cone to myself, too?" I bit.

His face flushed a little as he rubbed the back of his neck. "It's not what it looks like. She's just—"

"Better get those oxtails home, Wesley."

"Come on, man. Don't be like that. From one guy to another, you know how Avery can be. If she found out, she'd make it something it's not. She's a bit of a drama queen with a temper regarding this friendship between Drew and me."

"Hey, Wesley?" I said.

"Yeah?"

"Come closer."

He took two steps toward me.

I leaned over the display and whispered, "Say one more bad thing about Avery, and I'll slam your fucking face into this glass display."

That drained the color from his cheeks before he turned and left.

The second he was gone, Priya turned to me with a look of concern.

"I thought that guy was engaged to Ms. Kingsley?" Priya asked after Wesley left the shop.

"He is," I said, feeling a pit of doubt sitting heavily in my stomach.

"Wow," Priya said as she restocked the pork belly in the

display window. "Ms. Kingsley is a better woman than me. I would never be okay with my fiancé being all over another person like that."

I couldn't help but wonder if Avery knew about Wesley and Drew. I doubt she would've been fine with how close the two of them seemed within our shop.

The urge to kick Wesley's ass was a strong one, but instead, I debated if it was my place to inform Avery of what I'd seen. Then again, if it were me, I'd want to know.

Even if it hurt.

10

AVERY

I moved through the day as a zombie. I ran into a few people in town. None of them realized I wasn't myself that day—or maybe this was my true self. Still, they didn't notice how off I felt. They didn't see me because I'd worn a mask to hide my darkness so well.

Sure, they saw my grumpiness and cold persona, but they didn't see the heartbreak rippling through my system. They didn't see my sorrow and pain as they passed by me. I felt invisible to the world, and I couldn't help but think that even my partner couldn't see the hurt within me.

As I walked to my office before practice, I took a few deep breaths at my desk. I wished there was a button on my body to reset my system and be normal. Whatever normal was.

Nathan knocked on my door and peered inside. "Hey, Coach. I just wanted to stop in and check on our plans for today and..." He stepped into my office space and knitted his brows together. "What's wrong?"

"What?"

"You look...off."

My chest tightened slightly from his words.

No way.

There was no way he could see me—see the real me—when the rest of the world seemed so blind.

I crossed my arms and sat back in my chair. "I don't look off."

"Yes, you do."

"How so?"

"I don't know...You just look..." He studied me with a slight tilt of his head. "Sad."

I swallowed hard.

Sad.

Yes.

That's it.

"I'm not sad," I lied, standing from my desk. "What in the world would I have to be sad about?"

"You tell me, Coach."

His sincerity kept me from coming up with some witty remark. That, and my mind was still beating me up for calling him a bad guy the day prior. Yet there he was, Mr. "Bad Guy." The only one who could read my truths when the rest of the world seemed addicted to my misprints.

My lips slightly parted, but I couldn't bring myself to tell him that I was sad. Instead, I said, "I'm sorry."

He arched an eyebrow, perplexed. "For what?"

"Calling you a bad person. I don't think that about you."

His head tilted, and he walked over toward me. He placed a hand on my forehead.

"What are you doing?" I asked.

"Checking if you have a fever. You're speaking delusionally."

I shoved his hand away from my forehead. "I'm serious, Nathan. I haven't been fair to you, and I've made rude judgments. I guess the inner teenager in me still held a bit of resentment toward you, and I apologize for that. You didn't deserve it.

Truthfully, it was easier to call you a bad person than to face the reality of the situation."

"And what's the reality of the situation at hand?"

"That you're...good."

Which he was.

Maybe that bothered me the most—that he was a good person. A great person, even. Not only with me but with everyone he crossed paths with. Nathan made people feel seen and took his time to converse with anyone who approached him. He had a kind smile that made others grin themselves. He was respectable and humble, and a damn good coach, too. He was one of the good guys.

And that pissed me off because it was just a reminder of why I liked him so much all those years ago.

It was easier for me to hate him. When I hated him, my heart didn't feel so conflicted.

His joking manner settled into a serious look. "You really think I'm good?"

"I do."

"Then why have you been so hard on me? Because of our past?"

"Yes," I confessed. "And I'm a stubborn jerk."

"Or you're just someone who feels a lot and keeps it all to themselves. Either or."

"I like the idea of stubborn jerk. It has less emotions."

He smiled.

I liked it, too.

Damn me for liking it.

"Are you sure you're good, though?" he asked. "Coach to coach, I mean."

I nodded. "Yeah. I'm just a little overwhelmed with the wedding."

"Oh, right." It could've been my imagination, but I swear

Nathan grimaced at the mention of the wedding. "That's right around the corner, right?"

"Yes. Two weeks from today."

"Wow..." He cleared his throat. "That's a lot."

"Yeah. I'm sure I'm just getting wedding jitters." I glanced at my watch. "But we should get—"

"I saw Wesley with another woman today," Nathan blurted out.

My chest tightened as I looked up to meet his stare once more. He frowned and shook his head slightly. "I wasn't sure how to bring it up, but well...if it were me, I'd want to know."

"Was the woman a blond?"

"Yeah. They walked into my brothers' butcher shop earlier today. They went in laughing and seemed a little *too* friendly."

They were together today, too?

That felt like another knife to my gut. Yet this knife seemed to cut even deeper, seeing how Nathan delivered the news to me. I was humiliated. Though I tried to shake off the feeling.

"Drew," I muttered. "That's his best friend. Who just so happens to be his ex, too."

Nathan's brows raised. "I beg your pardon?"

"I know. I found out on Super Bowl Sunday."

The bewildered look flashing across his face would've been funny if it wasn't such a heavy topic to my spirit. "Get outta here," he said. "You're telling me he has a best friend who's also his ex that you didn't know existed?"

"Oh, I knew Drew existed for a long time. I just thought she was a man."

"*He didn't tell you Drew was a woman?*" he whisper-shouted.

I would've laughed if it wasn't so damn embarrassing. "Nope."

He gave me a blank stare before blinking a few times. "And you're okay with this?"

Absolutely not. Not in the slightest. "I don't really have a choice. She's his best friend. What am I supposed to say?"

"No," he sternly stated. "You're supposed to say no. There was something about them that made it seem as if they had some kind of—"

"Can we stop talking about my life and get to practice?" I snapped. I didn't mean to snap at him, but that was what happened when I was embarrassed or sad. Instead of tears, I found rage and annoyance.

He tossed his hands up in surrender. "Sorry. Breaking rules."

"All the rules."

"But..." He paused and grimaced. "They were sharing an ice cream cone."

"I'm sorry, what?"

"They were licking an ice cream cone together. One cone, two mouths."

The embarrassment seeped deeper into my soul as I stood still like a buffoon. "Let's just get to practice."

"Avery—"

"*Stop*," I begged. "Please."

"But—"

"I just told you that you're not a crappy person, Nathan. Please don't make me regret every single word."

His eyes flashed with compassion as he nodded. "All right. Let's go."

———

"Ice cream, Wesley?!" I barked, rage shooting through my system as I paced my living room. He sat on the living room couch, staring at me as if I'd lost my mind. "You were licking ice cream with her?! On Main Street?! You might as well have been licking her vagina in public, for goodness' sake!"

"Geez, Avery. Don't be so vulgar."

"Oh, screw you. What in the world were you thinking? Especially after yesterday."

He raised an eyebrow. "What was I thinking by getting an ice cream cone with my friend? Uh, nothing, other than I wanted ice cream."

"But you just had to lick hers, huh? In town, knowing how these people gossip. You don't even share ice cream cones with me."

"You don't like rocky road," he calmly replied.

I stared at him and silently prayed I wouldn't go to prison that evening for killing my fiancé. I'd seen enough episodes of *Snapped* before. I knew it just took one little thing to push women over the edge.

Apparently, mine was rocky road ice cream.

I took a deep breath as I closed my eyes. I quietly counted to ten before releasing the breath and reopening my eyes. "The whole town's coming to our wedding in two weeks. And now people are gossiping about seeing you with another woman, licking ice cream cones together. Do you understand how embarrassing that is for me? How stupid that makes me look?"

He removed his glasses and pinched the bridge of his nose. "I didn't mean for the day to go as it did. I went to get my car from work, and Drew was there talking to my boss. The repair center with my car called and said they'd have to keep it until tomorrow. Drew then started saying she'd drive me home again, but I had to go get groceries to cook dinner for you. So she took me, and there just so happened to be an ice cream shop. It was nothing serious, but I understand your frustration."

"Do you, though? Because it seems to me that you think I'm overreacting."

"Well, it's a known fact that women are a bit more emotional than men. Studies show—"

"Oh, screw your studies, Wesley!" I barked. "You've been weird for the past few months. Ever since that woman came to visit."

"Are you jealous of Drew or something?"

"*Jealous*?! *Of Drew*?!"

Yes.

I was.

Completely.

Wholeheartedly.

Yet still, he couldn't see me. Not the real, hurting me that was.

He dropped his head and put up surrendering hands. "Okay, you're not jealous of Drew."

I sighed. "Listen, if you don't want to do this wedding thing—"

"Whoa." He shot to his feet and headed over to me. "Slow down. What are you talking about? I want to do this marriage thing, Avery. And sure, I've been a bit off lately, but there's been so much going on with work. Plus, I understand that Drew has been a lot for you to take in, and I accept all my faults with how this came to be. I should've told you she was a woman and—"

"And that she licked your ice cream cone," I added.

He smirked slightly. "And that she licked my ice cream cone," he added. "But I was only having her help me cook your dinner because she loves to cook. I hate it. I wanted my apology meal to be amazing for you."

I arched an eyebrow and glanced over at the table set with a fancy-looking dinner. "You cooked me dinner to apologize?"

"Yes."

"With *her*?"

He swallowed hard, knowing this was going nowhere good. "Uh-huh."

I walked over to the plates of food. Fancy steaks with a compound butter and some cooked pork belly and peas.

I hated peas.

I glanced at Wesley, then toward the dinner, then back at him.

A big part of me wanted to ruin the whole meal. I wanted to throw the steaks against the wall and smear the butter in his face. What was he doing? Why was he working so hard to ruin what we had? We were supposed to be stable with one another. We were supposed to make sense. Sure, we weren't romantic, but we were supposed to be a team.

This wasn't teammate behavior. If anything, it was as if he'd benched me and I'd been replaced by another woman fourteen days before our wedding.

"I'm going to bed," I murmured, feeling slightly too exhausted and hurt to deal with any more interactions with him. All I wanted to do was crawl into my bed and stay there for the next few weeks.

11

AVERY

The next twelve days sped by faster than I was ready for them to move.

The air was thick with the scent of freshly mown grass and the lingering warmth of the sun. It was a much warmer start to spring than we were used to in Illinois, but I wasn't complaining. After the weekend, April was upon us, and I was thankful for more sunny days than snowy ones. The temps were even in the sixties, which seemed remarkable.

The guys threw me a pre-wedding celebration after our Thursday game. Although we didn't win the series that week, we came damn close to doing so, and the energy of the group was growing more and more each week. More students also attended the games to watch the team play. I had no doubt that we could pull out a win over the next few weeks with how the team performed.

When we walked back into the sports facility, a table was set up with balloons and a cake that read, "Congratulations, Coach K on your home run."

I couldn't help but feel loved by the scene in front of me. The guys had lost a game, but they smiled ear to ear as if the celebration was more exciting than a win. The gesture was so kind and warmed my heart even as it tugged at the threads of doubt woven through my excitement. I should've been more excited about the wedding taking place in two days, about *my* wedding. Yet with every passing second, I felt more and more anxiety in my chest. I felt more unsure, more unstable, more... scared.

I wondered if that was normal. Was it normal to feel terrified in the days leading up to "I do"?

Nathan stood back and took everything in. He'd been a bit quieter over the past few days, and I couldn't pinpoint why, but I also knew it was none of my business. He was my co-worker, not my friend. Anything going on in his private life was none of my business. Still, I couldn't help but notice his less-than-perky self.

Caleb cut the cake and handed everyone a slice. I took two pieces from him, and I walked over to Nathan, who was visibly frowning. I held out a slice of cake toward him. He took it and gave me a lazy smile, one that didn't reach his eyes.

"Thanks," he muttered.

"Yeah, sure." Curiosity hit me more with each passing second. "Are you upset about the game? Even though we lost, I think we had some amazing plays, and with some solid drills over the next few weeks, we can get the guys in better shape. I have no doubt we can beat the Graters when we play them and—"

"Don't marry him," he blurted out. His voice was low, only slightly above a whisper, and direct. My mind took a second to comprehend what he said. The seriousness in his tone broke my heart.

"What?"

"You heard me, Avery. Don't do it."

I blinked, and when my eyes opened once more, Nathan's

stare looked more dreadful. As if every passing second was breaking his heart.

"Nathan. I know Wesley and I have had a few rocky weeks, but that doesn't change the fact that we've had many more okay days than bad. And we love one another and—"

"He hurt you," he expressed through gritted teeth.

"He apologized."

"What's the point of an apology if he keeps doing the same behavior?"

I felt sucker punched by his words.

He stepped in closer, his voice a hair above a whisper. "Why do you do that?"

"Do what?"

"Accept the lowest form of disrespect and still consider it love."

Those words pierced through me as I stumbled back, shaking my head. "I'm not doing this, Nathaniel."

He sighed. "Aver—"

"*Two days*," I whisper-shouted so the guys wouldn't hear me. "I'm getting married in two days, and you think you have the right to sweep in and say these things to me? You think it's okay to tell me not to marry someone just because of a few moments of disconnect?"

"I'm thinking about you and what you deserve."

"Well, don't!" I spat out, feeling a mixture of emotions rocketing through me. "Don't think about me, all right? It's better when you don't." I started to walk away, and I didn't look back. The rest of the event went well, and everyone headed off to their homes. I crossed paths with Nathan in the parking lot, and I still couldn't comprehend our conversation that evening. My heart and mind were already at war, and Nathan didn't make that any easier.

His words echoed in my mind, making me dizzy with confusion.

Don't marry him. Don't marry him. Don't—

"Hey, Coach?" Nathan called out.

I grumbled as I looked over my shoulder. "What, Nathan?"

"I'm sorry." His hands slipped into his pants pockets as his duffel bag hung against his shoulder. "I was out of line."

"Yes," I agreed. "You were."

Still, I didn't know if that made him wrong.

"You'll make a beautiful bride," he stated softly.

The kindness in his words sent me for a loop. As I looked into his eyes, I saw the boy I once knew. The boy I once loved. The gentle boy who always made me feel as if I was the only thing that existed when his eyes landed on me.

That freaked me out.

He freaked me out.

"Thanks," I muttered before scurrying away with thoughts that shouldn't have belonged to me two days before my wedding. I couldn't think about the fact that Nathan had just accidentally given me butterflies. I couldn't allow those feelings to exist anywhere within my proximity.

YARA AND WILLOW stayed with me at my house the day before the wedding. Wesley was staying with his groomsmen at a hotel in Chicago. We had the rehearsal a few hours before, and everything went smoothly. Daddy was still calling Wesley by the wrong name, but I figured that was just a bit of Daddy's charm. I'd be weirded out if he called Wesley by his actual name.

Late into the night, Yara and Willow had retired to bed. My mind was moving too quickly to do such a thing, so I found myself trying to break through the thoughts racing through me.

"Avery?" Willow whispered, walking onto the back porch to find me standing there, staring out into the darkened sky. I hadn't been able to fall asleep. My mind had been spinning for days now. It was a little past two in the morning, the morning of my wedding, and I didn't feel...happy.

I was supposed to feel happy, right?

I looked over at her and pushed out a smile. "What are you doing up? It's late."

"I know," she said as she moved to stand beside me. Her eyes glanced up at the star-drunk sky, and a small smile curled her lips. "Do you know how much I love you?" she asked.

I laughed slightly and shook my head. "Go to bed, Willow."

"No, I mean it, Avery. I love you so much and have always looked up to you. I don't think I tell you that enough."

"You tell me all the time."

"I know." She nodded. "And still, it's not enough." We moved to the top step of the porch and took a seat. She leaned her head against my shoulder as we stared out. "Not only were you my big sister growing up but you were the mama I never had the chance to have. You were my Mary Poppins. I don't think I ever thanked you for that. For being a motherly figure to me all my life."

"I'd do anything for you."

"I know." She sniffled.

"Are you crying?"

"Only a little."

"Why?"

"Because sometimes love feels so big in my chest that it leaks from my eyes."

I chuckled. My sisters must've taken all the emotions and kept them for themselves. Sometimes, I wish I cried more. Maybe it would've moved some of the heaviness resting inside me.

She lifted her head from my shoulder. "But Avery...I was thinking about it earlier. You've been such a mother figure to

Yara and me all our lives, but you haven't had that for yourself,"
Willow said.

Her words felt like a punch to my stomach.

"I don't say that to make you feel bad. I only say that
because I want you to know that I can be that for you sometimes...the one you can lean on."

I bit my bottom lip. "What if my leaning gets too heavy?"

"It won't," she swore. "But if it ever did, I'd join a gym or
something and become stronger."

I laughed. "Thanks, Will."

"Always." She fiddled with her hands a little. "Can I ask you
a question?"

"Of course."

"Does Wesley make you feel?"

"Feel what?"

"Anything," she said.

I sighed and rested my head on top of hers. I couldn't
answer her question that night because it was too late to debate
such things. All the bills had been paid. All the flowers delivered. All that was left were a few "I do's."

"It's past midnight," I whispered.

"Yes."

"It's officially my wedding day."

Willow lifted her head and looked at me with the tiniest
smile. For a moment, I saw flashes of my mother within her
eyes. The kindest, softest comforting eyes filled with so much
love. It almost brought me to tears as I stared at her.

I rested my head back against her shoulder as she wrapped
an arm around my waist and pulled me against her side.

"Everything's going to be all right, right, Willow?"

"Everything's always all right. Even when the voices in our
heads tell us differently." She then stood and held a hand
toward me. "Now come on. It's time to get some rest before the
big day."

12

AVERY

It took me an hour to pull myself out of bed on my wedding day. Then once I was up, everything moved at warp speed. People ushered me around, makeup and hair were all a flurry. Willow added flowers to my hair, and Yara touched up my lipstick. Daddy didn't cry, but his eyes were misty. He still called Wesley by another name. Everyone in town was at the chapel.

Everyone but Nathan, I suppose.

My heart beat at the speed of light.

My brain filtered through a million thoughts.

"Can I get a moment alone with the bride?" Tatiana asked, ushering everyone out of the room. It was as if she'd known the overwhelm hitting me. She walked over to me, wearing the most beautiful strapless coral dress, which showed off every perfect curve she had. Gosh, I bet Mama and Tatiana were such a good time when they were younger.

Gosh, I wish Mama was here.

Tatiana walked over to me with a small treasure chest in her hands. She gave me her warm smile and led me over to the couch to take a seat. She sat beside me, placed the chest on her right side, and then took my hands.

"How are you?" she asked.

Don't ask me that, Tatiana.

I pushed out a smile and nodded. "I'm great. This is the best day of my life."

She narrowed her eyes, trying to tell if I was lying or not. But she didn't question it out loud. Instead, she reached for her chest and opened it. "I have a few gifts for you."

"You didn't need to—"

"Don't, Avery," she said. "Just accept my love."

I laughed. "We all know how hard it is for me to accept love."

"Yes," she said softly as she placed a hand against my cheek. "We do."

She began to take items out of the box. "Something old," she stated, pulling out an old pearl bracelet. "It was my great-grandmother's. She wore it on her wedding day, and it brought her great luck in love." She placed it on my wrist, then picked up the next item in the box. "Something new, diamond earrings."

"Tatiana," I breathed out.

She shook her head, knowing I would disagree, but she continued, placing the earrings into my ears for me. "Something borrowed and something blue kind of go together," she explained, reaching into the box and pulling out a ring with a blue stone.

My heart gasped as my hands fell to my chest.

Mama's wedding ring.

That made my eyes glassy.

The same something borrowed and something blue that Yara wore stitched into her wedding gown.

"Your father gave it to me, along with some thread and needle. May I?" she asked.

I nodded slowly. She threaded her needle and stitched the ring to the fabric of my dress right over my heart. Exactly where Mama's love belonged.

"Thank you," I whispered.

"Always," Tatiana replied.

She sat back and placed her hands in her lap. "How are you?"

I laughed. "You already asked me that."

"I know. I was just hoping we were past the lying stage is all." The knowing grin she gave me made me chuckle even more.

"Nervous," I confessed. "Scared. Terrified."

"That sounds more honest," she agreed. "Thank you for the truth."

I fiddled with my hands. "How does a person know if they've found the right one? How does one know that it's meant to be always and forever?"

She shook her head. "Sweetie, don't ask me. I thought by now I'd be married to Richard Gere or Idris Elba," she joked. "But honestly, I don't think anyone truly knows. We just hope. We hope and take the risk." Her brows lowered. "But, Avery...if any part of you is not sure..."

"I'm sure," I said. "Just scared."

"Okay." She patted my hand in hers and leaned in to kiss my cheek. "Because I was ready to start my getaway car."

"Sorry to interrupt, ladies, but I was told it's time for the father's first look at the bride," Daddy said as he stepped into my dressing room with the photographer behind him. His eyes fell on me, and he gasped, instantly growing misty-eyed. "And what a bride she is. My beautiful baby girl."

I stood and shrugged. "How do I look?"

He took my hands into his, giving them a light squeeze. "Like a dream come true." His eyes fell on the wedding ring Tatiana stitched onto my dress, and a moment of somberness found him. "Two of my favorite heartbeats resting against one another."

My father.

The romantic.

There were so many nights I'd wished his blood ran through my veins. I knew I would've been better with Matthew Kingsley's love in my DNA.

Tatiana excused herself as the photographer captured a few photos of my father and me. Then Daddy asked them to give us a moment of privacy.

"You look so much like your mama, Avery Harper." He sniffled, holding my hands to his chest. Tears fell from his eyes, and he shook his head. "You'd think giving away one daughter already would've made this easier. But it's just as hard."

I wiped away his tears. "You softy, you."

"Just you wait. It comes with age." His brown eyes locked with mine. "Are you sure you want to do this today?"

How many people were going to ask me that?

"Daddy," I scolded.

"I'm just saying. Ryan's fine and all—"

"*Wesley*," I corrected.

"Whatever. The rocket scientist is nice and all, but you... you're the shooting star. Don't forget that, will you?"

"I won't."

He kissed my forehead. "Okay. I'm going to wipe my face before we get this ball rolling. Ten-minute warning. I'll see you out there. I love..." he started, tapping my nose.

"You," I replied, tapping his back.

I was happy when I had a moment to be alone. I needed to remind myself how to breathe, yet my dress felt so tight that it was almost impossible to do. When I was alone, I allowed my smile to falter. When I was alone, I didn't have to pretend to be okay.

I stood in front of the oversized mirror, smoothing my

hands over the fabric of my gown and shaking my head slightly. "Mama, what should I do?" I whispered, praying she could hear me from wherever she was.

Before I could turn around, the dressing room door opened through the mirror, and Wesley appeared.

"Wesley! What are you doing? You can't be in here!" I shouted as I darted behind the couch in the dressing room. "It's bad luck to see the bride on the wedding day!"

"It's fine," he said, clasping his hands together. "You know superstitions are ridiculous. The probability of—"

"Don't come talking about scientific probabilities when it comes to seeing the bride in her dress on the wedding day," I ordered. "Let me be superstitious about this one thing. Leave."

"Avery," he said. The seriousness of his somber tone shot a wave of panic through my chest.

I rose and tilted my head toward him. "What's going on?"

He frowned and rubbed the back of his neck before sliding his hands into his pockets. "I, um, I just found out some pretty big news."

"Are you okay?"

"Yeah. It's just...Drew just called me with some big news. I got the job."

I narrowed my eyes. "The job?"

He brushed his hand over the back of his neck. "I didn't want to mention it until I knew for sure. Honestly, I didn't think I had a real shot at it. This is all surreal, but well, I wanted to tell you now before we...continued."

"Tell me what? What's the job?"

"I got accepted to a new program that will train me to go to outer space."

"Oh my goodness!" I gasped, my hands falling to my chest. "Okay. Well. That's a lot."

"It's based in Asia."

My eyes widened. "Asia? For how long?"

"For four years, that's before the space part, which would be three more years."

"Four years? In Asia? We'd have to move?" I questioned, my mind spiraling. Was I imagining this all? Was this some kind of fever dream?

"Well, you see, it would just be me going." The words leaving his mouth didn't seem to land correctly. What did he mean, it would just be him? "Which is why I think we should put a hold on this."

My stomach.

It dropped.

"A hold?" I breathed out. "A hold on what?"

"On this. On us. You know. Until I get my footing. Until we can see what this all becomes."

Oh my goodness.

He was leaving me ten minutes before we said "I do."

This dress.

It's too tight.

I hate this fucking dress.

I stumbled backward, hitting the edge of the couch as reality settled in.

"You're leaving me for a job?" I asked, getting flashbacks I thought I'd buried so many years ago.

"You're leaving me for your career?" I asked Nathan, tears streaming down my face. "But...we...I...I love you. Please don't, Nathan. Please don't go," I begged, rushing over to him and tugging on his T-shirt.

Just like that, I was eighteen years old again, having a man choose his career over me. Having him walk away, leaving me alone. I would've felt better if he'd left me for Drew. But for a job? Without warning?

I wanted to fall apart, but I couldn't.

I couldn't go back to that feeling from all those years before. I couldn't be weak. I couldn't feel.

Shut off the emotions, Avery. Stand strong.

"Okay," I muttered, shaking my head, still in disbelief. "Then go."

My shell hardened, but my heart?

My heart was in dismay. I wouldn't show him that fact, though. Instead, I'd be tough. Hard exterior yet fragile inside.

"*Then go?*" he echoed, looking at me as if I were insensitive. "Avery, you can't mean that."

"I do mean that."

He shook his head in disbelief, pinching the bridge of his nose. "I came here hoping you'd fight for us."

"Yes, well, I'm not feeling up to the challenge," I replied, crossing my arms.

He slipped his hands into the pockets of his expensive suit. "This is what I thought would happen. You'd be cold and dismissive."

"What do you want me to do, Wesley? You want me to fall to your feet and beg for you to stay? You want me to plead my case for why you should marry me five minutes before 'I do'? Because that will never happen."

"I know," he agreed. "Which is why I know I'm making the right choice."

"You could've chosen earlier, you know. Before I put on this stupid fucking dress," I hissed. "Your timing blows."

"Yeah, well, this all just unfolded. Drew just told me the news."

"Of course she did," I breathed out. "I'm sure that wasn't calculated at all. For a rocket scientist, you sure are naive."

"This whole jealousy thing is wild, Avery. Drew has been a great friend to me. She knew how much I'd dreamed of this opportunity."

"Why would she know and I not?"

"Because we don't talk about things like this. We don't talk

about stuff the way me and Drew do. You don't get me on that
level."

"Then why the hell would you ask me to marry you?"

He shook his head. "I don't mean it like—"

"No," I cut in. "Keep that energy. I don't get you like she
does. I'm not all sweet and bubbly and charming like little Miss
Drew. I don't like rocky road. I actually know how to play
charades. And I don't make inappropriate advances on another
person's partner."

"See, this is how she said you'd react."

"Oh, is that so?"

"Yeah, it is. And I know why you're reacting this way."

"Do tell."

"*Because you're hard to love!*" he blurted out. "You make it so
damn impossible to even have heart-to-heart moments, and
here I was, stupidly waiting years for the day that you'd open
up to me. I love you, Avery. I do. But you don't make it easy.
Which is why it's easier for me to go now."

Hard to love.

Those last few pieces of my fragile heart?

Eviscerated.

I shut my eyes.

I took a deep inhalation.

Then I released it slowly.

"Please go," I requested as I opened my eyes.

"What..." He sighed and pinched the bridge of his nose.
"What am I supposed to tell everyone? People are waiting for us
in the church. Maybe we can go tell them together."

"No way in hell am I going to do that."

"Avery..."

"Tell them exactly what you told me." I sighed, grabbing my
purse and cell phone. I slipped out of my heels and put on my
blue Chucks. "Tell them that you left me. Tell them that you got
a new job with your ex-girlfriend. Or tell them a complete lie. I

don't care, Wesley. Just..." I tried to hold back the tears brewing in the back of my eyes. "Leave me alone."

I left the room and went through the back of the church, avoiding making eye contact with anyone. The last thing I wanted to do was talk to anyone. The last thing I wanted to do was see people look at me with pity in their eyes. I hated pity. There is no worse feeling in the world than people feeling bad for you.

I knew I'd have to face the looks of others for a long time. I knew I'd be the gossip of Honey Creek for a good second. But before I could focus on that, I had to somehow find the courage to keep breathing.

13

NATHAN

oney Creek had a runaway bride on their hands, and the whole town was in a tizzy about it.

Avery didn't marry Wesley.

She didn't get married.

On one hand, I felt a sense of pleasure about that fact because Wesley wasn't good enough for her. I was happy she didn't tie herself to him for the rest of her life.

On the other hand, he broke her heart.

I knew Avery was heartbroken, even if she didn't show it. She had such a hard exterior, but I knew deep inside she was the most gentle, emotional person. I knew she felt things a lot deeper than others. So I hated that she was somewhere out there, pretending she was fine when she was far from okay.

Luckily for me, I knew Avery Kingsley.

I might've known her better than she knew herself.

So while the whole town searched to find where Avery had escaped, I knew exactly where I could find her.

As I strolled over to the batting cage, there she was, holding a wooden bat tightly in her grip. She wore a beautiful wedding dress along with a backward baseball cap. The train of the dress was covered in dust and dirt from the baseball field.

As the ball flung from the machine, Avery swung and knocked it out of the damn park. I'd never seen a person swing with so much power, and I worked in the Major Leagues. I was almost shocked that the bat didn't snap in half.

I leaned against the bleachers for a second, watching her as she knocked pitch after pitch toward outer space.

It wasn't until the machine was out of balls that I spoke.

"You get it out of your system, Coach? Or do you want me to reload it for you?"

Avery turned to face me. Her chest rose and fell from her weighted breaths as she tilted her head toward me. At first, she seemed confused by my presence, but then her face hardened again. She turned away from me and nodded. "Reload."

I flicked my thumb against my nose and did as she requested.

I reloaded the machine three times before I became concerned with how out of breath Avery had become.

"Reload," she requested once more.

"I think that's enough, Coach."

"No, it's not. Reload."

"Avery—"

"Fine." She dropped the bat. "I'll do it myself. I didn't need you to do it for me at all anyway. I don't need *anyone* to do anything for me." She huffed and puffed as she stormed over to the machine. As she reloaded it, I walked over and placed my hand over hers.

"Ave...come on."

"What?"

"You're burned out. How about you get some water and—"

"Stop it," she ordered, pointing a stern finger my way. "Don't you dare feel bad for me. I see it in your stupid brown eyes. I don't need you to feel bad for me, Nathaniel Pierce. I don't need your pity. Lord knows I'm going to get it from everyone else in town. You're the last person I need to look at me with those sad damn eyes."

"I don't feel bad for you," I lied.

She rolled her eyes so far back I thought they'd get stuck. "Don't lie to me. Have enough respect for me not to lie to me."

"Fine, okay. I feel bad for you." I almost forgot that for how well I knew her, she knew me too.

"Screw you, Nathan," she muttered. She bit her bottom lip, and I knew it was because tears were trying their damnedest to escape her eyes. "Screw you and screw *him*. Oh gosh." She paused and placed her hands over her face. "Everyone in town is talking about it, aren't they?"

"Who cares?"

"I do. I wish I didn't, but I do. This will be the worst thing for me to try to escape. Especially with the long weekend. Everyone's going to be looking at me as if I'm a sad puppy, which will only piss me off more."

"Let's leave, then."

She turned and arched an eyebrow. "What?"

"Let's leave. I have a getaway car parked right outside the school parking lot. You don't have to talk to anyone. You can escape to my penthouse in Chicago for the long weekend. I can even let your sisters know you're okay. I can set you up in my apartment, and you can decompress."

She narrowed her eyes. "You want me to run away?"

"Yes. I want you to run away."

"And you want to run away with me?"

"I want to run away with you." I gave her a half-grin. "I just want you to be okay, and I don't think you can get okay around this damn town. We know how these people are."

"Evil," she scolded. "And judgmental."

"Exactly. It's up to you, though. Say yes, and I'll get you out of here. You have my word."

"Why would you do that for me? I've been a dick toward you since you started coaching with me. Why would you help me?"

"Come on, Coach..." I whispered as I rubbed the back of my neck. "You know I have a kink for people who treat me like shit and talk down to me."

She smiled a little.

It was tiny, but it was there.

"You're a dumbass," she muttered.

"If you want me to get a hard-on, just say that, Coach," I joked.

"God, I hate you." She snickered, shaking her head.

I took a step toward her. "How much?"

"How much do I hate you?"

"Yeah?"

"A lot. Like, a lot a lot. But you're sort of my saving grace right now, so yeah, let's go."

WE SUCCESSFULLY GOT Avery out of Honey Creek without anyone noticing. I informed her sisters of her weekend getaway, and while Yara and Willow slightly panicked about the whole situation, I calmed them down by letting them know Avery was safe and taken care of.

Avery didn't say a word during the drive to the penthouse, but I didn't blame her. I didn't know what to say to her, either. The whole situation was uncomfortable and brought back many odd feelings.

The last time she sat in a car with me was when we ended things years prior. Now, seeing her sitting in my passenger seat —in a wedding gown nonetheless—sent me back into memories of us. Of who we used to be. Of how I'd wished we would've made it to the altar together. But that was a long time ago. We'd both changed so much since then. Still, some of my favorite moments in cars were rides with Avery.

The summer after senior year was one of the best damn summers of my life. That was until it wasn't.

After parking my car, we headed up to the private elevator of my building to the penthouse. As the elevator opened, I unlocked the front door as Avery shyly stood behind me. Her arms rested at her sides, and she kept biting her bottom lip. A nervous habit of hers.

Most of the time, she had her tough face on. When she showed any signs other than toughness, I felt as if I saw glimpses of the girl I once loved. The one who was strong but still so soft inside. The one who dreamed big and had sparkles in her eyes.

I opened the door and stepped to the side so she could enter. She walked in, glanced around the penthouse, and muttered something. She turned to face me and raised an eyebrow. "I read that you lost your penthouse."

"Can't believe everything you read online," I told her as I tossed my keys into the basket on the table in my foyer. "Especially when it comes from tabloids."

Avery took off her shoes, and I did the same. We placed them beneath the front hall table and stood still for a moment. She took off her baseball cap, revealing the flowers in her hair from her wedding updo.

I felt a tightness in my chest. I couldn't differentiate whether it was her aching or my own. All I knew was that I wanted to slowly pick those damn flowers out of her hair and tell her everything would be all right.

"Can I take a shower?" she asked. Her eyes lifted and she met my stare. A wave of tears settled in her eyes, but she didn't let them fall. That wasn't shocking. "I need to get out of this damn dress."

"Yeah, of course. I'll grab some of my sweats and get you set up. If you want, I can run you a bath in my primary bathroom. It's huge and relaxing. I got lavender bubble bath soap, Epsom salts, and bath bombs, too."

She tilted her head. "You still take baths?"

"Ever since you told me how good they were for muscle recovery, I'm kind of a bath snob."

"I always did give you the best ideas."

"Yeah," I agreed. "You did."

She almost smiled, and I almost loved it."Stop trying to make me not hate you anymore."

I laughed. "Did you already forget that I get turned on by your hatred, Coach?"

She rolled her eyes. "Can you draw me a bath?"

I stepped closer to her and removed one of the flowers from her hair. My hand slightly brushed against her cheek as I nodded slowly. "I can draw you a bath."

Her mouth slightly parted, and I was almost certain a sarcastic comment was going to fall from her lips. Instead, her eyes shut, and a single tear rolled down her cheek. I brushed it away with my thumb, and her body shivered.

"You don't have to do this, Ave," I muttered, watching her fight like hell to keep from breaking. "You don't have to pretend to be strong today."

"Yes, I do."

"Why?"

"Because being weak never helped me before." She shook her softness away, and I watched her eyes harden once more as her browns reappeared. She swiped away the tears that snuck past her stubbornness and rolled her shoulders back.

"Will you draw me a bath?" she asked once more.

"I will draw you a bath," I echoed.

"Thank you," she murmured.

"Be right back. Help yourself to anything in the fridge.

Though I haven't been here in a while, so I'm sure it's all expired."

"If I recall correctly, you had no problem eating expired food."

"Butter and eggs don't expire," I countered.

"Butter and eggs *definitely* expire," she disagreed. "And so does cheese."

"If there's no green, it's good to go."

She shook her head in disapproval. "That's how you ended up with food poisoning way back when."

"I still think it was a twelve-hour flu."

"That's because you're hardheaded."

"You always did know me best."

The corner of her mouth twitched.

Almost another smile.

Damn.

I missed her smiles.

"Bath, Nathaniel."

"On it, Coach."

I headed to the bathroom and began to draw her a bath. The number of bath products I had was a running joke with my brothers. Every time they come over to my place, they'd mock me for my drawer of bathtime goodies. From oils to bath bombs to skin conditioners, I had it all. The joke was on them, though. Due to my bath routine, I'd have baby-smooth skin into my late sixties.

I got the water running and added lavender bath salts because I figured that would help Avery relax a little. I could only imagine the thoughts swirling through her mind as she tried to process what she'd been through that afternoon.

What happened with her and Wesley?

Why did the wedding get called off?

Who called it off?

There were a million questions I wanted answers to, but I

knew it was none of my business until Avery made it my business. The only thing I knew was that if she was willing to run away with me—her sworn enemy—she must've been dealing with a lot of heavy thoughts.

Even seeing that single tear move down her cheek was a big sign of her hurting. One teardrop from Avery Kingsley was like a million tears from the average crier.

Willow was so in touch with her emotions that she probably would've cried enough to create her own river.

I lit a few candles around the bathroom, too, and poured her a glass of red wine. Before she came in, I tossed a jazz record onto the turntable. Was it odd I had a turntable set up in a bathroom? Maybe. But I took my bath time seriously. I was one to stay in until my fingertips looked like raisins.

As I walked out of the bathroom, I found Avery sitting on my couch, flipping through the baseball book I had as my coffee table centerpiece.

"Bath time," I said, breaking her stare from the book.

She shut it and held it close to her chest. "Can I read this in the tub?"

"You can do whatever you want here, Avery Kingsley."

She took a deep breath. "That's right. I'm still a Kingsley."

"Does that make you happy or sad?"

"Neither." She shrugged her shoulders. "It just makes me numb."

That made me sad for her, but I didn't mention that because I was almost certain she'd chew my ass out for being sad for her.

I walked her to the bathroom, and a slight gasp escaped her lips as she looked around the dimly lit room. "Oh my gosh. Your bathroom is the size of my bedroom." She paused and pressed a hand to her forehead. "Oh my gosh. *I don't have a bedroom anymore!*" Her voice cracked as the realization rolled off her tongue. "I lived with Wesley. In his house. Oh my goodness. I'm homeless."

"You're not homeless."

"I am! I don't have a home. Not having a home means homeless, Nathan. Oh my gosh, I don't have a home." She began pacing in my bathroom as the realizations settled in. "What am I going to do?"

"You have a home," I said once more.

"How so? How do I have a home if I don't have a home?"

"Well, I have a home. So if I have a home, you have a home. If you need one, I mean."

Her pacing stopped. She turned to me with widened eyes and tilted her head. Those full lips parted once more, and I prayed her thoughts would be released from her brain. Instead, she shook them away. "You need to leave. I have to get out of this damn dress."

"Right. Of course."

I turned to walk away, and she said, "Nathan, wait."

"Yeah?"

She placed the baseball book on the bath tray I had set up for her, turned her back to me, and moved the loose hair hanging against her neck to the side. "Can you undo my dress? I can't get out of this thing on my own."

"Yeah, of course."

I walked over to her and unlaced her dress from the top. I took my time with it, watching as the gown unraveled and loosened. She held her hands over her chest, keeping the fabric from falling to the floor. Each lace I loosened revealed more and more of her beautiful brown skin. I wanted my fingers to brush against her skin. I wanted to spin her around and hold her in my arms.

But I knew that would never happen for me.

She wasn't mine to hold anymore. Yet being that close to

her, I couldn't help but wonder what it would be like to have
her and to hold her once more.

I'd lost a lot of things in my life. I'd lost things I thought
would make me crumble into a million pieces. I've lost things
that meant so much to me. But nothing would compare to what
losing Avery did to me.

Losing Avery Kingsley would be one of the greatest regrets
of my life. If I could turn back time, it would've worked out
differently. If I could turn back time, I would've never played
another game of baseball if it meant I had her.

Yet that was the thing about choices. We'd made the best
ones we thought possible when we were dealing with the
different traumas at hand. Young Nathan was just...scared and
so deeply sad from the loss of his father. I didn't know how to
think straight at that moment, let alone have enough space in
my fucked-up head to love Avery right.

"I was right," I said as I kept removing the ribbon from its
loops.

"Right about what?"

"You being a beautiful bride."

She didn't say another word, and I didn't blame her. But her
body did tremble a little. Her soul did react. I just didn't know
what to make of the reaction. I wished I knew how to play it
cool around her, too, and pretend that I didn't feel the way I'd
felt, but I couldn't help it. She was beautiful, and I needed her
to know that.

"Done," I murmured, letting the ribbon drop to the floor.

"Thank you."

"Anytime."

"Hopefully, I won't need you to unlace me from a wedding
dress again."

One can hope, Avery. One can only hope.

14

AVERY

He left a bottle of wine on the bathtub tray beside the wineglass.

I was taking a bath in Nathan's gigantic bathtub.

Why was I taking a bath in Nathan's gigantic bathtub?

I skirted the water with my toes before climbing in. It was the perfect temperature. My body melted into the pool of comfort as the bubbles fizzled from my contact with them. The whole room smelled like I'd stepped into a lavender field, and the heaviness of my heart began to ease somewhat.

Until I turned to my left and saw my wedding gown pooled on the floor.

In a different world, Daddy would've already given me away.

My sisters would've been standing by my side. Both would've cried, but Yara a little more than Willow. Pregnancy hormones had a way of doing that to a girl. Willow would've performed the sand ceremony, giving us the symbolism of two words blending into one.

We would've exchanged our vows.

Wesley would've cried.

I wouldn't have.

He would've said, "I do."

I would've said, "I do," too.

Our reception would've been starting any second now.

We would've been introduced as Mr. and Mrs. Gable.

The room would've erupted into cheers.

There would've been cake cutting and dancing.

We'd be eating top-of-the-line food because Alex would've only prepared the best of the best.

There would've been a hot dog food truck for late-night snacks because I had an unnatural love for hot dogs.

Drew would've insulted me somehow, but I wouldn't care because I would've been drunk on prosecco and love.

We would've watched fireworks.

Wesley would've kissed me.

I would've kissed him back.

Yet a part of me would've wondered if I were happy. A part of me would've pondered if I made the right choice in going through with the marriage. We were good before Drew came into the picture. Well, we were okay. I did avoid accepting his proposal at first, but that was just because I had a fear of commitment. I loved him.

Right?

Yes.

Of course.

I loved him.

One hundred percent.

It was me who was hard to love, not Wesley.

Stop it, Avery. He literally left you on your wedding day.

My brain was trying its hardest to talk down my over-thinking heart. Yet it was next to impossible for it to happen. The thing about one's heart was that it felt so deeply, even if the brain told it to shut off.

I wanted to feel *less*.

I wanted my heart to stop beating, and the numbness that I told Nathan I felt to be true. I wanted to erase the tear that danced down my cheek from his memory so he wouldn't know that I was still capable of feeling pain.

The jazz music played in the background as I allowed my face to slip under the water. I held my breath as I hovered beneath the water and bubbles as long as I could. I wanted to disappear for a moment. Escape to a land far, far away from reality. I wanted to turn off my emotions for a little while.

I wanted my hurting to just…stop.

The worst part of being human was emotions. I didn't comprehend why we had to be able to feel. I hated feeling. I hated breathing. I hated Wesley.

No, I loved him.

Or maybe I hated and loved him. Perhaps both things could exist at the same time, and that was what upset me. I hated that I loved him, and I loved that I hated him.

After I stayed beneath the surface as long as I could, I came up for air and raked my hands through my hair. Willow's flower petals fell from my strands and landed in the tub.

I didn't even want flowers in my hair. I hated flowers in my hair. It felt so far from me, but I wanted to be right for him. I wanted him to look at me and call me beautiful.

A beautiful bride.

Nathan.

Oh gosh, I'm in Nathan Pierce's bathtub on my wedding day!

I instantly slipped back underwater.

———

AFTER THE LONGEST bath of my life, I climbed out and dried myself with the towel that Nathan slipped into his towel warmer. Yes, he had a towel warmer. I wanted to mock him about it, but it felt like stepping straight into heaven. I tightened

the towel around my body and poured the remainder of the
wine into my glass as I walked over to his sink countertop. I
looked at myself and saw how my makeup was smeared from
how many times I sank beneath the water's surface.

I looked awful.

As bad as a person who was left on their wedding day
would look, I suppose.

Without permission, I grabbed one of Nathan's black face
towels and began cleaning my face using his face wash on the
countertop. I scrubbed every drop of makeup away, and a small,
broken smile fell against my face as I looked at my reflection. At
least I looked a little more like myself again. A little more like
Mama.

I began digging through my hair, pulling out the million
and one bobby pins. Once I was free from the bondage of pins,
I shook out my wet hair and searched Nathan's cabinet drawers
for a hairbrush.

As I opened a drawer, I paused when I saw condoms sitting
stacked in the drawer.

With haste, I shut it.

With curiosity, I reopened it.

With more haste, I shut it.

With more curiosity, I reopened it.

Magnum.

XXL.

Heavy on the XXL.

I picked up the pack and read the side. For extra length and
extra width.

"Geez!" I muttered, tossing the condoms back in the drawer
and shutting it for good. When Nathan and I were younger, we
never crossed that line. I was waiting until marriage. However I
often wondered what equipment he was working with. My
imagination took me to all kinds of places, but my goodness.

XXL.

I shook my head, trying to erase the thoughts from my mind. The drunkenness was kicking in as I downed the rest of the wine in my glass.

Leave it to Nathan Pierce to be packing on his backside *and* his front. Just more reason to hate him.

"You good in there?" he called out, almost as if he knew I'd found out his dirty little secret. Okay, his dirty *big* secret.

"Fine!" I shouted, trying to shake off the bashfulness landing against my cheeks. "I'll be out in a second."

"Want me to order some dinner? I can get wings and tater tots."

"Yeah, okay." I shook my whole body, trying to remove the butterflies. "With—"

"Extra ranch and honey mustard?"

Jerk.

He still remembered how I liked my wings.

I sighed. "Yeah, that."

I opened one more drawer and found the hairbrush I'd been looking for. I quickly brushed my hair into a high bun and tossed the hair tie I'd pulled out earlier over it.

Afterward, I slid into Nathan's black sweatpants and his baseball sweatshirt, which I drowned in.

"What's becoming of your life, Ave?" I muttered to myself before combing my hands over my temple. I turned around one last time to see the wedding gown pooled on the floor before heading out to find Nathan sitting on his couch.

"Thanks for that," I said as I walked over to the opposite side of his couch than he was on and took a seat. I pulled my legs into my chest and wrapped my arms around them. "And for the sweatpants."

"They look good on you," he mentioned. "Want more wine? I can grab the bottle from the bathroom and—"

"I drank that all," I blurted out.

He arched an eyebrow. "You drank a whole bottle of wine?"

"Yup."

"Are you drunk?"

"Define drunk."

"Do you feel a bit better than when you went into the bath?"

"Well, yes. I feel..." I giggled a little and shrugged.

He smiled, and for some reason, his left dimple looked deeper than ever before. As if God himself carved it out a little more to pull me in.

"You're drunk," he said. He hopped up and headed toward his kitchen.

"Do you have vodka?"

"I have water." He poured me a glass.

"Is that code for vodka?"

"You don't need more alcohol, Coach. You said you were already numb before you drank one glass. I don't need you to flatline."

"Flatlining doesn't sound too bad to me right now. If I could, I'd take myself out," I semi-joked.

Nathan gave me a stern look and grew extremely somber. He walked over, kneeled in front of me, and said, "Don't ever say that kind of shit again."

"It was a joke."

"It's not funny," he scolded. "Suicide's never funny."

You're right.

It's not.

My hands wrapped around the edge of his sweatshirt sleeve, and I lowered my head. "Sorry. I didn't mean to..."

"It's fine. You're drunk."

"No." I shook my head. "I'm sorry, I didn't mean to tell you that secret."

"What secret?"

"That sometimes I'm so sad I want to run away from everything."

Why was I telling him this? Why was my mind buzzing so much, and why did I feel as if I were still underwater, drowning in my sadness? And why was I showing this part of myself to Nathan?

That was why I didn't drink.

When I drank, I became too truthful.

When I drank, my reality slipped out.

He placed the glass of water on the coffee table before turning back to me and placing a hand on my kneecap. "Should I be worried about you, Coach?"

"No. I'm the strong one, remember? No one worries about the strong one. The strong one worries about everyone else. We take care of others. We don't get taken care of."

"I'll take care of you."

Tears began streaming down my cheeks as I stared into his eyes. The sincerest looking eyes I'd ever seen. The same sincere eyes I'd once loved.

"I don't believe you," I whispered, not even trying to stop the tears from falling. I was too drunk, too heartbroken to even care that I was being vulnerable, which meant I was treading on very dangerous territory. The last time I was vulnerable—truly vulnerable—was with...well, him.

Over seventeen years ago.

Was that right?

Seventeen years of not feeling that deeply with another human being?

Wesley was right.

I was hard to love.

"Why don't you believe me?" he asked. His concern made my whole body break out into shakes.

"Because." I wrapped my arms around my body because

self-comfort was the only thing I could think of doing. "You said you'd take care of me before, but you still left."

I saw it—the heartbreak that flashed through his eyes. The hurt that almost swallowed him whole from the truth I chose to say. I hated that I was crying, but I couldn't stop myself. I couldn't stop the tears from gliding down my cheeks at an annoying speed.

I was drunk.

And sad.

And drunkenly sad.

His hand caressed my cheek, and I shut my eyes. His fingers swallowed up the tears that kept flowing. "Ave...if I could go back in time, I would've never left you. I've regretted that decision every single day of my life."

"Then why?" I asked.

"Why what?"

I opened my eyes and stared into his. "Why didn't you ever come back? I needed you, Nathan. I needed you to come back for me. And I waited, and waited, and, oh my gosh..." Reality stumbled back into me as a moment of soberness snuck in. I shook his touch away from my skin and hopped up from his couch. "What am I doing? I can't do this. I can't..." Oh, gosh. *Pull your drunk self together, Avery.* "We can't do this, Nathan."

He stood. "Do what?"

"*This,*" I urged, gesturing between us. "We can't be close like this. Physically and mentally. Especially when I'm drunk and sad. Especially on my wedding day."

"Why not?"

"Because we aren't us anymore. We haven't been us for seventeen years. And we can't be us. Not again."

"Exactly," he said as he stepped closer to me. "We aren't the same stupid kids who made the same stupid mistakes. We're grown now, Avery. I'm grown, and I wouldn't hurt you again. Trust me. I wouldn't hurt you."

"That's what he said, too," I whispered as the ache in my heart only intensified. "Because that's what you men do—you lie to get what you want. And then a better opportunity comes, and you leave. And then my mind will try to move on while my heart keeps breaking in the silence, wondering why I was never good enough to stay. You left me for baseball. He left me for space. And here I am once again—alone with the pieces of my heart that I have to repair on my own."

"Avery—"

"Can I go to bed?" I asked, still crying, still breaking, still drowning. "Please?" I whimpered, nodding down the hallway. "Can I sleep in your spare room?"

He hesitated for a moment before surrendering. "Yeah, sure. Second door on the left."

I hurried down the hall, into the bedroom, and shut the door. I crawled into the bed and wrapped myself in the blankets. I hugged the pillow and cried into it, having the first emotional release I could remember. I fell apart completely on his satin pillowcases as all my heartbreak caught up with me. Years of hurt wept out of my eyes; years of pain that I kept stored deep within myself poured from my spirit.

I wanted it to stop.

I wanted the tears to stop falling, but that was the issue with holding so much in for so very long. Once the walls began to crack, a deluge was released, and there was no turning back. I had to feel everything, even if I didn't want to do so.

And the only thing that kept crossing my mind as I sobbed into the pillowcase was how deeply I wished Mama was there to hug me. To hold me. To tell me everything would be fine. I deserved more time with her. I deserved more comfort through heartbreaks and more laughter during the happy days. I deserved to be able to call her whenever the world was swallowing me whole. I deserved her comforting voice to remind me that everything would be okay, even if it seemed like nothing would ever be okay again.

I deserved more of her love, and I wished she was there to hold me in her arms as if I were still her little girl.

It wasn't fair that mamas could die.

Their daughters still needed them so very much, no matter how much we grew up.

15

AVERY

I woke with a headache.

I wasn't sure if it was from the number of tears I'd cried or the abundance of red wine I drank. It took a moment for me to remember whose bed I was in and what had happened the day before, but once it all came rushing back to me, I felt an emptiness in my stomach.

I pushed myself up from the bed and walked over to the floor-length mirror.

My eyes were puffy from crying so much. It looked like wasps had stung my face due to the swelling. If I had any ounce of concern left in my body, I would've panicked at the sight of my face, but I didn't care. I didn't care about anything, really.

Moving over to the bedroom door, I opened it, and as I began to walk out into the hallway, I paused when I found a sleeping Nathan sitting beside the door. I tilted my head in confusion at the sight of him leaning up against the wall. His chest rose and fell slowly as I stood there, baffled.

"Nathan," I said, "wake up."

He didn't move.

I nudged him with my foot. "Nathan. Wake up."

Nothing.

"*Nathaniel*!" I shouted.

With the shout, he shook himself and opened his eyes.

"What?!" he quickly remarked, dazed and confused. He rubbed his hands over his eyes and tilted his head up toward me. "Oh. Good morning."

"What are you doing?"

"Waking up."

"On the floor."

"Yes."

"Why are you waking up on the floor?"

He pushed himself up to a standing position and stretched his arms to get the knots out of his body. "I must've fallen asleep sitting next to your room."

"But why were you sitting next to my room?"

"I wanted to know that you were okay. I wanted to stay next to the room until you stopped crying, in case you needed me to come in. I must've fallen asleep here."

I grimaced even though my tired heart wanted me to smile. "That's stupid."

"I'm stupid."

And sweet.

So, so very sweet.

"Can I cook you breakfast?" he asked.

"I don't want your old eggs."

He grinned. Ugh. That smile. "I ordered some groceries last night. I figured you might be hungry since you didn't eat dinner."

My stomach rumbled as if it knew exactly what he was asking. "Sure. Okay."

I moved into his living room and curled into a ball as he walked into the kitchen. I peered over at him, confused about what to say or do as he cooked breakfast for me. So I figured it was a good time to check my text messages.

Which wasn't the best idea.

Forty-three new messages from Willow, Yara, Tatiana, and my father.

Daddy's texts were very sweet.

DAD

> Just checking in, baby girl. I hear Nathan's looking after you. Always liked that boy. Call me when you're ready.

DAD

> I love you, Avery.

DAD

> I love you so much, baby girl. If you need me, call me. Day or night.

DAD

> I love you.

Leave it to Daddy to make my eyes almost tear up from his love. I knew he told me he loved me repeatedly because he knew how much my heart was hurting, and he knew how hard it was to say those same words to myself. Sometimes those three words made things a little easier to digest. Sometimes those three words from Daddy were the only thing that made me able to get up each morning and keep going after this thing called life.

A father's love was just as important as a mother's. I was lucky I still had Daddy around to give me his love.

Tatiana's messages were packed with love and a bit of revenge.

TATIANA

> I love you, Ave. Let me know if you want Wesley to go missing. I've listened to enough murder mystery podcasts to know how to get away with murder.

TATIANA

Call me when you're ready. I'll stay in the loop
with your dad and your sisters. No pressure.
Just love.

Willow and Yara's group chat messages, on the other hand, were a little more chaotic. I didn't expect anything else, truthfully.

YARA

Avery! Where are you? What's going on?

WILLOW

I'm sensing that something major happened,
but I can't pinpoint it.

YARA

Do we need to kick Wesley's ass? I'll kick
his ass.

WILLOW

I'm more of a lover, not a fighter, but I will
whoop someone's butt if they hurt you.

YARA

WHY DID NATHANIEL PIERCE JUST CALL
ALEX AND SAY YOU'RE WITH HIM?!

WILLOW

OH MY GOSH, WHAT?! ARE YOU TWO
HAVING A RUNAWAY BRIDE MOMENT?

YARA

IS HE YOUR RICHARD GERE?

WILLOW

DID YOU TOUCH HIS PENIS? WHAT IS
HAPPENING?! CALL US NOW.

YARA

Like right now! RIGHT NOW, AVERY HARPER
KINGSLEY!

> **WILLOW**
>
> I knew the two of YOU were twin flames.
>
> **YARA**
>
> Don't make the group chat hippie-dippie, Willow. You know hippie-dippie keeps Avery away from engaging.
>
> **WILLOW**
>
> That's because she has an avoidant attachment style.

I do not!

Okay, I did.

Avoidance was my favorite hobby. I truly wished I could've avoided having my mental breakdown last night, too.

> **YARA**
>
> Great, now Avery will never come back to the group chat. You can't just call people out like that.
>
> **WILLOW**
>
> Sorry. I met a therapist on a hike in Japan last month, and he told me all about attachment styles. Like you, Yara. You were previously an anxious attachment style that slipped into a secure attachment style after Alex and you got together.
>
> **YARA**
>
> What's your style?
>
> **WILLOW**
>
> Well, therapist man said I was an avoidant, too. So I blocked him.

I snickered lightly, shaking my head.

> **YARA**
>
> We love you, Avery. Call us.

WILLOW

We love you so, so much, sister. Please.
Call us.

I began to text back finally, first Daddy, letting him know I was okay. Then Tatiana. Then my sisters.

AVERY

I love you two, too. I'm okay. Just processing.
I'll be back in Honey Creek on Monday night.

They both instantly texted me back as if they'd been waiting by their phones.

YARA

We'll be here with hugs.

WILLOW

And wooden baseball bats if you want us to take out Wesley's kneecaps.

AVERY

I thought you were a lover, not a fighter?

WILLOW

Yeah, well. I go to war for my sisters. I know if it was the other way around, you'd take out someone's kneecaps with a bat. Love you, big sis.

AVERY

Love you, too.

At the same time, two messages came through.

YARA AND WILLOW

BUT NATHANIEL PIERCE?!

I chuckled again and placed my phone down.

"Talking to your sisters?" Nathan asked from the kitchen as he whipped eggs in a mixing bowl.

"How did you know?"

"Because you laughed a few times. They were always able to make you laugh, no matter what."

I smiled at that thought. It was true. Whenever I was at my lowest, my family had a way of making it seem as if the sky was no longer falling. And if the sky were falling, they'd toss themselves beneath it and hold it up as long as they could before it could crash over me.

"They want to kill him," I confessed. "Or, well, at least take out his kneecaps."

"With a metal baseball bat?"

"They said wooden."

"Oh." He grimaced as he kept whipping those eggs. "I would've gone metal."

A lazy smirk fell against my face, but it faltered quickly. "Thanks again for letting me crash here for the weekend. I needed to get away, and this worked out very well."

"Not a problem. And I know you probably thought I was shitting you, but you can stay with me in Honey Creek, too. I have a whole house to myself."

"Nathaniel," I scolded. "That's a terrible idea."

"Why is that a terrible idea? It's a whole house. You won't even see me if you don't want to. Or we could go over stats for our players and all the baseball stuff. Or, again, you can *not* see me at all. Whatever you need, I got you."

"It's a terrible idea because, well, I hate you, remember?"

Oh, the lies I told out loud.

He smiled the smile that made me want to blush. "I know, and I love your hate, but I want to make sure you have somewhere to land while you figure everything out."

"I can get an apartment."

"You shouldn't be alone."

"I'll be fine alone."

His stirring stopped, and he set the bowl down on the

counter. He walked over to me, pulled his coffee table closer to the couch, and took a seat. His brown eyes locked in on mine, and he shook his head. "You shouldn't be alone, Ave."

A nervous chuckle escaped my lips. "Why would you be concerned with..." The pieces started collecting in my head as to why he was so deeply concerned with me being alone and why he had slept outside my door last night. I started to recall the conversation the night prior, and a pit of nervousness slammed straight into my stomach.

I took a deep inhale and released it slowly as I started fidgeting with my hands. I stared down at them because looking into his eyes felt too intense.

"Listen, Nathan, I was drunk last night."

"Drunk people tell the truth."

"Yeah, but they don't mean to. You don't have to worry about me. I'll be fine. I'm always fine."

"You're not always fine."

Yes, you're right.

I shrugged. "But I'm a good actress."

"Not with me, Coach. I see you."

"I know," I whispered, tugging on the sleeves of his sweatshirt. "I always hated that you could see me."

"I kind of loved it myself." He clasped his hands together and tapped his feet against his living room rug. "I'm worried about you."

"Don't be."

"Can't help it."

"Why not?"

"Because I care."

"Well, stop caring, Nathan. Seriously. This is ridiculous. You're my coworker, not my friend."

"We could be friends, though," he offered. "And roommates."

"Nathan."

"Avery."

"Why are you pushing this?" I questioned. "Why are you being so damn pushy about this topic?"

His shoulders rolled back, and the corner of his mouth twitched. There was a heaviness in his stare that made me want to know his thoughts. What it was that was eating at him so much.

"You said you were extremely sad, Ave. That scares me."

"Nath—"

"Mickey Ray Phillips." He cut in. "Did you know him?"

I tilted my head and nodded. "Yeah, of course, I knew him. He was one of the best baseball players in the world. Wasn't he your...?"

"Teammate, yeah. And one of my best friends."

My stomach knotted up, knowing where this was going. Mickey Ray was one of the best Major League Baseball players of our time. He was one of the happiest-seeming individuals out there, too. I remembered when the news came out of his passing. It was shocking to hear that he took his own life. Nothing about Mickey Ray seemed to point to him being the type of person who would've taken his own life. Then again, what type of person took their own life? It was all types, all people, all levels of success.

Still, it stunned me.

I'd be lying if I said I didn't follow Nathan's career. He was one of my favorite players even though I hated him. I could never hate his talent. Studying how he and Mickey played was like studying the greats. It was clear that when those two were on the field together, they jived extremely well. Though I didn't know they were best friends. I'd only known what I saw on the television screen and during press conferences.

"I'm so sorry, Nathan," I expressed, placing a hand on his shaky leg.

He smiled, but it wasn't his normal, happy grin. It dripped in sadness.

"The night he passed away, he asked me to hang out with him. It was after a big win, and some of the guys were going out to celebrate. Mickey normally joined us, but he was in a weird mood. I figured it was because he didn't perform his best during the game. Sure, we won, but Mickey was hard on himself. He'd always go deep into his head when he had a bad game. But to me, on the other hand, a win was a win. And his worst game was my best. I wanted to celebrate." He grimaced and brushed his thumb against his nose. "I told him not to be a buzzkill and to come out with us. He asked me to stay in with him. And I didn't..."

"Nathan, what happened wasn't your fault."

"Wasn't it, though? Looking back on it, he was reaching out to me. He was asking me to be there for him, and I couldn't get my head out of my own ass for the life of me. I was so egotistical that I couldn't see past myself to realize my best friend, my best fucking friend, was suffering. He had suffered for a long time, too. And I didn't *see* it. I should've seen it."

"But still, it wasn't your fault."

"I hear you, Coach, I do. But I can't believe that. Because he asked me to stick around that night. He pretty much begged me not to be alone. And that's what he was—alone. They found him alone in his hotel room. That still haunts me. So the idea that you've been having dark thoughts...Avery...I'm sorry. But I can't leave you alone."

My tired, broken heart slowly began to beat for him. Maybe that was the exact second when my long-lived hatred for Nathaniel Pierce began to fade away. I had to admit, it was easier to hate him when he wasn't around. Yet when he was around, Nathan was the easiest person in the world to like. Especially in his older age.

"We'll figure out my living situation so I'm not alone," I

swore to him. "I can't stay with Yara because they have a baby on the way, and I don't want to put them out. And Willow's bus house is a little too small. And living with my dad..." I shivered at the thought. "Even though I love him, I can't live with my dad. He has one too many women who like sleepovers."

"So you'll stay with me."

"Maybe," I said. "Let's just make it through this weekend. How about that?"

He smiled—his real smile. The smile that almost made me smile, too. He held a hand out toward me. "Promise you'll really consider it?"

I shook his hand. "Promise."

He placed his hands on his thick upper thighs and pushed himself up to a standing position. "Okay. Let me finish your breakfast. Then we can figure out what to do for the day."

"Are you going to helicopter-parent me this whole weekend?" I quipped.

"I am going to helicopter-parent you this whole damn weekend," he replied with a nod.

Oddly enough, I didn't hate the idea of him looking after me.

16

NATHAN

I nstead of eating our meals at the dining room table, we sat on my living room floor, eating at the coffee table as we watched ESPN for hours.

Avery hadn't brought up the wedding over the past nine hours that swept past. Instead, she talked about everything else under the sun. We talked about our team's stats and how we'd tackle next week's games. She went over our practices and how we should switch things up. She even talked about how to make the best chicken wings. Anything and everything but the wedding.

It was going on so long that I finally burst while we were eating Chinese food for dinner. "What the hell happened yesterday, Avery?"

She turned to me and hesitated before placing her fork down. "What do you mean?"

"With the wedding. What happened?"

"Oh. That. Well, I'm cursed."

"Cursed?"

"Yup. When I was a kid, Betty Stevens read my tarot card on

the playground. She told me all men would choose their careers over loving me. I figured when you ditched me for baseball, it was just a coincidence, but then having Wesley leave for the same reason made it clear as day. I'm cursed to be second-string in men's lives."

"That's ridiculous."

"Maybe, but true. If it wasn't, I would've been married today. Instead, he showed up to my dressing room to tell me he got a new job and no longer wanted to get married."

"What a dick."

"I loved him. Or love him. I don't know. I don't even know what love is. All I know is I'm two strikes down."

"Two strikes down?"

"Well, Wesley was leaving me for a job opportunity. You did the same thing. One more strike and I'm out."

The amount of guilt that hit the pit of my stomach was enough for me to want to crawl into a hole. I wanted to explain to her why I'd left all those years before. I wanted her to understand that leaving her was the hardest and worst decision of my life. But that didn't matter in that very second. She didn't need my excuses. She needed comfort.

"Men are idiots," I murmured.

"You don't have to tell me twice." She huffed. "But still, it would be nice to be someone who people stayed for."

"I hate that he did that to you."

"Did you hate that you did that, too?"

That felt like a stab to my chest. "Avery—"

"Sorry." She shook her head. "I didn't mean to say that. I want to leave us, whatever we were, in the past. What happened with Wesley just triggered something in me."

"We can talk about it if you want. I have no issues talking about us."

"But it won't change anything. It is what it is." She combed her hair behind her ears and looked at me. "Can we talk about anything else but this? But us? Remember our rules?"

I wanted to say *fuck the rules*, but I knew she was too sensitive that evening for me to push it. So instead, we spent the rest of the night talking about sports.

17

AVERY

"**A**re you okay?!" Yara and Willow remarked as I pulled up to Willow's bus. After Chicago, Nathan dropped me back off at my vehicle Monday evening, and from there, I headed straight to Willow's.

My sisters came rushing outside, shouting in sync as I climbed out of my parked car.

Before I could reply, their arms were wrapped tightly around me. Their embrace made me want to melt into them more than ever before. I would've cried, but I'd hit my ten-year crying quota on my actual wedding day.

"I'm good, I'm good," I said. I felt emotionally spent, but it felt good to be back with my sisters after spending a long weekend with Nathan. A concept I was still making sense of. Even worse, I was considering living with him.

How could a life turn so far upside down in the span of seventy-two hours?

"I made some herbal tea for us. Let's go inside," Willow offered, wrapping her arm around my waist as she guided me to the steps of her mobile home.

Willow's home was beautiful. It was a school bus that she

and some guy she randomly knew transformed into a mobile home. It had everything a single girl could want, space-wise, including a living area, a kitchen, a shower, and a bedroom with a queen-size bed. It was remarkable how much space it seemed to have within it. Before she made the home, we watched dozens of RV and van transformations to make sure she had her dream home.

Some people probably judged her for her dream home being a mobile home, but Willow was like the wind and loved to move at her own will. That bus—or Big Bird as she called it —had seen more of America than I had.

The three of us took a seat on Willow's sectional couch. Willow began to pour the tea into cups that she had set up on her coffee table.

Yara struggled to cross her legs and get comfortable before turning toward me with a look of heavy concern. "Avery...what in the world happened?"

"I'm sorry I disappeared like that. I should've called you guys. I just wasn't in the right frame of mind to face anyone or anything. It was as if my brain shut down, and I just needed to get out. Nathan happened to find me at the batting cages, and well, he offered me an escape. So I took it."

"I'm not going to lie. Finding out you were with Nathan Pierce was the last thing I expected to hear. I figured you'd be on Mars before shacking up with Nathan Pierce at his penthouse," Willow expressed as she sat down beside me.

"I wasn't shacking up with Nathan Pierce at his penthouse," I urged. "I was running away from my life. Two very different things."

"Still. A little surprising," Yara said calmly, placing a hand of comfort against my kneecap. "Tell us what happened."

I sighed and told them the whole story.

"So he just called it off?" Yara asked.

"Yup," I replied.

"He's such a jerk," Willow griped.

I knew that was true, but still, a part of me hoped to find love, or something close enough, with Wesley.

When I was young, before Mama and Daddy found each other, it was just me and her for a while with my biological father. He didn't treat her well at all, and I remember from a young age watching her cry more tears than any person should've cried.

The day she found the courage to leave him, she packed up our things and put them in the back of her car. I'd never forget her turning to look at me and saying words that stayed with me for a long time. *"Go where you're loved, baby girl, and never stay a second longer when the love is removed."*

But what if there wasn't a place like that for me?

What if there was no place where I was loved?

"He also said I was hard to love," I murmured, feeling those words sting me the hardest.

Maybe because they were true.

"He said what?!" they shouted—again in unison. We Kingsley girls had a way of doing that—speaking in sync.

"Oh, screw him!" Yara yipped, shaking her head in shock. "I can't believe it. What a jerk. I truly can't believe he was bold enough to say that to you."

"And to think I gave him a friendship bracelet at the rehearsal dinner," Willow said, her words soaked in disgust. I knew it probably sounded silly, but Willow took her friendship bracelets very seriously.

I shrugged. "It's fine."

"It's not. It's very far from fine," Yara stated. Her eyes flooded with tears, and I grumbled a little, knowing the waterworks would flow soon.

"Yara, don't cry," I ordered.

"I'm not going to cry," she replied.

With a sigh, I picked up a napkin from the table and held it out toward her. "You *are* crying."

"I'm sorry, but this is just so heartbreaking. I can't believe he had the nerve to say that to you!"

Geez. She was crying harder than I'd been. And of course, Willow started tearing up, too, because she was a sympathy crier. If anyone within ten feet of her was teary-eyed, she'd burst out into an emotional tailspin. It quickly became clear why I chose to run away for the weekend instead of going to my sisters. I knew my sisters were more emotional than me, and if I had to comfort them during my own breakdown, I would've been a terrible mess.

I sighed and placed a hand on each of their shoulders. "There, there," I muttered. "Really, though. I'm okay."

"You're not," Willow replied. "I can sense your energy."

"Are you sure you aren't sensing Yara's hormones?" I asked.

"Well, actually, that might be true. A lot of energy mojo is going on in this room. I should get my sage stick and—"

"Oh no, that smoke makes me sneeze," Yara remarked as she wiped her tears. "I'll tame my energy." She took a few deep breaths and wiggled her body. "I'm fine. Everything's fine." She turned to me and frowned and then placed her hand in mine. "Are you fine, Avery?"

"Just peachy. So please don't look at me like that."

"Like what?" she asked.

"Like I'm some sad puppy left at a pound on Christmas morning." Yara's eyes filled with more tears, and I rolled my eyes. "Christ, Yara. Hold yourself together."

"Sorry, sorry. It's just that this little girl has me all wrapped up in my emotions," she said.

"Wait, what? Little girl?" I bellowed out.

Willow's eyes widened as she tossed her hands into the air. "It's a girl?! I thought you two weren't going to find out."

Yara nodded, and I frankly was happy for the shift in

conversation. "Alex and I just found out by mistake. A doctor mentioned it. Alex cried for the longest time—don't tell him I told you he cried. It would damage his bad-boy persona," she teased.

I think I liked Alex because he and I were so much alike. He didn't like people. He didn't like to smile. And he had a steady, resting bitch face. That was, outside of whenever he looked at Yara. I'd never seen another person's eyes light up with so much love when they looked at their partner. If it weren't for those two, I wouldn't have even believed love was real anymore. They were the opposite of one another, too. It was as if a golden retriever fell in love with a black cat.

As I watched them sometimes, I'd wonder about my relationship—well, past relationship—with Wesley. Wesley and I made sense in a technical manner. He wasn't romantic, and I hated romance. I didn't like grand gestures of love, and he didn't know how to perform any. Therefore, our lives matched up fine. What it lacked was...heart.

I didn't mind it lacking heart, though. Most things in my life lacked heart except for my love for baseball and my love for my family. The last time I opened my heart up to another—well, we all know how that turned out.

"A baby girl," I swooned, placing my hand over my heart. "We're going to have a little niece!"

"Can we revisit doing a water birth in a pool?" Willow asked. "I know a midwife who would be so good at that. I met her when I was in Peru, and I think—"

"No water births," Yara quickly stated. "I will be in a hospital with many doctors and nurses around, *thankyouverymuch*. And they can load me up with all the drugs."

"Okay, but holistic births are on the rise as of late. You can be an influential figure by diving in and having our baby girl in a pool," Willow expressed.

Willow would always live up to her name and free-spirited beliefs.

"Congratulations, Yar," I said, taking her hand. "Really. I'm so happy for you and Alex."

She smiled softly and shrugged. "I'm a little scared if I'm honest."

"Scared of what?" Willow asked.

"What if I can't do it as well as Mama? What if I'm not a good mother?" she quietly questioned. "I said the same thing to Alex, and he told me I was wrong, but those thoughts cross my mind sometimes. I just...I wish she was here to help me through this sometimes."

I knew that feeling too well.

"I wish she was here, too. Over the weekend, that was my main wish." Sadly enough, wishes like that never came true. Not in the way we'd hoped, at least.

"Oh, Ave. I can only imagine. I miss her so much—a lot more lately. You'd think it would get easier over time, but..." Yara shrugged. "Sometimes, it feels as if it only gets harder."

"Tell me about it," Willow murmured, growing somber.

My heart ached for my youngest sister. She never even got the chance to know our mother since Mama passed away during Willow's birth.

Sometimes I wondered if that was why Willow always ran off on her adventures around the world. She constantly sought something that was missing. Unfortunately, a mother's love couldn't be found in other places. It couldn't be replaced by other forms of comfort.

She didn't talk about not being able to have a relationship with Mama, though. Truthfully, her saying "tell me about it" was the closest she'd ever come to speaking about our mother. Usually, she was quick to shift the conversation to something that didn't involve Mama in any way, shape, or form.

"Willow…" I started.

She hopped up from the couch and clapped her hands together. "I have an idea!" She smiled brightly as if her heart wasn't just broken from the conversation. That was the thing with Willow Kingsley; she covered her sadness with smiles and conversation shifts. Maybe I had more in common with my little sister than I thought.

"Let's hear it," I said.

"Two words. Puerto Rico!" she exclaimed, wiggling her hips with excitement. "I was going to go next week to meet up with this guy I matched with on a dating app—"

"I saw this same plot in a horror movie." I sighed. I swear, my littlest sister gave me the highest level of stress from her travels.

"Anyway! I'm still going, but you girls should come with me! It will be a great three-month trip."

"Three months?!" Yara and I blurted out in sync.

"You can't go to Puerto Rico for three months with a stranger," I scolded. "I forbid it."

"Okay, Mom," she said, rolling her eyes. "Besides, it wouldn't only be to Puerto Rico. I'll be going to Europe to meet with a few of my lovers there, too. But I want you two to join me."

"Willow. I know this might come as a surprise to you, but I'll be having a baby next month."

"I know! I'll be back in town for baby girl," Willow agreed.

"Yes, but also, Avery and I have these things called jobs that kind of tie us down," Yara explained.

Willow made a face. "That sounds awful."

Trust me, it is.

"You really should consider getting one, maybe," I mentioned. "It wouldn't hurt for you to plant some roots."

"What? Just for someone to come rip them up? No, thank

you. I'd prefer to fly instead of staying grounded. Nothing good comes from being committed and grounded."

I wanted to argue with her, but there I was without a home or husband.

My life had been uprooted within seventy-two hours.

"Does Daddy know you're going to Puerto Rico with a stranger?" I asked.

"No, and he doesn't need to know. Not yet, at least. You know how he is. He'd worry."

"We all worry, Will," I said, shaking my head. "I would tell you not to go, but I know that would just make you want to go more."

She smiled. "At least you have a good idea of the person I am. If you change your mind, let me know."

I rolled my shoulders back and stretched. "I won't, but thank you for the offer. I have too much to figure out back here. Like where I'm going to live."

"Oh, crap. I didn't even think about that. You and Wesley lived together," Yara stated.

"In *his* house. Yeah. So I'm a bit shit out of luck on that front. I have to figure that out sooner than later."

"Oh gosh. Stay here! You can have Big Bird," Willow offered. "I won't be here anyway. This paradise can be all yours. Plus, having someone watching the place while I'm gone would be nice."

I glanced around the bus and had a moment of hesitation. Then I realized it was the perfect solution for the in-between period of my life. Like I said, Willow's place was highly impressive. I didn't hate the idea of it at all, and it took extra stress off me to try to figure out a living arrangement.

Even though Nathan ever-so-nicely offered me to be roommates with him.

"I'll watch over your place until I can find my own," I said. "Better than my other option."

"What was the other option?" Yara asked.

"Nathan offered me to be his roommate," I nonchalantly stated.

"What?!" they remarked.

Willow sat back down beside me, her eyes widening with the giddiest grin on her face. "Oh gosh, I can't believe we haven't dove deeper into the Nathan aspect of this whole situation. This is a big deal."

"It's not a big deal," I disagreed.

"You running off with your former secret lover after your wedding was called off? Uh, yeah, that's a big deal," she said.

Yara nodded. "Sorry, Ave. I gotta agree with Willow. This is wild."

"Did you two sleep together?" Willow asked.

"What? Oh my gosh, no." I lightly shoved her arm. "What's wrong with you?"

"Nothing. I think sex is a beautiful way to release some stress hormones. It's a beautiful, natural act that two people take part in, and—"

"And it didn't happen. I would never, ever sleep with that man," I sternly said as I crossed my arms. "There's no way in hell that would happen. I don't like the guy. I hardly tolerate him."

"You have to admit, though, it was nice of him to help you when you needed someone. I always liked Nathan," Yara said. "And it's even nicer for him to try to help you out with a living arrangement. Though, could you imagine the town's gossip if you moved in with another man after you called off your wedding?"

I grumbled. "I could, and I hate the thought. I bet they're already having a field day talking about me."

"Oh, it's not that bad," Yara replied in a singsong tone which told me it was *that* bad.

"Everyone's talking about it, huh?" I muttered.

"Literally everyone. Even Mrs. Carpenter, and she hasn't spoken since 1995," Willow said.

"Splendid," I murmured, pressing the palms of my hands to the back of my neck. "Nothing better than a gossiping town gossiping about me."

"Don't worry. Alex and I had people gossiping about us, too, when we first got together. Now, they're in love with us. Well, in love with me. I think they just put up with Alex and his grimaces," Yara said.

"I can guarantee you that Alex doesn't care that these townsfolk don't like him," I replied.

"Maybe that's the mindset you need to take on with them, too. Be like Alex. Tell everyone to piss off," Willow expressed with a smile. "He'd probably kick their butts for looking at him wrong, too."

"Pray for my daughter's first boyfriend," Yara quipped. "But really, Avery. Screw the townspeople. They are small-town people with small minds. If you want to live with Nathan Pierce, by all means—"

"*I'm not living with Nathan Pierce!*" I shouted. Even though, maybe just a little, maybe just for a small moment in time, I secretly considered the idea. I rolled my shoulders back and turned to Willow. "Do you have anything stronger than tea?"

LATER THAT NIGHT, I lay in bed beside a slumbering Willow, unable to sleep. My mind was spinning too quickly that evening. To my surprise, I wasn't the only one struggling to rest that night. My phone dinged with a message from none other than Nathan.

NATHAN

I should've asked you this before you left, but what do you want me to do with the wedding dress?

AVERY

Burn it.

18

AVERY

"How goes it, roommate?" Nathan asked Tuesday afternoon before practice. He walked into my office and leaned against the doorframe with a smirk as he chewed gum. "That is, if you're still considering being my roommate."

"I have thought about it, but I realize it would cause too much drama in a town with gossiping people. Plus, seeing as how we hate each other, it probably wouldn't be the best situation."

"Who is this *we* that you speak of?" he said with a smile that was so sweet I almost considered not being in a bad mood. "I couldn't hate you even if I tried, Avery Kingsley. And who cares what the townspeople have to say? They are already gossiping. Do you know that they gossiped about the size of the sausage at my brothers' butcher shop compared to the grocery store? They spent the past two weeks comparing sausage lengths, trying to prove that ours were overpriced. I'm proud to say we won. Us Pierce boys have the biggest and thickest sausages on the marketplace."

I stared blankly at him. "I'm not going to entertain that comment at all."

"I'm serious, though. The town's going to talk regardless. Might as well give them something to talk about."

He took a seat on the chair across from my desk and tossed his feet up.

I shoved his feet off my desk. "Willow is going out of town for a little while, so she's letting me stay at Big Bird until she returns."

"Her mobile home?"

"Yup."

"You'd rather stay on a school bus than with your devilishly handsome assistant coach?" he joked.

"Oh, I'd rather stay in a portapotty than with you." The insult should've offended him, but he chuckled to himself. Must've been that shame kink of his kicking into full gear. "But thanks for the offer, Nathan. Truly. And for the weekend. I didn't know I needed someone to take care of me as much as I did. I appreciate it."

"Of course." He clasped his hands together, and his eyes grew somber as his voice dropped an octave. "But...about what we talked about. With your...negative thoughts. Are you sure it's best to stay alone while going through all this, Ave? I'd honestly feel more comfortable with you staying with me, but I know it's not about my comfort. It's about yours. Still...my offer stands."

I wished he'd stop making my tired heart skip a few beats. I was supposed to hate him still, but he made it increasingly difficult to dislike him. Especially after the weekend we'd shared.

"I think I'm good. Thank you, though," I said, standing up from my chair.

He kept sitting and staring at me, uncertain.

I released a small laugh. "Seriously, Nathan. I'm good."

"I'm at 505 West Chipper Lane," he said as he pushed himself to stand. "In case you change your mind."

"I won't, but thanks. Let's get to practice."

It was a beautiful spring day in Honey Creek, the perfect weather to get out on the field to run a few drills. Truthfully, I couldn't have asked for better weather over the past few days. It would've been great weather for, say, a wedding celebration.

The moment Nathan and I met the players outside on the bleachers, I already hated the looks of pity they shot my way. I hated those looks. Nothing in the world was worse than other people feeling bad for me.

I cleared my throat and tossed on my baseball cap. "All right, team. Let's just address the elephant in the room. Was I supposed to get married this weekend? Yes. Did it get called off at the last minute? Also yes. But this should not distract you from the fact that we are in the middle of our season, and with one more win, we will be off to the playoffs. Therefore, we must stay focused on the game. I'm sure you've all heard some rumors about Wesley and me, but I want you to know that I'm okay. I'm fine, and we need to—".

"Coach K?" Cameron cut me off.

"Yeah, Cam?"

"Fuck Wesley!"

The rest of the guys cheered, agreeing with him. I glanced over at Nathan who had the tiniest smile curving his lips. I could almost hear him silently saying "fuck Wesley," too.

I rubbed my palm against my forehead. "Now, that's not needed. I know you're trying to make me feel better, but you don't need to. I'm fine and—"

"Coach K?" Jason called out.

A weighted sigh rippled through me. "Yes, Jason?"

"I think Wesley's a dumbass."

"Yeah!" everyone else cheered. "What a dumbass!" they echoed, clapping their hands together.

I felt a tug against my heart. If you looked up the word

loyalty in the dictionary, you'd find a picture of the Honey Creek Hornets baseball team.

I placed my hands against my hips. "All right. Anyone else have any thoughts on my current state of affairs? Let's get it all out so we can move on sooner than later." Everyone's hands shot up to add their commentary on my life. I pointed at Kyle. "Shoot, kid."

"If Wesley was such a great rocket scientist, then why couldn't he calculate the trajectory of the path to keeping a good woman?"

I smirked a little.

That was clever.

I pointed at Caleb next. "All right, Cal. You're up."

"I'm trying to figure out how the rocket scientist had a failure to launch."

Another good one.

"Steve"—I gestured—"what do you got?"

"I hope his love life is like a black hole after you, Coach K. Empty and meaningless," Steve said with a shrug.

"If I were your type, I'd marry the fuck outta you, Coach K," Eric said.

"Okay, okay, I think that's enough." I laughed. "And that's also highly inappropriate, Eric, so you'll run two extra laps today on the field. Anyway, now that we got that out of the way, can we get back to the game?"

Instead of agreeing with me, the guys all rushed over to me and wrapped me in a tight hug. For a moment, I froze, completely thrown off by their embrace. Then I felt myself start to get misty-eyed from the comfort they were showing me as they all whispered their apologies.

Those boys meant the world to me.

But I couldn't cry in front of them. Even though my eyes wanted me to fall apart. I'd already done enough falling apart over the long weekend. I glanced up to see Nathan standing back with the gentlest smile as his arms stayed crossed over his chest. His shoulders rose and fell. I shrugged back toward him.

"All right, all right, all right," I said in my best Matthew McConaughey voice. "I think that's enough of the emotional junk. Get on the field and start to warm up, will you?" I playfully shoved them away from me. They began to jog out to the field, leaving Nathan and me there alone for a few moments.

"Those damn kids," I said, shaking my head.

"They love you."

I nodded. "Yeah. I picked up on that."

"It's kind of hard not to, Coach."

My face flashed with heat as I shook my head. "Dang it, Nathaniel. You're making it harder for me to hate you."

BEING on the field and coaching was the first thing that made me feel okay over the past few days. It was a normality that I had been seeking. I knew that baseball was the one thing, outside of my family, that could make me feel better about anything that was bringing me down. The diamond felt like my haven. The place I could escape to when the rest of the world was too loud.

The guys played their best during that practice. That felt like a little gift they were giving to me. I appreciated it because I didn't have enough energy to shout at them for messing up any drills.

We ended the night with a few sprint drills, which they hated. I didn't blame them. I hated running, too. Nathan ran beside them as I blew my whistle, telling them to go faster.

Afterward, a few of the guys collapsed on the field, breathing heavily.

"I hope a guy never breaks up with Coach K again," Caleb

joked as he bent over from exhaustion with his hands on his hips.

I smirked to myself and ordered the guys off my field after they collected all the gear.

Nathan jogged over to me with a bag of bats over his shoulder. "They're getting pretty good out there, huh?"

"Yeah. I guess you weren't the worst addition to the team."

His lazy smile appeared, and he tipped an invisible hat my way. "Appreciate that, Coach."

"Don't let it go to your head. I don't need your ego to inflate."

He began to pretend he was floating away from his inflated ego. I rolled my eyes. He smiled bigger. Kind of our normal interactions as of late. Damn. I was really starting not to hate the guy. That was mildly concerning.

Nathan glanced up at the darkening sky. "You better get inside before a downpour hits town tonight. It's supposed to be a bad one."

"Night, Nathan."

"Good night, Coach."

After doing some paperwork, I gathered my stuff and umbrella. By the time I left my office, it was already raining. I opened my umbrella as I stepped outside, and as I grew closer to my car, a smile spread across my lips as I saw Daddy leaning against it, holding an umbrella and flowers in one hand and a picnic basket in the other.

A small sigh rippled through me as I grew closer. "What are you doing here?" I asked him.

He grinned the same smile that made Mama fall in love with him, walked over to me, and kissed my forehead. "I know I said I'd give you space to show up to talk when you were ready, but I was worried. So I made us a picnic for dinner. Figured we could eat it in your car."

My father, my hero. He was probably the reason no man

would've ever been good enough for me. My standards were quite high due to him.

We climbed into my car and tossed our umbrellas into the back seat. Daddy opened the picnic basket, and my heart felt the comfort from the simple act. When Mama and I moved to Honey Creek, I was only four years old. The town hosted an event called Snack on Hillstack, where people could buy picnic baskets for charity. Daddy and Yara bought ours that afternoon. That was the first time we'd met, and I'm pretty sure that was the exact moment Daddy fell in love with Mama.

Ever since that, each year, Daddy packed picnics for each of us girls throughout the year, and he'd add in extra baskets whenever we were dealing with heartbreak. The basket held the same foods that it did all those years ago on Hillstack— peanut butter and jelly sandwiches, barbecue chips, apple juice, and orange slices.

My father—the hopeful romantic.

It turned out that picnic baskets were officially my love language.

As he handed me a sandwich, he asked, "How's your spirit today?"

I shrugged my shoulders. "I'm fine."

He narrowed his eyes at me, not believing me, but he didn't question it. "I saw the asshole Henry in town over the weekend," he said nonchalantly, biting into his sandwich.

"*Wesley*," I corrected. Over the years, my father had never called Wesley by the right name. It was a running joke that Daddy never learned the names of my sisters' and my partners until he liked them. Wesley never grew on him. My father was convinced Wesley was too smart for his own good, which, in turn, made him stupid. Daddy said nothing good came from a know-it-all. Turned out he was right.

"Whatever," Daddy said, rolling his eyes. "He came up to me to talk."

"Really? What did he say?" I was somewhat surprised Wesley hadn't reached out to me to talk at all. I didn't know why, but I at least expected a few missed calls or long, well-written text messages. Yet it had been days, and not a whisper escaped him.

"He told me he was sorry for how much money I lost on the wedding and that he made his decision due to a lack of stability in your ability to filter your emotions and express real depth in a relationship."

My jaw dropped.

Then again, yeah. That sounded like Wesley.

"What did you say?" I asked.

"Nothing." He took another bite of his sandwich and tossed a few chips into his mouth. "I punched him in the fucking nose."

I laughed and rolled my eyes. That was until I saw the seriousness in his eyes. "What?! No. Daddy, you didn't!"

"Sure did. Got a nice cut on my knuckle from his big ole stupid nose that somehow cut me."

My eyes all but fell out of my sockets as they bugged out. "Daddy! You really punched him?"

"One hundred percent. I guess you get my bad emotional filtering from me."

The thought of my father punching Wesley was not something I saw happening, but I wasn't entirely shocked by the idea. If there was one thing about Matthew Kingsley, it was his strong papa bear skills. He might've been an amazing construction worker with his own business, yet he always said his first and most important position in life was being a father.

Unfortunately, Wesley found out what mess-around-and-find-out actually meant.

"Dad," I groaned. "Everyone in town is going to have a panic attack about you punching him."

"I'm fine with being the gossip. I don't care. And he

shouldn't have been speaking about you in such a way. Especially with that woman by his side."

"A woman?" My stomach slightly knotted up. "Drew?"

"Yes. He said it was his best friend. What's that about, huh? That's weird."

"What's even weirder is they dated for a long time."

"That's why I hate men," Dad exclaimed. "We're idiots. He had the diamond of the ball and ended up with rusty nails. I never did like Trevor."

"*Wesley*," I corrected. Though it didn't matter.

He brushed his hand against the back of his neck. "How's my girl, though? You okay?"

"Yes. I'm good."

"You're lying?"

"Yes. I'm lying."

He nodded. "Figured so."

"I'm staying at Willow's until I can find a place."

"You're both staying in Big Bird? That has to be cramped."

I shook my head. "No, Willow headed off to..." My words faded off, realizing I was not supposed to tell Dad where Willow was.

His brows shot up. "Where is Willow?"

I pressed my lips together and shook my head.

"Avery Kingsley, tell me right now before I go find out from Yara and make her pregnant self cry."

I sighed. "She's going to Puerto Rico for a few weeks, then off to Europe. She said she'll message you when she lands."

"Puerto Rico?!" he gasped. "With who?"

"Good question," I quipped.

He sighed. "If I had hair, they would all be gray because of you girls."

I laughed and rubbed his bald head. "Luckily for you, you started balding in your thirties."

He huffed. "Lucky me indeed. Remind me to kick Willow's

butt when she makes it back to Illinois." He then grew somber again. "Avery?"

"Yeah?"

"I love you."

"I know, Dad."

"Avery," he repeated.

"Yes?"

"I love you."

My heart skipped a few times as tears burned at the back of my eyes. I nodded slowly. "I know, Dad."

"You know, as a father, you're learning as much as your kids are learning, too. And you figure out that each kid needs a little something different because they're all individuals and unique. I think I love that most about you three girls—you all are so different from one another. But sometimes that makes it hard to know how I'm supposed to show up. If this whole situation happened with your sisters, I'd know what to do."

"What would you do for Yara?"

"Let her cry on my shoulder while I researched becoming a hitman."

"And Willow?"

"Go skydiving with her."

"And me?"

"That's the thing, you see...I'm not quite sure. That's what bothers me the most. I think the issue is you've always been the strong one. The one who never seemed to need help, yet you were always helping others. And I think you hate the attention and people offering help because it makes you feel weak."

"That's true."

"Yeah, but baby girl, asking for help doesn't make you weak. Sometimes asking for help is the strongest thing a person could ever do."

That was a concept I'd simmer on for a good amount of time.

"This is enough," I offered, holding up half of my sandwich. "You showing up, Dad. That's enough for me."

He smiled, and I felt it kiss my soul. "That's one thing I'll do for forevermore, my love. I'm always gonna show up for you."

We continued eating, and he managed to get a few laughs out of me, too, which made him feel like the biggest success that afternoon.

"What's this I hear about Nathan Pierce sweeping you away over the weekend?" he asked. "I heard about it over at the coffee shop."

I groaned. "People are talking already, huh?"

"You know this town. It's what they do best. What's the deal with you and Nathan?" He lowered his brows. "Is there something there?"

"Gosh, no. Not outside of his coaching with me. He just found me in a bad moment and got me out of town for a bit." Daddy's brows stayed lowered as he studied my face, and I laughed. "Seriously, Dad. There's nothing there. He was just a friend helping me out of a hard time."

"A *friend*?" he questioned. "Last I heard, you hated his guts, and he was going to ruin your coaching style."

"Right. No. I still hate him. I didn't mean friend. I meant coworker. He's fine. It's whatever. He's not that bad of an addition to the team. The guys like him. It's nothing, though. We are strictly professional. Nothing more, nothing less."

Dad smiled a "bullshit answer but I'll accept it" kind of smile, and we left the conversation at that.

After our meal, he headed home, and I drove to make one more stop before heading over to Big Bird. My house.

Well, my old house.

I knew Wesley was out of town doing training for his new position, so I couldn't think of a better time to pack my stuff and drive it over to the storage locker I'd rented.

After parking my car in the driveway, I climbed out of the vehicle and grabbed the boxes waiting in my trunk.

I stood still in front of the house that once was a home. My home. I felt the disconnect already. As if my spirit had already unplugged from the memories made within those walls.

Then again, I wasn't certain I'd ever truly plugged myself in.

I headed inside and packed up my things.

Later that week, movers would come and get most of the boxes and place them into a storage unit until I found my next stop.

After I finished, I grabbed two suitcases and put them into my car.

As I locked the front door, I figured that would be the closest I'd get to having a real goodbye with Wesley. We didn't get the closure I thought I deserved after three years. On the day of the wedding, I was in shock, but ever since, I'd wondered how he'd been more than once.

I wondered if he was happy.

I wondered if he missed me.

I wondered if he'd wished we had better closure, a better goodbye.

Goodbyes felt harder when they were one-sided.

19

AVERY

T he problem with staying in Big Bird? It wasn't exactly weatherproof. A few hours into the night, the roof started to leak over me. I placed a few bowls down to catch the rain, but unfortunately, the speed of the rain was coming faster and faster. "Geez, Willow. How do you live like this?"

I shot her a text message, though she might've been flying high in the sky.

AVERY

Water is getting all over the place. Any tips?

A few minutes later, she replied from her layover.

WILLOW

Do a rain dance. It's romantic.

Never in my life did I realize that my sister and I were more different than at that very moment.

WILLOW

It's nature's kisses.

AVERY

Shut up, Willow.

She followed that up with a kissing emoji.

I put my phone away and went to work, trying to patch up the ceiling where the water dripped from. Then I went to the bathroom, and when I tried to flush it, water began to rise in the toilet instead of going down.

"No, no, no," I barked as it overflowed. I grabbed the towels from the tiny shower and tossed them onto the floor. Just then, my patch on the ceiling came off, and water started rushing in quickly. "*Nooo!*" I screamed out, trying to grab everything I could of my stuff and Willow's to avoid too much water damage.

I tossed all the important things into my car, then stuffed the hole in the roof with a sheet, which was getting drenched.

The floor was flooded with no signs of it getting better.

AVERY

Really bad flooding. Not sure what to do.

WILLOW

Maybe take Nathan Pierce up on his offer for the night. Don't worry about Big Bird. She'll dry out when I get back home.

The amount of chill my little sister had was enough to give me gray hair. No wonder Daddy was bald.

20

NATHAN

There was a pounding at my door a little after midnight, and I was surprised to find Avery standing there with a suitcase sitting beside her. Her eyes looked exhausted and defeated. I could feel the heaviness resting against her soul as she grimaced.

"I need you," she said with a weighted sigh. "Is the spare room at 505 West Chipper Lane still available for rent?" she asked shyly, brushing a hand over her soaking wet hair. She then sneezed and shook the rain off her body. "Because I could really use a place to crash for a little while."

I grabbed the handle of her suitcase and pulled it into my house. She followed me.

"Let me grab you a towel," I said quickly before darting down the hallway into the bathroom. I came back with two and wrapped one around her shoulders as she took the other and began drying her hair.

"Thanks."

"Of course. I already have a room set up for you." I grabbed her suitcase and pulled it down the hallway. I observed her taking notice of all the family photographs against my wall, but she stayed quiet as she trailed me.

Once we reached her room, I flipped on the light, and she tilted her head. "What's that on the bed?"

"Oh. It's a welcome basket. I had it made up when I thought you might stay with me. It has all kinds of stuff in it that you might need, including a few snacks. I tossed some towels into the attached bathroom for you, too."

She arched an eyebrow. "You had a welcome basket made for me? What if I didn't show up?"

"I thought of it as a 'just in case Avery comes over' basket. I would've moved it soon enough, but I guess it worked out."

She looked perplexed by the idea of it but didn't argue with me. That was somewhat surprising. Avery's favorite pastime was arguing with me.

"Thanks," she murmured. "That's actually really nice."

"Don't thank me too much. My mom did most of the work. Perks of living on a family farm with a welcome-basket-loving mother."

"Your mom knows you were offering me a spot to stay here?"

"She asked if you were okay after the wedding situation. I told her I offered you a spot if you needed it. She got to work on the basket right away. She also made me straighten up my place, too. I'm not this neat on my own," I joked.

"I know. I remember sneaking into your place when we were younger. Your room was worse than the pigpens."

"I'm glad to tell you I'm not that bad anymore. I'll let you settle in. The fridge in the kitchen is stocked, too—with non-expired food this go-round. Let me know if you need anything. We can check in with one another in the morning."

"This isn't going to be a long-term thing," she expressed. "Willow's bus had a leakage issue, and the apartment complex in town has no vacancies until the end of the school year, but I'm going to keep looking for something else."

"You can stay here as long as you need, Ave."

"I think the last thing you want is to live with a bitter, almost-married woman while you're single and, well, mingling." She grimaced and tugged gently on her earlobe. "If you're mingling, that is."

"Right." I smirked. "Of course."

"Are you?" she asked as she glanced down at the carpet. "Are you currently mingling with anyone?"

"Are you asking me if I'm single, Coach?"

"It's none of my business, but if you're having women come in and out of this place—"

"I'm not dating."

"Oh." She nodded once. "Well, are you, you know... Is there a rotating door or something going on around here?"

I narrowed my eyes. "A rotating door?"

"You know. With different women coming in and out at mysterious hours."

I laughed. "Are you asking if I run a brothel?"

"No," she shot out. Then she shrugged. "Maybe. I don't know. Listen, I get it. You're single and famous and handsome. You can get any woman you want. You might not be dating, but you might be banging, and I don't want to be in here cockblocking you."

I snickered and grinned. "Did you just call me handsome?"

She rolled her eyes dramatically as she groaned. "That's the one thing you picked up on?"

"It sounded like the only thing that mattered."

"It's like there's nothing in that peanut-sized brain of yours. Nothing but energy drinks, pre-workout, and vibes."

I leaned against the doorframe as I flexed one arm. "What can I say? I'm just a simple, handsome guy with a rotating door of women coming to have sex with me."

"*Ugh.* You know what? Never mind. Forget I asked. I was trying to be polite and allow space for you to get your whistle wet, but forget I even brought it up."

I whistled low. "Don't worry, Coach. My whistle hasn't been wet in a mighty long time. Unless we are counting my faithful bottle of lotion and my own spit."

"Nathaniel. Have you ever heard of oversharing?"

"You're the one who made it sound like I'm the town's slut."

"I didn't! I just assumed that you were getting..." Her words faded off as a sly bit of shyness hit her cheeks. "Never mind, okay?"

"You thought I was going to pound town regularly in the land of pussy, huh?"

"Don't say pussy."

"Okay, vaginas."

"Don't say that either."

"Okay, lip land. The folds? The inverted hillside?"

"Oh my gosh. I get it. I now see why you're not getting laid. You're annoying and corny."

I nodded in agreement. "What can I say? This handsome face can only get me so far."

"Yes, it's your words that dry up a woman like the Sahara Desert."

"You'd actually be impressed at my ability to take a woman who's been in a drought to the wetlands within minutes."

She blankly stared at me before shoving me out of the room. "I need sleep. Sleep, and to erase this conversation from my mind completely."

"If you get lonely, my room is down the hall on your right. You are free to crawl into bed with me for roommate cuddles at any point."

"Roommate cuddling isn't a thing, Nathaniel."

"Then what's the point of having a roommate?"

She placed her hands against the edge of her door and gave me a small smile.

She *smiled* at me.

Damn...

Avery and her rare smiles.

"Good night, idiot," she said.

There was a slight twitch in my crotch area. Maybe I did have a real shame kink when it came to Avery Kingsley. "Night. Oh wait, I have something for you." I headed to my room and grabbed an item off my nightstand, then hurried back out toward Avery. "I know you said burn the dress, but I saw this stitched to it, and I figured you might want it back."

Her eyes glassed over as she studied the ring in my hand with the blue jewel. "Mama's wedding ring," she murmured, taking it from me. "Oh my goodness. I can't believe I almost lost this. My father would've been heartbroken. Thank you, Nathan. I'll get it back to him."

"Of course."

She reached out and placed a hand on my arm. "No, really. Thank you. You have no clue what this means to me." The flash of emotion in her eyes told me just how much it meant.

I smiled. "Good night, Coach."

———

"Is it just me, or is that Avery Kingsley wandering around on the farm today?" River asked me a few days after Avery came to stay with me. I stood in the chicken coops with him, collecting eggs. The guys at the butcher shop always sold fresh eggs to customers, and River somehow pulled me into helping him collect them, seeing how Grant had come down with the mysterious flu that had been moving around the farmland. It had taken out a handful of employees, leaving us short-staffed. Luckily, somehow, River and I were still free from the illness.

Easton recovered after a week and a half, which was good, seeing how he spent the past week or so being a pathetic crybaby.

I looked over at the horse stables, where Avery stood with Mom. Within seconds, my mind was transported back to the days we used to hang out beside those same stables.

"I love you, too, Nathaniel," Avery whispered, brushing her lips against mine. *"I love you more than I love breathing."*

Those words had been etched in my brain ever since she'd said them.

I shook my head back to reality as Avery and Mom walked into the stables. Tearing my gaze away from the area, I returned to collecting eggs. "Yeah. She's staying with me for a while."

River narrowed his eyes. "Staying with you? You hate roommates."

"Since when have I ever said that?"

"Uh, when my house was being remodeled, and I crashed in your spare room. You said you hated it."

"You were messy," I countered. "Avery isn't messy."

"You're messy, too!" he argued.

"I know. You can't have two messy people living together. Might as well be living in the pigpens if that's the case. Besides, I cleaned up my spot. It's not messy anymore."

"You cleaned for Avery?" He blew out a cloud of hot smoke. "I didn't know you had the hots for Coach K, brother."

I shot him a look. "I don't have the hots for her."

"Uh, you definitely do if you picked up your dirty boxers. You never clean when I come to visit."

"That's because I don't care what you think of me."

River smiled. "But you care what Avery thinks, huh?"

I rolled my eyes. "Don't make this a thing. She needed a place to stay after her weekend from hell. I had a spare room. That's all there is to it."

River kept giving me that goofy-ass grin. "Yeah, okay. Whatever you say, brother. Whatever you say." He picked up three more eggs. "That blows that her wedding was called off, though. It's been the trending story all over town."

"Yeah. It sucks." Screw Wesley and his "best friend." I hope they rode off toward unhappily ever after together. If you asked me, Avery dodged a bullet.

"Well, at least you can continue sleeping with her and not feel guilty about it," River commented.

"We aren't sleeping with each other!" I spat out. "What the hell are you talking about?"

He shrugged. "Just wanted to see your reaction." He narrowed his eyes. "But you do want to sleep with her, right?"

"I'm not answering your stupid questions."

"Because the answer is yes?"

"No. Because the question is stupid."

"Stupid questions can still be answered, and your avoidance of answering shows that the answer is yes. I wouldn't blame you, Nate. Avery is beautiful. Come to think of it... If you aren't sleeping with her and she's now on the free market—"

"*Don't you fucking dare go near her,*" I growled, shooting him a look packed with daggers.

He laughed and pointed at me. "There it is. The answer you didn't want to give. Don't worry, brother. I get it. Avery Kingsley is off-limits. I'll make sure the other guys know, too. She's all yours."

I grumbled and rolled my eyes. What a dumbass. "Finish up in here, will you? I'm gonna go check on accounting for a few hours," I said, shoving my basket into River's grip.

He still had that stupid smirk on his face as he nodded. "For a long time, I thought you were a loner like Evan. I didn't worry about Evan like I did you, though, seeing how he has Priya, but you don't have anyone. So I think this is good for you, Nathan."

"What's good for me?"

"You having a crush."

I didn't say anything back to him because he was right, and that sort of pissed me off a good amount. I *did* have a crush on Avery. How could I not? She was everything I loved about her when we were kids, but only now she have more fire. More passion. More bite.

There was no getting around the fact that my heart felt indescribable happiness whenever she came near me. But the messed-up thing about said crush was the fact that nothing would ever come from it. There was no way in hell she would ever crush on me back.

And that realization?

Crushing.

21

AVERY

For the next few days, I woke up in Nathan Pierce's home, dazed and confused at how my life turned out the way it'd been. Luckily, Nathan wasn't turning out to be the worst roommate in the world, and being on Honey Farms was a unique situation.

As a kid, I sneak over to the farm to visit Nathan. I was pretty sure I fell in love with him right outside the horse stables when he told me he wanted to marry me someday.

It was the same day he fake proposed to me with a RingPop candy, and we licked the thing as we lay in a pile of hay, staring up at the star-drunk sky and making up silly stories about the lives we'd live with one another.

Honey Farms was on over three hundred acres of land. They had a massive number of livestock, apple and pear orchards, a big barn house for celebrations, over fifty employees, and seven homes on the property. Nathan's mom, Laurelin, told me once that her only goal for the land was to make it a community for her loved ones to live on. So they'd all have a place to call home.

Each Pierce brother built his own house on the land. You

could tell a lot about the brothers' personalities based on the type of home they'd built. Easton's was a huge mansion-style home with a wraparound porch and a gigantic swimming pool. It looked like a remake of the home Noah built for Allie in *The Notebook*. Perfectly suitable for a lover boy like Easton. Evan had a rustic log cabin, big enough for him and his daughter, Priya. River and Grant had two houses, side by side, that had a Mediterranean feel to them. The homes were just like the twins —identical.

Even though the brothers all lived on the property, you couldn't even see their houses from the outskirts based on how they were situated. The family used golf carts to get to each other's homestead. Laurelin's farmhouse was at the center of the whole land. Nathan called it the heartbeat of their little community. That was where everyone went when their hearts needed a recharge of love.

My favorite aspect of the land, though?

The baseball diamond that had the best sunsets.

"Welcome back to Honey Farms, Ms. Avery," Laurelin said as she met me at Nathan's place a few days after I settled in. Nathan left me a note that morning stating that he was getting up early to get to work, but I was free to explore the farm if I so pleased and that his mom would probably stop by to see me since word got around that I was on the farm.

The air was humid from the rainstorms that passed through, and Laurelin showed up at Nathan's with a pair of rain boots for me to slip into. I couldn't help but smile when I saw her. I was always happy to see Laurelin.

Laurelin Pierce was one of the sweetest humans on the planet, and when I was younger, working at the farm, I always remembered her warmth more than anything else. I had a distinct memory of her as a little girl, too. It was right after Mama passed away. Laurelin showed up to our house with a care basket and a few cooked meals for Daddy. She stayed for a few hours, helping out with Willow. She cleaned up the house, too, and trimmed the flowers that people in town sent to our house. Then she came into my room and sat with me for a while.

She didn't say anything, and she didn't make me talk at all. She simply sat there and smiled at me. She did the same for Yara, too. I didn't know how much comfort it could bring to a person just to have someone else sit beside them.

Before she left my room, she walked over to me, knelt, combed my hair behind my ears, and said, "How lucky are you to have your mama's eyes? It's a little gift from God. You get to see your mama each and every time you look in the mirror."

Then she hugged me, kissed the top of my head, and said, "Sweet, sweet girl."

After that, I went to the bathroom, combed my hair behind my ears, just as Laurelin had, looked into the mirror, and said, "Hi, Mama. I love you."

I pretended that Mama whispered the words back, too.

That was my last interaction with Laurelin before I started working at the farm as a teenager. She was just as wonderful and kind as I remembered, too.

"It's good to be back," I told her.

"You want to take a ride with me on the golf cart over to the horse stables?" she asked. "If I recall, you loved those horses when you used to work here. I can introduce you to the newbie, too. I can also show you the new additions to the property."

"I'd love that."

I slipped into the boots she gave me, and we headed over to the stables. As we drove, I glanced over to see River and Nathan working at the chicken coops. A tiny smile slipped to my lips as my eyes stayed glued to Nathan. Something about seeing him working on the farm sent my mind back in time.

"Don't break an egg, or you'll have ten years of bad luck," Nathan told me as he juggled three eggs.

"Rumor has it that it goes the same for breaking pretty girls' hearts," I joked.

He caught all the eggs in his hands and stilled himself before he walked over to me. He placed a finger beneath my chin and tilted my head up to meet his stare. His face moved closer to mine, and he brushed his lips against my lips as he whispered, "And what kind of madman would ever break such a pretty girl's heart?"

If only he knew he would turn out to be the madman in question.

"A lot has changed since you've last been here," Laurelin said, breaking me from my memories. I was thankful for the snap back to reality. "We actually have an automatic egg collector machine that does a lot of heavy lifting for our poultry operations. It's being repaired this week, which is why the guys are collecting by hand today. We're at over five hundred chickens on our property, which is remarkable, seeing as we aren't strictly a poultry farm."

"Wow, that's amazing."

"Or batshit, depending on who you ask," she joked. "But I heard about a nearby farm that was abusing their chickens. It made me so mad, and I paid them a big chunk of money just to rescue those hens. The boys say I love these animals more than them, but that's just because the animals don't talk back."

I laughed. "That's a good enough reason to me. It's amazing what you've done here, Laurelin. You should be really proud."

That pride shone through her smile. "I am. What is even more amazing is that everything is free-range. Even with all the tech equipment we added, I still wanted to make sure we were putting out the best products for our customers and making the best life for the animals." We pulled up to the horse stables, and once the cart stopped, we hopped out.

"We have six horses in total now. The boys' horses and my granddaughter, Priya, just got her first one two years ago. Hugo."

"Hugo," I breathed out, loving the name. As we walked into the stables, my heart almost exploded with more love as I saw the beauty that was Hugo. The white coat of the horse was striking. Its mane and tail held the same bright, snowy hue. Sweet Hugo had beautiful hazel eyes, too.

"If you look up the name Hugo, you get a lot of different meanings, but I think this sweet baby lives up to them all. Heart, spirit, mind, and intelligence. I'd never had such a horse that was so loving and smart. Not since my Gracie."

My heart dropped a little. "Did Gracie pass away?" I asked about Laurelin's personal horse.

She nodded. "Yes. A few years back. I haven't had the heart to put a new one in her stable yet," she said as she gestured down the way to the empty stable where Gracie used to roam. "It's too hard to think about."

"I'm so sorry, Laurelin. I know how much she meant to you."

"That's the thing about life—we aren't promised forever. Even if we hope for it." She smiled as she opened Hugo's gate. We walked inside, and she picked up a brush and began to brush Hugo. "But thankfully, having this sweetheart here has kept me busy. After losing Gracie, I didn't know if I could have more room in my heart to love another horse. Hugo proved me wrong. I guess there is always room in us for a little more love, no matter how much loss we've experienced."

I smiled at her words, hoping they were true.

"Hugo won't be ready for riding for a while; we are thinking one or two more years so her muscles are stronger. But, if I recall, you had a nice connection with Nathan's horse, Lightning. You should go say hi. I think he still needs a good brushing," Laurelin said. "I can meet you over there in a minute."

I headed out of Hugo's space and walked over to Lightning, who was still as beautiful as ever. There was such an air of majesty and strength when it came to Lightning. His uniformed black coat was a deep charcoal-black with a glossy finish. His eyes were a deep brown that held such a calmness to them.

There was a time in my life when I thought I'd visit Lightning every week for the remainder of my life. Now years have passed, and my heart ached from knowing I'd missed so much time.

"Hey, sweet friend," I said as I opened his gate. "Remember me?" I walked over and picked up his brush. He pressed his face to my hand. I smiled as I began to pat him. "I know. I missed you, too."

As I began to brush him, a wave of peace washed over me. Something about Lightning made me feel so safe and serene. He was a massive horse, yet nothing was terrifying about that beautiful animal. He felt like coming home, and the way he showed me so much love with his nuzzling of my hand almost made my eyes tear up.

I brushed him for a few minutes before Laurelin walked over. She had that same grin on her face as she crossed her arms. "He still doesn't let anyone ride him except for Nathan. To this day, you and Nate are the only two who Lightning would let saddle up."

"I doubt he'd let me now. It's been years."

"The time doesn't matter," she said. "It's clear he's happy to see you. Maybe you could try to ride him when it's not so yucky outside. I think he'd like that."

"I'd like that, too," I said as I placed down his brush.

Laurelin leaned against the gate and nodded toward me. "I'm not sure how to bring this up without just bringing it up, but acting like I don't know when I do feels wrong." She took a deep breath. "I'm sorry to hear about what happened last weekend with the wedding."

My heart skipped a few beats. "Thank you."

"Is it silly to ask if you're doing okay?"

"It's not silly. I'm not really sure how I'm even doing. The weekend was hard, but your son helped me out a lot. I'm taking it day by day."

"That's all we can do, sweetheart. Take it day by day. I'm glad Nathan was there for you."

Me too.

I shifted slightly as I crossed my arms. "I will not be in y'all's hair too much on the farm, I swear. I'm getting my footing. As soon as a place opens at the apartment complex in town, I'll sign a lease and stay there."

"Avery, don't be silly. You're welcome to stay here as long as you need. *Mi casa es su casa*," she sang, winking my way. "Besides, as a mama bear, it makes me happy to know Nathan isn't living alone. The twins all have each other, and they lean into that. I worry about my eldest boy sometimes. I worry that he might be a bit of a workaholic in order to avoid the real issue that's eating at him."

"What issue is that?"

"That he's lonely." Her eyes flashed with a moment of sadness. "Nothing breaks a mama's heart more than knowing that one of their kids struggles with loneliness, but I know Nathan isn't doing much to put himself out there. That was why I pushed him to check out getting a coaching position at the high school."

"That was your idea?"

"Sure was." She placed a hand against my arm. "I hope I didn't cause any trouble. I just know you two used to be so close when you worked on the farm all those years ago. I thought it might be nice if you two could reconnect."

"Oh no. It's fine." She didn't know about Nathan and me and the way we fell for one another. From her point of view, we were two kids who would sometimes laugh together. Nothing more, nothing less.

"Oh good. I think it's good for him to be back on the field. I figured if he could get a grip on something he loved doing, he would start to wake up from this deep slumber he's been walking around in."

"You think he's in a slumber?"

"I know he is. He doesn't talk about being sad much. He's too manly to do such a thing. But I see it in his eyes. It's like he's moving through life but not living it. The other boys say I'm just overthinking it and being too motherly, but I don't know. My heart," she said, patting her hand over her chest. "My heart feels his sadness."

I didn't say anything because what could be said? Was Nathan really sad? I didn't notice that, but maybe that was because he was so good at putting on a brave face. Did he feel things deeply, like me, during his lonely moments? Did he ever struggle to get out of bed, too? Did he fill his days with helping others to avoid helping himself?

There was an odd tug at my heart as I listened to Laurelin talk about Nathan. Instant guilt hit me, too, because I didn't make the transition of his coming to join the team as a coach easy for him. If anything, I'd been a pain toward him, questioning every decision he made. In reality, he was using the baseball diamond and the coaching position the same way I'd been. He'd been using that place and its facilities to help him breathe.

I was such an asshat, and it was clear that Nathan deserved my apology, yet I wasn't exactly sure how to give it to him. I couldn't tell him what his mom revealed to me. That felt like a conversation meant to be kept between Laurelin and me. Still, I knew I'd been too harsh toward him. Especially after all he'd done for me over the past weekend.

"He's doing better, though," Laurelin mentioned as she gently petted Lightning. "I've been to your home games lately, and he looks like himself out there. He's not so uptight and business-forward. It's nice to see him let his hair down and have fun again. So I guess I owe you a thank-you for making space for him on your staff."

I pushed out a grin that was soaked in guilt. "Not a problem at all. We're lucky to have him."

That was a fact, too. Undoubtedly, the team was performing exceptionally well since Nathan joined the crew. He had a level of heart and intelligence that I didn't possess, and seeing the guys excel from his coaching made it more difficult for me to complain about...anything.

Later that night, Nathan came back to the house. He walked around a bit, clearing his throat as if he had a frog trapped in there.

I arched an eyebrow toward him as I sat on his living room couch. "Are you getting sick?"

"No. I don't get sick. I'm not a wimp like my brothers." He walked over and sat on the other side of the couch from me. He glanced at the television. "Are you watching some crappy reality show?"

"There's nothing crappy about *The Traitors*. It's fantastic."

"All reality shows are crap," he replied before once again clearing his throat. "I'm going to hop in the shower and head to bed."

I arched an eyebrow. "It's only seven."

"I'm exhausted."

"Maybe because your body is shutting down because you're sick."

"I'm not sick," he expressed as he pushed himself to a standing position. "Like I said, I don't get sick."

22

NATHAN

I got sick.

One would've thought I was Easton when I woke up sick to my stomach in the middle of the night. The flu from hell had finally hit me, and I spent a good portion of my night throwing up my insides as I hugged the toilet seat. My whole body shook with chills as sweat dripped all over me. After only a few hours of sleep that morning, I woke up and found my way back to the bathroom to finish throwing up even more. The bathroom floor was ice cold, a stark contrast to the ravishing fever burning its way through my whole body.

Maybe Easton wasn't being too dramatic. Whatever this bug had been, it was trying to take us out.

As I was expelling every single drop of dignity from my body, there was a knock on my bathroom door.

"Nathan? Are you all right?" Avery asked from outside the door.

I cleared my throat and grabbed the rag from the sink as I sat on the floor. I wiped it over my mouth. "Yeah, I'm fin—"

Before I could finish, I started violently throwing up again.

The door to my bathroom slowly opened, and Avery's soft

footsteps echoed against the tile. I glanced up for a moment to see her standing there, fully dressed and ready to head over to the high school for her job. And there I sat. Like a pathetic toad on the bathroom floor.

A flood of embarrassment enveloped me as I stayed plastered to the toilet seat. I knew I wanted Avery to take notice of me more, but not like that. Not as my insides tried their damnedest to exit stage right. This was not how I wanted her to see me—broken down and vulnerable.

"Hey," she whispered.

I tried my best to muster the energy to respond, but words seemed too much of a struggle to release. My mind spun as my fever grew, moistness soaking every inch of me. The only thing that I could release from my lips was a grunt.

Avery bent down beside me and placed the back of her hand to my forehead. "You're burning up," she said before grabbing another towel from my closet. She ran it under cold water for a moment before she wrung it out and placed it against my forehead. I leaned back against the sink cabinet, exhausted. My knees bent, and I rested my arms against my kneecaps as I closed my eyes.

The coolness of the cloth made it a little easier to breathe. Avery patted it gently all over my face and neck. She smoothed it slightly over my exposed chest. My breaths were uneven as I kept my eyes closed. Every time I tried to open them, the room began to spin all around me, so shut eyes were better.

"I'm okay," I muttered, hating that she saw me in the shape I'd been in.

"No. You're not," she replied as she gently placed her hand against my forehead again. The tenderness of her touch was a bit of a surprise to me. For the past few weeks, Avery had been very standoffish toward me. At that moment, it was as if her walls were coming down.

I leaned into her touch as her warmth seeped into me. "You

should not be this close to me. I don't want you to get sick. Plus, you should get to work and—"

"Nathan." She locked her eyes with mine, and her lips turned up slightly. "Let me take care of you."

I didn't know how much I wanted and needed to hear those words that morning. I wasn't used to people taking care of me. I was normally the one dishing out the care. A part of me wanted to argue with her offer, but a bigger part of me wanted to curl into a ball and have her hold me and tell me I would be all right.

Easton might've been onto something.

"Let's get you back to your bed," she said. She wrapped an arm around my body and lifted me as if I were as light as a feather. Clearly, Avery had taken advantage of the weight lifting facility at the high school.

She led me to my bed and pulled back my comforter. I sat on the edge of the bed, still shivering from chills, as she lifted my legs up into the bed. She covered me up, tucking me in, and then told me she'd be right back.

When she returned, she had a tray filled with goodies. Electrolytes, crackers, and an array of medicine. She set the tray on my nightstand and began collecting pills for me to take. "Now, I know you're probably not hungry at all, but you need to eat a few crackers in order to take the medicine," she ordered.

I grumbled and slightly pushed her approaching hand away.

She arched an eyebrow. "Nathaniel Grayson Pierce, open your mouth right now."

I shook my head.

She arched her other brow. "Now," she ordered.

I parted my lips slightly.

She shook her head. "No. More. Like this." She unlocked her jaw and opened wide. "Aah!"

If I were feeling more alive, I would've probably made an

inappropriate joke about stuffing her mouth with something tasty. Instead, I groaned like a sad puppy as I opened my jaw.

She placed the pills in my mouth and then fed me a sip of water. "Good job," she whispered, wiping her finger right below my lip where a drip of water was falling. "Now, eat one cracker."

"I can't, Coach," I muttered, shutting my eyes once more.

"Now," she ordered once more.

Something about her orders made me obey right away. I didn't know if it was her tone or the act of control that she had over me, but I opened my mouth once more and allowed her to feed me a few crackers.

"Good boy. I'm proud of you," she said as she gently rubbed her hand over my head. It turned out I didn't only have a shame kink but a praise one, too. "Now, rest," she told me. "I'll be back in a few to check on you."

"Don't you have to get to work?" I asked.

"I called in earlier when I heard you were sick. I notified the guys we wouldn't have practice tonight, either."

"What? No. They need—"

"Nathan. Everything's under control. You just rest."

I wanted to argue, but the heaviness of my eyelids told me not to do so. I shut my eyes and fell asleep, feeling a bit of comfort knowing that Avery was there to take care of me.

I SLEPT for over nine hours, only waking when Avery would come to give me vitamins and medicine, along with a few bites of bread. When I was fully awake, she came back and smiled my way. She held sheets in her hands.

"I think it's about time I switched out your sheets, seeing how you probably soaked your way through them," she said. "If you can sit in your chair in the corner, that is."

With a few grumbles, I pulled myself up from the bed and

moved over to the chair. I plopped down and sighed, feeling beyond exhausted from the few steps that I'd taken.

Avery went to work to change out all my sheets. She removed the dirty ones, along with my comforter, and replaced them with new ones. She even changed out the pillowcases. I didn't even know that I had extra pillowcases.

"Okay. You can come back. Unless you feel as if you can shower," she said.

I shook my head. There was no way I could stand up in a shower.

She walked over to me and offered her hand to help me. I took it for two reasons. One—I needed her help. Two—I always wanted to hold her hand.

"Thanks," I muttered as she led me back to the bed, only to tuck me in again.

She left the room for a second, getting rid of the sheets, and when she came back, she had a big bowl of soup in her hands.

I sat up on my bed with my back against the headboard. I could only breathe through my mouth, seeing how my nose was stuffed up. I closed my eyes as my breaths weaved in and out of my mouth.

"Why are you being so helpful?" I muttered, feeling the need to fall back to sleep.

"Because you deserve it. Open," she ordered.

I parted my lips more, she put a spoonful of soup into my mouth, and I swallowed it. The warmth felt good as it glided down my throat.

"I owe you an apology, Nathan."

That was enough to make me open my eyes again. "What do you mean?"

"Ever since you've come to coach, I've been a bit of a jerk to you. I'm sorry for that. You've been an amazing addition to the team, and I'm lucky to have you as a coach."

"I must look pretty bad, huh?" I let out a slight chuckle. "If I'm on my deathbed, just tell me now, Avery."

A gentle snicker fell from her lips, and even though I felt like shit, I loved the sound of that. Avery did not laugh a lot, so whenever one fell from her, I always tried to hold on to the sound as long as possible.

"You're not on your deathbed," she swore. "I just realized how much of a dick I've been toward you, and I'm sorry. You didn't deserve it." She fed me more soup.

"I'm sure parts of me deserved it."

"No," she disagreed. "None of you did. We aren't who we were when we were younger, and it was unfair of me to treat you as if you were the same boy who left all those years before."

"Just so you know, Avery, I hated that I left."

In her subtle reaction, I felt the weight of her pain. Or maybe it was my pain I was feeling. Maybe our hurts from the past we shared mirrored one another and sat packed with a quiet torment that we both carried. It just seemed that she hid hers better than I had.

She looked away for a moment and said so softly, "I hated it, too." Her voice was so low that I wasn't certain she'd actually said the words or if my fever-stricken mind imagined it.

"We don't have to talk about us," she said as she turned back to feed me more soup. The heaviness still stayed laced in her words. "You just need to get better."

I wanted to keep the conversation going, but the exhaustion set in again as I struggled with my heavy breaths. She smiled gently as she placed the bowl of soup down on the nightstand before she made me take a few more sips of water. When she finished, she stood to leave.

"Avery?"

"Yeah?"

"Thank you."

She smiled again, and within seconds, my eyes faded shut, and I went back to sleep.

IT TOOK me a week to recover, but Avery took care of me every step of the way. I did not know if she knew it, but she was making it next to impossible for me not to find myself falling for her with every second that passed by.

After my first day back coaching the third week of April, I approached Avery under the fading sunlight. She was busy organizing the equipment on the field, completely wrapped up in her task.

I leaned against the fence in front of her, taking her in for a moment. "Hey," I said, breaking the silence.

"Yeah?"

"I've been meaning to ask... How did you manage not to get sick after taking care of me for a week straight? What kind of superhero immune system do you have?" She went to grab the bag of baseballs, but I hurried over and lifted it for her, tossing it over my shoulder.

A mischievous smirk lit her face up. "Well, I figured one of us needed to suck it up. We couldn't both be little punks," she said, her voice dripping with a teasing tone. "Unlike some people, I can't afford to be a baby about it. I had a team to coach and couldn't afford to be sick."

I couldn't help but laugh. "A little punk, huh? Is that how you see me?"

"You cried for five days straight, tossing and turning, telling me to take you out."

I feigned a wounded expression, rubbing at my chest as if her words physically hit me. "For the record, I don't think I had a normal flu. I think I had a newfound plague of some sort."

"Sure, sure," she cooed, stepping a tad closer. As the distance between us shrank, my heart beat a little faster. "But you're lucky you had a solid nurse like me to look after you. You might've actually died if it wasn't for me."

"You don't have to prove that point to me, Coach. I already know I would've been fucked without you."

"Well, as long as you're aware of how good you had it."

"I am, which is why I want to make you dinner tonight as a thank-you for taking care of my punk ass."

The warmth that bloomed across her lips made me echo her smile. "You cook?"

"For you, yes."

She narrowed her eyes. "What are you going to make?"

"Baked ziti and garlic bread."

"Mmm," she moaned. The sound was enough to make me want to start humping her leg like the needy dog I'd turned into whenever she was near. She could've put a collar on me, and I would've allowed her to dog-walk me all around town with a smile on my face. "That sounds like a perfect Thursday night dinner. But"—she pointed a stern finger at me—"if I hear one sneeze from you, I'm calling you a punk for the rest of your life."

I laughed. "Deal."

"And don't read too much into this, Nathan. I still don't like you," she expressed as she started to walk off with that playful grin still on her face. "So don't you think for a second we're becoming friends."

I shook my head in complete awe of her stubbornness and inability to express that she and I were slowly but surely getting on better terms with one another. "Whatever you say, Avery. Whatever you say."

I liked her stubbornness.

I *craved* her stubbornness. Avery's attitude was one of the things I found most attractive. I didn't know if that meant I was mentally unwell, but that was where my state of affairs had been. The flu couldn't take me out, but my damn crush on Avery Kingsley might've been the thing to do me in.

23

AVERY

One Sunday morning, I suddenly awakened from my slumber due to the sound of a rooster crowing. I groaned as I pushed myself up to a sitting position and rubbed the exhaustion from my eyes. The sun was hardly up as I yawned and stretched my arms.

To my surprise, it wasn't a rooster shouting good morning to me. It was Nathan standing in my doorframe with a big goofy grin on his face, making the loudest rooster sounds I'd ever heard in my life.

"What in the living heck are you doing?" I grumbled.

He had a stack of clothes in his hand as he walked over to me. "Morning, sunshine. It's the third Sunday of the month."

I blankly stared at him, probably with morning gunk in the corners of my eyes, still. "What's your point?"

"It's Sunday Funday on the Farm!" he exclaimed, placing the clothes in my hand. "I guessed on your sizes. I let you sleep in a little longer, but everyone else is already out there warming up on the field. I wanted you to be on my team, Team Blue, but everyone said it would be an unfair advantage to have you play on the same team as me. So you're on the yellow team."

"Nathan, what the heck are you talking about?"

"Every third Sunday morning, starting in the spring, my family gets up and plays a baseball game at the crack of dawn. The losers have to go through the garden and prepare brunch for the winning team. It's a tradition. Sunday Funday."

"Oh my goodness," I groaned, covering my face with a pillow. "Don't tell me you're one of those families who runs marathons on Thanksgiving morning."

"Actually, we do." He pulled the pillow from my face and smiled. "Since you're here, you gotta play. Get changed. There are thirty people out there waiting."

"Thirty people?!" I gasped. My eyes bulged out of my head. "What do you mean, thirty people?"

"My cousins, aunts, and uncles come over for it, too. A lot just stay in the bleachers and watch, but they have to pick a team, too. Then they have to help out with the meal if their team loses."

"I hate everything about this," I muttered as I dragged myself out of bed.

His smile stayed in place as he patted me on the back. "You'll learn to love it."

———

I HATED that he was right, too, because the minute I got on the field, I was reminded of one of my favorite things about the Pierces—they took family to a new level.

Sure, I was close with my sisters and my father, but we weren't really that close with our extended family. We saw them around the holidays, but that was about it. Nathan's family—more than thirty of them—got together once a month to play baseball.

And they loved it!

The mood of the whole morning was light and fluffy. Young

kids were running around, taking bets on who they thought would win. My team—the yellow team—was led by Easton and River. That was until they handed the coaching position over to me. They were awful coaches, but at least they knew how to hit home runs. Each time we scored, I loved seeing the irritation sitting on Nathan's face.

The more the sun rose, the more excitement I began to feel. When it came down to the fifth inning—the final inning, because there was no way we would play a full nine innings— everyone was standing in the bleachers, cheering on team yellow.

The score was blue team five and yellow team four. Everyone was hungry for the win. We already had two outs. I was sitting on second base, and Easton was up to bat. He had two strikes, but I knew he could do it.

Nathan was pitching, and he had the smuggest look on his face, feeling as if he was about to take his brother out. I saw the sweat brewing on Easton's forehead. The opposing team's chants and mocking were getting to him.

"Come on, Easton, you got this," I cheered on. I tapped my hand against my chest and over my heart. "Think here, not here," I said, tapping my head next.

Think with your heart, not your mind.

A motto I'd learned from my father when he first taught me how to hold my first baseball. Heart over head. Daddy always said the game was over before it started if a person took their head into it more than their heart. It was something that stuck with me for a long time.

Easton nodded, gripped his baseball bat in his hand, and got into the right position. He had his game face on, with black pats smeared beneath his eyes. He was locked in.

Unfortunately, so was Nathan.

As Nathan threw the ball toward Easton, I held my breath

the whole time, ready to sprint faster than ever before if need be.

It all happened so quickly. The ball released from Nathan's hand, a perfect pitch, which wasn't shocking. Nathan might've played left field in the Major Leagues, but his pitching skills were always remarkable to me.

And Easton swung.

He swung like never before, making hard contact with the ball. It went soaring, too, farther than ever, making it nearly impossible for the other team to get.

I took off running as if my heart would explode from my chest. Right behind me was Easton, who was probably one of the fastest people I'd ever seen in my life. His track days came in handy that morning. The crowd erupted in shouts and cheers as I slid into home plate. Easton slid over the plate right after me, scoring us two points, making us the winners of the game.

I burst out in celebration with my teammates, wrapping Easton in the biggest hug. Before I knew it, he and River were tossing me up in the air to celebrate the win, calling me the MVP of the game. I couldn't stop laughing as I begged them to let me down.

That was what it was all about. The teamwork, the excitement, the game.

Gosh, that felt good.

It felt like a high I hadn't felt in so long. It was one thing to coach the sport, yet it was another to lace up your shoes and get out on the diamond. I missed it so much more than I realized.

They returned me to the ground, and Easton patted his chest. "Here, Avery." He tapped his head. "Not here."

I smirked. "Damn straight, buddy." I hugged him again, and he ruffled my hair with his hand in a victory cry.

"All right, Team Blue, you know the deal. Get to work," Laurelin said, clapping her hands together from the stands.

"Everyone else can head over to the barn house. I have a few snacks I tossed in there before brunch is ready."

My cheeks hurt from smiling so hard as Nathan walked over to me. He held a hand out my way. "Good game, Coach."

I shook his hand. "Great game. Too bad we smoked you."

His dimples deepened as he shook his head. "You always were a sore winner."

"What can I say? I get cocky with this game."

"Cockiness looks good on you. You can beat me every week at this game if it keeps making you smile like that."

An odd swirl of butterflies fell into my stomach from that comment.

I dropped my hold on his hand and rubbed my hands over my ponytail, trying to shake off the flurry of electricity that just raced through my system. I shoved him lightly, trying not to show him that he had some odd effect on me simply from his touch and his words. "I like my eggs scrambled, Nathaniel."

He smirked bigger. "It would be an honor to scramble your eggs, Avery." He slightly bowed and winked before he headed off to get the meal going.

Oh crap.

I think I just orgasmed on the field.

Screw Nathan Pierce and those damn winks of his.

I didn't think they still had that much power over me, yet there I was, feeling slightly weak in the knees.

"Can I sit with you?" Laurelin asked as I sat at one of the long tables in the barn, waiting to be served by the other team.

"Of course, please."

She sat across from me and quickly made herself comfortable. She grabbed a slice of the sourdough bread in front of us and started spreading butter onto it. "What a fun game it was today, huh?"

"Gosh, yeah. I forgot how much fun it was to play an actual game as opposed to just coaching it."

"I get the feeling Nathan felt the same way out there," she said, gesturing to her smiling son, who was bringing in a tray of hash browns to put on the bar with the food warmers. "You know he's been back in town for over a year, but this is the first time he actually took part in the Sunday Funday baseball game."

My eyebrows arched in disbelief. "What? He never played before?"

"Nope. He always said he was too busy doing stuff around the property. That was until today."

"He made it seem like he looked forward to these games when he told me. I wonder why that is or what changed."

Laurelin smiled. "Yeah, I wonder." Her eyes moved back to her son, and her smile slowly faded. "I do worry about him, though."

"Why's that?"

"Because he's like you. Resiliently strong. That worries me as a mother. I don't want him to feel as if he needs to always be strong. I don't want him to feel as if he needs to be so serious and driven every second of every day."

"My father says the same thing about me."

"The curse of being the eldest child," she semi-joked. "I was the middle child in my family. I never realized how much my sister Stacey dealt with until I grew up. She took on a lot more responsibility than she should've had to. Nathan did the same thing, especially after his father passed away. After that happened, I know Nathan felt a responsibility to the family. He struggled a lot to have a life outside of looking after us and the game. When he lost the game with his injury, after losing his good friend, too, he focused so much on the farm life. Nathan puts so much weight on his shoulders to help everyone out. I don't know the last time I've seen him have as much fun as he did today. It's good to see him like this," Laurelin explained.

"Like what?"

"Happy and free." She smiled at me. "Why do I feel as if you might have had something to do with that, Ms. Kingsley?"

I shook my head. "No. I honestly think it's just that he got back into coaching. I think helping the team is helping him. I felt it on the field today, too. I had nothing to do with his happiness. He just rediscovered something he loved again."

"Yes," she agreed in an all-knowing way. "He did." She smiled a smile that matched her son's and patted my hand. "Well, I should get to helping around here. But if there is anything you need, don't hesitate to ask."

"Thank you, Laurelin."

"Thank *you*, Avery," she said before she walked away. I didn't know exactly what she was thanking me for, but the words stayed dancing in my head for a while.

Not long after, Laurelin was standing in front of everyone, and she said a prayer over the brunch. When that was all done, the losing team began to go around and collect the winners' orders. When Nathan came over with my full plate of food, my stomach instantly growled.

"Here you go, your royalty," he sarcastically remarked as he set the plate in front of me.

"Thank you, my servant." I gestured toward the beverage table. "If only I had a nice, refreshing mimosa to drink with this meal. Fetch me one, will you?"

He snickered, shaking his head. "You're going to milk this, aren't you?"

I started to gesture me milking invisible udders. "One hundred percent." I patted my throat. "Make it two mimosas. I'm parched."

With a slight bow, Nathan hurried off to grab my drinks,

and when he came back, he took a seat across from me. He set down the mimosas in Mason jars and smirked my way as I was stuffing my mouth with a sausage link. I paused my bite as I stared at him, confused as to why he was smiling so dang hard.

I arched an eyebrow. "What?"

"Nothing, it's just..."

"It's just what?"

He leaned closer, a mischievous sparkle in his eyes. "You like that, huh?"

I glanced at the piece of sausage on my fork. "Clearly, seeing as I'm eating it." I took another bite.

His chest swelled with pride as his face glowed with a triumphant gleam. "I knew you'd like my sausage."

I almost choked on the piece of meat in my mouth as those words escaped his mouth. I started coughing, trying my best to clear my throat and swallow the meat all at once.

Nathan picked up my mimosa and held it out to me. "Don't worry. It's not uncommon for me to cause women to choke from time to time."

What a freaking idiot.

An idiot that somehow made me laugh. "Why are you such a moron?"

"I was born this way." He shrugged, then leaned in closer. "So tell me... How well did I scramble your eggs?"

"Are you just going to sit here and watch me eat while asking inappropriate questions?"

"Yes, actually, that was the plan."

"Don't you want food of your own?"

"I ate in the kitchen."

"What about drinks?"

He lifted one of my mimosas and took a sip. "Thanks, Coach. I was *parched*," he said, mocking me.

I rolled my eyes and took a sip of my own drink. "So what's

the deal with you? This morning, you woke me up like this baseball game thing was a huge deal."

"It is a big deal."

"Rumor has it that you haven't played a game since you moved back into town."

"It's a big deal for everyone else."

I narrowed my eyes. "Then why did you make it seem like it was such a big deal this morning and as if you wanted to play?"

"Because I did want to play." He set his Mason jar down and wrapped both his hands around it. "I just wanted to play with you."

"Don't do that, Nathan."

"Do what?"

Make my heart skip a million beats.

I shook my head. "Nothing. Never mind."

His lips curved up at the corners. "I know I can be a dumbass sometimes, but I'm serious, Avery. Lately, watching you with the guys at practices, you helped me to remember why I love this sport. Today was good for me."

"Today was good for me, too."

I looked down at my plate for a moment because sometimes it felt hard to stare into Nathan's eyes. It felt like staring into my future and past all at once.

"Your mom worries about you," I mentioned, needing to shift the conversation slightly so I wouldn't continue to be sitting in a pool of flurries. "Did you know that?"

Now it was Nathan's turn to uncomfortably shift. "I think that's what parents do best. Worry."

"Should she be worried, though?"

With a quizzical lift of his brow, he slanted his head slightly. His piercing look caused a tightness in my chest that was hard to breathe around.

"Now it's your turn not to do that," he whispered, his voice a blend of warning and pleading.

"Do what?"

"Make me tell you the truth," he said, his stare unwavering. The air between us felt heavy with the weight of his impending confession. My mind spun with what his truth may have been.

Before I could reply, Easton walked over and slammed his hands onto Nathan's shoulders, breaking the tension between us. "Sarah's here," Easton stated.

Nathan turned to face his brother. "No shit. Sarah's here?"

"Yup. She walked in like she still had a right to walk on in," he explained, sitting beside his brother. Easton looked at me and grinned. "Sorry to interrupt, Avery. It's just that Sarah's here."

"Oh, no. I understand," I said. I blinked a few times. "Who's Sarah?"

"The woman who broke River's heart," Nathan explained. "She cheated on him with his best friend."

"That's not much of a best friend," I muttered.

"You're telling me," Easton said, snatching a piece of bacon from my plate. "Can you believe that she had enough nerve to walk in here? With his whole family around?"

"Knowing Sarah, I'm not that shocked. Tact wasn't her middle name," Nathan said as he pushed himself up from sitting. "They are right outside?"

"Yeah. He's trying to get Sarah to leave, but she's having a full-blown freak-out," Easton explained. "Evan said he'd get rid of her, but you know Evan…"

"Yeah, I know. It would make a bigger scene if he handled it. Don't worry. I got it." Nathan glanced my way and gave me a small grin. "I'll see you later, Coach."

I stood from the table and shook my head. "Wait. Let me handle Sarah."

The guys looked at one another, then at me.

Easton grimaced. "You don't know Sarah, Avery."

"Exactly. And she doesn't know that River and I are *so* in

love," I stated, placing my hands on my hips, batting my eyelashes toward the guys.

Easton's grin stretched as he realized my plan. Nathan frowned.

"No way."

"Yes!"

They both said it at the same time, but I went with Easton's "yes" instead of Nathan's "no way."

"All right, Avery." Easton patted me on the back before he rubbed his hands together in bliss. "Batter up."

24

NATHAN

I hated this plan.

But dammit, it was a good plan. A great plan, even.

Sarah was the definition of a bad ex-girlfriend. Ever since River found out about her hooking up with his best friend, she'd been trying to get back with him on an unnatural level. Even with him blocking her number, he'd get calls from random phone numbers, only to find Sarah was trying to weasel her way back into his life.

I followed Easton to the front of the barn and peered out of the window as we spied on Avery walking out to where River and Sarah stood. Sarah, of course, was in a fit of emotions, tears streaming down her face, and poor River stood there looking as if he'd kicked a puppy. I knew whatever crap Sarah was feeding him was making him feel guilty, and that infuriated me. The poor guy had a heart of gold, and it made me angry that Sarah was manipulating his emotions post-breakup the same way she had during said "relationship."

Before Avery walked over to the two, she pulled her high ponytail out and raked her hands through her long hair, allowing it to fall past her shoulders. She then pushed out her chest and headed straight to River.

"Hey, babe. The food is getting cold and"—Avery's eyes moved to Sarah—"Oh, hi there." Without a moment of hesitation, Avery wrapped her arm around River's waist and slipped beneath his arm, forcing River to place his arm around her shoulders. "Who's this?" she asked with the sweetest voice I'd ever heard.

I wish she used that voice on me more often.

For a moment, River hesitated. The swirl of confusion sitting in his bent brow almost made me burst out in laughter. Then realization settled in, and he pulled Avery closer to him. My chest tightened from their proximity to one another. I knew they were acting, but still, a sting of jealousy slapped me hard.

"Oh, this is just someone I used to know, babe," River said, rubbing Avery's shoulder in a circular motion.

Sarah's eyes danced up and down Avery with a look of disgust. She wiped away her crocodile tears and huffed. "Who's this?" she demanded.

"This is Avery. My girlfriend," River said proudly as he puffed out his chest.

"Since when do you have a girlfriend?" Sarah barked with a disgusted tone, letting her true colors show.

"We're new," Avery mentioned as she stared at River with lovey-dovey eyes. "But I'm pretty sure we're going the distance." Avery stood on her tiptoes and kissed River's cheek.

I wanted to slug my brother in the jawline for getting that kiss on the cheek.

It's fake, it's fake, it's fucking fake, Nathan. Chill out.

"You moved on?" Sarah questioned, those fake tears falling from her eyes. Or maybe they were real tears from the realization that River was not wrapped around her finger anymore.

"Yeah," he said with a confidence that made me proud of the fucker. "I suggest you do the same."

With that, he pulled Avery in closer to him, turned around with her, and headed back inside to the barn. Sarah stood there with a look of shock for a second before walking back to her car and driving away.

And that, my friends, was what one called a mic drop.

The second Sarah was gone, Easton and Grant began jumping up and down all over River and Avery, celebrating the epic scene that just unfolded before us. Even Evan had a small smirk on his face as he stood there with his arms crossed.

"Not bad, Kingsley," Evan stated, giving Avery a slight nod. That was the biggest compliment in the world from Mr. Grump.

"You fucking rock star," River said, playfully shoving Avery. "First you get us a baseball win, then you gift me with another win."

"I had a good feeling you'd bring some good vibes to the property," Grant said, complimenting Avery.

She laughed and bowed. "What can I say? I'm a useful woman."

"Damn straight you are," River said, placing his hands against her shoulders in celebration.

"Drop the scowl, you're starting to look a little too much like me," Evan whispered as he nudged me in the arm.

I shook my head. "I'm *not* scowling," I said with, indeed, a scowl.

He chuckled slightly and shrugged. "Whatever you say, Nate. Whatever you say."

After the guys were done celebrating with Avery, she walked over to me with the kind of smile that made my own grumpiness dissipate.

I gave her a slow clap. "Not bad, Coach."

"I bet you didn't know I was such a good actress."

"Some might've said you weren't acting at all," I sarcastically remarked. "It seemed a little *too* realistic."

Raising an eyebrow, she shifted her stance, hands on her hips. "What's that, Nathan? A tinge of jealousy?"

Dismissing her accusation, I heavily sighed and shook my head. "Jealous? Me? Not in the slightest."

She stepped closer to me. "Maybe a little slightest?"

Her proximity felt foreign to me. Like a dream I'd been dreaming of for a long-ass time coming true. Was that...playfulness in her stare, too? Was Avery being playful with me again? This day was taking a turn I didn't expect it to take.

"Maybe a little," I confessed, stepping in closer, too. I'd move in closer and closer as long as she allowed it. "A tiny bit."

"Don't worry, Nathaniel." Her smile grew, and she placed a comforting hand against my forearm. "River's not my type."

"And what is your type, Coach?"

With a mischievous glint in her eyes, she gave me a once-over, a playful look on her face, before she coyly started off toward her table. "I need more mimosas."

This woman was going to be the end of me.

I followed her footsteps like a puppy dog in need of its owner's attention. "I'm just saying. Wesley didn't exactly seem like your type to me."

She glanced back at me and arched an eyebrow. "Is that so?"

"That's so."

"And what about Wesley didn't seem like my type?"

"He seemed weak."

"You think I don't have a thing for weak men?"

"I know you don't have a thing for weak men."

"Okay, wise guy. You seem to know me well. So you tell me," she said as she picked up her Mason jar and took a swig. "What do you think my type is?"

I swiped her Mason jar from her grip and took a sip, too. "Someone with a dash of cockiness and a sprinkle of charm."

"True. And maybe handsome, too. And funny."

"I'm hilarious," I said with a wide grin. "Knock, knock."

"Who's there?"

"Your future husband."

She rolled her eyes. I loved when she rolled her eyes at me. She did it so dramatically that I couldn't help but feel turned on.

"You're not my type, Nathaniel," she said.

"Why's that?"

She snatched her drink back. "Because you annoy me too much."

"That sounds like a compliment."

"That's only because your peanut brain doesn't know how to decipher insults from compliments."

I smirked. "Thanks, Coach."

Another eye roll. "Truthfully, I don't have a type. I don't like men, so that makes it next to impossible for me to have a type. Most of you just piss me off."

"You seem to like my brothers well enough."

"That's because they aren't major pains in my ass."

"I don't have to be a pain in your ass." I narrowed my brows. "Unless you request me to be a pain in your ass, if you're into butt stuff."

She laughed.

I liked that even more than the eye rolls.

"This conversation is over," she ordered as she took a seat back at the table.

I sat across from her. "Okay, what do you want to talk about now?"

"I was somewhat interested in our conversation before Easton interrupted it."

A knot formed in my gut as she said those words. The last thing I wanted to talk about was me and my mother's concern about me. I'd rather talk about anything else in the world but that. "That was a pretty boring conversation. I'd rather go back to talking about putting a pain in your ass."

Her eyes narrowed as she studied me, a seriousness finding her stare. "What does the rest of your day look like today?"

"Nothing too much. Why?"

She leaned in toward me. "Do you want to hang out with me today on the field here and hit some balls?"

I leaned in toward her. "Yes."

"Around seven this evening?"

"It's a date."

"It's *not* a date."

"It's hanging out between two friends."

"We are *not* friends."

"It's a batting round between two roommates."

"Okay. That works." She shoved her plate toward me. "Now, go get me some more of your sausage. I'm still hungry."

———

DID it seem like a setup that Avery asked me to hang out with her on the field? One hundred percent. Was I willing to overlook it since all I wanted to do with my time lately was hang out with her? One million percent.

I showed up to find her already standing on home plate with a bag of baseballs beside her. She wore black leggings, an oversized sweatshirt, and a baseball cap as she held a bat in her hands. The second she saw me, she said, "You're late."

"By two minutes."

"Late is late."

"I like to make an entrance," I joked, walking toward her. "So what's the catch here?" I asked.

"The catch?"

"Don't play dumb, Avery. That's my role. I know you didn't just invite me out to hit some balls for a casual conversation. So out with it."

She placed the head of her bat against the ground and held

it around the neck. "You didn't want to talk about your mom worrying about you at brunch."

"True."

"I figured it would be easier to talk about it on the field. This is my favorite place to talk about hard things. Or at least, think about hard things. I'm not big on conversation when it comes to my feelings."

"I guess we have something in common."

"Who would've thought?" she quipped. She held the bat out toward me. "So you want to talk while we hit balls around?"

"Since when do you care about my feelings?"

"Since I decided that I don't hate you as much anymore."

I arched an eyebrow. "No full-core hatred?"

"Trust me, I'm as shocked as you are," she stated. "Don't get me wrong, there's still hate. But the more time I've spent around you, the more I realized something major."

"And what's that?"

"We aren't that different, you and I."

I moved in toward her. "Is that so?"

"Yeah. We both suffer from the same disorder."

"And what disorder is that?"

"Oldest Sibling Syndrome."

I snickered. "Is that the official medical term?"

"Sure is. Look it up on WedMD. It's called OSS for short, though."

I reached into my pocket and pulled out my cell phone to search it. Avery held her hand out toward me and stopped me. "Later. Look it up later."

I slid the phone back into my pocket and crossed my arms over my chest. "All right, I'll play. What are some of the symptoms of OSS?"

"Oh, there are plenty. Especially when a parental figure is missing from the equation."

"Enlighten me."

She swirled the bat back and forth between the palms of her hands. "Well, for starters, you are extremely reliable and find yourself responsible for your siblings. Almost as if they are your own kids, seeing how you helped raise them."

I narrowed my brows. "Go on."

"You are overly protective over your family and go out of your way to make sure everyone's okay. You're a workaholic. You put your own wants and needs on the back burner in order to make sure everyone else is good. You let your dreams sit on the sidelines if it makes sure others are happier."

My mouth twitched a little.

She was hitting a little too close to home.

I took the bat from her and grabbed a ball from the bag. I tossed it up and swung, hitting the ball into the distance. "Go on," I said.

She took the bat from me and stepped onto the plate. "You suffer from a hyper-independence, which seems like a good thing, but it's not." She tossed a ball up and knocked it out. "It's actually a trauma response because you feel like you can't rely on others, seeing how it was always your job to be the reliable source."

"Too loud, Coach."

She handed the bat back to me. We switched positions.

"You also worry about messing up and letting people down. Which is why you are so achievement-oriented," she explained.

I hit the next ball.

She whistled low. "Nice hit."

"Thanks." I flicked my thumb against the bridge of my nose. "So with this OSS, what's the treatment plan?"

She shrugged. "Don't know. Still trying to figure that out myself. Because as someone suffering with OSS, I know that we hate all eyes on us, and we hate the thought of people worrying about us because it shows that we aren't as strong as we should be, and we should always be strong." She took the bat from me and performed another hit. "But I think it helps to struggle in numbers. Makes it a little easier to breathe."

"Are you suggesting we start an OSS club?"

"A secret society where we share our struggles with each other since only us eldest children can truly understand."

I put a hand against my chest. "Did we just become best friends?" I asked, quoting the movie *Step Brothers*.

She laughed. "No. Absolutely not. We aren't even friends. We are just two people who come to the field once a week to vent, to talk, and to feel better with one another."

"That's it?"

"That's all."

"Okay. I can get behind this secret society of two. Is this our first official meeting?"

She held the bat out toward me. "It is."

"Okay." I took the bat and swung. "So how does the conversation start?"

"Should your mother be worried about you?"

I glanced back at her and saw the seriousness in her stare. I considered lying, but that wasn't exactly the point of the OSS club. "Sometimes. Yes."

The corner of her mouth twitched as she frowned. "Should she be worried about you right now?"

I shook my head. "No. Right now, I'm good."

"Happy?" she asked.

"Right now? Yes. But I don't strive for happiness. It's a temporary, fleeting thing."

"What do you strive for?"

"Contentment," I replied. "It's a longer-term state of satisfaction. Happiness is fleeting. Contentment is stable and solid throughout life."

"I thought I was content in my last relationship."

"Oh." I shook my head. "That's different. One should never be content in love."

"Why's that?"

"I don't know. I just feel as if love deserves a word, a feeling bigger than that."

"And what word is that?"

"Don't know yet. But once I figure it out, I'll be the first to inform you."

She smiled a little, but then fell once again into a worried frown. "But you're okay, right?"

"For someone who isn't my friend, you sure show a lot of friendship tendencies."

"What can I say? I'm a good person."

"Yes," I agreed. "You are."

She grew bashful and snatched the bat from me to shake off her nervous energy. "Anyway, you didn't answer my follow-up question."

"Before we move on to if I'm okay, don't I get to ask you the same question about whether your father should be worried about you? Should *I* be worried about you?"

"Oh no. Today's OSS meeting isn't about me. It's just about you."

"That seems unfair."

"What can I say? I don't make the rules."

"That's funny because it feels as if you do, indeed, make the rules."

She bit her bottom lip. For a second, I thought about biting it, too. Then those moist, full lips parted, and she said, "Why are you single?"

"What?"

"Pretty straight-forward question, Coach," she replied. That was the first time she called me Coach, and it did things to my lower region. A twitch in my crotch area from a five-letter word. She wasn't lying. She didn't hate me as much anymore.

That was refreshing.

"I just haven't found the right person," I said.

"Are you looking for the right person?"

"No. I'm not."

She nodded with her lips puckered out as she pointed the bat at me. "You know what that is?"

"What's that?"

"Hyper-independence and a fear of intimacy. A classic case of Older Sibling Syndrome. You think that no one will be able to love you on a deep level because you haven't even managed to love yourself on said deep level, and you have a fear of letting go of the reins in your life, because you don't trust others to guide you."

Well, damn.

Okay, Dr. Phil.

I cocked a brow. "How did you get past it?"

"Oh. I didn't."

"Bull. You had a whole fiancé. You were minutes away from being married. You had to let go of some of that independence to get there."

"Yeah, that's the thing...I didn't. Wesley and I had a very scholarly relationship. When he asked me out, he used a pie chart and told me the statistics of a woman like me being paired with a man like him. When he proposed, he asked me with three different rings because he knew I liked to be in control of the outcome. At least, that's what I told myself. Looking back, I think it's just because he didn't know me well enough to know what I'd want."

"How long were you two together?"

"Three years." She almost smiled, but it fell short. "Turns out you can sleep in the same bed as someone for years and still not know who was lying beside you. Ask me three things that he and I had in common."

"What are those three things?"

She shook her head and shrugged. "I've been trying to figure them out over the past few days. I also have been trying to figure out why I don't miss him more. I feel like I should, you know? I should miss him."

"Maybe you're still processing the whole situation."

"Maybe," she agreed. She bit her bottom lip. "But can I tell you a secret?"

"I'm the best with secrets."

"When I called off the wedding, I was upset. Devastated, even. But after a little time, there was a moment when I felt... relief."

"You loved him, though."

"Yes, but that's the problem. I think I loved him up to my self-enforced limit of love. Which isn't saying much at all."

"Well, look at us. Two broken peas in a pod."

"I hate peas."

I smiled. "I know."

We stayed on the field for a while longer, then headed back to my house to call it a night. I watched television for a while before deciding it was time for sleep. While heading to my bedroom, and I knocked on Avery's door. She'd just hopped out of the shower. She had a towel wrapped around her body and one wrapped around her hair as she opened the door. It took everything in my power not to allow my eyes to move up and down her figure.

"What's up?" she asked, gripping the towel to her body.

"You never answered my question."

"Which one?"

"Should I be worried about you today?"

She smiled. It was so tiny and short-lived, but it sat against her lips for a moment. "No," she said, shaking her head. "Not today."

25

NATHAN

"I think you should take the lead today," Avery told me one afternoon before practice. "Let the guys get a feel of Coach P in his prime."

I didn't hate the idea. Truthfully, I was a bit shocked that she offered us such a position. Though lately it seemed as if Avery and I were not only in the same book with one another, we were finding our way to the same page. Sure, sometimes she wrote in cursive, and I didn't know what the hell was going on with her, but for the most part, we were becoming more and more of a team.

Especially when it came to baseball.

"I'd love that," I said. I gave her a slight head nod. "Thanks, Coach."

She nodded back. "I'm going to stay back and do some paperwork before our game this weekend. Have fun out there. I'll meet you all soon."

Not only was she letting me take the lead today but she was also giving me no reins. That felt fucking fantastic.

Over the past few weeks, I'd been getting to know the guys more and more. It was clear to me how different they all had been and how they each needed different coaching techniques from me. Some needed a gentler hand, while others needed to be shoved to reach their highest potential.

The one I connected to the most was Cameron, though. Something about him reminded me of myself as a kid. Not only that, but I could also relate to him having a drunk dad who showed up to games and embarrassed the hell out of him. Cameron was a good kid and a fantastic ball player. He could easily go to the pros with the right opportunities presented to him. He was a beast during practices and a natural-born leader. It was clear the rest of the guys looked up to him, and he made sure to help his teammates in any way possible.

It was just when he got on the field during actual games that he froze up, which was something I was looking to break him out of. Cameron Fisher suffered from stage fright. Call it nerves, call it pressure, call it whatever you want to call it. All I knew was that he lived too much in his head and not enough in his heart.

I used to have the same issue as him, which made me the perfect individual to help him break out of that mindset. Then when the scouts came to the games—and they would, due to a few calls I'd made—they could see how talented Cameron and the rest of our players had been. If I did anything for the team, it would be opening them up to the best opportunities for their lives.

During practice, I got the guys warmed up in the facility before shooting them out to the field to run a few drills. As all the guys started heading out to the field, I called out to Cameron.

"Cam, can you hang back for a second?" I asked.

He glanced toward me and raked his hand through his messy blond hair. "Yeah, Coach P?" he asked, jogging over to me.

I clapped my hands together. "Footloose."

Cameron arched an eyebrow. "What?"

"Footloose," I repeated as I started hopping up and down. "You need to embrace Footloose."

"I have no clue what that means."

"I know. There was a point when I didn't either. When I was younger, I used to be just like you. I used to overthink every play when it came to game days, and I'd get in my own head about it."

Cameron huffed as his face turned slightly red and his hands formed fists. "I know I've been messing up, Coach P, but I don't want you to bench me and—"

"Cam. That's not why I'm talking to you right now. I'm talking to you because you have a big game in a few days, and I know you can crush it. I'm not here to judge you. I'm here to help."

His embarrassment settled away slightly as he shook his head. "I don't know what's wrong with me. I just get in my head a bit, and I can't seem to focus out there."

"I know. Footloose."

"Why do you keep saying Footloose?"

"Because that's what got me through my tough period when I was struggling. I was about your age when I had scouts coming out to watch me play. I always froze up on those days and would have some of my worst games. It wasn't until I met a coach who gave me this technique that changed everything for me."

"The Footloose technique?"

"Yeah. It's where you take a moment and dance."

He laughed. "Yeah, right."

"I'm not shitting you, Cameron. And if you go back to watch some of my old tapes, you'll see me doing it on the sidelines before I went up to bat. Even in the Major Leagues. It's shaking off the pressure that is building inside you. It's finding out that no matter what, life isn't that serious. It's a game, yeah, but it's not the end of your life if you don't win or lose."

"Tell that to my dad," he murmured.

"That's the thing about Footloose," I explained. "You don't have to explain it to anyone else but yourself. Just try it, will you? If it doesn't work, fine. But if you do it, realizing that no one's opinion of you matters out there except for your own, then maybe you can get more out of your head and more into your heart. That's where baseball exists, Cam." I patted his chest, over his heart. "We play from here first. Otherwise, what's the point?"

"Footloose," he mumbled to himself. "And you just dance?"

"Hell yeah," I said as I started dancing around like a complete fool. "You let loose."

He laughed, shaking his head. "That sounds silly."

"That's the whole point. It's light. It doesn't weigh you down."

"And a coach taught you this technique?"

"The best coach in all of baseball. I promise you. If you allow yourself to be a complete fool, you also allow yourself to achieve greatness." I patted him on the shoulder. "Now, get out there with the guys. They need their leader to push them today before the game."

He nodded and started jogging out to join the rest of the team.

I hurried behind him, hoping that he might take my advice.

As the practice continued, Avery stood next to me with her whistle hanging around her neck and a clipboard close to her chest. As the guys performed a play to perfection, I noticed the small grin that fell on Avery's face.

"You're pretty good at this, Nathan. The guys listen to you," she told me.

"They like you more."

"Well, no shit. I'm amazing."

I snickered. "I think we can win this next series against Hamilton High. I think we're going to take it home."

"I sure hope so. The guys are working harder than they ever have. I would love to have a win under our belt. Then we can even make it to the postseason playoffs. Could you imagine that?"

"With you as their coach, absolutely."

She rolled her eyes. "Stop with the flattery. It's annoying."

I crossed my arms over my chest. "This does feel good, though, being back around the game. Coaching. For a while, I thought about coaching at a big college level. I got a few offers, but I wanted to help get the farm back on its feet. I felt as if my time was better used here."

"The farm seems to be doing really well."

"It is," I agreed. "But now I have the best of both worlds. Baseball and family."

"A big college-level team would be a lot more exciting than this little high school," she said.

"Yeah, but would that big college-level team have a coach who called me a dumbass on the regular?"

"Don't be silly, Nathan. There are plenty of coaches around the world who would love to call you a dumbass," she joked. She blew her whistle and started for the field. "Kevin! Run that play again, but step more into the pitch. You almost got it. Let me show you."

I smirked at her as she walked away to help the players.

Sure, maybe there would be coaches who called me a dumbass, but none would do it as insultingly as she did. There was something so sweet about hearing Avery Kingsley call me a dumbass. It held a certain level of prestige to it.

AFTER PRACTICE, Avery and I headed home to find a note on the front door from my mother.

Made you and Avery a pan of enchiladas that you can bake for dinner. Left it in your garage fridge.

-Mom

Avery smiled at the note. "You boys are so spoiled."

"The perks of living on a family farm. If you don't want to cook, someone else probably has dinner on the stove."

"I bet my mom would've been the same way," she mentioned.

That caused me to pause for a second as I was about to unlock the door. Avery hardly ever talked about her mother. Even when we were kids, the topic didn't come up much. I figured it was because some things were too hard to talk about.

"You miss her a lot, huh?" I asked as I unlocked and opened the door.

She nodded. "Every single day." She walked into the foyer of the house and began to take off her shoes. "Do you miss your dad?"

"No," I said without hesitation. "But I do miss the idea of a father."

She smiled a comforting type of smile that felt far from judgmental. "I know how tough it was for you when he passed. We didn't talk much about it, seeing how things between us ended abruptly, but I know how harsh he was toward you. You not missing him is completely understandable."

"But it comes with a level of guilt."

"Losing a parent always comes with a level of guilt. Even when you're young." She placed her duffel bag in the front closet before taking mine from me and doing the same. We were moving into a routine with one another after practice, and it felt so...good. "Do you want kids someday?" she asked.

"Yeah, I do. I just hope that I do better than him when it

comes to raising all my kids. I'd want to love each kid equally, unlike my father."

"He wasn't as harsh with your brothers?"

I shook my head as I walked to the kitchen to get water. "No. Mostly me. Maybe because I was the oldest. Maybe because I wouldn't allow him to snap at my brothers. It's hard to say."

"I read an article once about how no child has the same parent. Each one experiences their parents in a different light based on personalities, the time period, and the situations at hand. It's like how my dad has a completely different relationship with Yara, Willow, and me."

"Yeah. I just hope I don't have any of my father in me to pass on to my kids."

Avery shook her head. "You don't, Nathan. You're your mother's child, not your father's. And for what it's worth, you'd make a great dad."

"How can you know that?"

"I see you with our team. You treat everyone as individuals and care for them as if they were each the center of your universe. That's what a good parent would do. Treat each child as a unique individual."

"Those kids mean a lot to me."

"You mean a lot to them, too."

I poured two glasses of water and slid one across the island toward Avery. "We make a good team, don't we, Coach?"

She shyly grinned and nodded. "We do all right." She took a sip of water. "I'm going to go get the enchiladas from the garage fridge. I'm starving."

"Sounds good."

26

AVERY

The first game in the series against Hamilton High was off to an amazing start. The guys were on fire, and I couldn't help but feel hopeful that we could win this thing.

I felt the pressure of the game riding on Cameron. I sat in the dugout, nearly chewing my nails off, as Nathan stood near the field, clapping his hands. The other players stayed ready on their bases. We had all bases covered, and all Cameron needed to do was hit one good pitch to get Caleb and Tommy home from second and third base. Then we'd win the game.

Unfortunately, Cameron was two strikes down. I saw it happening—the anxiety of the pressure building up in Cameron. Our practices had been amazing, and I felt as if he was getting stronger and stronger each week, but I knew the nerves were still eating at him the same way I was eating at my nails.

He was all in his head and not in his heart.

This wasn't going to be good.

I stood from the dugout and began clapping along with the rest of our crew. "You got this, Cam!" I shouted out.

His body language said the complete opposite as his father, Adam, shouted at him from the stands not to screw up. That made my blood boil, but I couldn't focus on the asshat in the audience. I needed to keep my focus on my player.

The more Adam ridiculed him, the more I cheered him on.

Out of nowhere, Nathan called for a time-out. I shot him a look as he gave me a small smile before he jogged over to Cameron. Nathan placed his hands against Cameron's shoulders and whispered something into his ear. Then Nathan began to jump up and down and broke out into a silly dance, shaking his hips all over the place and waving his arms in the air like a madman. Cameron laughed slightly, and I watched as the heavy pressure on Cameron's shoulders began to dissipate. Nathan kept dancing like a tree in a windstorm, and he lightly shoved Cameron's shoulder. Cameron sighed for a moment before he began to dance like Nathan, too.

What in the world was happening?

Nathan clapped his hands together, pulled Cameron into him, and whispered one more thing before patting the top of Cameron's baseball helmet and swatting him back out to the batting diamond.

Nathan jogged back over to me and crossed his arms, focusing back on the field.

"What was that?" I asked, keeping my eyes on Cameron.

"Footloose," he replied. "Always helped me get out of my head and more into my heart."

My heartbeat quickened as those words left his mouth, knowing I was the one who taught him the Footloose technique all those years before. It was something I learned from my mom when I was a little girl and anxiety would swallow me whole. When life was too much, we would take a break to shake off the pressure that was building up. I hadn't used that technique in such a long time, but to see Nathan use it on

Cameron did something to my soul that I couldn't quite describe.

I tried to push the feeling away and went back to my focus on Cameron.

I held my breath the whole time I watched him get into position.

The pitcher was in his zone.

The players were ready on base.

The ball was released.

Cameron swung.

And he hit!

Not only did he hit, but he freaking smashed the heck out of the ball. It soared, too, going over the stadium, which meant Cameron Fisher just hit a grand slam.

A grand freaking slam!

And he made it look easy.

I started shouting and jumping up and down, with Nathan doing the same beside me as each player rounded the bases, hitting their home runs. The moment Cameron made it around, the whole team rushed over and started jumping all over him, cheering like wild.

We won...

We won!

Without thought, I wrapped my arms around Nathan as we continued to leap up and down in pure shock from Cameron knocking it out of the field!

I didn't know I could feel so damn happy from one hit. My happiness was more than winning the game, though. It was about Cameron finding his confidence, finding his strength in the midnight hour, and showing up not only for the team, but for himself, too.

That was why I did what I did.

That was why I loved this sport so much.

The crew all shook hands with the opposing team, and their coaches shook hands with us.

"That was damn impressive, Coach K," Coach Riley said from the opposing team. "It seems you and Coach P have a good thing going on over here. The other teams you have coming up should be prepared for challenging runs with your team. Great game."

I thanked him, still feeling as if my heart was going to explode from my chest. The amount of pride I had swirling in me was almost all-consuming.

After the game, I had all the guys meet in the stands to tell them how proud I was of them. The energy burst shooting through everyone was something worthy of the movies. I knew it seemed like a basic win to the outside world, but for us, it stood as a shift. Things were changing for us, and I knew if we kept moving forward, we could go far this year.

It had been a long time since I'd felt so hopeful.

After the team headed home, I went to my office, still high as a kite. Not long after, Nathan came in, clapping his hands together in celebration. "Can you believe that?!" he exclaimed, his energy still an eleven out of ten. I couldn't blame him because I was also still bursting at the seams.

I walked over to him and shoved his shoulder. "What the heck?" I laughed in complete awe, shaking my head. "That was fucking phenomenal."

He playfully shoved me back. "I can't believe it. Those guys were on fire."

I shoved him back, and he playfully fell backward, landing against the edge of my desk. "It was like they were high. Jackson, Caleb, Tommy, Cameron! Freaking Cameron! I can't believe it! What in the world did you say to him? I saw his energy lift before the dancing happened. What did you say?"

"I told him what I wish I would've heard during some games when the pressure felt so high and all on me," he explained, placing his hands against the edge of my desk. "I told him that he was good enough, no matter what happened, and that the world wasn't resting on his shoulders."

My breathing slowed as I stared at him in complete awe.

"Nathan?"

"Yeah?"

"You're a fucking remarkable coach."

His smile reflected our shared triumph that afternoon, and for what felt like the first time, we were coasting on the same wave, feeling the same feelings as one another, completely in sync.

"Avery?" he said.

"Yes?"

"You're a fucking remarkable coach."

And just like that, everything began to shift.

In the afterglow of the electrifying baseball victory, the air in my office felt supercharged with excitement and relief as I studied Nathan. His biceps were on full display as he held the edge of my desk with a wicked smile of bliss plastered against his mouth. My eyes danced around and peered at the walls adorned with strategies and team rosters, signs that spoke of the countless hours of dedication Nathan and I had put in over the past few weeks. This wasn't just my win. This was ours.

It was clear as day to me that I couldn't have gotten the team to where they were without Nathan's guidance because he added such an important part to the game that I'd somehow forgotten over time—heart.

He was the heartbeat of our team, and somehow, he'd managed to get my heart beating again after so much time of it being shut off.

I shook my head as I paced the room, replaying the game's final moments as the air between Nathan and me sat thick with an unspoken bond forging between us through the victory.

"Can we talk about Caleb, too?" I expressed as I recounted

the pivotal play that got the team to a solid spot in the eighth inning. As I turned to him, my stomach fluttered with butterflies that surprised me. Nathan's gaze met mine, with unspoken words lingering in the air. Did he feel it, too? The tension that I had no clue how to decipher? My pacing came to a halt as my eyes stayed locked with his. At that moment, the world beyond the office walls faded, leaving only the two of us suspended in the aftermath of our victory.

Without a full understanding of the impulse, I found myself closing the distance between us. Nathan, as if drawn by the same invisible force, straightened up, his attention fixed solely on me. The air shifted, charged with a new, unexplored tension.

My heart raced, pounding against my chest with a fervor that matched the adrenaline of our win. My mind, which was normally so focused and clear, was a whirlwind of emotions and a newfound desire. What was happening to me? What was this feeling taking over?

Words were lost to me as I stood there with his approach. Instead of running or pushing him away, I stepped out of character. I acted on a compulsion fueled by the high of our victory and the sudden, overwhelming realization of feelings for the man who stood before me. At that moment, I felt like eighteen-year-old Avery again, lost completely in Nathan Pierce's soul, uncertain if I wanted a roadmap out.

With a boldness that surprised me, I reached up to him, my hands finding the sides of his face, and I pulled him into a kiss that crackled with the moment's intensity. I fell into uncharted territory, and while I should've felt fearful of the dive I'd taken, I felt nothing but pure bliss.

He instantly responded to my kiss and didn't hesitate to kiss me back. Within seconds, he took the lead, wrapping his arms around me and pulling my body closer to his. The world around us, the office, the echoes of the game, the weight of our responsibilities—it all fell away, leaving only the truth of the moment we were creating.

He kissed me as if he'd been waiting decades to find his way back to my mouth, and I kissed him back, famished for his taste as his fingers dug into my back. At that moment, all common sense disappeared, and I was left with nothing more than the need for more.

More, more, more...

I didn't know how long we kissed, but it didn't seem long enough. His hands wrapped around my body as he deepened the kiss. When we finally parted, breathless and with a new energy flickering between us, my mind caught up with what had happened.

But I wanted more.

I needed more.

Yes...yes...my gosh, yes...

I didn't know kisses could taste like his. Powerful and sensual all at once.

I moved in to kiss him again, to get lost once more against his mouth, yet this time, he stopped me. I took a step back as a somber look fell over him, making my stomach turn. What was that expression? Regret? Disappointment?

His mouth parted, and he whispered, "Avery."

"What is it?" I asked.

Nathan grimaced and cleared his throat. His stare moved past me, over to the door. What was he staring at? Did a student catch our act? Was there a player taking in the passionate kiss he and I'd shared? I turned to see what caused Nathan to look so distressed, and I understood his expression within seconds.

My heart.

It dropped.

"Wesley," I murmured.

There, in the doorframe of my office, stood my ex-fiancé.

Wesley held a bouquet of roses in his hands while his eyes were packed with pain. Without a word, he turned and hurried away.

27

AVERY

"Wesley, wait!" I called out, chasing him into the parking lot of the school building. My heart pounded wildly, and I was completely uncertain how to slow down the intense thoughts shooting through my mind.

Wesley reached his car and started to open the door. As I approached him, I placed a hand against his shoulder. "Wesley, wait," I urged.

He turned around to face me, flowers still in his grip. His eyes flooded with emotions as he sat on the edge of tears falling down his face. "What, Avery?" he snapped as he pushed his glasses up the bridge of his nose. "What do you want?"

"I...we...it..." Guilt filled me as I swallowed hard. "What are you doing here?"

His shoulders dropped, and he waved the flowers around. "I thought I was coming to win you back, but clearly, that isn't a possibility."

"Win me back?" I asked, confused. "I thought you were supposed to be off getting prepared for your new...life."

He cleared his throat and sniffled. "It turns out the position wasn't locked in as much as I'd thought. Drew miscalculated the situation. The position went to another."

"Oh...gosh." I almost told him I was sorry, but I didn't like to lie to jerks who left me on my wedding day.

"As if you care," he huffed, his coldness stinging my system.

"Why do you have an attitude with me? You're the one who left me on our wedding day, not the other way around," I expressed.

A part of me was still stunned that he was standing in front of me. A part of me thought I might've got hit in the head with a ball at the game, and I was suffering from a terrible concussion. Over the past few weeks, I assumed Wesley didn't want anything to do with me. I figured he rode off into the sunset of his happily ever after. I made peace with that. Not all stories received decent endings. Some ended abruptly in the middle of a chapter.

Wesley's shoulders dropped. "I know...I know. Sorry it's just..." He took a deep inhalation and released it. "You already moved on with that freaking guy who you swore you hated! I didn't imagine I'd find you sucking face with him as I came to talk things out." He paused. "Is it true you moved in with him?" he asked with a tinge of disgust.

I shook my head slightly, thrown off by the question. "That's nothing that we need to talk about right now."

He huffed. "It's just funny...you gave me such a hard time about Drew, but then you end up playing house with your ex."

"Stop it, Wesley," I whispered, feeling chills race up and down my body. "That's not fair."

"At least it makes it clear why you were so okay with calling off the wedding. Who knows how long the two of you had been hooking up behind my back? I knew I got a weird feeling from him when I went into the butcher shop. I bet you told him to take the coaching gig, too, so you'd have more time together."

"That's not true."

“That sounds like a yes to me.”

“Then maybe you should fix your hearing.”

“So him snapping at me at the butcher shop weeks ago, threatening to slam my head into the glass display, was just out of the good nature of his heart? You can’t convince me that you two weren’t screwing around.”

Nathan snapped at Wesley? That was news to me.

“Wesley, I never once cheated on you.”

“You’re telling me that the two of you haven’t even kissed until just now, huh? You want me to believe that?”

My chest tightened, thinking about what happened between Nathan and me not that long ago in my office. It was such a flurry of events that I hadn’t even processed yet.

“When I was with you, Wesley, I was with you. I never stepped out on our relationship.”

“Right,” he huffed. “You just didn’t waste any time getting into your ex’s pants. Noted. After all the years we spent together, I was wrong about you. If I knew you were a cheater, I would’ve never wasted my time on you.”

"*I didn't cheat on you!*" I barked, feeling my rage building from the idea that he was painting me as a cheater when he was the one who left me. Still, somehow his words affected me. Somehow, I'd felt guilt filling my chest, and I wasn't the one who chose a career over a relationship.

But still, you weren't emotionally available for him, Avery.

Maybe if you weren't so damaged, he would've been able to love you right.

There they were again. Those intrusive thoughts that loved to poison my brain. Luckily, enough sanity floated through my mind as I thought about our past relationship.

"What's my favorite color?" I questioned.

He huffed. "What?"

"What's my favorite color?"

"Is this some kind of test of the strength of our relationship? Colors don't matter, Avery. Those are kiddish facts."

"Okay. What position did I play in softball?"

No reply.

I shifted. "What vegetable do I hate?"

"Carrots."

"I love carrots." I crossed my arms. "What's my middle name?"

He rolled his eyes. "We aren't doing this, Avery."

He didn't know.

I felt a wave of disappointment wash over me as the realization settled in that I'd been spending the past few years of my life with a stranger.

"What's something we have in common?" I questioned. "Anything, Wesley, that connects us."

He tilted his head before his brows lowered in thought. "We both enjoy tacos."

My heart sank at his reply. "Everyone likes tacos, Wesley. That's not a reason to fall in love, let alone get married."

"We made sense on paper," he argued. "We made sense."

"No," I disagreed. "We didn't. Be honest with me and with yourself. If that job didn't fall through, would you be here right now with flowers?"

He hesitated a moment, which was more than enough to tell me his answer.

"Goodbye, Wesley," I said.

He sighed and pitched the bridge of his nose. "Gosh, why are you like this all the time? How can you be so coldhearted?"

"Someone once told me that I'm hard to love," I sarcastically remarked. "So it probably has something to do with that." He didn't say another word, simply because there was nothing left to say. The two of us were done. Truth of the matter was, we were finished long before we made it to our wedding day.

As he climbed into his car and drove off into the night, I stood alone in the parking lot, under the glow of the streetlights, trying to remind myself how to breathe.

AFTER A WHILE, I headed back to Nathan's house. As I walked inside, I found him loading the dishwasher in the kitchen.

"Hey," I said, drawing attention to myself.

The moment he heard me approaching, he looked up at me. "Hey. Is everything okay?" He leaned back against the kitchen island and crossed his arms over his broad chest. "Are *you* okay?"

"I'm fine." I snickered a little as I shook my head and walked over beside him. I leaned against the island and crossed my arms, just as he had. "That was, um, unexpected."

"To say the least."

"But, well, I guess in the end, he and I got closure. So that's cool."

"I'm sorry, Avery."

"Don't be. It's for the best. Do you know he didn't know

basic things about me? Not my least favorite vegetable, not my middle name, and not my favorite color. I know those are silly, stupid things that don't hold meaning, but how did that man know so little about me? The only thing he said we had in common was that we liked tacos."

"Everyone likes tacos."

"That's what I said!" I huffed. "I mean, I can't put it all on him. I think I stayed with him because he didn't go deep with me. Which meant I didn't have to open up completely. He couldn't shatter my whole heart if I only gave him a few pieces."

He grimaced and slid his hands into his pockets. "You want to go out back and hit a few balls around on the baseball field?"

"Yeah"—I sighed—"I do."

"Here," he said, grabbing a sweatshirt off one of the barstools. "It's cold out there."

We walked to the diamond together, and Nathan threw me a few pitches. Some I missed, others I knocked across the field. The chilled air brushed against my cheeks as his sweatshirt draped over my body. The more balls he threw my way, the more my body relaxed from the interaction with Wesley.

After we finished, I walked over to the pitcher's mound where he was and took a seat. He sat beside me, bending his knees as he rested his crossed arms on them. I was slightly out of breath as I stared up at the star-laced sky. That was always one of my favorite things about Honey Farms. The amount of light pollution was much less than in town.

"I liked kissing you, Ave," he said, pulling me back to the moment in my office. He didn't look at me when he said the words. His stare stayed on the sky. Mine stayed on him. "I liked kissing you so damn much, but if it was too much for you, if you're dealing with all your stuff, I don't want you to think it had to mean anything. It meant something to me but doesn't have to mean anything to you. No pressure. Plus, I sort of like what we're becoming."

"And what's that?"

"Friends. We kind of skipped over the friendship thing when we were younger and went straight to love. Don't get me wrong, I liked that. A lot. I'm just saying it also feels damn good to be your friend, too."

I smiled and leaned toward him, resting my head on his shoulder. "I think I like being your friend, too, Nathan." I looked back up at the sky. "These were some of my favorite moments with you. Sitting out here on this mound after a long day of working on the farm."

"You'd always smell like the pigpens," he joked.

"And you'd always try to kiss me."

"What can I say? I liked my woman filthy."

I laughed. "You were my first ever kiss, you know."

"Yeah, I know." He snickered, shaking his head. "A part of me still wants to be your last one, too."

I lifted my head. "Nathan..."

He tossed his hands up in surrender. "Sorry. Friends. Nothing more, nothing less."

"It's not that I haven't thought about you in that way because I have. But I'm still trying to find my footing. And like you said, we are so good right now. I'm scared if we move too quickly or move at all like we did when we were younger, we might explode again."

His lazy smile spread, and he nodded. "I agree. Besides... what's better than a bit of a slow burn? But I should get a shower in after working all day."

"Turns out you're the filthy one tonight."

"You have no clue how filthy I can get."

The sudden tingling between my thighs sure did wonder exactly how filthy that man could become. It turned out my brain and my body had *very* different reactions to Nathan Pierce.

He pushed himself to a standing position and then held a hand toward me. I took his hand, and he helped me stand.

"Thanks, friend," I told him.

"Welcome, friend."

"Just to be clear, even though we're friends, I still hate you."

He chuckled. "I'd actually be worried if you didn't hate me anymore. It's kind of our thing. You love to hate me, and I just kind of love to be within your orbit as you do so."

We walked over to his house, and he held the back door open for me to move through. His voice made me pause as I walked down the hallway toward my room.

"Peas," he said.

My least favorite vegetable.

"Harper," he whispered.

My middle name.

His smile stretched, and his dimples deepened as his hand rubbed the back of his neck. "And midnight blue."

28

NATHAN

I t had been a week since Avery and I kissed in her office, and I hadn't stopped thinking about it. For a long time, I never thought I'd get the opportunity to kiss her again, yet on that fateful day, I somehow found my way back to first base with her. Kissing her felt like the only thing my mouth was made for. I could've kissed her throughout the night, but I wouldn't have complained if we rounded a few more bases with one another.

She tasted so good, too. I couldn't help but think about what other parts of her tasted like and how I'd like to glide my mouth over every single inch of her brown skin. I wanted to explore every piece of her.

Especially the location resting between her thick thighs.

The number of times I'd close my door at night and stroke myself, thinking about it being Avery's hand around my shaft, was almost embarrassing. Just the thought of her was enough to get me hard and my hand sliding into my boxers. I'd shut my eyes and envision her full, plump lips sliding up and down my length. I'd groan in pleasure as I stroked my cock, muttering to myself, "Yeah, right there, baby. I love that, Avery."

I lost myself in the moment, falling deeper into the idea of Avery's mouth on my shaft, taking me all in as my hands fell to the back of her head, gliding her up and down. I groaned as I grew closer and closer to getting off. "Please, Avery, right there...Yessss," I said aloud, allowing myself to continue to daydream about the women across the hall as I masturbated. "Ave, fuck, Avery..."

"Yeah?"

I heard my bedroom door creak.

My eyes flew open to find Avery standing in the doorway, her eyes widen as she stared at my cock sitting fully loaded in my hand. "Fuck!" I shouted as my hand continued stroking.

"Oh my gosh! I'm sorry!" she hurriedly said, turning away and rushing out of the room in a state of panic.

Fuck, fuck, fuckkkkk!

I groaned as my body took over my mind, and I came in my hand, my whole body shaking from the orgasm that overtook my system. Just locking eyes with her for that split second was enough to push me over the edge, and there was nothing I could do to stop the act from taking place. I was already over the cliff and had no choice but to finish the dive.

My whole body was soaked in sweat as I lay there, heavily breathing, with a dirty hand to match my dirty mind.

Like an embarrassed teenage boy who got caught jacking off, I dragged myself off to my bathroom and cleaned myself up. I slid on a pair of boxers, then tossed on my black sweatpants, and walked out of my bedroom. I knocked gently on Avery's bedroom door.

"Avery?"

"Sorry!" she blurted out, not opening the door.

I snickered, imagining how flushed she'd probably felt from walking in on me. "No, I'm sorry. I just..." *Was thinking about you, and I got hard, and then came hard, too.* I cleared my throat. "I was clearing my mind."

"It looked completely cleared, too," she mentioned, still not opening the door. "I just thought I heard you saying my name and came in. Sorry. I should've knocked."

"It's no big deal."

"Oh. It was a big, *big* deal," she said, emphasizing the word big.

That did a good amount for an ego boost. I was almost certain I'd get off on that statement the next time my hand slid down my pants.

"Can I come in?" I asked.

"I would rather you didn't."

"Why not? We're both adults. We've both seen the opposite sex parts before."

She swung the door open and shook her head. "Yes, we have seen them before, but I've never seen *yours* before, and you're my roommate, which makes it weird. I don't want it to be weird between us. But now I can't stop thinking about what I saw, and well, I saw a lot," she said, her face flushed. "A lot, a lot."

I bit my bottom lip and smirked. "Hell yeah, you did."

She rolled her eyes and shoved me. "Don't get cocky, Nathan."

"I can't help it. As you saw, cocky is my default."

"I don't want to speak to you about this anymore," she said as bashfulness hit her straight in the face. "So good night, Nathan."

"Night, Coach."

I headed back to my bedroom after she slammed her door in my face. A few minutes later, my phone dinged.

AVERY

I have a question.

NATHAN

Are you texting me from the next room?

AVERY

Yes, I am.

NATHAN

Want me to come back over to talk?

AVERY

No. I can't say what I need to say to you with a straight face.

NATHAN

It's all right. I like your crooked smile.

AVERY

I don't have a crooked smile!

I laughed because she had a crooked smile. I loved that damn crooked smile.

NATHAN

What's up, Avery?

AVERY

Were you envisioning me as you were...you know...?

NATHAN

There's a high possibility that I was, yes.

AVERY

Oh.

A few seconds passed before another text came through.

AVERY

How was I? In your mind, I mean.

NATHAN

Fucking fantastic. Better each time.

AVERY

This has happened more than once?

NATHAN

If I told you how many times it has happened, you'd probably think I'd need rehab.

AVERY

That's too much info, Nathan.

NATHAN

You asked, Coach. I'm just being honest.

AVERY

Too honest.

NATHAN

Do you think of me, too? When you touch yourself?

AVERY

We aren't talking about me.

I smirked and sat up in bed.

Oh shit.

She thought of me when she got herself off.

This was a new development to the story of us.

NATHAN

Can I come to your room?

AVERY

Absolutely not.

NATHAN

Are you blushing right now?

AVERY

Absolutely not.

NATHAN

Is your hand between your thighs?

AVERY

Absolutely not.

NATHAN

Can you slowly slide your hand between your thighs for me?

AVERY

Nathaniel. Stop it.

I knew well enough to know that Nathaniel wasn't said from a place of hatred anymore. It was said in the same way she used to say it when we were younger. Playfully. Man, I missed her saying my full name in a playful way. I missed being playful with her. I missed *her*.

It blew my mind how someone could be so close and still you could miss them so damn much.

AVERY

I keep thinking about it, though...

NATHAN

About you touching yourself?

AVERY

No. About kissing you.

It turned out I wasn't alone in my wicked thoughts as of late.

AVERY

So I've been thinking...

NATHAN

Go on.

AVERY

Maybe we can be friends with...benefits.

NATHAN

You're making a lot of sense right now.

AVERY

Only kissing benefits.

NATHAN

If you're in love with me, Avery Kingsley, just say it. Don't be shy.

AVERY

Shut up before I change my mind.

NATHAN

Can I kiss both sets of lips?

I heard her snicker from the other room. My favorite fucking sound.

AVERY

Only the ones on my face.

NATHAN

You're killing me here, but I agree to these terms.

I stood from my bed and walked back into the hallway, then I knocked on her door.

There was a moment of hesitation before I heard her footsteps growing closer to the door. Still, she didn't open it. "What are you doing? We're supposed to be texting," she whispered, as if she were nervous for all the ghosts of the house to hear us.

"Open the door, Avery."

"What? No. I'm not going to."

"Why not?"

"Because there's no reason for me to open it up right now."

"Yes, there is," I argued.

"And what reason is that?" she asked.

"I have to kiss you good night."

There was a moment of pause from her. The door slowly creaked open, and she appeared. She combed her hair behind her ears as she stood there in her pajamas, looking as perfect as she always did.

"Hi there," I whispered.

"Hi there," she replied.

I stepped closer to her. She stood still.

My hands fell to her lower back, and I pulled her against my body. I moved closer, our faces almost touching. "Hi there," I murmured.

She came a little closer. Her lips brushed against mine. "Hi there," she replied as her eyes fluttered shut.

I placed her bottom lip between mine and bit it gently before I kissed her, taking her all in. Her back arched against my touch as her hands fell to my chest. She kissed me back, deepening our connection. I felt her smile against mine, feeling dizzy from how high I grew from her simple kisses. I never knew a simple kiss could feel so important.

She moved back slightly and pecked my lips softly before pulling away from me completely. Her hand fell softly against my cheek as she held eye contact. "Good night, Nathaniel," she said with a bit of flirtation.

I rubbed the back of my neck, wanting nothing more than to kiss her more, but not wanting to push it too much. We had all the time in the world for our mouths to find their way back to one another. Maybe our hearts could do the same.

I wasn't in a rush at all.

"Good night, Coach," I replied.

I headed back to my room, already looking forward to kissing her good morning.

I wasn't sure if it was exactly friends-with-benefits. I'd call it friends-with-kisses, but I'd take it. I'd take whatever I could get from that woman. Friends-with-kisses was good enough for me because it held two of my new favorite facts. Avery and I were friends. And we'd sometimes kiss.

I'd call that a win.

29

NATHAN

W ith each game we played, the crowds grew more and more. It turned out the Honey Creek Hornets were finding a spark of light in the media realm. The boys were eating it up, too. I'd played the game long enough to know that a team always played better when they had a strong crowd behind them. Something about the energy of being cheered on from the bleachers pushed players harder.

Something was so rewarding about it, too. Not only for the players but also for Avery. She'd finally been given the chance to lead the team and had more than proved herself in that position. It wasn't every day you ran across a female coach in the league, so it was refreshing to see her do better than most of the men in our conference.

Still, it wasn't uncommon for someone to slip in rude comments along the way. After we beat the Parkway Giants, we shook hands with the coaches. Their head coach, Frank, shook my hand and gave Avery a dirty look. Then said, "I think it's nice that you're pretending to be the assistant coach, Pierce. Everyone knows this team was shit without you. Way to carry this team on your back. It's good to see this sport run by a man."

The dig was said loudly enough for Avery to hear it. I flinched, knowing that wouldn't sit well with Avery.

"I beg your pardon?" Avery snipped with a puffed-out chest. If there was one thing she wouldn't allow, it was disrespect of any kind.

Frank smirked and held his hands up in the air. "Don't get your tampon in a twist, Kingsley. You make a stellar assistant coach. But don't get confused. This ain't your sport, sweet pea."

"I'll show you a fucking sweet pea," Avery yipped, marching toward Frank with invisible smoke blasting from her nostrils.

"Whoa, there, slugger," I said, wrapping my arm around her waist and pulling her back behind me.

Avery's brows shot up as she stood there, stunned. She tilted her head and pointed a stern finger my way. "Don't fucking do that again, Pierce," she scolded, her warranted anger spewing toward me.

I took a deep breath and stepped toward her. I said softly, "He's a dick trying to get under your skin because we just smoked his team. Walk it off, Coach."

"*You walk it off!*" she hissed, a fire brewing in those brown irises. "That's some sexist bullshit."

"Yeah," I agreed. "But walk it off. Otherwise, everyone around us will label you the angry, unstable coach."

Avery glanced around to see all the eyes on her. She grimaced, seeing people staring at her, waiting for her to snap. It wasn't fair. She'd always be judged harder than any other coach in the industry because there wasn't a dick between her legs. Even though Avery was better than most, she'd always have a target on her back if anything went wrong in the slightest. People like Frank were waiting for her to lose her cool and snap so they could label her in such a way. It was bullshit, but it was the way of the world.

Women in the industry had to prove themselves fifty times more than men.

A male coach could have a meltdown for a whole season and be labeled as passionate, while a female coach could throw off their baseball hat after a bad play and be called overly emotional.

Was it right? No. Yet it was the world we lived in. And now, with more attention on our team, we had more attention on our Avery.

She glanced up at the bleachers, where her father was sitting. Matthew Kingsley showed up to every single home game, no matter what. I hadn't officially met him, but he was clearly his daughter's biggest fan.

Matthew smiled a sad grin toward her. Then he mouthed, "Breathe, baby."

Avery grumbled and took a breathe before she stomped her feet off toward the building.

"Is it that time of the month for her?" Frank snickered with his assistant coaches who joined in the laughing.

"Fuck off, Frank," I blurted out before walking off the field.

"Walk it off, Coach?!" Avery spat out as she stood on the baseball batting mound at my place, clearly still enraged with what went down. "Are you kidding me, Nathan?"

"That was me having your back."

"Really? Because it felt like you were stabbing me in it."

I slid my hands into my pockets and leaned back against the railing of my porch. "You're pissed at me."

"Thank you, Captain Obvious. It's nothing like having a man tell a woman that when she's pissed off. I almost didn't notice without you informing me what I was feeling."

Her sarcasm was at a new level. I watched as she took a ball from the bag beside her, tossed it into the air, and knocked it out of the park. I swore her swings became Incredible Hulk strength whenever she was mad.

"I'm sorry," I said.

"Screw you," she replied before hitting another ball. She then turned toward me. "Frank Stagg is a dick."

"The biggest dick, yeah."

She pointed the bat toward me. "But he's not the only one who thinks that way. Do you know I spent all the years before being told that stuff? I worked under a misogynistic head coach for years, Erikson, who would've laughed it off with Frank. I'd been told countless times not to get my panties in a frenzy whenever some crap happened. I was told countless times by Coach Erikson to"—she made quotations with her fingers— "*take a walk* whenever I was being disrespected. Do you know how belittling that is? I was the only woman on the field and the only Black coach being told to take a walk because I was too much."

I began walking in her direction when I heard her voice crack. "And then I went ahead and said the same bull as those assholes."

She nodded slowly. "And I had the stupid idea that we were...partners."

"We are, Coach. I'm in your corner through and through. I will never understand what it is that you go through, but I need you to understand that anything I do is to better our team and protect you. Nothing good was going to come out of that inter-action with Frank Stagg. He's a fucking clown who was trying to get under your skin because we whooped his team's asses. I just didn't want him to spoil our win with his ignorant commentary."

She frowned and grumbled a little before biting her bottom lip. She looked back up toward me, the rage in her eyes from before somewhat simmering down. "Can you say anything other than 'walk it off' next time?"

I moved closer, took the bat from her hand, and placed it down. "What would you like me to say?"

"I don't know. Anything but that."

I took her hands and brought her left palm to my mouth. I kissed it lightly. "How about 'leave it on the field, Coach'?"

"Oh gosh, no." She shook her head as she inched a little closer. "Try again."

I kissed her other palm. "Lap it out, Coach."

"Nothing about walking or leaving the field," she argued. "Something that wouldn't feel so belittling but makes it clear that the other coaches are baiting me. Something that others wouldn't understand. Something that's just ours."

I brought both of her palms to my mouth and kissed them. "Butterflies."

"Butterflies?" she questioned, moving even closer. So close that I could easily step in and kiss her again.

"Yeah." I nodded, leaning in and brushing my mouth against her soft lips. "Butterflies."

Her eyes fluttered shut. "Why butterflies?"

"Because I'd have to be close to you whenever I said the word, and whenever I'm close to you, I get fucking butterflies."

She reopened her eyes and shoved me away with a loud chuckle. "Okay, cornball."

I gasped and tossed my hands to my chest. "Here I am, speaking from my heart, and you call me a cornball?"

"I'm sorry. If you didn't say corny things, I couldn't call you a cornball."

"You know what? Take a walk, Coach," I joked.

She snickered and flipped me off before she reached toward me, grabbed my shirt, and pulled me closer to her. "Kiss me, corny Coach," she whispered.

"Is that an order or a request?"

"An order."

"God..." I shook my head slowly, moving closer to her mouth. "I love it when you boss me around."

I kissed her, and she leaned into it, kissing me back. My hands fell to the sides of her face as she tilted her head toward me. I loved this part of us. The part where we kissed and made up. The part where I was able to taste her lips against mine. The part where I could daydream about more when our mouths touched.

Oh, how I wanted fucking more.

"I'm having a case of déjà vu," someone said behind me, breaking up the connection between Avery and me.

She stepped back and gently brushed her hand against her mouth.

Don't brush away my kisses, Avery Kingsley.

I turned around to see Evan standing there with his arms crossed over his broad chest. "Sorry to interrupt," he said with an almost-smirk. "I didn't know you two were...you two again."

"We aren't," Avery and I said in sync.

I smiled at her, and she smiled at me, growing shy.

Evan narrowed his brows. "Then what was that?"

"Oh. That was just two friends who sometimes...kiss..." Avery said, her cheeks rising high. She looked down and shook her head bashfully.

"We were going over plays," I said.

"With your saliva?" he questioned. "Is that a baseball technique?"

"What's up? What do you need?" I asked, shifting the awkwardness.

Evan still looked confused, but he went with the shift. "Priya is baking and needed some almond milk. You got any?"

"We do!" Avery exclaimed. "I'll go get it." She darted off as if she were running from the police. I could tell how embarrassed she'd been as she hurried into my place.

Evan glanced toward my back door. "So you and Avery, huh?"

"It's nothing serious. We're just friends."

"Friends who kiss?"

"Yeah." I shrugged. "I guess it's a thing."

His brows lowered, and he shook his head. "I remember how heartbroken you were when you ended things with her, Nate. It will always be serious with that woman for you."

I didn't reply, knowing he was right.

"Just do me a favor, will you?" he asked.

"What's that?"

"Pri and Avery have been hanging out together around the farm. Avery's been a good role model for Priya. She doesn't have many female role models outside of Mom. Avery's a good addition around these parts. So don't fuck this up."

I smirked and nodded. "I'll do my best, brother."

"Do better than that."

Avery came hurrying out with the carton of almond milk. "Here you go, Evan!"

Evan took the carton from Avery and thanked her. He gave me a nod and a slight smile, then wandered back toward his house.

"Oh gosh, how embarrassing. We have to be more careful about that," Avery mentioned, moving closer.

"I'm not too worried about it. It's probably for the best that he interrupted. I was starting to think you liked me."

She leaned in and whispered, "If you'd like, I could call you a shithead to balance it out."

I inched closer, my eyes falling to her full lips. "That would probably help."

Her hand fell against my forearm, and her mouth slightly brushed against mine. "You're such a shithead, Nathan Pierce."

I smiled and kissed her gently. "Thanks, Avery Kingsley."

"Anytime." She pulled back and took her warmth with her.

What I wouldn't give to kiss that woman forever. Yet sometimes the small, playful kisses between banter were my favorites. It made it seem as if what we were doing was simply becoming our new norm. Did I love kissing her all over during the wild makeout sessions? Of course. But kissing her in the quiet moments? During the fleeting seconds? Those kisses fed my soul.

30

AVERY

Nathan Pierce drove me wild. In good, bad, and ugly ways. The good: kissing him. Oh, that was so, so good. The bad: my mind wanted to do a lot more than kiss that man. The ugly: my heart wanted to let him in more than I already had.

As we moved closer to our final series, the series that would make us head to the playoffs, I was a ball of nerves. Yet the team was at their best, and Nathan was a soldier at keeping my panics at ease. I felt as if I had a lot to prove, not only for my team but also for myself. There had been more and more whispering around about how I should've allowed Nathan to step up as head coach. That his experience would've been a better fit for the guys.

A few coaches even went as far as to call me a stuck-up woman with a resting bitch face. The low blows at times were enough to make me want to rage, but whenever the word "butterflies" left Nathan's mouth, I'd take a few deep breaths and remove myself from any situation that raised my blood pressure.

Plus, getting covered in his kisses when we got home each

night didn't hurt too much. Waking up to his good morning kisses wasn't a bad touch, either.

My mind tried to keep me steady with my interactions with Nathan, but I'd be lying if I said my heart didn't seem to be leading the plays more and more each day.

When we got to our final game in our last series before the playoffs and won, I knew my heart would fully take over for the remainder of the season. Nathan Pierce helped get us to the playoffs. He'd helped scouts see more and more of our players. He made a difference to Honey Creek Hornets, and he'd made a difference to me.

My hardened heart somewhat began to soften around him.

That both thrilled me and terrified me all at once.

Yet there was still a sliver of doubt within my system as I thought about what others were saying. Maybe our winning season had nothing to do with me at all. Maybe it was Nathan who improved the game, not me. That did a number on my ego, but my heart?

My heart just wanted to keep beating for him and his kisses.

"Oh my gosh, oh my gosh, oh my gosh. I can't believe we made the playoffs!" I shouted, my heart pounding as Nathan headed to his kitchen to grab a bottle of champagne. My body still buzzed with excitement as I paced his living room, clapping my hands together. I'd never felt prouder than I did that evening, seeing my boys celebrate the victory.

"It was the most intense game I've ever been a part of," Nathan said as he walked into the living room with two glasses of champagne.

He held one out toward me. I downed it instantly. He laughed and handed me another glass. I downed that, too.

"I should've just opened two bottles, and we should've drunk straight from those," he jested.

I cocked an eyebrow at him. "Well..."

Within minutes, we sat on his living room floor, each of us

chugging champagne straight from the bottles, laughing about how wild it was that the game went in our favor.

"I've never seen those boys put their all into something the way they did that. I almost threw up watching it happen. And for Cam to get the winning hit! A grand freaking slam at that! Gosh! That kid deserved it. He's one of the best players out there," I expressed. "I know you helped get him to that spot, too. I can't thank you enough for building his confidence, Nathan."

He narrowed his eyes. "Was that a compliment?"

"Don't get used to them," I said, playfully shoving his shoulder. "I still hate you."

He shoved me back. "With hate like this, who needs love?"

I shoved him back. "Hate is better than love anyway. But still, maybe Ray was right. Maybe you should've been head coach."

He shoved me back. "Bullshit. That team listens to you. Your tough love drives them. You were made for that position. I'm just happy to help."

I shoved him again. "Yeah, I appreciate the assistance even though I hate you."

As I began to pull my arm back, he gently wrapped his arm around my wrist. His eyes were gentle and packed with care as he looked at me. His stare fell to my lips before he rose back to my eyes. "How much do you hate me, Coach?"

My heart began beating faster as I placed the champagne bottle in my other hand down on the floor. Every butterfly that fluttered within my stomach from his touch began to intensify as he held his intense stare with mine.

Butterflies, butterflies, butterflies...

"A lot," I lied.

He pulled me closer to him. "A lot, a lot or a little, a lot?"

I bit my bottom lip. "Sometimes a lot a lot, sometimes a little a lot."

He pulled me closer.

So close that I was nearly sitting on his lap. So close that if I inched forward just a little, I'd be close enough to rest my hands against his chest. To feel his heartbeat against my fingertips.

"Nathan..."

"I read an article about how bonding exercises were important for coaches heading into playoff games."

A nervous laugh escaped my lips. "Is that so?"

He lifted me onto his lap and combed a piece of my hair behind my ear. I closed my eyes as heat raced through my whole system. He rested his forehead against mine, and I could feel his hot breaths against my lips as he whispered, "Yes. That's so."

"What kind of bonding exercises did they mention?"

"They didn't really give details," he explained, brushing his lips against mine ever-so-slightly. "So I figured we could make them up as we go."

My hands pressed against his chest as my heartbeat intensified. "That sounds dangerous."

"I like danger."

"That's funny. I tend to run from it."

"Don't run from this, Coach."

Gosh, I hated how he called me Coach. It sent a wave of electricity throughout my whole system. He made me weak in the knees every time and didn't even know it.

"We shouldn't be this close," I breathlessly scolded.

"Maybe we aren't. Maybe this is all make-believe."

"A dream?"

"A fucking great dream. A make-believe realm."

I tangled my fingers against the fabric of his shirt. "What kinds of things can happen in a make-believe world?"

"Well...this," he said, slightly brushing his mouth against

mine. "And this..." He parted my lips with his tongue before gently biting my bottom lip.

My knees spread to the outside of his legs, which allowed my core to brush against the hardness resting in his sweatpants. My breaths were erratic and uneven as I allowed myself to fall into the fictional world where heartbreak didn't exist and passion was abundant.

"What else?" I whispered, moving my mouth to the edge of his ear and sucking it gently. "What else happens in the land of make-believe?"

"I taste you," he said, allowing his mouth to move to the nape of my neck. His tongue slowly swept across it, making my toes curl and my inner thighs pulse as if they had their own heartbeat. His hand wrapped around my neck, making me tilt my head up to meet his stare. His lips pressed to mine as he said, "I taste all of you."

I got lost in the depths of his gaze. His eyes were so dark, so dilated, so packed with want and need. When he kissed me, my eyes fluttered shut as my hands landed against his chest. The moment our lips met, a surge of electricity rippled through my whole system, igniting every nerve within me. He kissed me deeper, and I felt it—every second of every minute that led us to this moment. The kiss was the culmination of every glance, every whispered word, every moment of the push and pull we'd experienced over the past few weeks. The kiss began as a question, and as it deepened, it gave me the answer to the inquiry my heart had been quietly asking over the past few days: does he feel it, too? Does he feel our connection? His first kiss said yes; his second one was a hell yes. As the kisses grew, they evolved from something soft and tender to wilder and more untamed.

Nathan's hands fell to my lower back, which arched against his touch the second his tongue slid into my mouth. A pool of heat fell to my stomach as our kisses deepened with a growing passion, as if we were discovering a hidden world between our lips, and the only way to unlock our universe of make-believe was to become fully addicted to the taste of each other's mouths. I felt myself melting into him as his hands began to massage my lower back, a ravish want dripping down every inch of me.

I wrapped my hands around the bottom of his T-shirt and pulled it over his head, tossing it to the side of the room. My hands fell to his hardened chest, my fingers rolling over his abs, taking in every piece of his beautiful, tight skin, knowing that there was no going back from here. I wanted all of him. I wanted every piece of Nathan Pierce and our make-believe realm.

He pulled back slightly and locked his eyes with mine. There was a moment of uncertainty in his stare as he looked my way. I wasn't certain why until I realized he was waiting for me to give him permission to...me, to *us*.

I bit my bottom lip and nodded. "Please," I whispered, a sound coated with so much want that it felt intoxicating escaping my lips.

It was all he needed.

He placed his large hand on the nape of my neck and pulled me back to him, kissing me harder than before, fucking my mouth with all he had as he somehow figured out a way to stand us up from the floor with a one-arm lift, with me still wrapped around his body. He carried me down the hall, tossing my shirt off along the way. When we reached his bedroom, he dropped me onto his bed.

I scrambled to undo my pants as he unbuckled his belt and jeans. He slid out of them, revealing his black briefs that were holding the beast that rested within them.

Nathan. F**king. Pierce.

XX. F**king. L.

I tossed my pants to the side of the room and lay there in

my yellow silk panties and yellow bra. He stood over me for a moment and shook his head as he bit his bottom lip.

"Fuck," he murmured, walking over to me. "You're so damn beautiful, Avery Kingsley."

My heartbeat intensified as I sat up slightly on my elbows and combed my wild hair to one side. My cleavage was bursting from my bra as his eyes danced all over my figure. I'd never felt so safe with a man in my life. I'd never felt so wanted, either. Nathan stared at me as if I were the only thing that ever existed, and I stared at him the same way.

He grew closer and wrapped his hands around my waist. With one tug, he pulled me to the edge of the bed, making my legs hang over the edge. He raked his hand through my hair and then kissed me once. Slow this time, controlled, and sweetly. "Fucking beautiful," he mumbled once more before his mouth moved down my body, inch by inch. His left hand moved to my bra, and he unhooked it with one flick. As the straps fell down my arms, Nathan removed the fabric from my skin, catching my breasts in his hands. His mouth began to worship them both as if they were his goddesses, and his only job in life was to make love to each one.

He sucked on my nipples, making me moan as my want for him built more and more with every passing second. His hand pushed me back, so I was lying down on his bed as he continued to suck and nibble on my breasts as he growled against my skin. His kisses then continued to trail down as his hands remained on my breasts, massaging them.

As his mouth made it to the top edge of my panties, his hands moved down to my waist. His fingers wrapped around the fabric, and as he pulled it down, his mouth kissed every inch revealed to him. As the panties dropped to the floor, Nathan spread my legs, placing his hands against my inner thighs. The tingling sensation intensified as I felt his hot breaths sweeping against my core. His tongue swept against my clit, and he sucked it gently before he slid a finger inside me, feeling how wet he made me from his kisses alone. He slid another finger inside and began to pump them in and out at a speed that made my body arch in his direction. His mouth kept licking up every drip from me as his fingers worked in sync with his tongue.

More, more, more...

I cried out in bliss as his mouth devoured my core, making me feel things I didn't know I could feel from oral sex. The more I moaned and whimpered, the more he worked me, eating me out as if he were on a mission to swallow each drop.

The intensity of the orgasm kept building more and more with each fleeting moment, my body growing to the point of no return as I wrapped my legs around his shoulders, placed my hands against his head, and glided his mouth against my core.

"There, there, *ohmygoshthere!*" I screamed as I reached the peak of my orgasm as he kept working his mouth against me.

I lay breathless on his bed, every inch of me dripping in sweat as Nathan's hands stayed pressed against my thighs as I wiggled to get loose to recover from the best round of oral I'd ever experienced in my life.

My whole body trembled against him as he gently licked up any remaining evidence of what he did to me between my legs. I felt like nothing and everything all at once. A galaxy of stars floating in a black hole. I didn't know mouths could do what he'd done to me. I didn't know I could scream out in need, in want, or in pleasure the way I moaned his name out into the air. I didn't know tongues could fuck the way his fucked me.

"Okay, okay, okay." I gently giggled, pulling his head from between my legs. If he could, he'd probably keep eating me until the sun came up in the morning.

He smirked as he climbed over me. He pushed his hands to my sides, flexing every single muscle on his arms as he brushed his mouth against mine, allowing me to taste myself against his tongue. "Sorry. I have a big appetite, and I love the way you feed me," he said. "I love the way you drip for me."

"I want to feel you," I begged within a whisper. "*Please.*"

"That all depends."

"On what?"

A wicked smile found both his eyes and his lips as his shaft brushed against my clit. My whole body trembled from the shot of desire racing through my system. He moved in closer, a hand sitting at the nape of my neck. A deep growl escaped him as he said, "You still hate me, Coach?"

"No," I cried out.

Not even a little.

Not even a bit.

I couldn't form any more words as my hips arched up, wanting nothing less than his all.

"I want you to take all of me in, do you understand, Avery?" he asked as he removed his boxers and slid a condom over his hardness. His words felt like an order, and it was at that very moment I realized I was fine with being bossed around by Nathan Pierce.

"*Yesss...*" My voice fluttered, unstable and raw.

"Good girl," he purred over my lips as he began to inch into me. A gasp fell from my mouth as he kept feeding his inches deeper inside me. His mouth stayed pressed against mine as I tried to contain myself from his thickness. He growled as his whispers fell onto my tongue. "You're taking it so well. Keep your eyes on me," he ordered, placing a hand beneath my chin. He tilted my head up to make sure our eyes stayed locked. "Yeah, that's right...just like that..."

I whimpered as he thrust into me, filling me completely. My hips rocked as his hardness slid in and out. My breaths were uneven as they tried to keep up with our make-believe. For something not real, it sure felt that way. It felt *so, so very real*.

I wrapped my arms around his neck, begging for him to

keep going, to keep fucking me as if his life depended on it. If I didn't know better, I would've assumed his life did depend on how he fucked me because he didn't leave any space for error.

Without hesitation, he placed one of my legs over his shoulder, one hand against the headboard, and held his eye contact. The way he looked my way both excited and terrified me. He looked at me as if he planned to spend the rest of forever making sure I got off from his touches.

Each thrust felt personal like he were trying to break into my soul and leave his imprint. Our bodies moved as one. As my lungs gasped for air, his exhalations filled me back up. My hips rocked against him as he pumped himself deeper inside me, the sound of his pounding thrusts making me wetter and wetter. I was dripping for him, wanting nothing more than to release the orgasm building up inside me with every passing millisecond. I didn't even know I could come as many times as I could until that very night.

Nathan must've known I was close because the wicked smirk that fell against his lips was enough to show he was proud of his work. If I were in my sober, non-sexed-up mind, I would've called him a dick for having full control of me. But as I parted my mouth to speak, only mumbles came out. Jumbled-up, wannabe words that had no meaning as my eyes rolled to the back of my head due to the intensity of the pleasure taking place.

I dropped my hands from around his neck and dug my fingernails into his back, gliding him in more and more, faster and faster, deeper and deeper as the explosion of pleasure built with every passing second.

"I...we...it..." I stuttered, still unable to form any words.

"*Avery*," he breathed out as his mouth rediscovered mine. "Use your words to coach me through this, or better yet..." He bit my bottom lip and whispered, "Go ahead and fall apart against my cock."

That was enough to take me over the edge. I wrapped my legs around his body as I fell into the hardest, most intense orgasm of my life. I could've sworn my soul left my body for a moment's time and went on a smoke break to recover from the overwhelming sensation of pleasure I'd found myself taking part in.

"That's it, Ave, that's it. Give me all of it, give me all of you. I love feeling you come for me. That's my sweet girl."

Oh my goodness.

That man could talk dirty to me for the rest of my life, and it still wouldn't be enough.

After I fell apart, I made it my mission to get him to do the same. I flipped him over to his back and placed myself on top of him. It was now my turn to be the head coach.

I began riding him as my breasts bounced in his face. I gripped the headboard and held eye contact with Nathan the whole time. "Now it's time for you to be my good boy and let go for me," I cooed, rolling my hips slowly against his hardness. His eyes fluttered shut for a moment, and he muttered under his breath.

"Shit, Ave...wait, when you...fuck, I..." he stuttered.

There it was.

My control over him.

It felt good to know it went both ways.

I smirked when I felt him throbbing inside me. I leaned down toward him and brushed my lips against his as a whisper escaped me. "Hey, Coach..." I bit his bottom lip. "Give me all of you."

Within seconds, his eyes shot open, and he thrust into me, his body shaking as he reached his climax. Something was so good about watching what I'd done to him—something so rewarding about seeing how he completely surrendered himself to me. He lost himself for a moment as he found me.

I rolled my hips against him a few more times, loving how

he shivered beneath me, before climbing off and falling beside him.

Our breaths were uneven as we lay there, dripping in sweat from head to toe.

Something changed between us, yet I wasn't ready to unpack exactly what it meant.

At that moment, I simply wanted to be there fully, unafraid of what the future could bring.

Nathan sighed as he pulled me into the curvature of his body. "After that, I feel like I should smoke a cigarette and head to the kitchen to make you a sandwich," he joked.

I snickered and rested my head against his chest. Against his heartbeat. "Extra mayo, please."

He pulled back slightly and looked at me with wonderment in his eyes.

I raised my eyebrow. "What is it?"

"Nothing," he said, falling back to his pillow. "I'm just trying to figure it out."

"Figure what out?"

"How I lived all these years without you."

G et up, Avery.

No, no, no.

It wasn't supposed to go like that. Not after the night I shared with Nathan. I was supposed to wake up and be okay. I was supposed to wake up and crawl out of my bed and be on cloud nine from not only winning the game the day prior but also for having the best sex of my life.

I wasn't supposed to feel so...defeated.

But what if I'd made a mistake sleeping with Nathan? What if what we'd done changed everything? We were doing so good. There was no reason I should've let it get as far as it did the night before, but I wanted it so badly. I wanted *him* so badly.

Still...

Now my mind was trying to convince me of everything that could've gone wrong.

If you don't work out, the team could suffer, Avery.

Why would you let him back into your life after he left you before?

What happens now? You fall in love? Get real. You don't do love. People don't love you. People leave you.

My mind was getting louder and louder as I turned in the bed. I looked to my right, and Nathan was still lying beside me, his eyes closed.

A small smile sat against his lips as he muttered, "You up?"

I held my hands to my chest. "I am," I whispered. "Have you been awake for a while?"

"Yes, but I wanted to wake up with you." He opened his eyes and moved the falling pieces of my hair from my face. "Good morning."

I tried to push out a smile, but it faltered. "Morning."

He pushed himself up on his elbows and looked down at me. "What's wrong?"

"Nothing. Nothing. Everything's fine."

He frowned. He fell back down to the bed and moved in closer, brushing his nose against mine. "Avery...what's wrong? Was it last night?" Guilt flashed across his eyes. "Did you not want to—"

"No." I shook my head. "Last night was...perfect. It's not you, it's me."

"That's the last thing anyone wants to hear after a night of sex."

"No, I mean it. It's me, Nathan. I'm a little messed up sometimes."

"How so?"

"I don't know. I struggle to..." I took a deep breath and closed my eyes. "Sometimes it's hard."

"What's hard?"

I blinked my eyes open, and a few tears trailed down my cheeks. "*Everything.*"

The guilt that once laced his stare shifted to care and concern. And understanding. Maybe that soothed my troubled soul the most—the understanding of his stare. "Are you sad, Avery?"

"Yes."

"Do you know why?"

"No."

"But sometimes, is it hard for you to get out of bed?"

I nodded. "Yes."

"Okay." He moved in closer and wrapped his arms around me. "Then we'll stay in bed today."

———

HOURS PASSED of him holding me. He didn't complain for a second, even when I kept offering him my apologies.

"Don't worry," he told me as he pushed himself up to a sitting position. His back leaned against the headboard as he looked down at me. "There was a long period of my life when I couldn't get out of bed, either."

I sat up and leaned against the headboard. "You too?"

"Me too." He brushed his thumb against his nose. "After Mickey passed away, I couldn't get out of bed, no matter how hard I tried. Then even when I felt as if I should've been able to get up, I still couldn't. It was as if my mind was cementing my body into the bed. No matter how many good things happened, it was just hard to...exist."

"Yes," I agreed. "Just like that. How did you get through it?"

"I found my beams."

"Your beams? What does that mean?"

"My therapist told me that when I was going through my darkest moments. She told me to look for my sunbeams. She said that people who are sad often try to dive headfirst into feeling better. They go to extremes and try hard to climb out of the darkness to feel the sun's full burst of joy again. They try so hard to get back to a feeling from their past when they felt the happiness."

"Yeah. I do try to chase the high of past happy moments."

"Many people do. Then they crash and burn because it was too much, too soon, too hard. That leaves a feeling of even more depression because you're hard on yourself, and you feel as if you've failed, when really, you just went too hard, too soon. And it's not about chasing the past. It's about allowing a new future through finding your sunbeams."

"Break it down."

"The sunbeams are the small bursts of light that break through one's window of depression. The little flickers of light that remind you of how life can feel. Those sunbeams can be anything. People, places, activities. Mine was my family. Coming back home and working on the farm. Holding a baseball bat in my hands. Laughing with my brothers. To the outside world, these aren't big things, but to me...they got me to the next day. Over time, I started finding more beams of light. Things that filled me with joy. Over time, the light grew. It's not a constant thing. Some days, the beams are more abundant than others. But still, the light always comes in. So I think that's what you need to do. Find your beams of light."

"I like that thought," I whispered. "But what if I don't even have enough energy to get out of bed to shower?"

"Then your sunbeam is your ability to open your eyes and lay still."

I shut my eyes and slightly shook my head. "But I want to shower. I *need* to shower. This is so embarrassing to even admit."

"In the deepest parts of my depression, I went weeks without a shower and stayed hidden in a motel, Avery." His hand fell against mine. "Never be embarrassed with me."

As I opened my eyes, tears rolled down my cheeks. "Thank you, Nathan."

"Of course. If you'd like, I can carry you."

"Carry me?"

"To the bath. I can bathe with you and hold you through it."

I tried to let out a chuckle, but it fell short. "No, Nathan. You don't have to do that. You've already done too much, and I can't ask you to do that."

He moved a piece of hair from in front of my face, and a lazy smile fell to his lips. "Like I told you weeks ago, Ave. I'll take care of you."

A small sob broke through my lips as I let his words envelop me. I felt weak. Tired. Ashamed. And still, he smiled at me and said he'd take care of me.

His thumb brushed away a few of the tears. "Just say the word, and I'll draw a bath."

I closed my eyes and nodded. "Please," I requested.

His lips fell to my forehead, and he kissed me gently. "Always."

He climbed out of bed and headed out of my room. I listened to the sound of running water as I stayed exactly where he'd left me. About ten minutes later, he returned to the room and lifted me from the bed in his arms.

I laid my head against his shoulder as he walked me to his bathroom. The room was dark, and I appreciated that. Only a few candles glowed as he placed me down on my feet. He began to undress me slowly, pulling my T-shirt over my head before he took off my sweatpants. He removed my bra and panties without taking his stare away from my eyes. There was nothing sexual about the interaction, but the heavy level of intimacy filled me up. He then removed his own clothing. For a few seconds, we stood completely naked. I should've felt exposed, but instead, I felt safe. Protected. Free to be broken within his realm.

Nathan took my hands into his and led me to the tub. He helped me step in first, then he stepped into the tub behind me. His body wrapped around mine, and I fell into him as if he were the safety net I needed. He reached for the bath soap and washcloth as I closed my eyes and focused on my breathing. He began to clean my body all over, the warmth of the water feeling like a balm to my soul. He didn't speak, and I was thankful for the silence as he washed us both from head to toe. After a while, he let the water drain from the tub and turned on the overhead shower. He then washed my hair as we remained sitting in the tub.

Water crystals rolled down my cheeks as I kept my eyes shut the whole time. Nathan's hands massaged my scalp, getting the conditioner deep into the roots. As he rinsed it out, I wondered if he noticed my falling tears intermixing with the shower water flowing down my face.

If he did, he didn't say a word. Instead, he just made sure I was clean from head to toe.

When we finished, he shut off the water and climbed out of the tub. He wrapped a towel around his waist and retrieved two more towels from his towel warmer. He helped me stand and wrapped a towel around my body, then took another and wrapped it around my hair.

"Thank you," I whispered.

He smiled in reply before he lifted me into his arms and carried me back to my bedroom. He set me down on the edge of my bed, went into my drawers, and pulled out clean panties for me to slip into.

He held them beneath my feet and slid them up my body. He then went to my bathroom and grabbed my lotions from the counter. Without thought, he knelt in front of me and began to lotion me up from the tip of my toes all the way up to my neck. Every inch of me was moisturized. As his hands rolled over my breasts, I let out a small breath. The care he took was almost overwhelming.

He then left the room for a few moments. When he came back, he was wearing sweatpants and no shirt. He held a blow dryer and an oversized T-shirt of his. He slipped the T-shirt over my shoulders and then plugged in the blow dryer.

I removed the towel from my hair, and he sat behind me, placing me between his thighs, and dried it. My back brushed against his rock-hard abs as he did so, holding me in place.

Once he finished, he unplugged the blow dryer.

I figured he was done, but he headed back to my bathroom and grabbed my toothbrush along with a glass cup.

"Open," he said. I parted my lips, and he began to brush my teeth for me. After he finished, he held the glass up to my mouth and said, "Spit."

I spat out the paste in my mouth. He then headed back to the bathroom, rinsed out the glass, and came back.

He gave me that same lazy grin. "Can I hold you again?"

"Please do."

He climbed into bed with me and wrapped me in his arms. He didn't ask me to talk. He didn't ask me to be okay. He didn't ask me for anything. All he did was hold me.

And there it was...

My beam of light.

He stayed with me the whole day, feeding me meals, lying with me on the couch, and watching movies that I didn't pay attention to because I was too invested in looking at him. Whenever I looked at him, he was looking at me.

He asked me if I needed anything every second our eyes locked, and I'd shake my head and whisper a "no." He'd then give me his lazy smile, and I'd feel that smile vibrate against my heartbeat.

When nightfall came, he carried me to my bedroom. I lay in his arms as he kissed my forehead again before closing his eyes.

"Nathan?"

"Yeah?" he whispered, eyes still closed, halfway asleep.

"Thank you."

"For what?"

"Being my sunbeam today."

His tired eyes flickered open and locked with mine. His lips turned up in an exhausted grin, and he brushed them gently against mine, giving me the tiniest kiss that felt so big before he fell asleep.

I fell asleep, too, in his arms.

When I woke up, he was still there, holding me in his arms.

32

AVERY

The following morning, I showered on my own and came out of my bedroom to find Nathan cooking breakfast for me. I could get used to the current living arrangement.

When he turned to see me, he smiled. "Morning, sunshine."

"Morning." I moved over and gave him a small kiss. "Food smells good."

He buried his face against my neck, covering me in kisses. "You smell good."

We moved to the living room and did one of our favorite things—watched ESPN with our plates in our hands. After we finished, Nathan turned to me. His eyes were slightly somber, and I could tell something was up.

"What's wrong?" I asked.

"I want to give you something, but I'm not sure if you'll think I'm an asshole."

I narrowed my eyes. "That lead-in makes me nervous."

He slipped a hand into his back pocket and pulled out a business card. "It's the name of the wellness clinic I went to in Chicago when I was going through a hard time after losing

Mickey and my injury. My therapist was amazing and helped me get back on my feet. Yet they have a lot of different, extremely talented individuals. Some of the best in the industry. I still go bimonthly. Just wanted to offer that up to you if you ever want to speak to someone other than me."

I smiled shyly as I took the card from him. "Thank you, but I don't think I can afford the same level of treatment that an MLB all-star receives."

"Don't worry about the cost. I'll cover it."

I shook my head. "No, Nathan, I can't let you—"

"I'll cover it," he assured. "You don't worry about that. I just want you to feel the best you can. That's all that matters to me."

"Oh no..." I murmured, moving closer to him. "You must really like me a lot if you want me to be mentally stable, huh?" I joked.

The seriousness in his eyes remained. "I like you so damn much that it scares me, Avery Kingsley. I'm around you all day, and then I still dream about you, too."

Butterflies.

Butterflies and Nathan Pierce.

"Thank you," I breathed out, glancing down at the card in my hand, because looking into his eyes was becoming too intense. "I don't know if I'm ready yet, but I'll keep this in mind. Is that okay?"

"More than," he agreed. "When you're ready, just say the word, and I'll get everything in order," he said, kissing my forehead.

I didn't know it was possible for forehead kisses to feel like the ultimate kind of affection until that very moment in time.

EACH DAY THAT PASSED, I found myself falling more and more for Nathan. On my dark days, he made me smile, and on my bright days, he made me laugh. It was becoming harder and harder to ignore the feelings developing in my chest for that man.

I sat in my bed, flipping through social media late one Saturday night. I knew Nathan was out with his brothers in Chicago to celebrate Evan's and Easton's birthdays, but I still wished he was home. Never in my life did I think I'd get to the point of missing having him around on the regular.

The house seemed lonelier without his voice bouncing off the walls.

It was around two in the morning when I heard him stumble inside. He must've run into the coffee table or something because I heard him holler, "Fuck!" after a big thump sound.

I snickered at the idea of him being wasted out of his mind. That was what he got for hanging out with his younger brothers. He couldn't keep up with those guys.

"Ouch!" he muttered once more as he crashed into something else.

A few moments later, a text message popped up on my screen.

NATHAN
Your light's on. You up?

AVERY
I am.

There was a knock on my door.

"Come in," I said.

He turned the knob and opened the door. He stood there shirtless, with his belt undone and his jeans unzipped, revealing his black boxers. He placed his hands on the top of the doorframe, revealing every muscle tensing against his body.

"Hey, Coach," he whispered.

I smiled. "Hey, you. You're drunk?"

"Wasted. Took a taxi home. Rest of the guys stayed at my penthouse in the city."

"Why did you come back?"

He bit his bottom lip. "I missed you."

"Don't say that."

"Too real?"

I nodded. "Too real."

"I missed you," he repeated.

Heart skips and butterflies.

I sighed. "I just said don't say that to me."

"I wasn't talking to you," he swore as he drew closer. He pulled my blanket off and placed a hand between my thighs, separating my legs. His thumb brushed against the fabric of my silk panties. "I was talking to her."

A slight moan slipped from me as he edged the fabric of my panties to the side so his finger could massage my core.

My eyes fluttered shut as I shook my head. "You're trouble."

"You like it."

I loved it.

Before I could reply, he lowered himself to the floor, getting on his knees. He wrapped his arm around me and pulled me over to the edge of the bed.

"Nathan"—I laughed—"what are you doing?"

"*You*," he replied with that wicked grin on his face. "I'm doing you. I was out all night thinking about coming home to you."

"It sounds like you're an addict."

He began to pull my panties down my thighs, trailing kisses along my inner thighs as he did so. "I never want to sober up from this," he swore before he slid a finger inside me.

Within seconds, my body reacted, my back arching in his direction.

He placed a hand against my shoulder and gently laid me

back down. "*Relax.* Take it easy... Get comfortable," he said. "I'll take care of you from here on out."

He spent the next few minutes getting me off, and when he finished, he licked his fingers clean. I tried to offer him a happily ever after ending to his night, too, but he said he just wanted to please me before falling asleep with me in his arms.

He stood and took off his clothes, turned off the light, and crawled into bed with me.

As he wrapped himself around me, he said, "I missed you."

"Talking to her again?" I joked.

He shook his head. "No. Not this time. Night, Coach."

"Good night," I muttered as my heart did a few cartwheels before falling asleep that night.

33

NATHAN

verything about Avery drove me wild in the best of
ways. That woman did things to my mind—and body
—that would leave me reminiscing for days after.
Outside of that, she was just a remarkable person. She was a
brilliant sister and daughter. A loyal friend. An outstanding
coach. I didn't think she knew how impressive she had been,
either. Whenever someone complimented Avery, she shrugged
it off quickly, never wanting the attention on her for too long.

Now that our team was doing so well, people were showing
up to our games, wanting to interview her and find out what
her secret had been. She hardly ever did interviews unless the
guys were being interviewed. She liked to be there with them to
make sure their words weren't taken out of context. She was a
very protective mama bear when it came to our guys, and she
wasn't afraid to bite if someone crossed the line.

I loved that about her.

I loved a lot of things about her.

Finding a list of qualities that made that woman lovable
wasn't hard. I saw it at the farm, too. When she wasn't working
at the high school, she was helping my mom, River, and Grant

around the farmland. Or she was making up goodies with Priya. My favorite moments were when I'd come home from checking in with our local restaurants to find Avery wearing some barn boots while milking cows, collecting eggs, and hanging out with the horses. The farm life looked good on her.

Sometimes I'd get a little bit jealous if I'd find her laughing a little too hard at River's or Grant's jokes. Those fuckers weren't *that* funny. It was like they went out of their way to make her laugh. It made my skin crawl.

Any man who looked at her a little too long made my whole system heat with rage. It wasn't shocking, though. Avery was the most beautiful woman in the world. It was no secret to anyone with eyes. And now that she wasn't with Wesley, it was a known thing to the men of Honey Creek that she was a free agent—at least to their knowledge.

Yet she wasn't free.

She was mine.

At least, in a way.

We'd never talked about it, but the more I saw men drool over her, the more I knew that conversation was needed. Besides, I didn't want to just be her friends-with-benefits anymore. I wanted to be her everything, just as I wanted her to be mine. I didn't know how she felt about the whole thing, especially since she had been about to be someone's wife not even that long ago, but I knew if I fucked up another chance to be with her, to have her by my side, I'd never forgive myself for missing that opportunity.

Avery Kingsley was all I'd ever wanted, and for some reason, the universe gave me another chance at her heart.

The last thing I wanted to do was strike out on that chance.

If she allowed me to be hers, I'd be hers forever.

Even if she didn't...I'd be hers forever.

I had my mind made up. It was either Avery for me or no one.

Now, all I had to do was build up the courage to come to her about it and ask her to be mine. I knew I'd hate myself for the rest of my life if I didn't.

ONE SATURDAY NIGHT, after she finished working at O'Reilly's, I waited in the living room for her to come home. When the front door opened, I stood.

Avery's smile stretched. I loved that lately, she smiled instead of grimacing when she saw me. "Isn't it past your bedtime, old man?" she asked.

I nodded and slid my hands into my sweatpants pockets. "It is."

"Let me guess." She tossed her keys and purse on the foyer table. "You're still sad at how badly our team lost the game earlier today?"

"No, that's not it."

She kept smiling as she took off her shoes before walking toward me. "You ate spicy food and got heartburn?"

I shook my head. "Nope. Not it."

She arched an eyebrow and placed her hands on her waist. "You had nightmares and needed a cuddle buddy?"

"Nah. Not that."

She narrowed her eyes. Her playful look grew somber as she stepped closer. "Are you okay? What's wrong?"

I brushed my thumb against the bridge of my nose. "I'm falling for you, Avery."

Her lips parted, but no words came out. So I continued.

"It's not shocking because you're you, but I don't think it's fair for me to bring this up without also bringing up our past. And I know I promised you early on that we wouldn't talk about our past, but the more I fall for you, the more I understand that our past was a defining moment for us that still needs to be ironed out."

"Nathan…"

"That is, unless you don't feel yourself falling for me. If you don't feel it, say it now, and I'll bury these feelings and deal with them on my own. If you don't feel the same way, I'll swallow my pride and never bring this up again. But if there is even a slight chance that you feel the same way for me, just tell me to go on."

Her eyes flashed with complex confusion for a moment before she moved to the couch. She sat down, crossed her legs, and placed her hands in her lap. "Go on," she whispered.

A slight breath of relief slipped through my lips as I moved over to her. I sat down on the coffee table in front of her and clasped my hands together. "I loved you back then, Ave. I know you probably doubted that because of how things went down, but I did. We only connected for a short period of time, on the diamond and off, but during that season of my life, you were the best thing that happened to me. Losing you was the hardest thing that I ever had to deal with."

"Then why?" she asked. "Why did you let me go?"

"I was a mess. My family's farm wasn't doing well. No one knew that except for my father. He got into a bit of gambling issues and owed some guys a lot of money. As you know, he and I had a rocky relationship. He, um, was my greatest hero and my biggest villain. I never understood how that could be the same person. How the person in charge of my biggest highs could also be the cause of my lowest lows. How he could be my cheerleader and my opponent. But that's who he was to me. The only reason I took up baseball was to be closer to my father, and then I realized that no matter how good I became, I wouldn't get him to love me the way I wanted to be loved. His love came with conditions, and his goalpost kept moving. He was proud of me for seconds until he saw someone doing better than me. Then he'd expect more from me.

"You were the part of my life where I could be myself fully. The good and the bad. About a week after I realized how deep and real my feelings were for you, he and I got into the biggest fight. I told him I didn't want to play for the pros. I didn't want to pack up my life and sign a contract for something that would take me away from you. He had a heart attack that night."

"That was the night he passed away?"

I nodded. "Yeah. Needless to say, I blamed myself for it and took it as my responsibility to care for my family. I pushed you away because I thought I had no choice. I thought I'd let my whole family down if I didn't do what my father wanted or fully focus on my career. It was his dying wish for me, and I handled it awfully."

Her eyes were soft with compassion as she placed a hand against my forearm. "Nathan...I would've understood all this. I just wish you would've communicated that with me instead of cutting me off so abruptly. You left and never looked back. You wrote me out of your life without giving me any reason as to why. It was unexpected and harsh."

"I know. I was grieving, and young, and scared. I didn't think it through. And by the time I did, I figured I missed my opportunity. I didn't think it was right for me to try again with you after I blew it so massively. But I do owe you the biggest apology for how things ended, Avery. You deserved more, and I'm sorry for how I handled it."

She smiled gently. "Thank you for that. I've waited a long time to hear you say those words."

"It took too long for me to say them." I cleared my throat and rubbed the back of my neck. "My mom believes that each person has three big regrets in life. Three defining moments in a person's life. If they had the chance, they would've gone back and changed the choices they'd made. My three include that final conversation I had with my father, the night I went out to drink instead of staying with Mickey, and the night I ended things with you. Losing you, Avery, is one of my top three regrets."

She stayed quiet for a moment, studying me. I was trying my best to read her mind and tap into the thoughts flying through her brain. Yet all I could do was wait for her to say something, anything. I wouldn't blame her if she didn't want to give me another chance. I wouldn't be shocked if she thought this was too much. Yet I needed to hear her say it. I needed her to push me away so I could officially let her go. Though, a part of me figured that a woman like Avery wasn't something a person just let go of.

I figured that no matter what, she'd always linger within my heart.

There was no other woman for me. It was Avery Kingsley or no one.

She reached for me, holding her hands in my direction. I gave her my hands, and she took them into hers. She slowly raised them to her lips and kissed my palms gently before pulling me over to her to join her on the couch. She bit her bottom lip, nervously breaking her stare away from mine. Then she looked up at me. Those brown eyes that I loved so much smiled more than her lips. "If I let you in this time, Nathan, you have to promise you'll stay."

I pulled her closer to me. "I swear."

"I'm scared," she confessed, her voice slightly cracking as those two words fell from her tongue.

"I know." I took her palms and kissed them gently. "Me too."

"But I want to try." She nodded slowly. "I want to try to be us again with you. But the grown-up version of us that communicates our feelings, no matter how big or little they may be. Because this feels good," she swore, placing my hands against her chest, where her heartbeat fell against my touch. "This feels right."

"I promise I'll do whatever it takes to keep you, Ave. I promise you all that I have. I was an idiot back then, and I'm pretty sure I still have idiot moments now, but I will spend the rest of my life making up for my past mistakes and proving to you that I'm fully here for this. For us."

"Well, then, what are you waiting for?" she asked. "Kiss me, you idiot."

And so I did.

34

NATHAN

For the next few days, thunderstorms rolled through Honey Creek. After a Saturday practice, I ran out to my car to avoid getting drenched in the rain. I hopped into my vehicle quickly and put the car into drive. The rain was coming down hard, making me take the roads a little slower than normal. As I was driving, I noticed a boy walking on the side of the road with a duffel bag over his head.

The closer I grew, the faster I realized it was one of my guys. I pulled the car over to the curb, rolled down my window, and shouted, "Cameron. What are you doing?!"

He turned toward me, soaked head to toe, and shook some water away from his blond hair. "Hey, Coach P. My dad forgot to pick me up. I was just walking home."

I put my car in park, leaned over to the passenger door, and swung it open. "Get in."

He hurried over and hopped inside, dropping his duffel bag into his lap as he slammed the door shut. I rolled the window up for him as he buckled his seat belt. "Thanks, Coach P."

"No problem."

"Normally, when he forgets to get me, it's not raining that bad, so the walk doesn't suck so much."

"Does he forget you a lot?"

Cameron went quiet for a second before shrugging. "He's had a lot on his plate since my mom passed away last year."

"Oh...I had no clue, Cameron. I'm sorry."

He nodded. "Yeah. It sucks." He cleared his throat and raked a hand through his wet hair. "I'm good, though. Not a big deal. I live about ten minutes from here. I'm on the outside of town." He gave me his address, and I plugged it into my GPS.

"I've seen your dad at the games," I mentioned. "He shows up to all of them."

Cameron huffed. "If you consider that showing up."

I tried to push out a smile, but reality wouldn't allow it. Cameron's father was a drunk. He was always the loudest one in the stands, shouting out rude commentary toward his son whenever he was up to bat. He had a lot of damn nerve acting the way he had in public. It wasn't shocking that Cameron had stage fright when it came to the game when the person who was supposed to be his biggest cheerleader was his biggest villain in the stands.

"My dad used to heavily drink, too, you know. He'd show up to my baseball games and embarrass the living shit out of me."

"Yeah? How did you deal with it?"

"Tried my best to ignore it. Focused on the game in front of me and not on my wasted, unstable parent."

"Did he ever get himself together?" he asked.

I shook my head. "Unfortunately, he passed away from alcoholism. The drinks finally caught up to him. He didn't even get to see me play in my first big league game. Even though he was the reason I got into baseball."

"Yeah? My dad is why I play, too. When I was younger, it was the one thing we connected to each other with."

"Same with me and my dad. I was his oldest, and he tried to

make me into his puppet. I had no problem with it, though, because I thought my father was the coolest person in the world. When he was sober, at least. When our family farm started to go to shit, he put a lot more pressure on me to perform better, to get the big contract to help take care of my family."

"I get that kind of pressure, too."

"Yeah. I figured." I glanced over at him before looking back at the road. "Can I give you some advice I wish someone would've given me when I was your age?"

"Sure."

"It's not your responsibility to parent your parents. It's your job to be a kid as long as possible."

"Easier said than done."

"Yeah," I agreed. "Unfortunately, I know that, too."

As we approached his house, I noticed Cameron's dad standing at the door of his car, fumbling with his car keys.

The amount of embarrassment that crept over Cameron's face took me back to my own childhood. I knew that feeling. The humiliation of others seeing your father drunk and stumbling.

I pulled into the driveway and put my car in park.

"He wasn't always like this, you know," Cameron stated softly. "Not before my mom died."

I placed a hand against his shoulder. "Then maybe he'll figure it out and turn the ship around. There's always hope if we're still breathing."

He gave me a lazy smile and nodded. "Yeah. He'll get there. I know it. Thanks, Coach P," Cameron said before he hurriedly got out of my car and tossed his duffel bag over his shoulder. He headed over to his dad, patted him on the back, and the realization that Cameron had made it home was shown all over his father's face.

His father dropped the keys again. Cameron picked up the

keys and then placed a hand on his father's back. Adam reacted harshly and shoved Cameron as he tried to get his keys. Cameron went stumbling backward, hitting the ground hard.

I flew out of my car and shouted, "Hey! Take it easy!"

"What the fuck do you want?" Adam slurred, his words dripping with confusion. He looked so drunk that he didn't even realize we were there.

"Get back in my car, Cam," I ordered.

"I'm sorry, Coach P," Cameron said as he pushed himself up to a standing position.

"It's fine. You'll stay with me tonight. Keep his keys," I told him. "He shouldn't be driving anywhere tonight. I'll get him back inside."

Cameron looked at his father, then at me. He nodded slowly. "Yeah, okay."

I dragged Adam back inside the house. He didn't make it easy, but I was much stronger than him. I plopped him down on the couch, and he muttered slightly before he lay down and passed out.

I headed back to my car and hopped into the driver's seat.

"Thanks, Coach. I'm sorry again about that..." Cameron stated.

"Don't be sorry. It's fine."

I'd been Cameron before. I used to apologize to my team-mates for my dad's outbursts at games. I used to be ashamed when he'd get locked up for DUIs, and everyone in town would talk about it. I used to give the same waves of heartbreak to my own coaches.

No kid should've had to deal with that kind of situation at home. It was clear from the small interaction who was parenting who.

I just hoped Cameron's father could figure it out in time before leaving his son with too many dark memories.

35

AVERY

I sat confused as Nathan approached the house with Cameron beside him. I arched an eyebrow as the two walked into the living room, where I'd been watching a movie. I stood and crossed my arms over my chest.

"What's going on?" I asked.

Cameron had a duffel bag over his shoulder and a look of defeat in his eyes. "Hey, Coach K. You and Coach P live together?" he questioned. "Are y'all dating?"

"What? No. No." I shook my head. "I needed a place to crash after the whole wedding situation. Coach P was just helping me out." I narrowed my eyes. "What's going on here?"

Nathan patted Cameron on the back. "Cameron, too, needed a place to crash for a short period of time. Cam, you can take my room for the night."

"Oh no, Coach P. I'm fine sleeping on the couch or something. I don't want to put you out."

"Two doors down on your right," Nathan said, gently guiding Cameron down the hallway. Cameron gave me a broken grin before walking off, leaving me there, perplexed.

"What's going on?" I whispered to Nathan, taking a few steps closer to him. "Is he okay?"

"I doubt it, but he'll be fine. I found him walking home in the rain, picked him up, and his dad had a full-blown meltdown. He was screaming at Cameron. Even took a few swings at him. I was going to call the cops, but Cam begged me not to. He said he didn't want his dad to get into trouble."

"That man has been a loose cannon for a while now."

"Yeah. Makes me worry that he might abuse Cameron when no one's around, but I could tell that he really didn't want me to call the cops on his father. He said he couldn't lose his dad, too."

That tugged at my heart. I knew Cameron's mother, Erika. She was a stand-up woman and went above and beyond to support her son. When I heard she had passed away, my heart broke for Cameron. He was a mama's boy through and through. I knew what that was like. Losing my mom was a defining moment for me. Even though I was young, it still shaped the person I'd become. I figured loving someone so much and then losing them was why I didn't allow myself to fall so deeply with others. Why I didn't connect with many people. The fear of loss was very strong within me.

"I feel like I should leave," I said, glancing in the direction that Cameron headed. "You're his coach. That's one thing. I'm his coach and his teacher. I don't want any rumors to start swirling about the situation."

"It's fine. He's exhausted, and he's just going to sleep tonight. I'm going to sleep on the couch. No one will know come morning when I take him to school. It's all good." He must've noticed my unease because he placed a hand against my shoulder and squeezed softly. "I promise it's going to be okay, Avery."

I nodded, somehow trusting that he was telling the truth. I didn't know when I began to trust his words so much, but lately, they felt like a warm blanket of comfort resting over me whenever my mind began to overthink.

"I should check in on him. Get him some dinner, maybe," I said.

"I'll handle the food. You go check on him."

I did as I was told and walked down to Nathan's bedroom, where Cameron was staying. I knocked twice on the open door.

Cameron was sitting on the edge of the bed, fiddling with his hands. He looked up and pushed out a tired smile. "Hey, Coach K."

"Hey. Can I come in?"

He nodded.

I walked over and grabbed the chair from Nathan's desk. I pulled it over to Cameron and took a seat in front of him. "Coach P was telling me some of the stuff that's been happening with your dad."

He blew out a breath and waved me off. "Oh, yeah. It's no big deal. Dad just had a bad night tonight. Nothing major. I actually don't even know why Coach P thought I should come over here tonight. It's all good."

"It's okay if it's a big deal, Cam. You don't have to downplay it."

He laughed and shrugged. He didn't look at me, though. His head stayed low as he tapped his feet repeatedly against the carpeted floor. "Nah. Everything's fine. Dad just needs to sleep it off tonight. He'll be better in the morning."

I reached out a hand and placed it on his forearm. "Cam."

He shoved off my hand and stood. "No, you know what? I should probably get back home to him. I bet he's worried about me. He didn't mean what he did, Coach K. That's not my dad. My dad would never..." His voice cracked as he began pacing the bedroom. His hands sat on top of his head. "My dad would never say that kind of shit to me, you know? My dad would never hurt me. My dad would never piss himself and pass out from being a hot fucking mess. My dad would never hit me. No. Not my dad." His voice began to rise as the reality of his situation built more and more with each word that stumbled from his tongue. "My dad would never call me a dumbass for fucking up on a math text. My dad would help me. My dad would coach me through it. My dad wouldn't lose his job. My dad wouldn't miss our mortgage payments. He wouldn't snap at me for forgetting to pay the light bill for him. He wouldn't push me. He wouldn't fucking push me, Coach K. He wouldn't hit me because I'm stupid." He smacked the side of his head. I cringed and shot to my feet. "He wouldn't hit me because I struck out." He smacked himself again. "He wouldn't, he wouldn't, he wouldn't..." he said, smacking himself repeatedly as the tears began to stream down his face.

I didn't know what to do other than to rush over to him and grab his arms to stop him from hitting himself. I pulled his arms to his sides as he tried his best to go back to beating on himself. My heart broke into a million pieces as he began to break down completely. "That's not my dad, Coach K. I don't know who that is, but he's not my dad. Because my dad wouldn't...he wouldn't..." His breaths weaved in and out as the reality of his world began to seep in. How his father was currently far from the man Cameron once knew.

I wrapped him in my arms as he began to crumple. Each sob that ripped through his system made my eyes water. I held him so tight, not only so he wasn't able to hit himself, but so he could also feel me. So he could realize he wasn't alone, even as he cracked.

After a while, his body relaxed against mine, his buckling knees sending him to the floor as he cried. I fell with him, still holding on, still knowing that he needed the reminder that if he went down, I'd go with him.

"Why did she do that, Coach K?" he sobbed, grabbing the fabric of my hoodie and resting his head against my shoulder.

"Why did she have to die? She ruined everything. She ruined fucking everything, and I'm so sick of missing her. I'm so fucking pissed that I have to miss her for the rest of my fucking life," he cried.

I held him tighter because I knew that feeling.

I knew it too well.

I knew it too deeply.

The feeling of resentment for a loved one dying. The feeling of abandonment. The feeling of emptiness.

No child should've lost a parent at such a young age. It was unfair and cruel of life to allow such things to happen.

I noticed Nathan appear in the doorway. His beautiful brown eyes were packed with worry and concern. He started to walk toward us, but I shook my head and mouthed, "He'll be okay."

I meant it, too.

If I knew anything about healing, it was the fact that sometimes one had to fall apart before they could fall back together again.

I held Cameron that night for as long as he allowed me. It could've been forty-five minutes. It could've been an hour. I didn't know. I wasn't counting. I was just holding him. Letting him know that he wasn't alone.

36

NATHAN

When Avery came out of my bedroom, she shut the door behind her. When she turned to face the hallway, she found me sitting against the wall across from my room.

Her eyes were teary, but she smiled a little. Not the happy kind of smile, though. The kind of smile that broke hearts.

I stood. "You okay?" I asked.

She parted her lips to speak, but instead of words, a small whimper fell from her. She shut her eyes and shook her head as she whispered, "That poor boy." Her hand covered her mouth as she began to cry, and I wrapped my arms around her, pulling her into me. "It's not fair." She quietly cried against my shoulder blade. "It's not fair."

WE WENT into her bedroom to talk, closing the door behind us. I sat on her bed beside her as she fiddled with her fingers.

"I feel like a shitty person for not paying close enough attention to him after he lost his mom. I think maybe I avoided it because I feared it would unlock some hard emotions within me, and I wasn't ready to face those feelings. It was selfish of me," Avery whispered.

"You're human. You also didn't know everything that he was going through."

"Yeah, but I should've noticed. I should've pieced it all together."

"You can't beat yourself up for not knowing, Ave. That's not fair to anyone. And when he needed you the most tonight, you were there. Those are the moments that matter."

She sighed and allowed her head to fall against my shoulder. I wrapped my arm around her waist and pulled her in closer. "I was ten when my mom passed away."

"You never told me what happened with her."

"That's because it's still one of the hardest things to speak about." She bit her bottom lip. "She passed away from complications during labor with Willow. I'll never forget when Daddy told us the news. Our grandmother was staying with us while he was at the hospital with Mama. Yara and I were so excited about having a new sister any time now, yet I didn't fully understand what it meant when Daddy came home with Willow and without Mama. The look in his eyes will forever be burned into my memory. I remember him setting down in the car seat with sweet Willow resting inside it.

"I remember Grandma's whimpers as she covered her mouth in disbelief. I remember Yara moving to Willow with a big smile and a bracelet she'd made for our little sister. I remember her asking where Mama was. I remember Daddy crashing down to the floor—just as Cameron did. I remember him calling Yara and me over to him. I remember him telling us he loved us. He kept saying that. He kept saying that he loved us. And then I asked him when Mama was coming home. I asked if she had to stay at the hospital to get better. He just cried more and told me that he loved us so much."

"I'm so sorry, Avery..." The words fell from my tongue, but they felt empty. Condolences didn't do much at the end of the day. They didn't bring back the ones who were lost. They didn't heal the cracks within one's spirit.

She wiped her tears. "It was traumatic. On top of that, we had a newborn baby in the house that needed all of Daddy's attention. He didn't even get to grieve properly because he knew he still had to raise three daughters."

"I still think your father is one of the strongest men I've ever come across."

"Oh gosh." She blew out a big breath. "Everything I know about love, I've learned from my father. He's not even my biological father, but you could never tell me any different. I am his, and he is mine. He's Superman. He's the definition of what a real man is, but still, he's only human. Sometimes, I'd wake up from hearing Willow crying, and I'd sneak into the nursery to find him sitting in the rocking chair, crying tears against her face as he sang her mama's favorite lullabies. He'd be whispering..." She placed a hand against her heartbeat, shaking her head slowly. "He'd be whispering to her that she was loved, too. So deeply loved and how he was so thankful that she existed."

I listened to every word Avery said to me that night. Every syllable of her story that she hadn't shared with me before. I took her in—all of her, all her soul—wanting nothing more than to know every piece that made her into the woman she'd become.

"I avoided Willow for a long time," she confessed. "I hated her for a while because I thought she was why I no longer had a mother. I blamed her for stealing that from me and for not having a mom to hug each night. For not having a mama to say prayers over me each night before I went to sleep. That was until Daddy came to me one night and asked if I wanted to hold Willow. I told him no. He asked me why, and I told him the truth. I told him that I hated her and wanted nothing to do with her. I saw how that broke his heart."

"What did he tell you?"

"He said Willow was a gift from Mama. That in her eyes, I could see my mother forever. That Willow's laughs were Mama's giggles. That her cries were Mama's tears. He then told me how blessed I was to have known Mama the longest out of all of us. Before Mama was theirs, she was mine alone. Then he told me how special that made me. Because Mama's imprint was on Willow, yes, but I was covered in Mama's memories. And he told me how special it would be if I shared that with Willow. If the mama in me could kiss the mama within her. So that very night, when Willow woke up crying, I went to her nursery and held her close to me. I fed her as Daddy stood back and watched me. I kissed her forehead and said the prayers that Mama used to pray over me, over her. From that moment on, Willow was the living image of my mother's love. I couldn't believe I avoided her for as long as I did because she was, and still is, something so special. I couldn't imagine life without her. A world without Willow is like a world without air."

I grinned, feeling grateful that she shared so much of her story that evening, even though it was probably hard for her to do.

"Sorry," she blurted out, wiping her tears. "I don't know why I just told you all that. It kind of poured out. I never pour out my heart like that. I'm sorry."

"I'm not complaining. Thank you for sharing. I know that's not the easiest for you."

"You made it easy tonight." She smiled gently. "Thank you for listening. I should get some sleep, though. I'm exhausted. I would offer to let you sleep in here, but I don't want Cameron getting the wrong idea."

"Understandable." I kissed her forehead. "I'll see you in the morning."

I got off the bed and started for the door.

"Nathan?" she called.

"Yeah?"

"Do you think Cameron will be okay? Do you think he can get through this?"

"I do. He's strong. And on the days he can't be, we'll make sure to be there in his corner. We're better together."

Her smile wasn't heartbreaking anymore. There was a flash of hope resting against her lips this time. "Okay. Good."

"And Avery?"

"Yes?"

"If you ever need to pour out your heart again, please pour it onto me."

37

AVERY

I learned a few things about my third Sunday morning when it came to staying at Honey Farms. The first being get up early or be awakened by a loud ass rooster screaming outside your window.

"What the heck is going on?!" Cameron asked as he emerged from Nathan's bedroom, rubbing the sleep from his eyes.

I stood in the kitchen, pouring myself a cup of coffee. "Morning, slugger." I held the cup out toward him. "You drink coffee?"

"I do today," he mumbled, taking the mug from me. He picked up the creamer on the countertop and poured some into his coffee. "What's with the rooster?"

"It's Sunday Funday on the Farm," I explained. "Trust me, it's not as annoying as it sounds. The Pierce family all heads out early as heck to get a round of baseball in on their diamond before going to the garden to pick out vegetables and such for a big brunch. The winner gets to relax as the loser gets to cooking."

Cameron blankly stared at me before taking a sip of his coffee. "They do this every Sunday?"

"Every third."

"And the rooster only crows on Sunday mornings at the ass crack of the morning?" he asked.

"Oh, that's not a rooster," I started. The back door opened, and in came Nathan, wearing his old baseball uniform. He tossed a ball up and down in his hand. "That's Coach P."

"*Cock-a-doodle-doo!*" Nathan shouted, walking over to Cameron. He patted him on the back with triple-shot of espresso type energy. "Are you ready for some baseball?"

"Uh, you can actually take me home—" Cameron started, but Nathan cut that off quickly.

"Nope. You slept over, which means you take part in Sunday festivities. We needed an extra player anyway. So you get to pick. Are you on Team K or Team P?" Nathan asked, gesturing between me and him. "Fair warning, I will be butthurt if you choose Coach K over me."

Cameron snickered a little. "Sorry, Coach P. I gotta go with my original coach this go-round, seeing how she wasn't cock-a-doodling in my ear at a crazy hour this morning."

I beamed with pride over the fact that I was chosen over Nathan.

"Suck on that one, Nathan," I said, smug as ever.

"Don't get too cocky about it. You'll both lose, which means you'll be cooking a huge brunch for thirty people."

"Thirty people?!" Cameron gasped. "You have that many people coming over for a baseball game?"

"Not just any game. It's Sunday Funday on the farm! All my aunts, uncles, and cousins will be here for the game. You might want to go warm up for a while. Avery pulled a muscle during her first game because she didn't know how seriously we took this sport."

"Don't let him get in your head, Cam. We got this one in the bag."

"Uncle Nate! My dad is asking you if you have his lucky glove. He said he left it in your—" Priya came barging into the house and paused the moment she saw Cameron standing there. Her eyes widened as she froze in place. "You're Cameron Fisher."

He gave her the kind of smile that would've made any teenage girl go wild. "Yeah. Do I know you?"

"Oh, no. Gosh, no. Of course not. You're Cameron Fisher, after all. I'm just me. I mean, Priya. I mean, I am me, I am Priya Pierce. I'm a sophomore. You're a junior, so it's not shocking that you don't know me, but, well, I know you, and well." Priya's cheeks flushed with a red shade. "Well, I know I don't *know* you, but I know of you. I mean, everyone knows who you are. You're like...a big deal."

Cameron raked his hand through his messy hair and gave her another of his golden boy smiles. One that was almost strong enough to get poor, shy Priya pregnant. He held a hand toward her. "It's nice to meet you, Priya."

Nathan's eyes narrowed as he darted his stare back and forth between the two teenagers. The energy in the space was strong and vibrant, sending Uncle Nathan into a panic. As Priya reached out to shake Cameron's hand, Nathan stepped between them, stopping the connection from taking place.

"All right, that's enough. Priya, here's my keys. Go get your dad's glove from my car. Cameron, go take a damn shower with your greasy-ass hair," Nathan ordered.

"I like your hair," Priya chimed in.

Cameron smiled bigger.

That kid deserved to smile. It also tickled me that Nathan was nearing a strong panic attack from the idea of his niece flirting with Cameron.

Nathan shoved Priya and Cameron away from each other,

leaving me standing there sipping my coffee with a goofy grin. Nathan walked over to me and grumbled as he poured himself a mug of coffee.

"Can you believe that? What was that all about? All the googly eyes and stuff?" He grimaced as he sipped the black coffee. "That was highly inappropriate."

"How so?" I laughed. "They are around the same age. I thought it was cute."

"*Cute?*" he barked, rolling his eyes. "It's not cute how Cameron tried to put his hands all over my poor, sweet baby niece. The girl's hardly out of diapers, and here he is trying to hold her hand."

"I hate to break it to you, but those aren't diapers in Priya's bathroom. They're tampons."

He pointed a stern finger my way. "Watch your words, Avery Kingsley. My niece is still a little girl."

"Not so little. I think it's sweet that she and Cameron had a moment there. I recall having the same kind of moments with a handsome boy when I was around her age, too."

He narrowed his brows. "Are you talking about me?" he grumbled.

I lightly shoved his shoulder. "I'm talking about you."

A bashful grin fell against his mouth. "Oh, well, I guess that wasn't too bad of a thing."

"It could've been worse."

He set his mug down and stepped in front of me, boxing me in as my back pressed against the kitchen counter. His hands went on both sides of me, and he leaned in slowly. "I really want to kiss you right now," he whispered.

"I can tell you a million reasons you shouldn't," I whispered back. "Especially with Cam here."

"That's fine, but I just need one reason I should, and that reason needs to be that you want to kiss me, too. So...do you want to kiss me, too?"

I bit my bottom lip. "You know I want to kiss you."

"Can I?"

"Maybe."

"Fast?"

"Fast."

He pecked my lips quickly.

I sighed.

I wanted more.

"Again?" he asked.

I sighed, hearing the water turn on from Cameron's shower. A sign that perhaps we were in the clear. "Again."

He kissed me again, this time a little longer. He didn't pull his lips away from mine this go-round. "Again?" he murmured as he pressed his body against mine more.

My hips arched toward him, feeling his good morning greeting sweeping against my leg. "Yes," I sighed. "Again."

This time, he parted my mouth with his tongue and kissed me deep and hard. His hands fell to my lower back, and he pressed his body against mine. I placed my coffee cup down, then wrapped my arms around his neck, deepening the kiss. He lifted one of my legs and wrapped it around his waist before he smacked my behind, making me giggle against his mouth.

"Uh, Coach?"

Within seconds, Nathan dropped his hold on me, I shoved him away, and I turned my back toward Cameron, who was standing there in the kitchen archway, staring at us. I wiped my hand over my mouth as humiliation settled in.

Nathan cleared his throat. "Hey, yeah. What's up? I thought you were showering."

"I was about to hop in, but you're out of body wash. I figured I'd ask," Cameron explained. He pointed two fingers toward Nathan and me, a big grin on his face. "I knew you two were into each other!"

"*We're not!*" I called out, still not turning to face him. "That was just, uh, I had something stuck in my teeth."

"And Coach P was sucking it out?" Cameron sarcastically asked.

Nathan snickered, and I swatted his arm. "Don't laugh!"

"You don't have to explain it to me, Coach K," Cameron said. "I already know about the birds and the bees. I think it's good for you both. The team plays better when the two of you get along. Now that I know you both are banging, we'll probably win the whole series," Cameron joked.

"Hey! That's enough. Body wash is under the bathroom sink. Get going," Nathan ordered.

"Okay, thanks, Coach P. Oh, one more question. Is your niece Priya single?" he asked.

I giggled with my back still turned.

"Get out of here, Cameron!" Nathan shouted, hurrying Cameron off.

The moment he was gone, I turned around and raised both eyebrows and tossed my hands up in defeat. "That's bad."

"The fact that he's asking about Pri? Yeah. That's awful."

"No." I shook my head. "The fact that he saw us together like that."

Nathan smirked as if he were unfazed by the fact that Cameron walked in on us tonguing the heck out of one another. "It's fine. He's not going to tell anyone."

"Are you joking? He's probably texting the whole team about how, quote, 'Coach K and Coach P are banging' unquote."

"The fact that you said quote and unquote is adorable."

I shoved his arm. "It's not funny."

"No, it's not. But you're sexy when you're nervous. Your little nostrils flare and steam comes out of your ears."

"You're a pain in my ass."

He narrowed his brows and smirked. "Is that in reference to what I did to your ass the other night, because—"

I swatted his arm as a small chuckle fell from me. "Shut up! Gosh. I can't stand you. At least you'll be cooking me brunch today."

"Don't hold your breath. I got this in the bag."

"That would be true if I didn't have Cameron Fisher on my team." I grabbed an apple from the basket on the counter and tossed it into the air before catching it. "Batter up, Coach." I smirked before walking off to change into my uniform. As I walked away, I called out. "Stop looking at my butt, Nathan Pierce."

"Can't help it. There's so much goodness to take in."

"Shut up before I take off my shoe and throw it at you."

"Don't stop there," he urged. "By all means, throw me your panties, too."

38

NATHAN

The game was a hit, and unfortunately, I lost to Cameron and Avery. That was a game I'd never live down based on how the two mocked me nonstop during brunch.

Afterward, Avery stayed back and helped Cameron with his homework and talked to him through some things. I figured it was good for them both to talk about their mothers. Sometimes talking about the hard losses in one's life made them easier to deal with.

On the other hand, I figured it was a good time to check in on Cameron's father and have a heart-to-heart with the living.

"Coach Pierce, hey," Adam said as he opened his front door after I knocked. He looked as if he'd come down slightly from his drunken binge. He had dark circles beneath his eyes as if he hadn't gotten much sleep. He was still wearing the same clothes he had on the day prior, too, and smelled like booze. He scratched his head and cleared his throat. "Is Cam with you?"

"No. He's still at my family's farm."

"Shit. Listen, last night, I was a mess. I've been meaning to figure out a way to apologize to you and Cam for how I was acting. That's not who I am normally."

"But it's who you've been lately."

He grimaced. "Listen, I don't need a lecture—"

"I'm not here to lecture. Just here to talk. Can I come in for a second?"

Adam glanced over his shoulder. "Gee, Coach, it's actually pretty messy. I don't want you to get the wrong idea. Things have been a bit rough lately without..." His words faded away, but I knew he was speaking of his wife.

"I don't mind messes. I won't take up much of your time, I swear."

He nodded and stepped to the side. He led me into his house, to his living room, where empty food containers and beer bottles were spread all over the place. Adam scrambled to gather the stuff from the coffee table and tossed it into the kitchen sink. He then tossed the dirty clothes piled high on the couch into an already overloaded basket sitting by the laundry room.

"Sorry," he grumbled, hurrying back over to me. "Please, take a seat."

I sat on the couch, and he sat in the recliner across from me.

I noticed the photographs sitting on the fireplace mantel, photos of Adam smiling with his family, before the darkness tried to swallow him whole.

"Look, Coach, I just owe you an apology for how you saw me last night. That wasn't my norm, and I don't want you to think anything awful about me," he started. "And I know Cameron probably painted a bad picture of me, but that kid can be a bit dramatic with everything. He's a good kid, but he's a bit of a drama king. I like to say he got that from his mother." The moment he mentioned his wife, I saw the sadness flash through his stare. "She was a drama teacher, after all."

BRITTAINY CHERRY

"I'm sorry about your loss, Adam."

He grimaced and sniffled a bit. "Yeah. That's what most people say. After a while, those words feel empty."

"Do the words feel empty, or do you feel empty?"

He hesitated for a moment before clearing his throat. "Can you tell Cameron he can come home now? I got everything under control. Last night was just a bad night."

"Cameron mentioned you've been having a few bad nights. And you seem to get a bit too excited at games, too."

"What can I say? I'm a big baseball guy." He laughed, trying to play it off. He went to stand. "Listen, I hate to break this up, but I have a lot—"

"My father had a drinking problem. Drinking and gambling. He almost lost our family farm due to his addictions. He used to come down hard on me whenever he was in one of his drunken slurries. Never came down on any of my younger brothers, only me. And only in private. My mom never knew. I think it was because he thought I was strong enough to take his abuse."

Adam lowered himself back down to the recliner and narrowed his eyes. "What's your point?"

"My point is that Cameron is your son. Not your punching bag."

"Now you hold on right there, I ain't never laid one hand on my son. Sure, I might've shoved him a little last night, but he fell alone. How dare you even accuse me of such a thing? Was last night bad? Yes, but I'd never—"

"He needs you, Adam." I cut in. "You might not be physically abusing him, but your words and actions...those are hitting him deeper than you'll ever know. Yet that boy loves you more than anything. You are his hero, and I think watching you struggle after the loss of your wife has been the hardest thing for him. Because he knows this isn't you, Adam. Cameron knows that this version of you isn't his father. I know you might find the need to get defensive, but you don't have to do that. I'm not here to shame you. I'm here to help."

"To help?" he huffed, shaking his head. His hands clasped together, and he looked down at his hands. "How the hell could you help me?" he smugly asked. "How the hell could you make anything I've been going through better? You don't know half the shit I'm dealing with."

"You're right," I agreed. "I don't. But I've been your son. I've had someone like you as my father. And I would've done anything I could've to get my father back."

"I wasn't supposed to do this without her," he whispered. I saw tears falling from his face as he kept staring at the floor in front of him. He shook his head. "She wasn't supposed to be the one who left first."

"I can't imagine how hard it was to lose your wife."

"No," he agreed. "You can't. Because she was the lighthouse. She was the way home for Cam and me. And without her, there's just darkness."

At that moment, I thought of Avery and what she had shared with me about Willow and her mother. If that was true for her, I was certain it was true for Cameron and his mother, too.

"But you still have that light of her in him, Adam. Cameron is a walking miracle of his mother. He is the living legacy of something you and her crafted. And you're missing it. She's in every piece of him, and you're just too lost in grief to see how much of a miracle that is. She left you the greatest gift she could've ever given you...a son who loves you more than life itself. You might have lost your wife, but Cam...he lost his mother. Don't let him lose his father, too."

"Damn." He sniffled, wiping his eyes with the back of his hand. "I'm messed up, man. I know I am, and I don't know how to fix it. Cameron doesn't deserve this. But I don't know how to get better."

"I think that's the first step. Realizing that you're not okay." I cleared my throat and clasped my hands together. "The second step is getting help, which is why I'm here. Cam mentioned some money issues. I can help with that. You can get a position at my family farm. I'll look after Cameron whenever you need an extra hand. All I need you to do is get help. Whatever it takes, I'll do it. You can't keep going like this. I need you to recognize that you need help. Then things can start to change."

"Why, though?" Adam asked, looking back up at me. "Why would you do this for me?"

"I'm not doing it for you. I'm doing it for a son who just wants his father back. He has already lost part of his heart. He doesn't need to lose the other half, too."

He sniffled some more and stood from his chair. "All right. I'll do it." He held a hand out toward me. I stood and shook his hand. "Thank you, Coach."

"Anything for Cam."

"You're a good role model for those kids."

"They're better ones for me. We'll figure out a game plan, but first...I got a call from Prest University, down in Georgia. A few scouts came out and want to have Cameron come down to explore their campus in a few weeks."

"Prest University?" he asked. "They have one of the best baseball programs in the country."

"Same one I went to before the big leagues. Those coaches take the game seriously. Cameron would excel at that."

"Wow..." He shook his head as his eyes flashed with more emotions. "My son at Prest University, huh?"

"Yeah. I want to plan a trip where I take him down and show him around for a weekend. I'd love for you to come with us. It might be a great bonding opportunity for you both."

"Oh, yeah. Okay. I'd be interested."

I smiled. "Good. All right. We'll be in touch soon."

I turned to walk out of his house, and he called after me, making me turn back to face him.

"Can you tell my boy I love him?" Adam asked.

"He'll be back tonight," I said. "You tell him yourself."

39

AVERY

verything was going well.

I feared when life seemed good because I always seemed to wait for the other shoe to drop. So nothing could be *too* good for me. I lived in a constant state of pessimism, even though life seemed good. But lately, things have been good. Great, even.

The other day, the apartment complex in town told me they had an apartment coming available. I told them I wasn't interested because I didn't hate the idea of staying with Nathan on the farm. I felt like my best self at Honey Farms. Nathan and I were closer than ever. There wasn't a night when I fell asleep without being in his arms.

The team was on a roll, too. We'd been winning game after game, and the crowds in the stands grew each week. With us being in the playoffs, a ton of eyes were on our team. I didn't expect the season to take such a dramatic shift, but it had. I was not one to complain about it, seeing how my guys were all getting noticed by scouts. Their names were now entering rooms with higher-ups who could change their lives for the better.

Nathan, Cameron, Adam, and I were off to Prest University in two weeks to meet with their baseball team. Prest University! I couldn't think of a better match for Cameron.

It was impossible for me not to admit all of this was due to Nathan. He was such an asset to the team, and I couldn't have been more grateful for him joining us.

Due to his Major League success, the Honey Creek Hornets were making nationwide coverage. Just last week, there was a segment about the team on *Good Morning America*, and we went viral on TikTok, landing on baseballtok and booktok. I didn't see how those two things crossed paths, but it seemed to have been a great way to get our team's name out to a wider audience.

Unfortunately for me, with all eyes on us, came interviews.

I despised interviews.

On the other hand, Nathan was convinced that any press was good for the guys. The more we made our presence known, the more individuals would take notice of our players.

Everything was still going fine until one night after an annoying practice. After everyone left, I stayed on the field in the darkening night. The silence slicing through the space was a heavy contrast to the turmoil of noise racing through my head.

Then the other shoe dropped.

The glow of my phone screen illuminated the latest headline that came through of the last interview I did with Nathan. "Miracle Season or Male Influence? The Real Reason Beyond the Honey Creek Hornet's Success."

My heart sank to the pit of my stomach as I scrolled through the article, taking in every word.

Coach Kingsley's coaching skills weren't strong enough to carry the team alone. They hadn't won a game in years. Perhaps having a woman coach a man's sport is more trouble than anything.

Before two-time World Series-winning Nathan Pierce joined the staff, the Honey Creek Hornets were dead on arrival. Without the addition of Coach Pierce, it's sufficient to say that the team would still be down in the dumps.

If I thought the article was rough, the comments were even harsher.

Keep women out of our coaching positions.

Maybe she took a wrong turn on her way to the cheerleading practice.

It's not a shock that someone who looks like her doesn't know how to coach. It looks like she'd cry over a hangnail.

The air around me felt heavy, thick with unspoken doubts that were now being formed within my thoughts. A wave of nausea hit my stomach as I read the article again. And again. And again. Each time I read it, the invisible pressure resting against my shoulders felt as if it was pushing me further down. I felt so little at that moment. So heartbroken. Mainly because a big part of me believed the article.

I wished I could say that was the first article I'd seen, but it wasn't. Over the past few weeks, more and more alike had been flooding in. Articles questioning my capabilities and suggesting that Nathan should take the head coach position. Stories stating that perhaps baseball wasn't for me, and I should look into starting a softball team of my own. Think pieces about how women weren't meant to exist in men's realms.

I locked my phone, the screen going pitch-black, but the words lingered in my mind. They were embedding themselves into my spirit, into my soul, and I couldn't stop it, even though I tried. I worked really hard for my team over the years. I went to bat for those boys time and time again, and all the achievements I did make, like getting better equipment and getting a facility built so they could be the best they could be, were all being diminished. What was even worse was them saying it was because I was a woman. I'd be fine if they said I sucked. But saying I sucked because I was a woman? That set up a completely different kind of hurt brewing within me. It felt like I was on trial for my gender as if my every decision was being scrutinized and judged based on my sex.

Unfortunately for me, when I was hurt, I grew angry. And when I was angry, I was no fun to be around.

"Hey, Avery?"

I quickly composed myself at the sound of footsteps approaching. I knew it was Nathan coming to check on me. Normally, after practices, we'd meet in my office to go over our game plan for the following day.

I slid my phone into my pocket and shook off my nerves as I turned to face him. I tried to push out a fake smile, but it fell short. "Hey," I said.

"I was waiting for you inside." He narrowed his eyes. "Everything okay?" His voice was laced with concern. Had he read the articles, too? Surely, he saw the one from today. It was on one of the biggest sports websites out there. I had no doubt people had been tagging him in it.

"I'm fine," I curtly replied, walking past him. "Can we talk about the plan for tomorrow later? I'm not in the mood."

His footsteps hurried behind me as he caught up to me. He placed a hand on my shoulder, pausing my movement. "Ave, wait, slow down."

I shook his grip from my arm. "I don't want to slow down. I don't want to talk right now, Nathan."

He grimaced. "You read the article, huh?"

That felt like a punch straight to my gut. The realization that he'd actually read it, too. The heat of embarrassment pierced my face like little needles stabbing against me. My emotions were all over the place, yet I knew the last thing I wanted was to witness Nathan's pity stare. His worry felt like an intrusion, a reminder of everything spiraling out of my control.

"What does 'I don't want to talk' mean to you?" I snapped, more sharply than I intended. The words felt bitter as they somersaulted from my tongue. They were laced with frustration building like a quiet storm within me. Poor Nathan didn't even know that he'd just stepped right into the eye of the storm. He was in the danger zone, and with how I felt, I was more than willing to make him my target.

He recoiled slightly, tossing up two hands in surrender. "Avery, slow down. It's me you're talking to."

There was an instant regret for my coldness, but the floodgates of my anger had been torn open, and I was unable to stop myself from lashing out. Unfortunately for him, he was just in my target range.

"I know who you are." I griped as my breaths heavily weaved in and out. "You are Mr. World Series! The redeeming knight in shining armor for this damn team. Without you, I'm nothing. Without you, this team is shit. You're fucking Superman, and I'm Lois Lane, the weak woman who needed to be saved by a man."

"Avery—"

"Or better yet, you're Tarzan and I'm Jane. The stupid love interest. How about you throw me over your shoulder and pound your chest because you're a big, strong man who is the king of the jungle?"

"I get it. You're upset right now and—"

"*Screw you! I'm not upset!*" I screamed, highlighting that I was, indeed, upset. My chest heaved with rapid breaths. "Do you have any idea how hard it is? To constantly prove yourself only to have it all be undermined because of baseless speculations? I worked just as hard as you this season!"

"No one is saying you didn't, Avery."

"*Everyone* is saying I didn't!" I cried out, tossing my hands up in frustration. "You don't know what this feels like. You don't know how it feels to have everything I love and worked hard for questioned by the whole world. You just get to be the shiny hero in the story. So congratulations, Nathaniel. You're a winner."

I started to storm off, but he reached for my wrist and swirled me back around to face him. "No," he said, his voice dripping in control. "No, fuck that, Avery. You don't get to make me the villain in this. I'm sorry they said what they did in that article. It was fucked up and stupid, but I'm not your enemy."

"Yeah, well, it didn't really sound like you were my partner, either."

"What do you want me to do? Go burn down everyone who ever printed a bad word about you? Because I will. I will burn them all to the ground, but you don't get to snap at me like this when I didn't do shit wrong," he growled. His eyes were dilated, and now his chest was the one rising and falling at an uncontrollable speed. "You said that I don't know how it feels to be questioned by the whole world, and that's bullshit. I've been in your shoes before. I've walked through that shit. It fucking hurts."

I went to respond, but he held up a hand. "I'm not done speaking. You got to yell at me, so now it's my turn to respond. I remember the headlines like they were yesterday. 'Nathan Pierce: From World Series Hero to Suspected Junkie.' Or, oh, how about 'Legends of the Fall: Nathan Pierce's Fall from Grace: How an all-American all-star let the pressure ruin his life.' Oh, or what about 'The world would be better if players like Nathan Pierce were six feet under instead of on the field.' You think I don't know what these vultures are like? I've been dragged through the mud and called every nasty name in the book. Yet I never took it out on anyone else."

His words halted my storm as he verbally slapped me in the face with a taste of reality. He moved in closer to me, not backing down. His presence somehow dripped with challenge and support all at once.

"The media loves a downfall story," he told me. "They love

to make you feel like you're nothing so they can somehow feel as if their own lives are good enough. Don't fall into their booby traps. They'll feed off you until you're nothing. Don't let their words define you, Avery. Otherwise, they then yield the pen to write your tragic ending, too."

I stood frozen as he somehow made the boiling rage within me come down to a simmer. The tempest within me clashed with the raw honesty of his words. My hands unclenched by my sides as a small tremble slipped through my lips. "I'm sorry. It just hurts," I whispered as the anger residing within me began to ebb and be replaced with nothing more than pain. "It hurts," I said, revealing a truth I had come to terms with.

"I know," he agreed. "And that's fine. It's okay for it to hurt. But we're more than their stories. We've worked too hard to get to where we are. We're too strong to let this kind of shit get us down. We are almost to the finish line, Avery. Don't let this sidetrack you. I know how deep the pit of self-doubt can pull you."

I could tell that he meant that. Nathan had faced demons in his life that he probably never even spoke of. There were parts of his story that he ripped up the pages to. He'd been through the wringer of public opinion, and somehow, he not only managed to escape it and become stronger—but he still remained humble and kind.

He extended his hand toward me. "Let's go to the batting cage and get this energy moving out of your system."

"It's fine. You don't have to stay and make sure I'm good."

He extended his hand once more.

I sighed as I looked at his hand and then at his eyes. I saw it, too. The care that he had the moment he first approached me. At that time, I was too hot-tempered to allow his kindness to take care of me.

I placed my hand into his. The moment I felt his touch, my whole body relaxed.

He walked me over to the batting cages. He grabbed a

helmet and placed it over my head. As he put his hands on the side of the helmet, he placed his forehead to mine. "You are more than those articles, Avery Kingsley. And stop trying to push me away, will you? I'm not going anywhere, no matter how much you tell me to piss off." He leaned in and kissed the tip of my nose before he smacked my behind and said, "Batter up."

"I love you," I blurted out, the confession hanging in the air between us. That felt more frightening than any article that could've been written about me. He froze in place as my whole body began to tremble from the words that freely fell from my lips. I shook my head in confusion because that was the last thing I expected to say in that batting cage after my outbursts. "I love you so much, and I don't know when it started. I don't know when I started to fall for you or when you started to mean so much to me, but I do. And I'm sorry for everything I said and how I reacted, and how I said so many hurtful things. I know I'm hard. I'm a hard person to see and to get, and every time I think you're going to run away, you end up moving in closer, even when I don't deserve that, even when I don't deserve you, and well, it's silly and stupid and completely unexplainable, but I love you, Nathan Pierce. I love you so much that it scares me, but still, I'll love you anyway. And well, I just—"

He stepped toward me and wrapped his hand around the bat in my grip. "Wait. Stop." His gaze intensified as he searched my eyes. He placed a finger beneath my chin and tilted my head up. "Say it again," he requested, his voice barely above a whisper.

"I love you," I repeated as warmth wrapped around the fear sitting heavily within my chest.

He placed his forehead to mine once more. "Again," he murmured.

I closed my eyes. "I love you," I breathed out.

He took the bat from my hands and dropped it to the

ground. His fingers laced with mine, and he pulled my hands to his chest. He shook his head slightly. "Sorry, it's just...I've dreamed of you saying those words to me again," he confessed as his thumbs gently caressed the palms of my hands. "Because I love you too, Avery. I've loved you since I first met you, and I'm certain I never stopped."

We stood there for a moment in the batting cage, surrounded by the echoes of our past and the promise of our future, holding one another in a moment of complete surrender. I forgot about everything else. I forgot about the articles and the cruelty of the world outside of us and I allowed myself to slip back into our make-believe. Where happily-ever-afters existed and conflict didn't lead to goodbyes. Where my heart could shatter, and he'd pick up the broken pieces.

I kissed him in the batting cages, allowing myself to fall completely for the man he was that day. Still, even if I wanted the lingering thoughts of doubt placed by the media to disappear, those quiet voices in my head were still trying to convince me otherwise.

Love didn't cure self-doubt.

Sometimes it only made it louder.

40

NATHAN

"Calling for your suitcase in the car, Avery! The plane will leave without us!" I shouted through the house as I carried my duffel bag to the front door. Last night, I saw Avery packing two suitcases. We were going to be gone for forty-eight hours, not forty-eight years.

She walked over to me with no suitcases.

I chuckled a little. "I know I mentioned you should pack a little lighter, but this is a bit extreme."

"I can't come," she mentioned.

"What do you mean? Is everything okay?"

"Yeah. Everything's okay. Everything's better than okay, I think, it's just...Yara's in labor. I just got the call."

"Oh shit," I said, shaking my head in disbelief. "That's crazy!"

"I know. I want to be there at the campus with you and Cam, but—"

"Don't worry about it. I know that campus inside and out, and I'll be fine with Cam and Adam. You get to the hospital to be with your sister."

"Okay, okay, okay. I need my keys." She paced the foyer as if she were forgetting something.

I placed my hands against her shoulders. "Avery."

"Yes?"

"Your keys are in your hands."

"Right. Yes. Okay."

"Take a deep breath, Auntie. You're gonna do great. Tell them I said congratulations."

She nodded. "I will. And update me with how everything goes for Cam, will you? I'm so excited."

"Talk about a victorious weekend." I kissed her forehead and smacked her ass. "Congrats, Auntie Avery."

"Can you believe it?" She smiled, her cheeks rising high. "A baby," she sang, tossing her hands in the air from excitement. "*We're having a baby!*"

We're.

I knew she wasn't talking about her and me, but then again...I didn't hate the idea.

THE WEEKEND at Prest went as amazing as it could've. Seeing Cameron in his element was the best thing to witness in the world. Having Adam there with him was the icing on the cake.

Cameron even joined in on one of the workouts with Prest's team. As he ran drills on the field, I stood in the dugout, watching it all take place.

"How does it feel to be back on your stomping grounds, Pierce?" Coach Reed asked me as he walked over with a clipboard and a brown envelope in his hand. Coach Reed was an older gentleman who'd been the head coach at Prest for the past twenty years. He was the one who got me into the big leagues. He was one of the best, and I was excited that Cameron might have the opportunity to work with such a legend.

"Feels like coming home," I told him.

He nudged me in the arm. "I was hoping you'd say that." He nodded in Cameron's direction on the field. "The boy's good. One of the best we've seen in a long time."

"He can take it all the way."

"I have no doubt about that. He has all-American written all over him. It would be a treat to coach that boy. He needs a little bit of work, but nothing I can't help him with."

"I know he'd be in good hands here," I told him.

"You should know that," he agreed. "Seeing how you'll be joining the team as one of the head coaches, too."

I narrowed my eyes as I looked at Reed. "I beg your pardon?"

"It's no secret that you've had quite the turnaround with your career, Pierce. I've been watching you, like the rest of the industry, and your small town turned the game upside down. I even saw some articles on your team on ESPN."

"They're a solid team."

"Because they had a solid leader."

"That's true, they did. Avery Kingsley has done remarkable things with that team this year."

He waved a dismissive hand my way. "I'm not talking about that girl. Don't get me wrong, I'm sure she's talented, but this is about you, Pierce. We want to offer you a position at Prest. You would be the coach of our dreams, and I couldn't think of a better one to take over once I retire."

"Retire?" I asked. "You're planning on retiring?"

"I'm old," he explained. "My wife said if I don't, she'll leave me. So you know." He shrugged. "I figured I should start looking for a replacement."

I smiled and patted his shoulder. "I'm honored, but I think I'm good."

He held out the brown envelope. "Inside this is a contract. One that is probably much more impressive than that lil' ole high school one you got. You have a big talent, boy. Not many people get second shots like this. Just give me your word that you'll consider it."

I took the envelope. "Thanks, but I think I'm settled where I am."

"Just consider it," he echoed.

Knowing that he wouldn't let up on it, I agreed. Even though I knew in my heart of hearts that I wasn't leaving Honey Creek. I'd found my way back home after years of wandering. I'd be an idiot to leave when everything I'd ever wanted was in my lap.

"Attaboy." He patted my back and then looked out toward the field. He blew the whistle hanging around his neck. "Run that play again, boys. And don't make it look like a toddler's doing it, all right?"

He walked off the field as Cameron came jogging over toward me. "Coach P! Did you see me out there?"

"Hell yeah, I did. That was amazing."

"Did Coach Reed tell you about the coaching position? Could you imagine? Us both being at Prest? We'd be unstoppable."

"Yeah. He mentioned it." I smiled an uneasy grin and patted his back. "But we should probably get going to the airport. I just wanted you to get one more run on the field before we headed out."

Adam, Cameron, and I headed to the airport, and the flight was easy enough. After we walked out of the Chicago airport, I said my goodbyes to the two and thanked them for the weekend.

"Hey, Coach P?" Cameron called out.

I turned and looked back toward him. "Yeah?"

He rushed over and hugged me. "Thank you for this."

"You did this all on your own, kid. Your talent got you here."

"No, I don't mean Prest. Don't get me wrong, I mean, this is an amazing opportunity, and I'm grateful. But I meant him." He gestured toward his dad, who was decked out in Prest University gear from head to toe. "Thank you for making him feel like my dad again. He said he's getting help, and I can't help but think you had something to do with that."

I smiled. "Being human is complex, and sometimes we fall off our tracks. He deserved another shot."

Cameron nodded. "Thanks for putting him back on the tracks, Coach. See you tomorrow at practice."

I headed back home, excited to see Avery and tell her how great the weekend had been. I also wanted to see more photographs of her sweet niece. I'd missed her over the past few days. I knew it was silly, seeing as we'd been spending more than enough time with one another, but the second I left, I missed her.

"Welcome home, Coach," Avery said as I walked into the front door. She wore an oversized graphic TLC T-shirt, red panties, and a bottle of wine in her hands. "Dinner's on the table."

I dropped my bag in the foyer and kicked off my shoes. "I could get used to these kinds of welcome home greetings." I moved toward her as if there were a strong magnetic pull and found her lips against mine. "I missed you."

She laughed. "You're such a simp."

"Simp?" I kissed her again. "Learning some slang words from your students?"

"Yup."

"And what exactly is a simp?"

"I googled it. It's a person who's perceived as overly submissive or even desperate for the attention or affection of someone without receiving anything in return."

"Oh." I pulled the palm of her free hand to my mouth and kissed it. "I am such a simp for you, Avery Kingsley."

She giggled, and I wanted to swim in that sound.

Simp, simp, fucking simp...

"I love you," she said.

"I love you," I replied.

"Dinner?" she asked me as she took off my jacket.

"Yes"—I nodded—"dinner."

She led me to the dining room, and I took a seat. She opened the wine and poured two glasses. She then placed a pasta dish with garlic bread on our plates. She went to sit in the chair beside me, and I held a hand out, stopping her.

"What?" she asked.

I patted my lap. "Here."

She laughed and placed her hands on her hips. "Do you want me to feed you or something?"

"Yeah. Like I said, I missed you. I need you as close as possible right now. So come here and sit."

She hesitated for a moment, probably debating a sassy reply, but instead, she climbed into my lap, facing me, with her legs hanging to the sides of the chair. She kissed me gently. "I missed you, too."

I chuckled to myself and shook my head. "Gosh, Avery. You're such a simp."

She reached behind her and lifted the plate into her hand. "Shut up and eat." She fed me a forkful of the pasta. "Tell me everything about your weekend. Tell me all about Cameron."

I did. I told her all about Cameron's adventures on campus and how it was remarkable watching his dreams come true.

She told me about Yara and how amazing her beautiful niece was as I fed her the pasta.

"Teresa Marie," Avery stated. "Named after Alex's great-aunt and our mom." Her eyes lit up with complete bliss as she talked about the meaning behind her niece's name. "Gosh. You'll have to meet her. She's something special. She's equal parts Yara and Alex. I swore she even had Alex's grimace when she was born."

I laughed. "That would be a sight to see."

Her stare fell to the floor as her smile faltered.

"What is it?" I asked.

"Nothing, it's just..." She shrugged defeatedly. "I thought I'd have what they have, too. I always wanted a little girl, and I wanted to name her after my mother. I'm not mad at Yara for using the name. Trust me, I'm not. She didn't even know about that dream of mine. But still...it feels like that idea died a little today."

"You still have time to be a mother," I told her.

"Yeah. But..."

"My name is Nathan," I explained.

She narrowed her eyes and let out a confused laugh. "Yes, it is."

"That's my cousin's name, too. And my other cousin. I also have an uncle with the middle name Nathan. We were all named after our grandfather. Nathaniel Pierce. So what I'm saying is, one day you can have your little Marie if you have a little girl. It's kind of nice...to have a history of love showcased through names."

The smile reappeared against her lips as she took the plate from my hands and placed it back on the table. She then cupped my face and kissed me long and hard. "I love you," she muttered before kissing me again.

I wrapped my arms around her waist. She arched toward me as I kissed her deeper. "I love you," I swore. My mouth moved to the nape of her neck where I trailed kisses. "I love you," I repeated, slowly swiping my tongue against her smooth skin.

She gently began to rock her hips against my crotch, making my dick instantly wake up. Her hands moved down as I kept kissing her skin, and she began to unbuckle my jeans. Without struggle, she got them off, and I shook out of them, only lifting her body for a slight moment. With the jeans went my boxers, revealing my hardened shaft that was more than ready to slide inside Avery.

My hand moved down to her red panties, and I shifted them to the side, exposing her warm, wet pussy. My thumb began massaging her clit as she pressed her hands to my chest and closed her eyes. A whimper fell from her lips as she rocked against me. I lifted her slightly, allowing my cock to rub against her lips before I slid her down against it.

"Yes, yes, yes," she moaned as I filled her up. She wrapped her arms around my neck as my arms wrapped around her body, and she began to ride me right there, gliding up and down my dick, making me feel as if I was on a damn water ride based on how wet she'd been.

"You did miss me, didn't you, Coach?" I growled against her ear, holding her closer to my body, feeling my heart race faster as she bounced up and down against me. "Because you're riding me like you did."

She leaned back against the table, resting her elbows against the edge. She arched an eyebrow, and a wicked smirk spread over her full lips. "Yeah, I missed you. Now show me that you missed me more, big boy." She slowed her hip rolls, teasing my cock as she took control of the speed of entrance.

I arched a brow. "Is that a request?"

"No," she purred before rolling her tongue slowly across her bottom lip. She leaned back toward me, placed a finger beneath my chin, and tilted my head up slightly to lock my eyes with hers. "That's an order, Coach."

Fuck...

Something about the words and the actions combined almost brought me to the finish line sooner than I'd wished. If I had it my way, Avery Kingsley would be ordering me around for the remainder of my life, and like the good, faithful simp I'd been, I would've allowed her to dog-walk me every single step of the way.

With haste, I lifted her from the chair, off my cock, and flipped her around so she was facing the table. Her feet hit the floor, and I tossed off my shirt before placing my body against hers. My hand wandered up her shirt, and I grasped her breasts, massaging them as my dick rubbed against her perfect ass. My mouth found the edge of her ear before whispering, "After this, I'll make love to you, I swear..." I licked her earlobe and bit it. "But first, I'm going to fuck the everlasting shit out of you until you scream my name in cursive."

I then bent her body forward, and she spread her hands over the table, grasping it the best she could as I slid back inside her from behind. I wrapped my hand around her neck and tilted her body toward mine, loving the sound of the screams of pleasure escaping her as I thrust into her deeper and deeper, filling her up with all of me as she gave me all of her.

"Look at me," I demanded.

She tilted her head slightly around to see me, her eyes fluttering open as moans of desire kept escaping through those plump lips of hers. My hand stayed at the base of her neck as we locked eyes for a moment before my mouth slammed against hers, and my tongue fucked her at the same speed and intensity as my dick fucked her.

"*Yours,*" I breathed into her. I wanted to fill all her holes with me, and I wanted to feel her moans vibrating off my tongue as she surrendered to me and our love. "*Forever,*" I promised.

I twisted her body back around so she faced me, and I laid her against the dining room table, shoving the plates and glasses of wine to the floor, not giving a damn what shattered along the way. Her eyes were on me, and mine on hers. I climbed on top of her, rocking my throbbing cock deeper into her as she wrapped her hands around me and dug her nails into my back.

"Nat...Natha...We...I...Nat..." She shuddered, unable to form my whole name with her words. I felt her growing closer and closer to her orgasm as she deepened her nails against me, holding me as if I were the key to her greatest victory. "I, so, so close," she muttered, her eyes fluttering shut. "Right there. Don't stop, don't stop, *don't you dare fucking stop!*" she growled with an order.

The closer she grew to her climax, the closer I inched to mine. As her legs began to tremble against me, I lost myself, too, falling into the hardest orgasm I'd had in a while. I took a few moments before sliding myself out from inside her, and I fell backward into the chair in front of the table.

My breath weaved in and out as I stared at Avery, who was now sitting up on her elbows. She bit her bottom lip with a wicked smile. "This is a sturdy table."

"As sturdy as they come."

She pushed herself up from the table and began walking down the hallway. I watched her ass move side to side the whole time.

"Where are you going?" I asked.

"To shower." She glanced over her shoulder. "Join me."

41

AVERY

My legs felt like Jell-O the following day when I went to school. I had Nathan to blame for that, seeing how he'd kept me up all night long. Then again, I wasn't complaining. Not in the slightest.

Students buzzed around with a lightness to them. School was coming to an end, and graduation was right around the corner for many of them. The energy felt fresh, renewed in some way.

"Coach K!" Cameron said, rushing over to me in the hallway after first period finished. He looked like he was still floating on cloud nine from the weekend. That made me happier than I could've ever expressed. "Dude! I wish you were there this weekend!"

I smiled. "I wish I was, too. But rumor has it that you had the best weekend ever."

"It was amazing! My dad loved the campus, too. And Coach P showed us all around his old stomping grounds."

"I love that. I'm glad."

"Me too!" He grinned ear to ear, grabbing the straps of his backpack tightly around his shoulders. "Plus, the idea of him coaching there when I attend is so exciting. I mean, I wish I had both of you coaching me, but at least a part of Honey Creek is coming to Prest, too."

My heart skipped a few beats as I tried to grasp the words leaving his mouth. "Wait, what do you mean?"

"Coach Reed at Prest offered Coach P a head coaching position. He gave him a contract and all." He narrowed his eyes. "Oh crap. I thought he would've told you when he got back. I'm sorry if—"

I pushed out a smile and patted Cameron on the shoulder. "No, no, it's fine. I knew. I just didn't know he shared the information with you," I lied. The bell rang, and I cleared my throat. "Get to your next class, will you? We can't have you falling behind on your studies."

"All right."

"And Cam?"

"Yeah?"

"I'm really proud of you."

He grew bashful and nodded. "Thanks, Coach K for... everything."

After he left, his words grew heavier and heavier in my mind with every passing hour. When my lunch break came around, I left school and headed to Nathan's house. I knew he was in town that afternoon, so when I went into the house to snoop around, I knew I'd be fine.

As I walked into the house, I noticed an envelope on the kitchen island that Nathan left there the night prior. With nerves bubbling up inside, I opened the envelope to find the contract that Cameron told me about. A contract for a lot of money.

I felt sick.

He was leaving me.

He was leaving and didn't bother to tell me about the offer.

Just like Wesley had done. Just like Nathan had done years before, too. There was no way that was possible.

Just like that, the make-believe world I had created with Nathan crashed straight into reality.

With a busy mind, I pulled out my cell phone and called the apartment complex in town. "Hi there. I was just calling to see if that one-bedroom apartment was still available. I'd like to come through today and sign a lease for it if possible."

After I hung up the phone, I texted Nathan.

AVERY
Can you lead practice tonight? I have some things to handle.

NATHAN
Yeah. Is everything okay?

AVERY
Everything's good.

NATHAN
Okay. I'll see you afterward.

AVERY
Yeah. All right.

I headed back to school for the remainder of the day, and afterward, I headed to the apartment complex to sign the lease. That took some time, then I headed back to Nathan's place and began to pack my suitcases. I needed to get out of that place and away from him as soon as possible. My heart couldn't take much more breaking. I was reaching the point where I had little to nothing left.

Unfortunately, I didn't end up packing fast enough because Nathan showed up early from practice to find me about to walk out with my suitcases.

He arched an eyebrow. "Avery. What are you doing?"

I blinked a few times and shook my head. "I signed a new

apartment lease. I should be able to move in next week, but for the time being, I'm going to go stay with my dad."

His brows narrowed as confusion swirled in his eyes. "Wait, what? You're leaving?"

"We knew this arrangement was temporary, Nathaniel. I was always going to get an apartment," I said as I started to walk toward the front door.

He stepped in front of me, tossing his hands up in confusion. "Wait, I'm sorry, slow down. You're acting weird."

"No, I'm not."

"Yes, you are. Why didn't you tell me you were signing a lease?"

"Since when do I have to tell you everything I do?" I snipped at him.

"You don't, but..." He shook his head. "This just feels like I'm being blindsided a bit."

"Yeah," I agreed. "Isn't that a shitty feeling?"

His brows knitted. "What's that supposed to mean? What's going on, Avery?"

"Nothing," I argued. "I'm just leaving."

"Why would you stay at your father's place instead of staying here for the week before moving in? Why would you even want to leave? I don't get it."

"Yeah, well, I don't get why I had to hear about you getting offered a position at Prest University from Cameron. Then again, I guess that's what we do. Keep shit to ourselves."

His eyes grew somber as the reality of the situation settled in. "Shit."

"Yeah. Shit," I echoed. "Please move."

"Listen, Avery...I didn't know Cameron even knew about the offer. He misspoke."

"Doubtful. He made it very clear that it would be great having you as his coach when he headed off to Prest. I think this is great. I think it's great that I had to hear it from a student instead of from you," I sarcastically remarked.

"I was going to tell you…"

"Why not last night? Did it slip your mind when you were fucking me against your dining room table? Did it somehow go forgotten while you fucked me in the shower and told me you loved me?"

His eyes widened as if I were speaking in a different language. "Like I said, it was a misunderstanding. Let me explain—"

"No," I spat out. "I don't want your explanation. I want to leave."

"Yes, Coach Reed offered me a position, but I'm going to turn it down."

"Going to? So you made him think there was a chance? You're considering it?"

"No, but in person, he wouldn't take no for an answer and—"

Tears.

They wanted so desperately to fall.

"Nathaniel, move," I ordered as he continued to block the front door.

"Avery—"

"*Move!*" I shouted, my rage building more and more each second.

"You're scared."

"Excuse me?"

"Should I have told you last night? Yes. But it wasn't at the forefront of my mind, seeing how I had no plans of taking the job. I'm sorry I didn't tell you. I fucked up with that."

"Okay. Cool. Now move."

"No. I won't because you're scared. You're scared of this—of us—because we are getting serious. You're trying to push me away before we can get closer because you're scared."

"Don't tell me what I am!" I spat out. "The last thing I need is Nathaniel Pierce to tell me what I am!"

"*You're fucking scared, Avery!*" he shouted, his hands tossing up in frustration as he paced the room. "You're so fucking scared of being left that you are trying to run before that could happen again, and I get it. I fucking get it, but I'm not Wesley, Avery, and I'm not that fucked-up, scared kid that I was when I left before. I'm here. I'm solid," he swore, pounding his hand against his chest. "I'm not leaving. So you can either be scared with me, and we work through this together, or you'll have to be the one to walk because you don't get to rewrite this story. You don't get to go ten years down the road from now and tell the story that Nathan Pierce left you because I made a promise to you. I promised you I wouldn't fucking do that. I'm staying, Ave. I'm standing here, and I'm staying. *So fuck*...just stay here with me, too."

My mind was spinning as the words fell from his mouth. I could hear him, yet my thoughts wouldn't allow his sentiments to stick. My mind was working too hard on trying to make me retreat because my messed-up thoughts were already certain he'd leave at some point. Maybe not today. But what about tomorrow?

Why wouldn't he?

He left before.

Wesley left.

Mama left.

Maybe that was the one that cut the deepest. Maybe that was the one where my fear of abandonment truly took flight. Mama left me with nothing but trauma and a jaded mindset of what love could be because, in the end, that was what love did. It went away. Nothing in life was promised, and every human would leave this planet the same way—alone.

Even if I held on to Nathan for the rest of my life, there would be a day that I'd lose him, a day I'd have to let go, and I wasn't sure that my heart could take that. I wasn't certain that I could face a realm where he'd left me.

So I'd leave first.

I'd pretend to be hard when weakness was all I felt.

"Better to leave now than ten years down the road," I murmured, my voice shaking from fear.

"What happened to heart over head?"

"I realized that was a stupid way to live," I replied.

The flash of pain that hit his eyes almost made my own eyes cry. I'd never seen him look as broken as he had at that very moment. He swallowed hard and stepped to the side of the door, making a clear path for me to leave. "Just like that, huh?" he asked.

"Yup." I sniffled and rolled my shoulders back. "Just like that."

"Then go," he whispered, his voice cracking.

I stood as tall as I could even though I felt extremely fragile. As I stepped out of the front door, Nathan said, "Congratulations, Avery, you did it. You pushed me away. You can have your life, and I'll go on with mine. But just so you know, all I wanted —all I've ever wanted—was for this. For us. I just wanted another chance to love you."

He turned and walked into his house, leaving me standing there to close the door for him. It only seemed right, seeing as I was walking away this time, not him.

I got into my car, and I only made it a few minutes down the road before I burst into tears. I couldn't breathe, let alone drive. After pulling the car over, I reached for my phone and dialed Willow's number.

"Hey, Ave. What's up?" Willow asked.

I sobbed on the phone, unable to get any words out.

"Okay, okay. Hey, it's all right. What's going on? Where are you?"

I somehow managed to state where I was located. She heard me loud and clear.

"Don't worry," she swore. "I'm on my way."

When she showed up in Big Bird, she parked right behind my car. She climbed out of her vehicle and rushed to my passenger seat.

"I'm sorry," I cried as she pulled me into her arms. "I'm sorry, I'm sorry," I kept repeating. I wasn't certain if I was apologizing for inconveniencing her time or if I was still apologizing to Nathan for leaving. Or maybe I was apologizing to my own heart for breaking it again.

"You're okay. You're fine. I got you," she swore, pulling me closer to her as she hugged me. "Everything's going to be okay."

I sobbed even harder when she said those words.

Because I knew they were a lie.

42

NATHAN

The problem with breaking up with Avery was the fact that the baseball postseason wasn't over yet. We still had two weeks left together. We'd still had to interact in front of the guys, day in and day out, as if nothing was different between us.

She'd do her best to act unfazed by the fact that she ripped my fucking heart out and stomped it out while she went over strategies. I hated everything about it. What I hated more was that she seemed...okay. She seemed fine with the fact that we weren't us anymore. We didn't even get long enough to really become us, either. It felt like déjà vu. Our shot at happiness was once again being ripped away prematurely.

"You got everything for the final tournament games?" she asked me as I stood in her office. She began packing up her paperwork. She'd been avoiding eye contact, but that wasn't unusual over the past few days. She'd been working her ass off to avoid looking my way.

Her damn stubbornness was going to be the death of me.

"Yup. We're all set. The bus will be here at two to transfer us to Ridgedale."

"Perfect." She picked up her duffel bag and tossed the strap onto her shoulder. "If there's anything else you need before—"

"How the hell are you all right?" I snapped, getting more and more annoyed with her nonchalant persona. "How are you acting like everything's all fine and dandy when I'm sitting here fucking broken?"

Avery's lips parted as she froze for a moment's time. A flash of hurt shot through her eyes, showing me that she wasn't handling it as well as she had me believing. She still cared. She still felt. She was just working her damnedest to suppress those emotions. She blinked a few times before a hardness returned to her stare. She rolled her shoulders back and cleared her throat. "Do you have any more questions before Ridgedale?"

The coldness of her words sliced through me.

"Nope," I said. "Nothing else."

"Okay. I'll see you tomorrow," she stated, walking my way to leave.

As she crossed my path, I grabbed her arm and pulled her close. "Why are you doing this, Coach?" I whispered. "Why are you pushing me away?"

Her voice cracked, and she closed her eyes for a moment. "I have to, Nathan. I can't...I can't..." Her eyes opened once more, and I saw it again—the aching of her soul seeping out from her irises. "Please let me go," she said, her voice barely audible.

"Are you sure that's what you want?" I asked. "I don't want to let you go. Not again. I'm trying to love you, Avery."

"I know." She nodded, a few tears rolling down her cheeks. There it was again—her truth.

"Then let me."

"I can't," she murmured.

"Why not?"

She turned her lips up into the saddest smile I'd ever witnessed. I never knew a smile could break a heart until that very moment. She shook her head slightly and shrugged her shoulders. "Because how can you love me when I don't even know how to love myself?"

Fucking hell.

How could seeing her broken, struggling heart so easily shatter my own?

"Avery—"

She pulled her arm away from my hold and wiped her tears, shaking her head. "Please, Nathan? Can we just make it through the rest of the season and then move on?"

No.

I wanted to fight with her. I wanted to tell her that she was being irrational and that she shouldn't have allowed the demons in her head to keep her from being loved, but I knew how it was to be so deep in the darkness that you thought you didn't even deserve the slightest touch of love. I hated that she felt that way. I hated that there was nothing I could do to help her shift those dark thoughts filtering through her mind. So I did the only thing I could think of doing at that very moment.

I gave her the space she'd requested.

"Okay," I agreed.

"Thank you," she muttered, a small sigh of relief rippling through her words.

She started for the door, and I called out one last time. "Hey, Coach?"

"Yes?" she asked, looking over her shoulder.

"We'll get our boys to state and win. I'll be the best assistant coach for you. You have my full commitment to this team. I also won't bring us up again," I promised. "I get it. You're done, so I'm done. We're done. There's no going back for us, so let's just make it through the rest of the season."

My words landed against her, and it looked as if they broke her heart. Which, in turn, broke my own. Because that was how our two hearts worked—when hers broke, mine shattered.

"What do you mean she's gone?" Easton asked as he and my other brothers sat on my front porch, confused as ever as to why Avery wouldn't be joining the Sunday game. I wasn't going to play, either. I wasn't up for that shit.

"I mean exactly what I said. She's gone. She left on Monday," I told them.

"*On Monday*?!" River hollered, tossing his hands in the air. "How have you gone a week without telling us Avery was gone?"

"I didn't figure it was worth mentioning," I said as I headed for my car. "I won't be playing today. I got too much stuff to take care of."

"Whoa, whoa, whoa, pause, time-out!" Grant shouted, chasing me. "You can't just tell us you lost the love of your life and leave it at that."

"Don't be so dramatic, Grant. I thought that was Easton's job," I muttered.

"But she is," Easton said, walking toward us. He leaned against my driver's door, blocking my entrance. "She is the love of your life."

"Yeah, well, sometimes shit doesn't work out in life," I barked. "Now move, Easton."

"No," he said, standing stern. "Not until you get Avery back."

"Easton," I growled. "Move before I move you."

Grant shot over and stood beside Easton. "You'll have to move me, too."

River hurried over and stood next to the two of them. "Me too, brother."

I grumbled. "Stop being dicks and get on with your own lives, will you? At least Evan has enough nerve to mind his own..." My words faltered as Evan stood in front of my car, too. I pinched the bridge of my nose. "Not you too, Evan."

"Sorry, brother. It's just you've been grimacing more than me this past week. I can't have someone taking my sultry looks. I got that copyrighted. Tell us what happened," Evan said.

"Yeah. What did you do?" Grant asked.

I narrowed my eyes. "What did I do?" I barked. "What makes you think that I did something wrong?"

They shrugged in sync as if they were quadruplets instead of two sets of twins.

"Avery just seems...perfect," River said.

"*Well, she's not!*" I blurted out, tossing my hands up in frustration. I paced the space with irritation filling every inch of my being. "She's messed up and hard and confusing and abrupt. She makes rushed decisions and sees everything as black-and-white with no middle ground. It's an all-or-nothing mentality with her, which leaves almost no room to let other people in. She's hardheaded and mean. She's so damn mean to me sometimes, but even meaner to herself. She's damn rough around the edges, too. She's so rough that if you even look at her wrong, you'd end up with papercuts somehow, and I, I, I—"

"You love her," Easton expressed quietly.

I paused my footsteps.

I took a few deep breaths.

I felt a tug of my heart as I nodded. "More than breathing."

"Then go get her back," Evan said, patting me on the shoulder. "I don't believe in that love stuff for myself, but I believe in it for you, Nate. You've been a completely different person since reconnecting with Avery, too. You've been happy. Don't lose that."

"It's too late. She wants nothing to do with me. This whole week, we've had games, and she has hardly looked my way. It's torturing me, and I can't take much more. I know she has her issues, but fuck. She won't let me in. What the hell am I supposed to do?"

"Keep trying," a voice said from behind me. I turned to see Priya standing there. "You're supposed to keep trying, Uncle Nate."

I sighed and shook my head. "It's not that easy, Squirt."

"I didn't say it was easy. I just said you had to keep trying," she replied.

Evan started toward Priya. "Listen, Pri, this is grown folks stuff and—"

"No offense, Dad, but you're a guy. And guys are a little stupid when it comes to what we women need."

"Women? I thought she was a little girl," Easton whispered with a pout.

"Well, I'm not, Uncle East. I'm a grown woman, and I know what Avery is going through. We've talked a lot over the past few weeks of her being here, and I think I get her. She has trust issues."

"I know. Because of what I did to her when we were younger, but—"

"No." She shook her head. "It's because her mom left her when she was a kid. We talked about that together...losing our moms."

Evan's brows lowered. "You've talked about that with Avery?"

"Yes," she said.

"You never talk about it with me," he urged.

"That's because I know it hurts you still, Dad. Even if you say it doesn't." Priya turned back to me. "But that's not the point. This is about Avery, not me. When she lost her mom, she lost her trust in the world. She had flashes of trust, but it's easier for her to run away from something good because she has a belief that nothing can stay that way. That things can't stay...good. That's why she pushed you away. She got scared."

"Yeah. I know. It still doesn't change the fact that she doesn't want anything to do with me," I expressed. "I'm not going to pressure her to let me in. That's not fair to whatever it is that she's going through."

"I'm not saying to pressure her," Priya said. "I'm saying keep trying. Maybe not as a romantic partner, but as a friend. Sometimes people don't need romance. Sometimes they just need someone in their corner."

I crossed my arms over my chest and lowered my brows. "When did you get so smart, huh?"

Priya smiled. "Last week after my AP Chemistry test. Now, come on, guys. I made a new batch of cookies I want you all to try for me."

The guys shot from in front of my car with haste and started in the direction of Evan and Priya's place. If I knew cookies would get them to move, I would've offered that up from the jump.

Evan hung back with me and grimaced as he watched his daughter walk away. "I still have no clue how she became so wise," he said.

I patted him on the shoulder. "She was raised by a good man."

"No," he disagreed, gesturing toward the other three guys who were playfully pushing Priya around. "It takes a village." He smirked slightly. "She's right, too, you know. About Avery. Just keep making her feel seen. Besides, you've waited how long for her to come back around? What's a little bit longer?"

43

AVERY

Daddy and Alex moved all my things into my new apartment while Yara, Willow, and I sat on my new couch, watching the men work hard. I held Teresa Marie in my arms as she slept peacefully. I couldn't believe there was a new generation in the family. She was as perfect as ever, too.

"Okay," I said, looking up from the sleeping baby toward my sisters. "I know you're both thinking a lot, so go ahead and let it all out. I will give you the next"—I glanced at my watch—"three minutes to ask me anything you please about Nathan and me."

Yara went first. "Do you love him?"

"Yes," I said.

"Did you freak out because you love him?" Willow questioned.

"Also yes," I replied.

"Do you miss him?" Yara asked.

I sighed, feeling a flip in my stomach. "More than words."

"Then go get him," Yara said, resting a comforting hand against my forearm. "You deserve love more than anyone else, Avery."

Her words left her mouth, but they didn't hit my soul. I couldn't believe them to be true because my self-love was lacking. How could I accept love from anyone else?

"He got offered a job. A dream job at Prest University in Georgia. I won't stand in his way of that opportunity, especially when I'm so wishy-washy with him. It's not fair. It's not right. Besides, he's made for more than this small town. More than me," I told them.

"Avery," Willow scolded. "Stop making yourself sound so small. Anyone is lucky to get you. Nathan would stay for you. I know he would."

"I do too," I confessed. "Which is why I pushed him away. I can't have him give up his dreams because of me. This is for the best," I said. "He'll go to Prest and become an amazing coach, and I'll stay here. Everything will go back to normal. I'll coach at the high school, and I'll return to my life as if nothing happened between Nathan and me."

"But so much did happen, Ave. So much good," Willow stated. She took my hand in hers. "Avery...does Nathan make you feel?"

"Feel what?"

"Anything," she said.

Tears burned at the back of my eyes, and I nodded slowly. "Everything. He makes me feel *everything*."

Yara's eyes flashed with tears as she reached out to wipe mine that decided to slip down my cheeks. "Ave—"

"Time's up," I said with a forced smile. "And I think Teresa needs a new diaper."

———

THE TEAM'S talent only grew more and more as we made our way to state. Which we did—we made it to state!

I couldn't believe the transformation that took place over

the past few months with the Honey Creek Hornets, and I knew so much of it had to do with Nathan Pierce getting on board. He wasn't only the best thing that happened to me, but he was the best thing that happened to the team, too.

With the flurry of everything going on, we'd had interview after interview leading up to the final series. The last interview we did was with ESPN, which felt as close to the big leagues as I'd ever get. I was nervous doing an interview, especially after how the media had been toward me, but I knew it would be good to shed light on our team. The more attention we got, the more attention the boys received from the scouts.

As I sat mic'd up beside Nathan during the interview, I tried my best not to look nervous. Nathan naturally took the lead on a lot of the questioning. At some points, I felt as if the interview was trying to make little digs at Nathan about his past career and how it went up in flames. Nathan, being the professional that he'd always been, handled it with grace.

"That's the thing about our past...it doesn't have to shape our future," Nathan expressed. "I'm not who I was yesterday, though. I'm not embarrassed by my past mistakes. Those missteps led me here." He glanced over at me, and a small smile appeared before he looked back at the interviewer. "And I would walk every broken road twice over if it led me back to this."

I swallowed hard at that comment but remained quiet.

The interviewer turned to me next. "And what about you, Coach Kingsley? I know you've been paid a lot of attention by the press. Something you're probably not used to."

"Not in the least." I nervously laughed.

"How are you handling the pressures as we go into the final game of the series? Do you feel as if you have something to prove as a woman? It's said that you are in the wrong sport and you only got here because of Nathan. I'm not saying I believe that, but it's clear that a majority of folks do. They said it's all

Nathan carrying the team and not you. Clearly, the majority couldn't have all gotten it wrong, right? How much of this team's success was truly yours? Or, like many are saying, was it all Pierce, and you just got pulled along the way toward victory?"

I felt it happening. The tightening of my chest. The rage building from the rude question that was being asked. My vision began to blur as every negative thought that lived within me started to come back to the surface. Every suppressed feeling of doubt was awakened at that moment.

"Oh shit," Nathan said, looking out into the distance. "Did you see that?"

The interviewer turned around to see what it was that Nathan was speaking of. "What's what?"

"Oh, nothing." Nathan shook his head. "I just thought I saw an array of butterflies."

"Butterflies?" the interviewer questioned.

"Yeah." He turned toward me and nodded with a tiny smile. "Butterflies."

A laugh of comfort escaped me.

Butterflies.

Nathan gave me a comforting wink. "Go ahead and continue, Coach," he said. "Sorry for the interruption."

I cleared my throat and turned back toward the interviewer. "I, like most, have read the comments about my position as head coach at Honey Creek. I'd be lying if I said the words didn't hurt me; I'm human, words can hurt. And the truth of the matter is that Nathan has been such a blessing to our team. There's no way we would've made it this far without him."

"Or without Coach Kingsley. We're a team," Nathan added. "That's what we are, Avery and me—we're a team. One isn't more important than the other. We were both focused on the season's success this year, and we ebbed and flowed like magic with one another. Avery Kingsley is one of the best coaches to ever coach the game, and it has been nothing less than an honor to coach beside her. The whole game of baseball is better with her in this industry. Frankly, I think we could use more women coaches on the field. I think it's beyond time that we expand our realm."

Oh, Nathan...

How badly I want to love you.

After the interview finished, we were un-mic'd, and free to go. As we were walking out of the building, I paused beside Nathan. "Hey, Nathan?"

"Yeah?"

"Thank you for having my back in there. I know things between us have been...strange. But that meant a lot to me."

He nodded once. "I'll always cover your base, Coach."

WE WON.

We won state.

We freaking won state!

The second it happened, I felt as if my heart was going to explode in my chest. I shot out to the field from the dugout and began to celebrate with all the guys on the field, who were losing their minds over the fact that we were the state champions. I couldn't control my excitement as I jumped up and down, hugging the players.

Before I knew it, my arms found their way around Nathan, and we embraced.

"We did it!" I shouted, my heart pounding rapidly against my chest. "We did it!"

"You did it, Coach!" he said, swinging me around from pure excitement. "I'm so fucking proud of you!" he told me. He placed me back down on solid ground, yet the world kept spinning faster and faster around us.

I stared into his brown eyes, shaking my head in amazement. Then my excited heart shifted to feeling as if it wanted to cry. Because all it wanted at that very moment was to kiss him. To fall into his arms again and never let go. To celebrate with him on the field and off. But I couldn't.

We couldn't.

"Nathan..." I whispered.

He gave me a sad smile as if he could read my thoughts. "I know," he said softly. "Me too, Coach. Me too." He then moved in and gave me another hug, holding me close to his chest. He kissed my forehead and whispered, "I miss you so much it's hard to breathe."

Then he let me go.

He let me go and celebrated with the rest of the team as if his heart wasn't breaking, too. I didn't know what to expect because I told him to do that. I told him to stay away, and he did what I'd asked.

But my breathing was suffering, too. I knew exactly what he meant when he said those words to me. Because, without him, it was so hard to breathe.

AFTER THE GAME, the team headed off to celebrate with a late night of pizza at the hotel where we were staying. I told them I'd join later on, but first, I needed to take in the moment on the field now that it was cleared out. I needed to come down from the busyness of the day and take it all in by myself.

Though it turned out I wasn't alone.

"Way to go, Coach K," a voice said from the stands.

I turned to see my father sitting there. The crowd was gone, and the only things remaining were the floodlights on the field and my father in the stands.

"Not too bad, huh?" I said with a smirk.

"I like Nathan," he stated, throwing me completely off-kilter.

"What?"

"I said, I like Nathan."

"Are you about to give me a father-daughter talk?" I asked as I walked over to the stands to join him.

"I'm about to give you a father-daughter talk." He patted the empty spot beside him, and I took a seat. He turned his stare back to the field. "Do you remember when your mother and I used to take Yara and you to the baseball field for family time?"

I laughed. "Yeah. She and Yara would sit up here making artwork while you and I hit balls on the field."

"Those are some of my favorite memories."

"Me too. You're the one who made me fall in love with the game."

"You're the one who made me stay in love with it," he expressed, clasping his hands together and resting them in his lap. "I like Nathan," he repeated.

I sighed. "Yeah. I heard that the first time."

"You like him, too," he said, certain. "You love him."

I blinked a few times. "What does that have to do with anything?"

"Baby girl, love has to do with *everything*." He stared forward and shook his head slightly. "I don't know much about life. I'm a simple man who does construction and enjoys a good beer on Friday nights. But there are so many complicated things in life that I don't know much about. But I do know about love. I think love is the reason we humans decided to come to this damn planet in the first place."

"If that's true, then we're stupid. It's stupid," I countered.

He arched an eyebrow. "You think love is stupid?"

"Yes," I confidently said. "Because if we came for love, then why wouldn't we come solely for love and love alone? If we only came for love, then why is there so much hurt, too?" I shook my head and shut my eyes. "Because all the hurt in the world seems so much louder than love. It feels more as if we humans came here to suffer. To break."

"You don't really believe that, do you?"

I shrugged. "Sometimes. Because if it was all about love..." My voice cracked as I rubbed my hands against my legs. "Then why would this world allow a little girl to lose her mother? Why are there children suffering, wars, violence, pain? There's so much pain, Daddy," I cried, placing my hand over my chest. "There's so much hurt. Why would we do this? Why would we come for love but then make hearts that could break so easily?"

"I think you're confusing the opposite of love with hurt."

"No," I disagreed. "I know the opposite of love is hate."

"No," he replied with a headshake. "The opposite of love is indifference. The feeling of emptiness. That's what the opposite of love is. Love allows you space to feel everything—joy, bliss, sorrow, and pain. Grief is love, Avery. Love and grief go hand in hand."

"Why is that?"

"Because grief is the realization that you could care for another so deeply. That your heart could shatter a million ways, all due to how much you adored another. Being able to feel so deeply is a gift, baby girl. It's the indifference, the inability to feel, that is the curse."

"It's scary to feel grief..."

"It's even scarier to feel nothing." He flicked his thumb against the bridge of his nose. "I once read a quote by a person named Jamie Anderson that said, 'Grief is just love with no place to go.' And I felt that deeply. Yet then I realized that the gift of grief is that there are still other types of love that surround you. When I had so much grief after losing your mother, I thought I had nowhere else to put said love, but then I saw it within you three girls. My love for her spread into the love I had for you. And don't get me wrong, that doesn't cancel out the love I have for your mother. That grief will always be a part of me, but the love from you girls...that refilled my tank. I think after all these years, that's what you need, baby girl. You need a refill of your tank."

I sniffled, knowing that Nathan had started to refill my empty tank over the past few months. Still, I was so scared that I created a leak in the tank because I was terrified of what would happen if that love went away again. "I'm scared of loving him, Daddy," I quietly confessed.

"I know," he agreed. "Tell me why."

"Because..." Tears streamed down my cheeks as the reality settled in. "I think I'm so broken that no matter how hard I try to be enough for him, I'll never live up to what he deserves. What if my love isn't enough for him to stay?"

Daddy took a moment, taking in my words. He wasn't one to speak out of turn without thinking his thoughts all the way through. Then his mouth parted, and he said, "I've sat in the stands at the home games this whole season, Avery. I didn't watch the game, though. I watched Nathan watching you." He gave me a small smile and wiped away my tears. "I've only been in love—real love—once in my life, with your mother. That kind of love doesn't come around often; it's rare. But I see it when he looks at you, sweetheart. His love for you is only growing with each passing day. Don't run from something real just because you're afraid of getting hurt or that you're not good enough. Life is hard, and hearts do break, but those hearts can heal, too. Just don't think that your heart needs to heal on its own when someone out there is interested in fixing it with you."

I bit my bottom lip. "You think he'd stay through my lows?"

"Sweetheart...you're in a low right now, aren't you?"

"Yes."

"I saw him this whole game looking at you, baby girl. He

already stayed. He's standing on the front porch waiting for you. It's up to you to open up the door and let him back in."

And there it was...

My turned-off heart began to beat slowly again.

"And for what it's worth, Avery Harper Kingsley, you're more than enough. Especially on the days when you don't feel that way."

"Thanks, Daddy."

"Always." He reached under the bleachers and pulled out a picnic basket. "Now. How about a victory PB and J sandwich?"

44

NATHAN

W e won state.

The sun was already setting by the time we got home the next day.

I was exhausted but so proud of the team, so proud of Avery.

But even though I was proud, there was a heaviness that felt so hard to face reality with. The fact that we won and I still felt as if I'd lost was something so hard to come face-to-face with.

After being greeted by my family with a little dinner celebration at my mom's house, I headed back to my place to find a surprise on my porch.

Avery.

I narrowed my eyes as I approached her. "Hey. What are you doing—"

"Can we have an impromptu OSS meeting on your field?" she blurted out.

"What?"

She shook her head. "You know... OSS. Oldest Sibling—"

"Oldest Sibling Syndrome, yeah, I know what it means." I tilted my head, studying her for a moment's time. I wished I

The Problem with Players   371

could understand that messy brain of hers and help her shift through her files. But she was there, in front of me...

I could tell she was scared, but still, she showed up.

That had to mean something.

I gave her a nod and walked her out to the field. I grabbed a bat and handed it over to her. "I'll pitch you some," I told her as I placed a helmet on her head.

"Sounds good."

She took the bat from me. I grabbed a bag of balls and moved out to the pitching mound. I pulled a ball from the bag before dropping it beside me. She moved over to home plate and kicked off some dust resting on it.

I tossed the ball in the air a few times. "I'm glad you're here, Coach, but there's going to have to be a few new ground rules to the OSS."

"New rules?" she nervously asked. "Like what?"

"Rule number one," I said, getting into the pitching position. "You can't run away just because you get scared."

She nodded. "Okay."

I threw the ball; she hit it.

"Rule number two," I said, grabbing another ball. "We have semimonthly meetings out here on the field. No breaking that rule."

"Okay."

I threw the next ball. She hit it, and it skirted over third base.

"Rule number three, we find reasons to laugh. Even when it feels hard."

"That works for me." I threw another ball, but she missed it. "Is that all the rules?" she asked.

"Yup. That's all the rules."

Her head lowered for a moment as she fiddled with the bat in her hands. "Can I add one more rule?"

"Shoot."

When she looked up, tears were falling down her cheeks. "Rule number four. You set me up with the wellness clinic in Chicago?"

Geez...

Avery Kingsley and my fucking heartbeats...

I stood there frozen, because I wasn't certain what to make of her words. My brain was spinning, uncertain if I was even allowed to comfort her when all I wanted to do was wrap my arms around her and tell her that everything would be okay. She pushed me away. She wanted distance, not me. Still...I wanted to hug her. But I couldn't.

That killed me.

She began crying harder, shaking her head as the bat fell from her grip. "I'm so sorry, Nathan. I don't mean to be this broken and scared."

"It's okay, Coach. You're okay."

"But that's the thing. I'm not. I know I'm not, and even though I want to give myself to you fully, my mind won't let me with these thoughts I have. I need something more than hope. I need real help."

"We'll get you what you need, Ave. I promise."

"How are you so...so...*good*?" she asked. "I've been awful toward you."

"Shame kink," I joked. "Seriously, though, Avery...I've felt broken before, too. I had a lot of people who didn't show me grace, but I had plenty who did. It's what we all desire in life—

a few moments of grace as we walk through the darkness."

"I'm not sure what I have to offer you right now," she confessed, shame written all over her face.

"Just be my friend, Coach. I don't need anything else. All I need is for you to feel better. All I care about is you walking down that path of healing, and all I want to do is walk that path right there beside you. If that means we are only friends, then that's more than enough for me."

"Swear?" she whispered, looking up at me.

"Swear."

"Can I give you a hug?"

"Always."

She fell into me, wrapping her arms around me. I held her close. I'd hold her for as long as she needed me to do so.

"And don't worry about the journey to healing, Ave. It's okay to go slow," I swore.

"*Go slow*," she echoed with a nod. "I think that's what I need to do. I need to go slow."

"Take your time."

"I know I don't deserve it, but..." She stepped away and gave me a small, broken smile. "Thank you for walking with me."

I grinned back. "My favorite steps yet."

We did exactly as we said we would do, too—we went slow.

45

NATHAN
JUNE

In June, we met on the baseball diamond twice a month for our OSS meetings. We caught up on things, and Avery mentioned the bad reality shows she was watching. I started watching them, too, so I'd have even more to discuss with her the next few times we'd spoken. It turned out that I loved bad reality shows. I spent a whole weekend binge-watching *The Traitors*. I couldn't stop myself if I wanted to.

I stopped working so much, too. I allowed myself to sit with my thoughts more. Figured if Avery was working on herself, I should take a page out of her book, too.

"Should I be worried about you today?" I asked her after we finished hitting around balls on the field. I walked Avery to her car and opened the driver's door.

She climbed inside, smiled, and shook her head. "No. Not today."

"Happy?"

"Happy."

"Good. See you in two weeks, Coach."

46

AVERY

JULY

I n July, Nathan and I not only spent time at our twice a month OSS meetings, but we texted one another a lot more, too.

NATHAN

How did they not know that Phaedra was the traitor?

I smiled at my phone at the new reality show fanatic.

AVERY

She plays a good game.

NATHAN

I would've figured it out if I was on the show.

AVERY

If I was on the show, I'd want to be a traitor.

NATHAN

I'd guess it was you right away. You're a bad liar.

AVERY

What?! Take that back.

NATHAN

Never. Side note, do you think CT and Phaedra Parks are in love? I think they are in love.

AVERY

You should watch the old seasons of CT on The Challenge.

NATHAN

He was on another show? Down the rabbit hole I go…

I WOKE one morning to find eleven missed text messages from Nathan sent through the night.

NATHAN

Did you watch The Traitors Australia?

NATHAN

It's just as good as the US version.

NATHAN

OH MY GOSH! THERE'S A PSYCHIC!

NATHAN

Psychic is as good as I am at making guesses. She shouldn't go to Vegas.

NATHAN

Dammit, Avery. Why did you get me watching this show?

NATHAN

It's three in the morning, and they are about to vote off my favorite player.

NATHAN

Yup. He's gone.

NATHAN

I'm FREAKING OUT.

NATHAN

Oh crap. It's five in the morning. Good night.

NATHAN

Or, well, good morning.

NATHAN

If we happen to cross each other's paths today, please bring coffee.

Later that afternoon, I found myself standing on Nathan's front porch. I rang his doorbell, and an extremely exhausted Nathan approached the door. He was shirtless, rubbing the exhaustion from his eyes.

"Ave. You okay?" He yawned, stretching his arms out, revealing every muscle resting against his body. "What's going on?"

I held a cup of coffee out toward him. "Crossing your path. Good afternoon, Coach."

His tired, lazy smile spread as he took the coffee from my hands. "Good afternoon."

I SAT ACROSS FROM REBECCA, my therapist, nervously fidgeting with my hands in my lap. I still wasn't used to expressing myself in this fashion. Yet Rebecca was patient with me. She never pushed me to dig deeper, which somehow made it feel like a safer place to dig deeper.

"So you were engaged," she asked me.

I nodded. "Yes. We were together for three years. It didn't work out. We weren't a match."

"Three years is a long time, though, yes?"

"Yeah, maybe."

She smiled. "But within those three years, how much did you actually open your book to your partner?"

I laughed and shook my head. "I don't really open my book to anyone."

"What about the person who you were connected to over the past few months? From what you've told me, it seems that he may have read some of your pages."

"Nathan," I said, nodding. "Yes. That's because he had a way of figuring out how to undo the lock on my book."

"Was it good? The two of you?"

"Yes." I nodded. "So very good."

"Which is why you shut your book so swiftly," she explained.

I arched an eyebrow. "Huh? Why would I do that? Why would I shut my book when it felt so good?"

Rebecca sat back in her chair with a smile. "Because sometimes in life, we get triggered by the idea of letting someone else read our books, having someone else see our messy, dark chapters. Love only triggers us more. Sometimes we believe it's easier to shut said book and mark it as a 'did not finish' instead of moving through the hard chapters toward the happily ever after. This is because we fear losing said love. But this Nathan, do you think he liked what he read of you?"

"Yes," I confessed.

"I think that's what happened. You feared that he liked it. That he loved it even, because that went against a core belief in your system."

"What belief is that?"

"That you, Avery, are unlovable. Nathan coming along to

challenge that belief is a lot for your system to break down and understand."

Tears pinched at the back of my eyes. I looked down at my hands for a moment, but no words came out.

"It also scares you," she continued. "Having him love you, I mean. Because you like to control tasks, and you can't control the outcome of his love. You can't pace it or shape it to fit beside your triggers. That's his ship to sail. How he loves you is something you cannot steer. Love has no reins. That scares you."

"Terrifies me."

She nodded. "Understandable. But do you know the cool thing about love having no reins?"

"What's that?"

She leaned forward and whispered, "It has *no* reins. Imagine how much love he could feed you if you opened up said book again. Imagine how deeply another could care for you, how much you could care for them, if you found the courage to read each other's hard pages out loud together. Imagine a love that doesn't rot. Imagine a love story that only grows."

"Dang," I muttered, shaking my head. "You're worth every penny."

She grinned. "I'll see you next week."

47

NATHAN
AUGUST

s Avery walked up to the field for our August meeting, she narrowed her eyes toward me with a suspicious stare. "Why are you looking at me like that?" she asked, waving a finger in my direction.

"Like what?"

"Like you have something up your sleeves, with that wicked smile and all," she urged, gesturing toward me.

I took a few steps in her direction and crossed my arms over my chest. "There's nothing wicked about my smile."

Her brows rose. "Oh, there's something extremely wicked about your smile. What's going on?"

"I figured maybe for today's meeting, we could do something a little different."

She pulled out a hair tie and tossed her long hair up into a high ponytail. "Like?"

I flicked my thumb against my bottom lip. "I figured maybe you'd like to ride my stallion."

"*Nathan!*" Avery gasped, her eyes widening as if I'd just asked her to fuck me on home plate.

Though, I wouldn't be opposed to that idea...

"Chill. Not this stallion." I gestured over to the horse walking around the fenced in field. "That one."

Her eyes wandered over to Lightning, who was wandering around, eating some grass. It was a perfect day for a ride, and I knew Avery had been thinking about giving it a go from what my mother told me.

A shot of nerves raced through her body as she shook her head. "Oh, no. It's been so long..."

"He loves you. He'll let you ride."

"I don't know..."

"You scared?"

"A little," she confessed.

I held a hand out toward her. "That's all right. We can do things scared."

"What if he doesn't want me to ride? I don't know. I'm just..."

"Coach," I cut in.

"Yeah?"

"Do you trust me?"

She hesitated for a moment before she placed her hand into mine.

I got Avery saddled up, and Lightning was more than willing to allow her on board. I leaned against the fence as Avery took my big boy for a few spins. They looked good together. Always had. Always would.

In that split moment, I was a young boy watching a young girl riding my Lightning for the first time. And there, once more, I began to fall in love all over again.

I didn't know falling in love was a repeated action. I used to think it happened once and then it was locked in. But it was clear to me now that the falling never ceased. I was in a free fall, tumbling down more and more for the woman in front of me.

When it came to my love for her, I'd hope I'd never touch solid ground.

In August, Avery laughed more than ever before.
    She laughed at my good jokes.
    She laughed at my bad ones even more.
    That made it a good month for me.

48

AVERY
SEPTEMBER

"Rumor has it that it's someone's birthday," Nathan mentioned as he walked out to the pitcher's mound, where I was already waiting for our first OSS meeting of September. He had a box in one hand and a food container in the other.

I smiled. "Let me guess, a sister of mine told you about it."

He sat down beside me and shook his head. "I remembered it from when we were younger."

"Then you also recall how I don't like celebrating birthdays."

"Yeah, but a little homemade cake never hurt anyone." He opened the container and revealed a beautiful cake with lavender frosting and beautiful yellow piping around the edges. "I present to you a hummingbird cake."

My mouth parted slightly. "That's my favorite dessert. My mom used to make it for me all the time."

He smiled.

He remembered.

"You made me a hummingbird cake?" I echoed, stunned.

"Yes." He shrugged. "Actually, Priya made it. But I did add the eggs."

I laughed. "Close enough. Thank you."

"Always."

My cheeks flushed as he placed a candle in the middle of the cake. He pulled a lighter from his pocket and lit the candle. He held the container in front of me. "Make a wish, Avery. Make it a good one."

I closed my eyes, and I wished for him.

When I opened my eyes, his lazy smile was smiling at me. Gosh. *To love a smile like his...*

He placed the cake down and then handed me the small box.

"You didn't have to get me a gift," I said.

"To be fair, half of the gift is mine," he explained.

My curiosity increased from his comment as I opened the small box. I laughed instantly as I stared down at the item in front of me. "Best Friends necklaces?"

"Yup," he said, picking up one of the necklaces that said "Best" on it. "Figured we could each wear one to highlight this beautiful union."

I moved my hair to the side to allow him to put the necklace on, shaking my head in amusement. I then placed his necklace on.

"You're so freaking ridiculous," I told him.

"Don't shame me, Coach," he teased. "I'm not trying to cross those friendship boundaries with you tonight." He picked up a fork and dug into the cake. He fed me the first bite. "Happy Birthday, Avery."

Happy birthday, indeed.

49

NATHAN
OCTOBER

W hen Halloween came around, the Pierce brothers and Kingsley sisters linked up and went out in downtown Honey Creek to celebrate. One thing about a small town was that we took our holidays to heart.

Everyone dressed up except for Evan. I wasn't shocked about that, though. He wasn't one to take part in costumes. I was almost certain he only come out because he knew whiskey would be involved.

My brothers and I walked into the bar before the Kingsley women showed up. Easton was dressed as Quailman from the cartoon *Doug*. River and Grant showed up dressed as Ken from *Barbie*. They didn't plan to match costumes and didn't even notice that they had until they arrived at the bar.

Identical twin behavior.

I, myself, was a tube of mustard.

When Willow, Yara, and Avery walked in, I couldn't help but smile.

"For fuck's sake," Evan muttered. "Don't tell me you and Avery agreed on being ketchup and mustard."

Pride beamed through me as I saw Avery walk in dressed as a tube of ketchup. The most beautiful kind of ketchup, too.

"Part of me thought she wouldn't follow through," I said as I grinned ear-to-ear.

"That's why I don't fall in love. People do stupid shit when they fall in love," Evan said.

I laughed. "We aren't in love. We are—"

"*Just friends,*" my four brothers echoed, rolling their eyes as if they didn't believe me.

The women approached us, and Willow smiled brightly. "Hey, you guys. I see most of you went ahead and dressed up," she said, eyeing Evan.

He grimaced yet didn't say a word.

"Nice costumes, ladies," Easton said, already having shots ready to hand out toward the three sisters. "Willow, you are...?"

Willow spun slightly, showcasing the leaves and flowers all over her body. "Mother Nature."

"You look like a flower shop vomited on you," Evan dryly remarked. Clearly, it was meant as an insult, but Willow's eyes glistened with joy as she curtsied.

"Thank you," she replied.

"No Alex tonight?" I asked Yara, who was dressed as a witch. That was comical, seeing how Yara Kingsley was one of the sweetest women alive.

"Are you kidding me? Socializing on a holiday when people are drunk, loud, and rowdy? He'd rather peel a million onions than be here. Mama's having her first night off to party like wild!" she sang, downing the shot Easton passed over to her.

She shivered with disgust from the taste, making me chuckle. "Another one!" she cheered.

Avery smiled at her sister, then she smiled over at me. A shyness touched her cheeks as she slightly nodded. "Hey, Mustard."

"Hey, Ketchup. Red looks good on you. Brings out your eyes," I joked.

Evan rolled his eyes. "Fuck, you're corny. I need air." He pushed past us with his whiskey in his hand and headed outside.

The rest of us took more shots and partied even more.

AFTER A WHILE, I realized Evan never made it back inside. I took a break and went to check on him, only to find him sitting on a bench outside of the bar, staring down at his hands, which were gripped together. I knew my brother could be grumpy, but he seemed more than his normal grump that evening. He seemed troubled.

"Brother," I called out.

He looked up and frowned. "Hey."

I walked over and sat down beside him. "What's up? What's going on?"

"Nothing. A lot on my mind. Sorry. I don't want to bother you. Go have fun."

"Evan. Spill."

He grumbled a bit before clearing his throat. "It's about Priya."

Worry filled me. "Is she okay? What's going on?" I asked, my uncle protectiveness growing quickly.

He shook his head. "Not that Priya. Her mother, Priya."

It was the first time I had heard Evan talk about that woman in years. Sixteen years, to be exact. After Priya surrendered parental rights to her daughter, Evan never spoke of her again. I knew the whole situation was hard for him, but he kept a lot of it to himself, not even sharing with his own twin, Easton.

"What's going on?" I questioned.

"She's pregnant again."

My eyes widened. "By you?"

"No, you dipshit. I don't know who she's pregnant by. She stopped in the butcher shop. Thank goodness my Pri wasn't working that day. She told me she was pregnant, and she didn't want to keep it. She offered me the opportunity to adopt the baby once they were born, seeing how the kid would be Pri's brother or sister."

"Shit," I muttered.

"You're telling me," he dryly replied. "What the hell am I supposed to do with that?"

"I have no idea. So the father isn't in the picture?"

Evan shook his head. "I guess he overdosed. Passed away. The past sixteen years haven't been kind to Priya. She doesn't have any connection to her family or anything."

"That's crazy."

"That's life. Bad shit happens all the time."

I grimaced and clasped my hands together. "So...what are you leaning toward?"

"Truthfully?"

"Yeah."

"A big part of me wanted to tell her to piss off and never come back to this town."

"But...the other part?"

He frowned and glanced into the streets sprinkled with people in costumes, living their lives. "The other part knows that Priya deserves a chance to know her little brother or sister. I grew up with my brothers. I couldn't imagine my life any other way. I wouldn't want to take that away from her."

"Even if the kid isn't yours?"

He paused for a moment, falling deeper into his thoughts. Then he shook his head. "If they are her family, they are mine, too. If that little baby came into my house, they'd be mine as much as I'd be theirs."

And that, folks, was why Evan was the best father in the galaxy.

"Well," I said, patting him on the shoulder. "If that baby comes to the farm, we know one thing for sure: they'll be loved and cared for. If they don't, we can't be certain what will happen to them."

"Yeah," he agreed. "And I don't think I could risk that outcome."

"Well, little brother, it's about time I got another niece or nephew."

He huffed and chuckled lightly. "This was probably the only way you'd get another one out of me." He pushed himself to a standing position. "I better get home and tell Pri before it spreads around the farm too fast."

"What? You think I can't keep a secret?"

"I know you can, but I told Easton already. And you know he can't keep a secret if his life depended on it."

I laughed. "True."

I stood and hugged him. "Proud of you, brother."

"Take another shot for me," he ordered as he glanced behind him and looked into the bar to see everyone else still having a good time. "Mother Nature, huh?" he mentioned, speaking of Willow's costume. "That's fucking stupid."

I snickered and shoved Evan in the direction of the farm. "Night, brother."

"Night."

He walked off, and within a few seconds, my bottle of ketchup burst out of the bar. She looked in one direction before turning to find me. "Nathan, come on!" Avery said, her glassy eyes filled with drunkenness. She held a hand out toward me. "We're taking cherry bombs!"

50

AVERY
NOVEMBER

We almost kissed on the pitcher's mound in November.

We ate pumpkin pie cheesecake on the mound and talked about our hopes for next season. We talked about our hopes for our next lifetime.

We talked until we ran out of words. Until our stomachs were stuffed.

He fed me one last bite.

I leaned in.

He did, too.

Then his brothers came over, demanding some of the cheesecake.

That was when I realized how much I'd missed it.

I missed the taste of his lips against mine.

51

NATHAN
DECEMBER

The farmland was covered in snow when the holiday season rolled around. Like all the years prior, we hosted a big Christmas Eve party in the barn. Holiday music blasted through the speakers, and eggnog was poured at remarkable speeds as the spirit of the season took over in full force.

I wandered off to the horse stables to get a few breaths of air. For the most part, I did okay with Avery's and my friendship. Over the past few months, we'd become professionals at taking it slow, but I had to admit, a big part of me wanted to pull her under some mistletoe and place my mouth against hers.

I missed her kisses.

I missed holding her.

I missed her.

The version of her when she was mine.

Sure, we had this newfound friendship, but I couldn't help but wish it was more.

I figured I'd always want more with that woman. She was the only thing I couldn't get enough of.

"Walking off the eggnog?" a voice said, breaking me from my thoughts.

I turned to see my mother standing in the doorframe of the stables with a smile on her face. Her arms were crossed over her large puffer jacket as she walked toward me. She gently nudged me in the arm. "Or are you overthinking things?"

I gave her a smile. "Me? Overthink? Psh. Never."

She frowned and shook her head. "I'm sorry, sweetheart."

"Sorry? For what?"

"For not seeing how much pressure your father put on you."

I narrowed my eyes. "What are you talking about?"

"I had a heart-to-heart with your brother Evan. Lord knows how much eggnog it took for him to open up. You know that boy's stubborn with his feelings. But he told me he was scared about being a father again. Then he told me about a conversation you and he had on Halloween."

"Oh...that."

"Yes. That. Sweetheart..." Her eyes were packed with emotion. "Were all the choices you made back then an outcome of what went down between you and your father the night he passed?"

I hesitated to reply because it didn't matter anymore. "That was a long time ago."

"Still...it matters."

"Why would it matter?"

"Because it would mean you gave up your life to save this farm. A farm that wasn't your dream."

"This place is home to me, Mom. We would've lost everything."

"And we would've found something new." She placed a comforting hand against my cheek. "You've done more than enough for this family, Nathan. You've saved enough people. Now it's time for you to put yourself first. It's time for your life to take flight. And I am so sorry that I didn't notice the way your father was with you. I was too lost in the ways he was hurting me that I didn't even know that he was doing the same to my boys."

I leaned toward her and kissed the top of her head before pulling her into a hug. "We're all okay, Mom. We boys turned out all right because we had a strong woman leading us."

She hugged me back. Once she let go, she wiped away her falling tears. "Well, since it's the holiday season, I figured I could give you one Christmas gift early before tomorrow. Don't tell your brothers. Lord knows they'll give me a hard time and claim I was playing favorites."

"A gift?" I asked. "What is it?"

"Who," she corrected. "Who is it, you mean."

Right then, Avery stepped into the stable with a small smile on her face. I stood confused for a moment before Mom leaned toward me and kissed my cheek. "Merry Christmas, Nate. Momma loves you."

She walked away, leaving me standing there a bit dazed and confused by Avery's appearance. Avery took a few steps toward me, her nervousness apparent.

"Hi there," she said with a small smile.

"Hi there," I replied, moving closer. "What's going on?"

"Remember when I lived with you and we had a conversation about happiness versus contentment?"

"Yeah. I recall."

"You said that when people are in love, being content wasn't good enough. You said there needed to be a word to express the meaning behind that kind of love. Well, I figured out the word that encompasses what love is and that full feeling. The feeling that fills you up from your head to your toes. That feeling of a nature high, where all hurts stop hurting and joy exists tenfold. I know what the word for that is."

"What is it?"

"You." Her eyes glassed over, and she shook her head slowly. Her shoulders shrugged. "It's you, Nathan."

I shut my eyes for a moment and took a deep breath. "Coach, don't come in here on Christmas Eve and play with my emotions. Because it's getting a lot harder for me not to wrap my arms around you every fucking day."

"I know, and I have this whole speech in my head that I want to say to you. I've been playing it over and over for weeks now. I get that I'm negative and expect the worst outcome. I hardly let my guard down, and if I do, I build it back up quickly. I jump to conclusions. I'm mean—"

"Avery—"

"Wait, let me finish," she urged as a flash of emotions sliced through her eyes. "I'm also moody, and scarred, and scared. Mostly that. Mostly, I'm scared, Nathan. I'm scared of being abandoned. I'm scared of being alone. Which is ironic because I self-sabotage and push everyone away in order to avoid being left behind, which ends up leaving me alone. I'm grumpy and don't smile enough. I pick fights that don't need to be picked. I get it. I know I'm hard to love, okay? I know I'm a mess and all over the place, and I'm just learning how not to be all these things, but I can't let this year go by without telling you how I feel.

"I love you, Nathan. I love everything about you. I love your heart and how gentle it is. I love how you are patient. I love how you laugh. I love how you push my buttons. I love how you listen. I love how you see all our guys on the team as individuals. I love that you take extra time to serve them. And I love how easy you make it to fall for you. I love you, Nathan. I love you so much that it scares me, but I don't want to waste another day not loving you out loud."

I narrowed my eyes, baffled by everything she was saying. Yet one comment stood out more than the others. "Who told you that?"

"Who told me what?"

"That you were hard to love."

Her bottom lip trembled as she shook her head. Tears began to roll down her cheeks, and she didn't try to stop them. As she let the tears out, she was letting me in. "It doesn't matter. I just know it's true."

"Avery..." I stepped toward her, wanting nothing more than to wrap my arms around her and pull her in closer to me. I wanted to wipe away her tears and fill her with the comfort her soul needed and deserved. "It's true. You are all those things you mentioned, except for that one. You are not hard to love."

It was only six words, but I saw how they cracked her. She shut her eyes as her body began to shake from her emotions taking over.

I moved in closer and closer. So close that I was able to wipe away her tears and speak the words once more, hoping they'd land against her heartbeat. "You're not hard to love. Trust me, I know who you are. I know your ins and outs. And you're right. You're grumpy, moody, and you do have walls built up. You also leave a shit ton of hair in bathroom drains," I joked.

She snickered quietly as I kept going. "But you're so much more than that. You're an amazing coach. A great friend. You're loyal. You're consistent. You always show up whenever someone needs you. You're humble, even when your gifts deserve more praise. You're an amazing sister and daughter. You're funny and clever and the smartest person I've ever met. The hardest-working one, too. You challenge people to think in a way they never have before. You are an amazing person, and I need you to understand one thing and one thing only."

"What's that?" she asked as her eyes opened.

"Loving you is easy."

She bit her bottom lip and tugged on her sleeves. "Really?"

I moved in more, softly kissing away the tears falling down her cheeks. "Really."

"You still love me? After making you wait all these months?"

"I loved you, I love you, and I will love you, Avery Kingsley. This love will never stop."

"I'm still working with the therapist. I'm still working on me, and I'm trying so hard to be perfect for you. I want to be everything you deserve because you deserve so much, Nathan."

"Avery..." I took her hands in mine and kissed each palm before holding them to my chest. "You don't have to be perfect to be loved by me."

Her eyes fluttered with surprise. "I don't?"

"You don't. All I'm waiting to hear from you is when it's our time to try again. I'm here. I've been here this whole time. I'm waiting in the dugout. Just call me out, Coach, and I'm yours. Give me a sign, and it's game on."

The next thing I knew, her lips were pressing against mine. She kissed me as if she was apologizing for every hurt she'd ever caused, and I kissed her with all the forgiveness in the world. I didn't need Avery to be perfect in order for me to love her. I needed her to be real. And that evening, as she stood in the stables—the same stables where we shared our first-ever kiss—I knew we were ready.

I knew we were finally getting a real shot at us. I also knew I'd spend the rest of my life stepping up to the plate to let her know that I'd always show up to bat for her, no matter if she had good days or bad. Because loving her was, and always would be, easy.

EPILOGUE

Nathan
Seven Months Later
Fourth of July

"You're going down, Kingsley," I said, rubbing my hands together as Avery finished putting on her uniform for the Fourth of July Pierce baseball game. Everyone from our small town was invited to the family farm to celebrate the holiday, including Avery's family and the Honey Creek Hornets. Evan and Easton were doing what they'd done best, grilling up some meat as Mom, Tatiana, and Matthew made sure everyone had a drink in their hands for the afternoon game.

I couldn't think of a better way to spend the holiday—baseball and family.

Avery smirked my way as she headed toward the front door. "Don't get your hopes up, Nathan. I get Jackson on my team, and you have Willow."

I narrowed my eyes. "What's wrong with having Willow on my team?"

"I'm pretty sure the girl has never held a baseball bat in her whole life." She smiled my way. "But don't you worry, I know you're not a sore loser."

"I am a sore loser. I am the sorest of losers," I pouted. "Maybe I should get out there and give Willow some pointers before we get started."

As we headed out the front door, I saw Yara, Alex, and Willow pulling up to the property. Little Teresa was in the back seat with Willow.

Willow hopped out and rubbed her hands together. "Are you ready for some football?!" she shouted.

Oh, hell.

We were going to lose.

Everyone began to arrive, and the size of the crowd was outstanding. We had easily over sixty people laughing and joking around with one another. Cameron brought his father along with him, who seemed to be doing much better than he had been a few months ago. The other day, Cameron told me that Adam landed a new job at a construction company— Matthew's company, to be exact. Leave it to Avery's father to offer a hand toward a guy who needed help.

"Is it just me, or does your brother have a stick up his butt?" Willow asked me at one point as she walked over to me with a smile on her face.

"Let me guess, Evan?"

"Yeah! I asked him if he had any vegan hot dogs to toss on the grill, and he said that wasn't a thing. To which I told him it was indeed a thing. To which he said not on his grill. To which I told him he should expand his mind a little. To which he told me that he didn't need to expand his mind because it was expanded enough. To which I said 'I bet you're a Aries.' To which he said 'I don't believe in astrology.' To which I said 'that's a very Aries thing for you to say.' To which he said 'go away.' So here I am now."

I laughed. "That sounds about right. Evan's a bit hard around the edges."

"He's grumpy."

"Yeah."

Willow glanced over at him, a small smile still on her face. "And he frowns a lot."

"It's his signature expression. He's not much of a people person."

"But he's a good person?"

"One of the best."

She paused for a moment and shrugged with a hopeful expression. "Anyway, I'm looking forward to kicking the ball with you later, teammate. We are so going to win!" she said before she danced off. I wasn't being dramatic, either—she danced away. Willow always seemed to be floating off in a dancing manner. As she pranced away, I looked over at the grill, where I found Evan watching Willow dance away. His grimace was still apparent, but curiosity was there, too. I hadn't seen my brother appear curious about a person in a long time.

Wait a second.

Did Willow just say kick a ball around?

Cameron came rushing over to me before I could comprehend what she said.

"Hey, Coach P? I have a question for ya. I was just wondering..." He grew bashful and shrugged his shoulders as he wore his catching glove on his right hand. "Is Priya single?"

My eyes moved from him to my niece, who was tossing a ball up and down on the field, laughing with Yara and Alex.

I gave him a stern look. "Yes. She's single until she's in her nineties. Don't get any ideas."

"I don't know, Coach," Avery said, walking up behind me. "Rumor has it, Priya was asking about Cameron, too."

Cameron's eyes lit up. "Seriously?"

"Yup. You should go see if you can give her some tips on throwing. I bet she'd love that," Avery stated.

"Gee! Thanks, Coach K! I'll do that."

I turned and gave Avery a stern look. "Why would you do that?!" I whisper-shouted. "Now he's going to think she likes him."

"She does like him. I think it's cute."

"It's awful. My sweet niece...liking boys." I shivered. "That's traumatizing."

She laughed. "Don't be so dramatic. But speaking of...I think it's time we tell everyone about us."

I arched an eyebrow. "Really?"

"Yeah. I think so."

We'd spent the past seven months secretly dating one another. We wanted the privacy of getting back together without too many outside voices getting involved. She still had her apartment, but I figured that was good. It gave us time to grow closer to one another. One day, she'd be living with me for the rest of her life, but I wasn't in a rush to get us there.

Okay, I was in a rush. If it were up to me, we'd be married tomorrow.

We'd kept our relationship pretty much on the hush-hush, just to make sure we were moving in the right direction.

Now, we were ready to share the news with everyone else.

We headed out to the pitching mound before the game, and I got everyone's attention.

"Hey, everyone. I just wanted to thank you all for coming out to Honey Farms to celebrate the holiday with us. It's been a damn good time so far, and I'm really looking forward to smoking Avery's team during this game. But before we start, I thought it was a good time to announce that Avery and I are dating."

The space stayed quiet as everyone stared blankly at us.

Avery swallowed hard and gestured back and forth between the two of us. "Each other," she added. "We are dating each other."

Someone in the stands shouted, "Well, no shit, Sherlock. We all knew that."

Everyone agreed, shouting out the same kind of comments, leaving me a bit stunned.

"No, I mean, like, we're in love," I explained.

"Yup." River nodded. "We picked up on that fact."

"What? You all knew?" I asked.

"Yup, sweetheart," Mom said, shrugging her shoulders. "Just like we all knew you two had a thing all those years ago."

Avery's eyes widened in shock. "What? You all knew about that, too?"

Everyone who knew us back then nodded in agreement. Grant announced, "We weren't idiots. Now are we gonna play ball or what?"

I turned to Avery. "They knew about us."

Avery snickered, shaking her head in disbelief. "I thought we were sneaking around."

"You're terrible at sneaking," Matthew added. "But we're happy for you both."

"Right, okay, well, all right then." I placed my hands against my hips. "So does anyone have any questions about the two of us being together or...?"

The guys from the Honey Creek Hornets all shot their hands up.

Avery pointed a stern finger toward them. "Any questions that aren't inappropriate in any nature, which would lead to you all running extra laps during our summer practices?"

All their hands slowly recoiled.

I smirked. "Well, that was anticlimactic."

"I kind of like it that way." Avery leaned into me and kissed me. "This is all amazing, but we still have a game to play, and

I'm not going to take it easy on you just because you're officially my boyfriend now."

I snickered, shaking my head. "I wouldn't expect you to take it easy on me, Coach. You never have."

"And I never will. Now, come on," she confidently said before smacking my butt. "Let's play ball."

As she jogged away, I couldn't help but smile. I shook my head in disbelief that, somehow, I'd become lucky enough to call her mine once more.

Avery Kingsley was my best friend. My partner. My greatest grand slam.

With her around, my world would never again become too dark.

She was, and always would be, my very favorite sunbeam.

The End.

ACKNOWLEDGMENTS

Hey there!

Thanks for taking the time to read The Problem with Players! Avery and Nathan were such a thrill to write! This story flowed out of me, and they made it a joyous adventure for me. As I wrote this story, I couldn't help but think about my older siblings, who have inspired me through so many hard times. This book is for all the eldest siblings. The ones who might have felt overlooked, overworked, and overextended. I want you to know I see you, and thank you for all you've given to others, but now is the time to give to yourself.

Keep dreaming, keep growing, keep your hearts soft, and find your sunbeams.

There's a handful of people I'd love to thank for helping this book come together, and that starts with you, sweet reader. Thank you for taking the time to read my words. It has been so fun writing this novel, and I'm excited to dive in deeper with other characters from Honey Creek, Illinois.

A big thank you to my amazing editing team that went above and beyond. Ana Teresa, thank you for being the first to view Nathan and Avery's story. Your developmental editing skills blow my mind, and it is a privilege to work with your creative mind. Thank you to Jenny, Virginia, and Ellie for all editing the novel to help polish it up! Without editors, I'm just an author lost in a world of misplaced commas.

A shout out to Tanya, Christy, and Betül for being the best

betas ever. I'm so grateful for you helping me shape this into the best book it could be!

To Flavia and Meire, my agents from Bookcase Agency. Thank you for being in my corner for almost a decade. I couldn't imagine a better team to have in my corner.

To Good Girls PR, Shaye and Lindsey, I am blown away by your talents. Thank you for getting my novel into spaces that I would've missed out on before.

Thank you, Valentine PR for helping me promote this book and reach a bigger audience. Your team is extremely gifted and talented and it's an honor to work with you all.

Staci Hart, thank you for designing my favorite cover to date! You knocked this one out of the park, pun intended.

This was a fun one.

Here's to many more!

Always,

-BCherry

Printed in Great Britain
by Amazon

61415095R00234